Main crew

Johnny Martin

MAIRI CRAW

BEYOND THE HEDGE

Illustrations by Johnny Milne

authorHOUSE™

1663 LIBERTY DRIVE, SUITE 200
BLOOMINGTON, INDIANA 47403
(800) 839-8640
WWW.AUTHORHOUSE.COM

First published by AuthorHouse 11/02/05

ISBN: 1-4208-8576-6 (sc)

Printed in the United States of America
Bloomington, Indiana

This book is printed on acid-free paper.

www.mairicraw.com

Illustrator Johnny Milne was born in the Scottish county of Lanarkshire in 1933. He simultaneously survived World War Two and school, going on to study at the renowned Glasgow School of Art. This was followed by National Service which was spent  in RAF Radar Intelligence. Marriage, children and mortgage forced Johnny to give up the carefree life of an artist and seek gainful employment. He first met the author while teaching at Wellington School in Ayr where she was a pupil. Their lives followed different paths for many years until they met again at a school reunion in 2002. Mairi's debut novel inspired Johnny to embark on a series of drawings which blossomed into the illustrations which are now so much a part of this book. Both parties were reluctant to attend that reunion but remain delighted they were persuaded to do so!

Author's note: Mairi is Scottish Gaelic for Mary and sounds exactly like the word 'marry'. Sandy's Mum's name, Tina, has the unusual pronunciation, 'Tyna'. As for the town of Irvine, that's pronounced as if there is no 'e' on the end and Corvine is exactly as it looks.

With special thanks to:

My parents, especially Dad, who introduced me to Wee Alfie Elf in the first place.

My family: Kirstine, Billy, Ewen, Elaine and Emily Dyer; Pete, George, Nicky, Paul and Margaret Freshney; Dave Mulkeen; Bill and Catherine Ritchie.

My agent: Darin Jewell.

My friends and 'Hedge' enthusiasts: June Axon; Norna Bell; 'Bernadette'; Chris Black; Mike Black; Henry Buckton; George and Barbara Brockie; Jan Burnett; Cheryl Cott; Ted Dougherty; Dick and Jean Esmond; Jacqui Cox and Phil Ham; Liz Drysdale; Jude Dunn; Valerie Ferguson; Jo Gardner; Iain Goldsmith; Frances Harris; Michael Hehir, aka 'Mick the Post'; Rob and Louise Hickman; Karen Hornby; Sheila Hunt; Gini Hyde; Rosanne and Phil Jacques; Paul and Chris Kent; Sheila Mahoney; Maureen and Jim Mather; Johnny and Jean Milne; Paul Nickson; Bernard Palmer and Tim Woodward; Ellie and Roddy Payne; David Rintoul; Larry Sellyn; Do Senez; Tamsin Shearn; Paul Strudwick and Lynda Furnival; Barbara and Laurence Tarlo; Anne Thornberry; Terry and Rose Walker; Ray Warleigh; Phil Warren and Janine Morgan; Sean Willey; Gill and David Willoughby; Marion Wood; Jennie Workman.

Angelic Crystal; Cairn o' Mohr Winery; Fox Mountain Essences; Friars Moor Veterinary Clinic; Mike Porter of the Scottish Maritime Museum, Irvine; Richard and Judy; Michael Russell.

Beasts multifarious.

FOR EMILY

1

The extraordinary events that took place on Sandy Henderson's 11th birthday began to unfold with no hint of what was to come. It had all started uneventfully enough as she played with her Abyssinian cat Leo in the back garden of 'Woodburn', Bank Street. But then the inexplicable happened.

'Woodburn' is a sprawling Victorian house in the town of Irvine on the south-west coast of Scotland. In those days Irvine was a quieter place with a gentler pace of life. At the time that concerns us, the house had a vast, overgrown garden with a neglected apple orchard. Old rambling tracks led to forgotten secret places. A twisting, narrow path stopped abruptly at a bricked-up old doorway that had once led who knows where. It was an intriguing garden, a strange, mysterious place that appealed to a dreamy child like Sandy.

This jumble of a jungle was her favourite place. It seemed there was always something new and diverting to investigate, be it a flash of tiger stripes through the waving grass, or the flicker of flamingo wings in the reeds and bulrushes of the sunken lily pond.

Leo leapt through dense shrubbery at the farthest edge of the orchard intent on some cat pursuit or other. Sandy, dark ponytail flying out behind her, scrambled through ancient rhododendrons and brambles trying to keep up with him. Fierce, spiky tendrils caught at her bare legs as she ran along brushing aside dewy spiders' webs with a grimace and a shiver.

The cat was heading for an arch in the hedge which separated the orchard from the wilderness that made up the rest of the garden. Sandy was sure she'd never seen the structure before but she rarely ventured this far as the vegetation was virtually impenetrable.

She stopped a few yards short of the wooden construction. The arch was heavy with swags of late summer roses and intricate spirals of honeysuckle and looked inoffensive enough, but there was something distinctly unsettling about it and she experienced a stab of unease. She called out to Leo but in true cat fashion he didn't react so she shouted his name again more insistently. He glanced at her disdainfully and strolled through the arch.

It was a genuine case of now you see him, now you don't. The cat-shaped space where he'd been filled with a running, swirling kaleidoscope that rushed in like the tide to cover his tracks. The garden swam back into focus through the arch and the orchard echoed with a hushed, conspiratorial whisper, "Cat? What cat?"

Leo had vanished into thin air.

The strong, heady scent of old-fashioned roses was intense and overpowering, and the late morning sunlight darkened to the bruised purple hue of winter twilight. For a second or two the air was filled with the tinkling of tiny bells.

The crow had seen the whole thing from his precarious perch on the highest branch of a huge sycamore. The branch was barely more than a twig and the crow could not be described as insubstantial.

2

The Hendersons knew how to look after their feathered chums. They were fed regularly with kitchen scraps and leftovers, and we're not talking small portions. Life for the wild birds was good, in fact it was a piece of cake, the odd stale bun or two and the occasional slice or three of fusty bread. A particular favourite was cold, dance-on thick porridge which Sandy had valiantly struggled to eat. She was Scottish after all but, try as she might, she never quite made it to the other side of a bowl. That was just fine with the birds. They were delighted to help out.

The crow realised what he'd witnessed would take some sorting out, and the sooner he made a start the better. He shook out his feathers, gave them a quick appraisal and flew effortlessly up into the warm autumn air. Turning smoothly down Bank Street, he flapped off in the direction of the harbour past the imposing yet graceful architecture of Trinity Church which sits on high ground overlooking the River Irvine. He was unable to resist the urge to fly under the station bridge at the bottom of Montgomery Street and, when he came out the other side, performed a nifty 360 degree victory roll. Even in an emergency the crow couldn't help showing off.

It may be apparent by now that this is no run-of-the-mill crow. He's fully conversant with the language of humans and likes to introduce himself in the same flamboyant way. "The name's Craw, Jock Craw, Special Secret Agent, Double-O-One, the-one-and-only."

In some quarters the big guy is affectionately known as 'not-so-secret agent' for reasons that aren't hard to deduce.

The crow was approaching the Harbour Office when he found himself in the slipstream of his chum, Peg Leg, another regular diner at 'Woodburn'. He called out as he drew level with the seagull. "I've got to find the Captain urgently. I haven't time to explain. Just tell him Jock says he should come home right away. He'll understand. I'm going back to keep an eye on things."

"Leave it to me, pal; he's with Captain Robertson on 'The Garnock'. They're just about to dock."

With a "catch you later" Peg flew arrow-straight towards the tug.

Yes, I know you've noticed, the seagull can talk too, but Irvine, in spite of its apparent normality, is a very unusual place where just about anything can happen.

It was a working port then and Sandy's father, Captain Ralph Henderson, was the harbourmaster. He had just stepped onto the bridge of 'The Garnock' when he spotted the seabird heading his way. The gull landed on the guard rail beside him which was a tricky manoeuvre with just the one leg.

The harbourmaster looked at him quizzically as the tug rolled towards the wharf and its usual mooring behind the dredger. "What's up, Peg Leg? It's not like you to be so familiar when we're in company. Is something wrong?"

The seagull leant forward gingerly and in a loud whisper relayed the message from Jock.

Jim, as Peg Leg was formerly known, lost a limb during a short but violent storm off the coast of Northern Ireland. The gull was forced to take refuge on an Irish fishing boat carrying a cargo of Dublin Bay prawn, lobster and crab. Sadly for Jim, he chose the wrong creel to land on, the one occupied by a large, angry lobster. This was the absolute limit for the trapped creature who was already beside himself with distress and panic. That upstart gull was going to regret his impudence BIGTIME.

With a single lightning-fast movement the lobster thrust a gigantic claw up through one of the gaps in the lobster pot. There was a sickening crunch as the desperate beast, in a fit of spite, snapped Jim's left leg clean off just below the knee. The gull screeched in pain and flew out to sea leaving a trail of blood behind him.

"That'll teach you," muttered the crabbit crustacean. "Now it's not just me who's had a thoroughly ghastly day."

The lobster was immediately ashamed of his uncharacteristic behaviour. He could hardly blame his predicament on the unfortunate gull: he'd managed to get into this mess all by himself.

Jim was a seasoned campaigner who'd had more than one brush with death, so the partial loss of a limb was not about to burst his bubble. He was used to life being extremely harsh but he'd always managed to keep his head above water. Seagulls have guts, and I don't mean fish guts, although on a good day this is also true.

Jim's generous and forgiving nature is the only reason the lobster didn't end up as 'Speciality of the House' in some posh restaurant. Faced with a similar fate, any one of us might be less than rational.

The seagull managed to staunch the bleeding with a skilful tourniquet of seaweed which was the perfect remedy, stuffed as it is with healing minerals and nutrients. Jim rested on the stern of the boat until he felt better then flew towards the creel where the subdued lobster was contemplating his imminent demise. The trapped beast was feeling remorseful. Why had he been so vicious? He was undoubtedly going to die and, as if that wasn't bad enough, he now had the burden of this dreadful last act on his conscience.

"Psst!"

The lobster looked up dolefully. His heart was heavy and he was consumed with shame.

"I'd like to help you if I can. Is it safe to come closer?"

The crustacean was amazed to see the very same seagull hobbling towards his rope prison. "*You* want to help *me* after what I've just done? No way, why would you? I must be hallucinating. It's the shock, of course. I've gone bonkers; the stress has tipped me over the edge and left me three barnacles short of a rock."

The lobster was more than a little distracted and Jim was beginning to lose patience. "I'm as real as you are and, if anyone should be in a state, it ought to be yours truly. I've just had my name changed to Peg Leg, thanks to you, and I think I've taken it pretty well under the circumstances, don't you?"

"You really have come back! Why on earth would you do that? You're having me on, toying with me... pulling my leg." He hesitated before adding, "I'm so sorry, I can't believe I said that. How tactless. I'm afraid I haven't had much use for diplomacy being a lobster."

Jim's good nature was being sorely tested. "Look here, Crusty, do you want to stay in that creel? I can leave you to it, if you'd rather, but if I am going to help you, there's no time to lose, so what say we get stuck in? Do you have a name?"

"Forgive me for not introducing myself. I'm Lorimer and I'm much obliged to you."

Jim pecked furiously at the ropes from the outside while the lobster worked relentlessly at the unforgiving bonds with his over-developed claw. They took turns at keeping watch while they worked.

A matter of minutes that seemed more like hours later, a grateful, grovelling lobster scuttled joyfully from his erstwhile prison towards the seagull. Lorimer had his claws outstretched and would have heaped the equivalent of lobster kisses on his saviour had it been feasible. Their different anatomy put paid to that idea which, all things considered, was probably for the best. Instead he gestured to Peg to jump on his back. "Take the weight off your feet... Yikes, I've done it again, I'm really sorry. I keep putting my foot in it. Did I just say "foot in it"? On balance, no perhaps balance isn't a good choice of word either." He fell into a perplexed silence.

"No problem, Lorimer. I'm not in the least offended. You had very pressing reasons, I seem to recall."

The embarrassed lobster was turning a fetching shade of pink. "You're right, I was in an awful state, but it's still no excuse; it's unforgivable."

The seagull took to the air; it was definitely time to skedaddle. "Head for the port-side scupper," he shouted. "It's your only chance."

Lorimer clattered across the deck and squashed himself through the relevant hole. He made a satisfying splash when he hit the water.

Peg Leg was bobbing about at a safe distance waiting for his unlikely new friend.

The gull thought it was only right that the lobster underwent a name change as well and decided 'Thermidor' had a good ring to it. It was a bit obvious but Lorimer readily agreed. Thermidor was more than OK with him. The lobster would always be indebted to the seagull; he owed him his life.

A reminder of what might have been helped focus the mind. It was also time to make provision for his failing eyesight. A pair of glasses modified for use underwater, goggles with special lenses would do the trick. He might receive a few odd looks but so what. At least he wouldn't end up in another creel because he was too vain to admit that he couldn't see properly.

Peg Leg and Thermidor never looked back after their fateful meeting.

The seagull was a bit tottery on his one leg but as he spent a considerable amount of time in the air or breasting the waves it wasn't too inconvenient. For formal occasions when he had to stand around for ages, he would strap on a short wooden leg, fashioned from driftwood in the style of

Long John Silver. As for Lorimer, he was one very lucky lobster who was overjoyed to be alive.

That afternoon an unusual and indestructible friendship was forged, but they had no inkling then of what lay ahead.

When the crow came to rest again at the top of the sycamore, he found Sandy very much as he'd left her. She stood with her hands firmly planted on her hips, pale legs with scratched knees showing beneath scarlet shorts. The turquoise and red striped tee-shirt, fresh on that morning, was already stained with blackberry juice.

Whatever had taken place was way out of the ordinary, unnerving but nonetheless intriguing. Sandy wanted to inspect the archway up close, but still felt unsettled by its very presence. She was sure she'd never seen it before because it simply hadn't been there before, and yet it did look very old. The arch held the key to Leo's sudden disappearance but instinct suggested she would be wise to remain this side of it. She needed time to think and decided not to involve an adult for the time being.

Jock was relieved that he could stay put. The shock of being approached by a talking crow might well prove too much for her after the other bizarre goings-on.

The bird heard the distant but familiar sound of the harbourmaster's car as it turned into the drive and he flew up to the garage to fill Ralph in on the morning's developments. Jock didn't see Sandy's Mum, Tina, or anyone else around so he landed on the Captain's shoulder. If someone happened to find them like this, Ralph could say the crow had become extremely tame. Moreover, Jock was able to whisper in his ear which was less noticeable than talking directly to him.

Ralph walked calmly down the long garden towards the old orchard with Jock sitting comfortably on his shoulder.

He nodded thoughtfully while the crow told him what had taken place.

The harbourmaster ducked down and pushed his way through the fretwork of shrubs that led to the far end of the orchard with the crow clinging tightly to his Harris tweed jacket. The unlikely pair struggled out from the maze of bushes into the autumn sunshine.

Ralph Henderson, a tall, slightly stooped figure, stepped carefully over the uneven ground towards his daughter, trying to put his thoughts in order. This was a very delicate situation that had to be approached with the utmost care. The next hour or so was going to be very tricky.

Leo was unwittingly causing pandemonium on the other side of the arch.

Sylvanian residents in the shire of Crawdonia quickly realised something unprecedented had taken place. The first indication was the unmistakeable sound of three loud blasts from the leader of the boundary patrol. Someone or something had managed to come through without an invitation.

Wee Alfie Elf, dressed in his best Lincoln green tunic, hose and boots, and his wife Pogo Pixie heard the alarm from the kitchen of their cottage while they were tucking into steaming bowls of Pogo's homemade sweetcorn and banana soup. The elf put down his spoon and looked across at his wife who had fallen silent. Her eyebrows were arched in surprise.

"What do you suppose that's about? I can't remember when I last heard the alarm."

Before Alfie could utter a sound there were three even louder blasts.

"Good grief, Pogo, something momentous must have happened. The Boundary Warden sounds very upset. Let's find out what's going on. Perhaps we can help."

Alfie rushed out into the hall, making a grab for his jaunty green hat with its bold plume of raven feathers which he plonked unceremoniously on his head.

Pogo Pixie is no shrinking violet and her husband knew better than to suggest she stay at home while he went off to investigate alone. Their daughter Estella was still at school, so she was in safe hands.

Pogo placed the saucepan on the pot-bellied stove next to the kitchen range. "I might as well keep the soup warm."

Ever the practical one, thought Alfie affectionately as he dashed out of the front door. He sprang over the gate onto the path that wound through the wood in the direction the alarm had come from.

As he sped along, he heard his wife call after him. "I'll catch up with you on my pogo stick."

She turned to look at her dog who was sitting in a basket by the stove, his ears pricked up in hopeful anticipation. She smiled fondly at the tousled little beast. "Come on, Pongo, but you'll have to be really quiet and well-behaved."

"I promise I won't bark too much," he yelled in a frenzy of excitement and charcoal curls.

The dog leapt from his basket and bundled out of the door behind Pogo who was bouncing along at a cracking pace having cleared the gate in one athletic manoeuvre.

"You won't bark at all, boy," she said firmly when he caught up with her.

"Only kidding, PP," said the dog cheekily.

He tore along beside her with his tail wagging frantically. This was the sort of day when anything might happen and Pongo loved an unexpected adventure; it gave him something to get his teeth into, possibly literally if he was really lucky.

The little figures were quickly swallowed up by the dark canopy of trees.

Pogo Pixie was originally called Priscilla, a name she came to detest when she was old enough to give the matter serious thought. The sniggers of the other elves and pixies when she started nursery school were the final indignity.

She was an energetic, enthusiastic child with not a smidge of Priscilla-ness about her. Positively exhausting was how her Mum would have put it.

The day Priscilla discovered her first pogo stick was an unforgettable occasion for all concerned. It took her a while to get to grips with it but she has never been one for giving up easily. Priscilla was a determined young pixie. A pogo stick was certainly not going to get the better of her.

Boing! She back-flipped over the garden fence right into the middle of a group of her Mum's toffee-nosed friends, scattering them to the sound of "Goodness, whatever next", "Would you look at the state of that?" and "It's her poor mother I feel sorry for".

By then she was completely out of control, narrowly missing her mortified Mum. Poink! She landed on her head. Boing! She was briefly the right way up. Poink! Boing! Poink! She executed a spectacular but none-too-graceful arc and landed smack in the middle of her father's cherished vegetable plot. Whoosh! Splunk! Splat! Her Dad's prized marrow turned to squash. Cripes! He was not going to take that at all well.

All the months of hard work and devotion, the midnight feeds with his secret, homemade tonic had been for nothing. Her father was going to explode in a manner not too dissimilar to the marrow if the Norgan boys took 'Best Marrow in Show' for the third year running which had just become the inescapable outcome, thanks to her little escapade.

When Priscilla looked up from the middle of the chaotic mush she had just created, she found Big Tam standing over her with a face like fizz. He was spluttering with rage and disbelief, unable to utter a single coherent word.

From that day forth she was known as Pogo, a nickname none too affectionately given to start with. Big Tam did eventually see the funny side of his daughter's impromptu display, but only just, and quite some considerable time later.

Pogo never managed to shake off the name as she grew up, but anything was better than the dreaded 'Priscilla'. She didn't go in for pretty, impractical clothes like many of her peers. If your preferred mode of transport is a pogo stick, skirts are out of the question. A brightly coloured plaid tunic and knee-high boots were more Pogo's style.

She only put her pogo stick aside when she was expecting her first child many years later. Shortly after Estella was born out came the pogo stick again and off she bounced with the infant strapped securely to her back. Estella would chuckle and gurgle with obvious delight. She was undoubtedly her mother's daughter.

Alfie ran through Old Rook Wood as if pursued by malevolent demons which is not as unlikely as it might seem. Lately some pretty unsavoury types have infiltrated the dark, forgotten corners of the ancient wood.

On this occasion, Alfie was desperate to avoid the Banshee who frequented the path he had to take. This creature needed no excuse to play to the gallery. At the drop of a hat she would screech and wail, howl and caterwaul, scream and yowl until the cows came home, which of course they never did when she was around. She just had to get things off her chest. She was that kind of girl.

Alfie knew he was bound to bump into her, worse luck, and it was sooner than he feared. When he sprinted round the very next bend she leapt out in front of him dressed in a grubby white nightie. Marta waved her thin, pale arms in the air and her haggard features were twisted in dismay. She looked a veritable fright which, come to think of it, was exactly the effect she was striving after.

"For goodness sake!" cried the elf with a start. "You gave me an awful scare, you daft gowk." The situation called for decisive authority. "Now, be a good Banshee and get out of my way."

Fat chance of that. Marta wasn't going to let him out of her clutches without putting up a fight. She took an enormous lungful of air and launched into her all-time favourite rant, right in Alfie's face. "Nobody loves me, nobody cares, as I topple head first down the stairs. Woe is me! Woe is me!"

They were practically nose-to-nose. "Right, that's enough of that nonsense," Alfie said, taking a hasty step backwards. "You don't even have proper stairs in that hollow tree of yours."

"Oh, you're no fun," she said in a dejected tone. "I'm so fed up and nobody ever stops for a chat. Everyone's in a rush when they see me."

"Why do you think that might be?" asked the elf with undisguised amusement.

Marta shrugged. She genuinely didn't have a clue.

"I can't hang around all day, dearie. Didn't you hear the alarm?" She shook her head glumly. "Too busy wailing and howling, I'll warrant." Seizing the moment, he broke into a trot. "Sorry, gotta go!"

With a wave of his hand he belted off in a blur of bright green, leaving the Banshee open-mouthed, her pathetic, scrawny arms outstretched beseechingly.

"Don't leave me! I haven't even warmed up yet."

Alfie felt a pang of guilt as he ran through the trees. Marta really was her own worst enemy. Maybe if she got a new frock and had her hair done, that might be a start.

Perhaps if she could cheer up a bit, too. All that moaning and whining doesn't half put people off. But then she's supposed to be a wet blanket, poor soul; it's in her job description.

When Alfie emerged from the shadow of Old Rook Wood the first thing he noticed was the odd behaviour of the pedigree flock of strunties that were out to pasture in the lush meadow at the north end of the wood.

Strunties are a cross between fairy sheep and elven pigs and they are cute with a capital 'C'. Their fleeces are as smooth as the most expensive silk and their gloriously soft wool is highly prized.

By nature strunties are docile, amiable creatures but if they are threatened in any way they become over-excited and extremely silly. They snort and bleat as loud as they can in an attempt to scare off potential predators.

The elf realised something was causing them major stress, judging by the racket, but there was no clue as to what it might be. He reacted to a sound behind him and discovered Grimpen, the dignified leader of the royal wolf pack, at his side. He was certainly not the cause of their distress, strunties and wolves are the firmest of friends. The wolves take care of the flock and strunties are not on their menu.

Life is never perfect, sadly, and the wee beasts do have some pretty unpleasant enemies. Struntie steaks are highly prized by some of the more disagreeable elements of Sylvanian society and there is a sizeable reward for information leading to the arrest of anyone who harms, never mind eats, a struntie.

Grimpen and his pack take their responsibilities seriously and operate a round-the-clock patrol. Nothing can ever be left to chance for the flock belongs to the Sylvanian Fairy Queen. They are one of Her Majesty's 'Special Projects'.

Grimpen had a grave expression on his wise face. "I've no idea what's happened, but the Boundary Warden is very concerned. Our security has been breached and your Uncle Angus was spotted rushing off from the scene with a mighty peculiar look on his face."

"I might have known. He always seems to invite trouble. I wonder what he's been up to this time; it doesn't bear thinking about. Another magic spell that's gone wrong, most likely. I've tried to persuade him to put his wand out of harm's way, but you know Angus, he's a stubborn, carnaptious old devil."

The wolf laid a reassuring paw on Alfie's arm. "Everybody knows what he's like. We don't call him 'Steam and Whistles' for nothing."

The elf laughed in spite of himself. "Maybe Angus is not to blame for this, but perhaps I'd better not get my hopes up."

"That's probably wise," said the wolf.

Pogo and her little dog had just come out of the wood and were making good progress across the field. They too had fallen victim to Marta the Banshee.

Grimpen raised his noble head and let out a long, plaintive howl. Wolves appeared from every direction and in a twinkling encircled the flock. The pack leader nodded his satisfaction at their speed and efficiency. He knew his wolves were the best but there was never room for complacency. They were living in dangerous times.

Hosepipe Snout the Hairy Hedgehorn was very upset. As Boundary Warden he had raised the alarm twice with three loud blasts. In the whole of Sylvania there is no one who can outblast him. His snout is a finely tuned instrument which is why he holds one of the most prestigious jobs in a land where security is paramount.

Sylvania is protected by massive, constantly changing, impassable hedges which are the ideal habitat for hairy hedgehorns, the only creatures who can penetrate their restless, thorny interiors.

Hedgehorns are equipped with sharp spines like a garden hedgehog. They also have copious amounts of long, coarse hair which proves very useful if they're attacked by some nasty piece of work who thinks they'd make a quick, tasty snack. The hapless creature is likely to receive a mouthful of barbed spines for its trouble, with a blood-curdling fanfare of snout-blasts thrown in at no extra cost. Hairy hedgehorns have the ultimate body armour, with that built-in element of surprise.

Hosepipe Snout was used to sleeping peacefully in his cosy bed of twigs and leaves, but he was in for some sleepless nights if he didn't get to the bottom of this breach of security, pronto. He was relieved to see the familiar little trio coming towards him.

Pongo enjoyed the company of his friend the hedgehorn and made as if to chase him. They liked nothing better than a bit of play fighting when Hosepipe Snout was off duty.

Pogo Pixie was quick to intervene. "Not just now, boy," she said, gently restraining him. "He's very busy. Some other time, eh?"

The dog was disappointed but he could tell the hedgehorn was engaged in matters serious.

Wee Alfie Elf is well regarded for his sound common sense. He holds the strictly unofficial post of adviser to the Fairy Queen who firmly believes the royal household must never lose touch with the needs of the people. Alfie provides a valuable link between Queen Celestina and her subjects and he's not afraid to speak his mind.

Hosepipe Snout scuffled towards the group with his brows

knitted together in a deep frown.

"It's an awful carry-on, WAE. I haven't known anything like this since that mix-up years back when the rat came through at his original size. One minute the rehearsal for Sandy's visit's going beautifully and the next everything's gone pear-shaped. It's an absolute disgrace and we so rarely have visitors from 'Woodburn'." He stopped to catch his breath. "Did I say pear-shaped? Cat-shaped would have been a more accurate description but it all happened so quickly, so unexpectedly."

Pongo reacted eagerly to the word cat. Maybe things were looking up after all.

Alfie paced backwards and forwards with his hands clasped behind his back. "Are you telling me a cat accidentally came through from 'Woodburn' and wasn't even miniaturised?"

The hedgehorn fell in step with him. "I only caught a brief glimpse but I'm pretty sure it was Leo. He was definitely Sylvanian sized, thank goodness. We've had enough problems with the Giant Rat."

Alfie abruptly came to a halt. "Uncle Angus must have had a hand in this. It bears all the hallmarks of his recent, unpredictable magic."

The hedgehorn sighed. "I'm afraid he was here. He shouldn't have been as it was a restricted area, but the old buzzard won't be told. I'm sorry, that was rude of me. He is your uncle, after all, and a highly respected spell weaver in his day."

"Don't trouble yourself, I've heard Angus called worse. He's impossible these days. Maybe something on this scale will make him stop and think. We can only live in hope. In the meantime I must find out what he's been up to."

"You really have no idea where the cat is?" Pogo said, cutting to the chase. "He must be very confused and frightened."

"I don't have a clue and, to make matters worse, I caught a brief glimpse of Sandy who saw the whole thing. As if that wasn't bad enough, the cat was understandably traumatised. To be met by me raising the alarm at the top of my snout was too much for him. He was so shocked, he bolted. There are patrols searching for him as we speak. What a trying business, it's nothing short of a catastrophe."

"A 'cat'astrophe indeed," said Alfie with the ghost of a smile.

Sandy was startled by the sound of snapping twigs and whirled round to see what was going on. She was surprised to find her Dad coming towards her and her eyebrows shot up even further when she noticed the crow sitting on his shoulder.

Ralph saw the look on her face and in a hasty whisper suggested Jock ought to refrain from speaking. The crow readily agreed. The morning had been strange enough already for her.

Sandy spoke first. "I'm so glad you're here, Dad, but shouldn't you be at the Harbour Office and what on earth's Jock doing on your shoulder?" She recognised the bird by the distinctive patch of white feathers on his chest. He'd always been a cheeky bird, but never *that* cheeky.

Ralph waited to see what else she'd say before he was forced to answer her questions.

She didn't even hesitate. "Something really odd happened a wee while ago and I swear I'm not making this up. Leo disappeared when he walked through that arch over there and I'm dreadfully worried about him. I don't know where he is now or how to begin to search for him."

Ralph sat down on an old tree stump and beckoned his daughter over. "As it happens, I do know what's going on and I'm pretty sure we'll be able to find Leo, but there are a few things I need to explain first. You remember I promised you'd meet Wee Alfie Elf and Pogo Pixie one day?"

"Yes," she replied with a bewildered smile, "but that was years ago and I've known for ages you were pulling my leg." Jock leant forward on Ralph's shoulder, his bright, beady eyes fixed on her face. She glanced at the crow then back at her father. "Has Jock got anything to do with this?"

"Yes, he has, but I'll get to that later. Those bedtime stories I told you about the fairy folk who lived in our garden were exactly that, stories. But, and this is a very big 'but', I didn't invent the characters and when I said you'd meet them all one day, I wasn't kidding. They're as real as we are, although they're an awful lot smaller, with the exception of the Giant Rat who's…em, rat sized." Ralph paused to let what he'd said sink in. "It looks like you're going to get to know them sooner than I'd thought. I was expecting to have more time to prepare you for your visit which was arranged for half term, but after the shenanigans here this morning, you'll have to leave early. Jock came to fetch me when he saw what happened to Leo."

His daughter's open-mouthed expression was nothing short of comical.

The crow was fit to burst and couldn't contain himself any longer. "I flew down to the harbour as soon as I…"

A broad grin spread across Sandy's face. "Whatever next, a talking crow! What a birthday this is turning out to be."

"Thank heavens for that," said Jock with a satisfied chuckle. "It's been an awful strain keeping my beak zipped."

"I'm sure it has," said Ralph with a knowing smile. "You'll have to go after Leo straight away. I wish I could come with you, Sandy, but I can't. Only children are allowed to visit Sylvania. I was lucky enough to go there myself a long time ago to search for the Craw Cauldron. It was stolen and Alfie and Pogo helped me get it back. It's not just an old heirloom; it has some very special powers and was a gift from the Sylvanian Royal Family to our ancestor Rory Craw who helped rid them of a terrible evil."

Jock chimed in. "My cousin Crawford will have to bring forward all the arrangements. I'll introduce you to him myself and naturally you'll be staying with Alfie and Pogo while you're away. You have some dear friends in Sylvania who, frankly, can't wait to meet you."

Sandy was as still as a statue but her emotions were in turmoil.

The family's chocolate and cream Siamese cat had turned up and was rubbing himself against her legs. Ralph leant forward and tickled him behind the ear. "Perhaps Jamie could go with you. What do you think, Jock? He's devoted to Leo and if anyone stands a chance of finding him, he might just be the one."

"We'll need special clearance. Sandy is expected but after the carry-on with Leo, who knows? I'd better go right away and see how the land lies. I'll be back before you know it."

The crow flew towards the old archway and vanished as he passed under the roses and honeysuckle.

Crawford was waiting for his cousin on the Sylvanian side of the arch. "Thank goodness you've come. What a to-do! We were running through the procedure for Sandy's visit when that silly old fool stuck his wand in where it wasn't wanted. It really is too bad and the whole thing's a total mess. And, can we find him or the cat? Absolutely not. Mark my words, Angus has gone too far this time. Queen Celestina is very forgiving but I hope she'll put her dainty little foot down this time. He really does need squashing."

Crawford straightened his bow tie fretfully and the monocle fell from his left eye. "Would you look at the state I'm in, my nerves are in shreds!"

"It's not that disastrous, surely? Leo's just a cat."

"That's easy for you to say, but there have been a lot of changes since you last deigned to pay us a visit. Sylvania is not the happy-go-lucky place it once was. We have treachery in our midst. Can you imagine what that might mean for all of us? Sandy's visit was very much touch and go, but there's no going back now. Queen Celestina is determined she'll come, particularly in view of Leo's unscheduled trip, so that's that. You know how she is if her mind's made up. Her Majesty can be very pernickety and she's insisting on the full festivities." He shook his head anxiously. "My priority is to find the cat at the earliest opportunity and send him home again where he belongs. If I have my way, the child will go straight back with him. There's too much at stake but, sadly, that's not for me to decide."

Crawford repositioned his monocle and cleared his throat. "I'm sorry about that outburst, it was most unprofessional. You'll be wanting an audience with Her Majesty. I'll just call ahead and make sure she's ready to receive you."

He pulled a crumpled leather-like object from the pocket of his waistcoat and gave it a good shake. "Come on now, I know you prefer the nightshift, but this is urgent."

The bundle slowly unfolded its umbrella-like wings and hung on clawed feet from the dapper little crow's wing tip. A small pair of eyes blinked sleepily at Crawford.

"Bat mail," he said, nudging Jock with his other wing. "Moriarty, dear boy, please let the palace know my cousin has arrived and be quick about it. My pocket awaits your speedy return." He shook the bat into the air and watched him fly off towards the Sylvanian capital, Corvine, which is in the shire of Crawdonia.

Jock and Crawford moved away from the enchanted boundary hedge where their two worlds touched towards the bank of the Sprinting River which at this point, contrary to its name, meanders through fertile fields of maize and watermelons which grow abundantly in the sunlight of the Sapphire Valley.

The river enters Moonglow Lake before tumbling out over the Flighty Fairy Falls on its way to Corvine where it is joined by its tributaries, the Pinkie and the Bloodrock. The Sprinting River canters cheerfully through the capital into the natural harbour before it reaches its final destination in the Whiteraven Sea.

On a precipitous outcrop overlooking Corvine and its busy port sits the whimsical confection that is the royal palace.

Queen Celestina received Moriarty personally in her private drawing room. She playfully spun the bat around her bejewelled wrist, much to the wee chap's delight. "I shall return you to Crawford personally," she said airily. "It must be business as usual. The arrangements for Sandy's visit have been in place for weeks. It would give out entirely the wrong message if we were to cancel now."

She tossed her mane of blue-black hair in a defiant gesture and flounced onto the balcony in a swirl of silk and lace. Those flamenco dance classes were starting to pay off.

The palace guard of red and gold liveried imps leapt to attention at the sound of her voice.

"Prepare Kismet at once and ask the Royal Raven to tell Crawford that I shall greet Sandy and Jamie personally." The Queen attached the bat to the shaft of her wand and twiddled him round to check he was hanging securely. "And make sure Crawford knows I'm looking after Moriarty." Her voice softened and she smiled warmly. "We wouldn't want Daddy to worry, would we, cutie-pie?"

"Fetch the Royal Steed," shouted Twitchett, the Captain of the Impfantry. The rotund, rosy-cheeked officer turned to a freckle-faced imp at his side. "You boy, summon the Royal Raven. I want to brief her for a very important mission."

"Yes, sir," said the imp. He turned smartly on his heel and marched towards the raven's luxurious quarters above the barracks. He climbed the spiral staircase which gives access to Indigoletta's suite of rooms for those unfortunates who don't have the power of flight. The imp knocked on the carved oak door and called through the bevelled grill. "The Captain of the Impfantry would like to see you right away, ma'am."

The Royal Raven was perched in a walnut tree in the beautiful roof garden conservatory that adjoins her spacious apartments. She called out imperiously, "If you wish to speak to me I insist on seeing your face."

The inexperienced foot soldier swallowed nervously. Crumbs! An audience with the Royal Raven. What the heck, might as well get it over with. He turned the ornate handle and pushed the door open. "Don't be silly," he mumbled to himself. "It's only a bird."

Indigoletta's reputation was formidable. She never suffers fools and can't abide inefficiency of any sort.

The imp was dazzled by his splendid surroundings and his eyes busily took in everything as he walked uncertainly through the hall towards the conservatory.

"I'm here, boy." He looked up at the tree where the majestic bird was seated. "What's your name?"

"It's Will, ma'am."

The raven was the colour of a perfectly ripe aubergine and just as shiny.

Indigoletta introduced herself. "Now that we're on first name terms, Will, go and tell Twitchett I'll receive him in my quarters. If that pompous little twerp thinks he can summon me then he's barking up the wrong tree."

The lad sniggered at her involuntary joke and the raven gave a throaty laugh. "I'm too funny for my own good."

"Not at all, ma'am," he replied with a shy smile.

"You'll go far, dear boy. I can feel it in m'feathers. I'm never wrong, you know." Indigoletta had a flash of inspiration. "Perhaps you might like to work for me. How's that for an idea?"

Will knew he was facing a life-changing situation and wasn't about to let it slip through his fingers. "It would be an honour to serve you, ma'am."

The imp didn't know what to make of these whirlwind changes in his circumstances but he knew life was definitely going to be a lot more interesting.

"I don't know what your position will be yet, but I pay my staff well. You'll be much better off than you were in the Impfantry, and the perks are excellent." The great bird beamed at him. "Run along and tell Twitchett about your promotion, and have the little fool report to me at once."

Will was feeling extremely chipper. Indigoletta seemed to have it in for his old boss which was fine with him.

If you can soar into the air on a whim, then perhaps the Impfantry does seem rather limited and pathetic by comparison.

There were stirrings deep in the enchanted cave below Moonglow Lake. A spider dropped silently on a thread from a formation of stalactites on the roof and hung by the right ear of the huge snake who was slumbering in a coil that encircled the most magnificent gemstone. The Giant Sapphire was glowing gently as it cast a benign blue light across the other treasures heaped around the vast cavern.

Wooden chests overflowed with rubies, diamonds, emeralds and doubloons. Heaps of pearls, iridescent opals, zircons, jade, lapis lazuli and gold nuggets lay in glorious profusion next to chunks of quartz crystal, amethyst and aquamarine.

In the far corner, by the inner entrance to the cavern, was a black and white bird. She was diligently polishing moonstones and placing them in an intricately carved ebony casket.

Morgana the magpie whistled contentedly while she worked in the positively charged atmosphere of the cave. This was one happy and fulfilled bird. She adored all things sparkly, glittery and shiny, so this cave was a dream come true. Hey, they even paid her to keep the whole shebang catalogued and in immaculate order.

The spider cleared his throat. "SSS, it's time to shake your tail. Morgana is ready to attend to the Giant Sapphire, if that's OK with you. She has to knock off early today as one of the chicks has a touch of featherbane."

The stately serpent raised his head and focussed his steady gaze on the little arachnid. His gold and blue skin gleamed in the crepuscular light of the cave. "S-s-spondoolicks, my diminutive chum, it's more than OK. Where would we be without Morgana's superlative dedication to the well-being of the Sapphire?" His forked tongue flicked in and out as he spoke. The spider was unmoved by this disturbing display for he had nothing to fear from the mighty reptile.

Sammy Slithering Snake, Prince of the Royal House of Cobalt-Sibilance, to give him his full handle, languorously uncoiled himself from the fabulous gem. With one practised switch of his tail he flicked his platinum and sapphire crown from its velvet cushion onto his noble head. "There now, Spondoolicks, that's me dressed. I have some serious thinking to do, dear friend. My third eye was working tirelessly while I slept and I've received troubling news. I must talk to Wee Alfie Elf, so that's where I'm headed first. I'd like to be there to meet Sandy when she arrives so I'd better get a move on."

Sammy zig-zagged expertly through the maze of stalagmites on the cave floor and, with an ironic, "Do your worst, Morgana", disappeared behind a wall of rock.

The magpie flew towards the Giant Sapphire and the gem began to glitter in anticipation. The colour at the heart of the stone intensified and the cavern glowed with warm peacock-blue light. She cleaned and buffed the stone, facet by facet, with a finely spun duster of struntie wool infused with lavender.

The bird worked tirelessly.

"You're going to be very busy soon and I want you to be in good shape when SSS comes back. There's evil around, I can feel it, can't you?"

2

The Island of Long Forgotten Dreams is a desolate, forsaken place off the west coast of Sylvania. It lies due north of Corvine and is protected by a reef of jagged rocks whose treacherous currents and deadly whirlpools are un-navigable for all but the most skilled mariners.

Needless to say, Long Forgotten Dreams is not the No.1 destination for Sylvanian holiday-makers. It's virtually unoccupied and is likely to stay that way. The very atmosphere is poisonous, not just in the physical sense, but spiritually as well. The island is draining, debilitating, barren, bleak and, as such, is a magnet for all negativity and despair. It induces melancholy and feeds greedily on depression and neurosis. It is a place to be shunned as several unfortunate souls have found out to their cost. Shipwrecked sailors who have managed to survive the malevolent reef and reach the shore almost immediately begin to feel wretched and lethargic. They gradually lose the will to live and soon die of despair and extinguished hope.

It was not always like this.

The benevolent Isle of Muckle Mirth was once home to a prosperous population of fairy folk, but those days were long gone. The island had found itself at the centre of a dispute between an ancestor of Queen Celestina and a brilliant spell-weaver with an over-inflated sense of his own worth which convinced him he was more powerful than anyone else. When the wizard was challenged and ultimately proved wrong, he invoked an immutable curse which blighted the island he had longed to possess.

In the decaying heart of Long Forgotten Dreams is a deep, dank sink-hole where Maligna the Harpie has been imprisoned for years. The source of her power is an engraved anklet of black gold studded with clovenstone from the ancient, now defunct mines in the shire of Kelpien. The Harpie has been deprived of this precious item which is kept at a secret location far from the island.

Sylvania's future hinges on Maligna never being reunited with her precious anklet, so naturally that is her sole preoccupation. She has thought of little else since the first day of her incarceration. But what can she do? She is alone in her deep dungeon and can never escape unless her fortunes change dramatically.

The Harpie is a resourceful creature who has tried to bribe the only people she has contact with, namely her ever-changing shift of guards. No jailer is left exposed to her wiles for more than a day or two and they must also be protected from the island's increasingly negative influence. She can be very persuasive and silver-tongued when she wants to be, with or without her anklet, but she has never made any progress and is pretty well resigned to her fate.

Maligna has been in female form for so long she's experiencing a rising sense of panic. On top of that, she's suffering from the first symptoms of claustrophobia in her wretched, disgusting sink-hole.

Her preferred incarnation is that of a sea serpent. It's invigorating and revitalising to take to the waves whenever you fancy a change. How she misses and longs for the oceans, the freedom of skimming through the water, racing schools of dolphins and swimming with mermaids. Maligna has

enjoyed these simple pleasures for she has no grudge against the creatures of the deep. The sea runs in her veins.

Sometimes in the dead of night when the relentless wind drops a little, Maligna is sure she can hear the waves breaking on the reef. It's a comfort to her and brings her solace. On those rare occasions, lying on her wooden pallet in the dark, she resolves never to give up hope.

Sammy Slithering Snake managed to catch up with Wee Alfie Elf in no time, thanks to the accuracy and precision of his third eye. Had it not been for this rare gift, he might well have been a prisoner to his job. As it is, he can be wherever he needs to be and still keep tabs on the Cave of Sublime Spirit and its fabulous centrepiece, the Giant Sapphire. He can also move at incredible speed and be back at the cave almost before he's left it.

Alfie's first priority had been to locate his meddlesome uncle who, as luck would have it, is a creature of habit. His stomach's requirements come way in front of his good common sense.

Angus felt he'd stayed out of sight long enough for the heat to have died down. Well, that's what his stomach was telling him for pressing reasons of its own.

Alfie knew his uncle's weakness for food and visited a couple of his preferred taverns on the outskirts of Corvine. He caught up with him at The Staggering Parrot, an out-of-the-way inn to the east of Old Rook Wood in the hamlet of Skelter.

The old spell-weaver was holding forth in his usual booming tones to some of the locals who were gathered round his table with suitably impressed expressions on their faces.

Angus was in his element and enjoying a fine supper as well. He plunged a fork into a plump, juicy 'Kilted Sausage'.

For the uninitiated, a 'Kilted Sausage' is a banger wearing a skirt of bacon, skewered with a generous slice of grilled tomato.

"Goodness knows what else might have gone wrong if I hadn't been there to salvage the situation."

Before he could say another word, his nephew's voice rang out across the crowded tavern. "What's that you're saying? I suppose you're explaining your part in today's events. From what I just heard I'm not sure your version matches anyone else's."

Angus's face turned beetroot red. "Now, be fair, WAE, you weren't even there."

The old elf had been revelling in all the attention and his nephew had just managed to ruin his moment of glory.

Alfie's features grew less severe. "You still have a fair few sausages to get through. What say I get us an ale and we can have a proper chat later?" He drew closer and lowered his voice. "We think it's best if Estella goes to stay with Pogo's brother and his wife. They're far enough away from the trouble that's brewing here in Crawdonia."

Angus's face lit up at the mention of his great niece.

"She wants to see you before she leaves. Pogo's preparing a special supper tonight, Estella's favourite carrot and walnut loaf with mashed peas."

"Carrot and walnut loaf, eh? Perhaps I'll skip pudding. It'd be rude to sit back and watch you three tuck in. I wouldn't want to offend Pogo."

"Of course not, but I'm not sure Pongo will see it that way," he muttered, watching his uncle guzzle the rest of the sausages.

The dog would be majorly miffed if Angus deprived him of his usual big bowl of nosh. It was one of Pongo's 'Top Ten Teas'.

Alfie reacted to a loud hiss as they left the tavern.

Sammy slipped out of a tree by the inn porch. "We need to talk. I felt it was best if I waited outside. I didn't want to cause any panic, folks are nervous enough as it is."

"We're on our way home," replied the elf. "Have you time to come back for a spot of supper? We can have a pow-wow afterwards."

"That would be most agreeable, WAE."

Angus puffed vigorously on his briar pipe. Telling Alfie what he'd been up to was bad enough, but to have to do so in front of the snake was going to be seriously unpleasant.

Perhaps Pongo was not going to lose out on the grub front after all.

It had been a long, horrid day. All Leo wanted was to be back at 'Woodburn' with the Henderson family, safely curled up on the hearth rug with Jamie, the Siamese cat, and Trixie, the boxer dog.

What had happened to change his well-ordered existence? Where was Sandy? And, even more pressing, where was he now and how was he to get home again?

The cat shivered as he considered his predicament. A familiar face or voice would be so good. But there was nothing familiar, reassuring or welcoming in this peculiar place.

A pair of curious, pink eyes were watching the cat from the cover of an elderberry bush. The eyes belonged to the Giant Rat, the most misunderstood creature in the land, Public Enemy No.1, until recent events had wrenched this dubious honour from his claws.

Gilbert was forever finding himself in incriminating situations. There was the time he blundered into the Cave of Sublime Spirit after a few too many ales and, tripping over an enormous pile of doubloons, knocked himself senseless and was discovered with his front paws wrapped around the Giant Sapphire and a silly big grin on his face.

Sammy Slithering Snake had seen the whole thing through his third eye and knew the daft beast meant no harm but many fairy folk were prejudiced against Gilbert simply because he was a rat and Sammy was finding it more and more difficult to protect him.

In the end the Giant Rat himself deemed it sensible to lie low for a while, particularly as the dust had not quite settled from his latest catastrophe with explosives.

Gilbert has always been fascinated by anything that goes BANG, particularly if it looks spectacular as it does so.

He almost destroyed one of the bridges over the Sprinting River when he overdid the gunpowder in a mortar while setting off the most splendid array of fireworks to celebrate his own birthday.

It had been seen initially as a possible act of war by an unidentified enemy.

When Gilbert was discovered with gunpowder burns all over his fur, it was hard to convince anyone that he was having a birthday party for one.

"Aye, that'll be right," was the general feeling, "and I suppose the band played 'Believe It If You Like', eh rat?"

But it was true; Gilbert had no friends.

For all that, the Giant Rat is a decent, caring soul and he immediately identified with the plight of the cat.

Gilbert is intelligent but lacks that important commodity, common sense. He tends to be a trifle ingenuous and hapless. It was time to get a grip on himself, stop making so many mistakes and *definitely* stop messing around with explosives.

More than anything Gilbert wanted a pal, someone to look after and share things with. Perhaps this kitty might fit the bill. If anyone needed a friend it was the little cat, but the rat knew he must tread carefully.

He sat back on his ample haunches and, with his whiskers twitching busily, put on the rat equivalent of a thinking cap.

Indigoletta arrived at the boundary fence with her attendant, a young hooded crow who sported a pair of fancy gold epaulettes. Jock and his cousin Crawford were deep in conversation, so much so they didn't notice their royal visitor, resplendent in her own exquisitely coiffed feathers. Indigoletta was not impressed and the young 'hoodie' stepped in at once. He coughed discreetly. "Ah'hem, gentlemen, the Royal Raven is here and wishes to speak to you urgently."

Jock and Crawford jumped in surprise and nearly tripped over each other in their rush to greet their eminent visitor. They bowed deeply and Jock took the initiative. "At your service, ma'am. May I say it's truly wonderful to see you. It's been far too long. And, might I add, you look absolutely magnificent."

Indigoletta smiled her most radiant smile then fixed the swaggering crow with her steady gaze. "I thought I was never going to clap eyes on you again, Jock Craw. I've felt positively abandoned. It's not good enough. It's time you took notice of my position in the royal household."

"Oh but I do, you *know* I do, ma'am." He executed a natty little pirouette and advanced towards her. "I worship the ground you walk on and for that matter the very air you fly in." Jock bowed for a second time and made as if to kiss her outstretched wing-tip.

"Steady on now, don't overdo it. I might think you were indulging in idle flattery." Indigoletta inclined her magnificent head coquettishly. There's no fool like an old fool, she thought, but she wasn't about to complain. Jock's approach made a refreshing change from palace protocol.

Crawford sighed and shook his head ruefully. What was it about his cousin that made birds of the female variety go weak at the knees? Whatever it was, he wished he had some of it. Jock's raffish, flirtatious quality appealed to the ladies. It really was most annoying. Crawford felt decidedly cheesed off. He straightened his bow tie irritably.

"Ah'hem, will that be all for now, ma'am?" asked the 'hoodie' politely, taking a couple of steps backwards.

"Thank you, Cough. I'll deal with this."

Indigoletta instantly became distant and professional. "Now, Jock, you must go back to 'Woodburn' straight away and prepare Sandy and Jamie for their visit. The Queen insists on being here to greet them. It will take some time to organise Her Majesty's entourage and, taking that and the time difference into consideration, Sandy and Jamie ought to come through late afternoon Irvine time, say five o'clock. If all goes to plan that should coincide exactly with Queen Celestina arriving here. There will be the full royal reception, of course."

Jock's beak dropped open. "I'll need longer than that to sort everything out."

"Out of the question," snapped the imposing bird. "I suggest you get a move on unless you'd prefer to fly to the palace and tell the Queen personally that you're unable to meet her schedule."

The dazzling raven turned her attention to Crawford. "I'm relying on you to make sure everything goes seamlessly at this end. You know how Her Majesty hates inefficiency."

Jock gave her a cheeky salute and, with a nod to his cousin, rose into the air and flew back through the arch.

The Royal Raven walked over to the crow who was dwarfed by her sheer size. "Well, good luck, Crawf."

Jock's cousin practically swooned on hearing her use the familiar version of his name. Who was going weak at the knees now? "Thank you so much, Your Majesticness."

He felt frivolous and light-headed and had to take a couple of steadying breaths.

Indigoletta signalled to Cough that it was time to go. The expression on Crawford's face was one of pure rapture and she barely managed to suppress a giggle. Ah, the power she could command when the notion took her. It was fortunate she didn't believe her own publicity.

The little crow watched until Indigoletta and Cough were two distant points on the horizon. Crawford was besotted and, as such, beyond hope.

Estella galloped round the kitchen of 'Corbie Cottage' with an exuberant Pongo barking up a storm in her wake.

"Don't forget your new pogo stick, the one with built-in stabilisers," said her mother, battering the peas into submission.

"I won't, Mum. I'm getting to grips with it, aren't I, Pongo?"

The dog belted out into the hall and grabbed the pogo stick between his perfect white teeth. He rushed back into the kitchen and dropped it at Estella's feet. He was so full of beans it seemed as if the tail was wagging the dog.

"There you go, and don't let that cheeky nephew of mine give you any trouble when you're staying with your Uncle Mervyn."

"Scruggs will be no bother. He's related to you after all." The child's eyes twinkled wickedly.

"That's what worries me," said the hairy wee dog, glancing up at Pogo. "We're not renowned for our quiet temperaments and rational behaviour."

"That's as may be, boy, but your family are good to have around when the going gets tough, and you know it. Scruggs is an excellent chap, very like you, come to think of it."

The dog gave a self-conscious smirk. He hopped into his basket, turned round several times and settled into his crocheted blanket.

Estella and Pogo nearly jumped out of their skins when he suddenly let rip with a barrage of extremely loud barks, announcing the imminent arrival of Alfie and his guests.

The pixie rounded on the dog. "Good grief, Pongo! Can you not be a bit more subtle?" She scanned the kitchen in an exaggerated, theatrical manner. "Where's my wee bairn? Oh my, there she is up on the ceiling; where else would she be after your performance?"

The child and the dog were rolling around on the floor, overcome with hysterical laughter. "Stop it, Mum," gasped Estella. "My ribs are aching."

Pongo recovered enough to dash to the front door. "Great to see you, Dad," he quipped. "Uncle Angus, too. How nice." The dog was about to follow them into the kitchen but stopped when the snake swished past him into the hall. "SSS, it's always a pleasure. You're looking bewitchingly well."

Sammy acknowledged him with a hiss and a gracious nod of his head before going into sidewinder mode round the kitchen table.

"Snazzy manoeuvre…"

"It comes in handy s-sometimes. I learnt it from my cousin in Aridzonia."

Pongo was amazed that the snake's headgear stayed firmly in place throughout. "Lovely crown, can I try it on?" He was pulling out all the stops on the cute and appealing front, something that came naturally to him. "Oh, go on, *plea-s-se*."

Pogo was affronted. What if Sammy thought the dog was being over familiar or making fun of the way he spoke? "Pipe down, for goodness sake. What do you think you're playing at?"

The pixie rushed forward to kiss her husband and his uncle but stood uncertainly in front of the snake. She couldn't shake hands with him and kissing him might be construed a bit forward.

The Prince of Cobalt-Sibilance took charge of a potentially awkward moment with a deft double coil of his tail round her outstretched arm. "You look radiantly well, Pogo. It's wonderful to see you."

The serpent spun himself into a multiply coiled figure of eight on the kitchen rug.

"I'm glad we're not standing on ceremony," trilled the dog. "Do make yourself at home, SSS. *Mi casa, su casa.*"

That was the last straw but before Pogo could react the others started to laugh.

"What a character," chortled the snake. "I didn't know he spoke S-s-spanish." Sammy flicked the crown from his head in the direction of the dog. "Here, Pongo, catch!"

"No problem!" The dog hurled himself into the air and caught it neatly between his teeth. He placed the crown carefully on the floor in front of him. "Anyone going to help me put it on?"

Sammy gestured to Estella with his tail. "Would you oblige, my dear?"

She dived across the room and, in a perfectly choreographed sequence, curtseyed to the snake, picked up the crown and placed it on Pongo's curly head with mock reverence.

"There you go, my wee lamb, or should I say, Your Highness?"

Estella then joined the serpent on the rug. She felt rather shy being so close to him but that didn't prevent her from asking if she could sit next to him at supper.

"I wouldn't have it any other way, s-sweetie," he replied gallantly.

It was a jolly affair and Estella had the sort of send off that was just right. She's so smart that any other way might have aroused her suspicions and she could well have suggested she ought to stay right where she was after all.

When she was safely tucked up in bed, the two elves, the pixie and the snake sat down to discuss the situation threatening their security. Pongo lay quietly in his basket listening to what they had to say.

Angus confessed to his part in the events that had led to Leo's unexpected arrival. What else could he do with the cold, dead eyes of the Prince of Cobalt-Sibilance gazing at him hypnotically from a mound of cushions on the sofa?

"I thought I was helping with the dress rehearsal for Sandy's visit. A bit of extra magic to ease things along. I'm as excited as everyone else that the time is right for her to come here. I have wonderful memories of her Dad's visit. My heart was in the right place, but sadly my brain was on a day off."

Pongo raised a sympathetic eyebrow.

Angus gave an involuntary shiver, struggled to his feet and walked over to the kitchen range to warm himself. "I simply didn't know the cat was there. That's no excuse. I should have seen him but I didn't." The old elf was choking with emotion. "I'm so dreadfully sorry. I shouldn't have been there, I knew the arch was out of bounds, but I let pride colour my judgment. That poor cat must be very frightened."

Alfie rose from his chair and embraced him. "Please don't distress yourself. We'll sort this out, and find Leo, but there are even more pressing concerns tonight."

Sammy slid from the couch onto the floor. He too was affected by Angus's plight and found himself in an uncharacteristically untidy heap at his feet. "The cat's arrival was unprecedented, but it's happened so there's no point dwelling on it. We must do our best to limit the damage and stop those who are determined to destroy all that we love and cherish."

The snake's sibilance vanishes when he's under pressure.

"I've stepped up security at the vaults, particularly in the chamber that contains the anklet. Maligna is secure on the Island of Long Forgotten Dreams but the guards have reported a distinct change in her behaviour. Her despondent mood seems to have lifted and wild, disturbing laughter has been heard in the dead of night."

Earth tremors are not that uncommon in Sylvania but earthquakes are rare. It so happened that the forces of good and evil came together one night and brought about a small seismic shift that was enough to alter the Harpie's circumstances. It was not immediately apparent that she might benefit from the quake as she was consumed with fury at being woken up and thrown so violently from her hateful pallet bed.

The earthquake lasted no more than a few seconds and the guards in the chamber above her dungeon shone strong-beamed torches through the huge metal grating that sealed the sink-hole. Everything seemed to be in order and there were no obvious signs of damage.

Maligna was flustered and angry. She was trying to salvage a modicum of dignity from a particularly undignified situation. Once the guards were satisfied they exchanged grins and went back to their game of peggity.

During the day a dim shaft of light shone through a gap in the rocks above the sink-hole. It was feeble at the best of times but the Harpie was grateful for it nonetheless. She had a small supply of candles which she could light at night but they were strictly rationed and she was reluctant to use them.

Maligna knew every inch of her prison and had no trouble finding one. She carefully lit the candle and, waiting for her eyes to adjust, glanced round to see if anything had changed.

At first she thought it was just the same dreich dungeon but then she spotted something lying on the rock floor partially concealed by the blanket which had slipped from her bed. She glanced up at the grate high above her head to make sure she wasn't being spied on.

The Harpie pushed strands of lank hair back from her dark, soulless eyes and moved the blanket aside. The object rolled towards her. On closer inspection she discovered it was an egg and a large one at that. She knelt down and shone the candle at the wall underneath the bed. There was a hole in the limestone which hadn't been there before.

Maligna rocked back on her heels when she noticed a small crack developing on the surface of the coarse shell. She stared in fascination as a split appeared in the inner membrane and a head popped out.

"And who might you be?" she asked in a hushed, reverential tone.

She crouched down, with her hands cupped under her chin, and found herself eye to eye with a baby dragon.

The creature was cautiously unfolding his scaly wings when he noticed Maligna's intense gaze. He smiled his very first dragon smile. "Hello, Mum," he said with relief and pleasure.

Maligna managed to stifle what would have been a very loud laugh. Fate had just been kind to her for the first time since her incarceration.

"Hello, my darling boy. I'm so glad to see you." She extended a translucent, bony hand and patted him lightly on the head. "You'll have to be ever so quiet, I'm afraid. No one must know you're here. They'll take you away from me if they find you and we'll never see each other again."

The tiny dragon tried to scramble onto her lap.

"Don't worry, I'll make sure they don't find you, but you must always do as I say."

She clutched him to her scrawny chest and blew out the candle.

"I need to rest now. There's much to think about, not least of all how to feed and take care of you without the enemy finding out."

Maligna placed him carefully on the bed between her two soiled pillows.

"Have a sip of milk, that's all they've left me with." She fed him small droplets from a chipped cup. "You must rest now. Good night, darling one."

The dragon cuddled up next to his 'mother' and fell into the deep, contented sleep of the very young.

No more than a few feet away, on the other side of the rock wall, a scattered clutch of dragon eggs was starting to hatch. The adult dragon was distracted and anxious as she tried to rescue her offspring and failed to notice that one of her eggs was missing.

Ralph Henderson was not one for open displays of affection but he embraced his daughter and kissed her goodbye. Sandy stood uncertainly in front of the shimmering arch with the Siamese cat beside her, a serene expression on his fine-featured face.

They were travelling light. Everything they might need was waiting for them in Sylvania.

Jamie rubbed his cheek against Sandy's leg and purred encouragingly. "We'll be just fine, you'll see."

"What will you say to Mum and Kirstine when I don't turn up for my tea? And Maureen and Liz Drysdale are coming for the weekend, I've got to be here for that."

Her Dad smiled reassuringly but Jock could tell he was worried.

"Your sister won't be back until Friday night and there's no way you'll miss your own birthday party. Time here moves at a much slower pace than it does in Sylvania and Leo shouldn't be that hard to track down."

The phrase 'famous last words' popped uninvited into his head.

All at once Ralph was gripped by a powerful sense of unease. He was sorely tempted to call the trip off but realised his daughter would never abandon her cat. As a mortal child she couldn't come to any real harm while she was in Sylvania and intuition told him it was already too late to stop the chain of events that had been set in motion.

Children, birds and animals are open-minded and non-judgmental. Their innocence of spirit and sense of wonder enable them to move between two different worlds quite comfortably. Fairy folk prefer not to have grown-ups in their world because they are invariably pompous and patronising. In no time they start interfering in a misguided belief that Sylvanians can benefit from their superior knowledge. It's a blanket rule which is strictly enforced no matter how nice the grown-up might be. Ralph and people like him are as rare as hens' teeth and certainly wouldn't upset the apple-cart, but the fairy world is not willing to risk damaging the status quo during unsettled times.

"I know this sounds ridiculous," Jock said with a chuckle, "but we'll have an easier passage if we link hands, paws and wings, like holiday makers in a Greek taverna after a good few drinks. We're different shapes and sizes so it'll be awkward but it will reduce the turbulence and we're more likely to arrive together." The crow offered up a silent prayer that nothing would go wrong. "It doesn't hurt a bit and I promise you'll love every second of it."

Jock was right on the button.

Sandy was delighted with her remarkable journey from Scotland to Sylvania. It felt as if she were dreaming and floating at the same time. It was an exhilarating experience, made up of fleeting images of warm, sparkling sunlit fields; of meadows peppered with fragile red poppies and delicate blue cornflowers; tantalising glimpses of mysterious reflections on deep, dark pools; cold, silvery shafts of moonlight reflecting on myriads of intricately sculpted snowflakes which could only have been created by Jack Frost himself; children in woolly hats and gloves laughing and smiling as they warmed themselves in front of flaming bonfires. In essence it was a kaleidoscope of those experiences that make childhood so special.

Jamie's journey was tailor-made for a cat. Kind, loving families, scrumptious food, endless snoozing in front of roaring fires, and a cat's ultimate pleasure; lazing in a warm, comfortable bed. These scenes were interwoven with cats and kittens indulging in a most absorbing pastime, the ancient art of cat yoga.

When your cat is fast asleep, belly up, with his legs all over the place, I hope you realise he's not taking it easy. Far from it, he's indulging in a challenging mental and physical workout to keep himself in peak condition.

Oh, *of course*, I hear you exclaim sarcastically. Let me put it this way, when push comes to shove, who's the fitter, you or your cat, and when exactly was the last time *you* ran up the curtains?

I rest my case.

The Giant Rat was still in serious thinking cap mode, considering how to befriend the cat without giving him the collywobbles.

His preferred course of action, after much deliberation, was to approach Leo with understated dignity and serenity, thereby introducing a calm note of reassurance and authority.

This was perhaps not the wisest choice for a star-crossed creature like Gilbert but he is one of life's optimists, bless him.

He tiptoed towards Leo who was sitting miserably by the Sprinting River watching a vast magenta moon climb into the navy-blue sky.

"Right then, chocks away."

The Giant Rat was dramatically silhouetted against said moon when he inadvertently tripped over an exposed tree root which catapulted him into the air. He let out a series of wails, punctuated with terrifying yowls, and landed in an earth-shaking heap right where Leo would have been were he not several feet in the air, having been scared witless.

The best laid plans of rats and men, to paraphrase Scotland's favourite son, the poet Robert Burns.

Gilbert and Leo had well and truly made each other's acquaintance.

The Giant Rat lay on his back with the tiny cat sprawled on his vast stomach. This was Gilbert's only chance to put things right but he could tell the cat was about to leg it.

"Please don't go, I didn't mean to frighten you. I'm afraid I'm clumsy and accident prone. I'm the wrong scale for this little world." Leo crawled onto Gilbert's chest and looked uncertainly into his kind eyes. "I'd like to help you if I can. You've just arrived here from 'Woodburn', haven't you?"

"Have I?" The cat was very confused but he did brighten at the mention of home.

"Yes, indeedy. I'm Gilbert, by the way, and it's very nice to meet you."

"My name's Leo and I'm an Abyssinian cat who belongs to Sandy Hen…"

Gilbert swiftly cut in. "I know who Sandy is, Leo."

"You do?"

"Uh huh." He gently lifted the cat up and placed him on the ground. "I'm going to get to my feet now, so don't be scared."

Leo could barely conceal his excitement. "Will you help me find Sandy?"

"I promise I'll do everything I can to bring about a happy reunion." Gilbert had a sudden urge to cheer Leo up. "I tell you what, why don't you come home with me? I've got a few sparklers left. We could set them off if you like."

Leo desperately wanted to go with the Giant Rat, but he was apprehensive about the sparklers.

"I'd really like to come with you, Gilbert, but I'm not very good with fireworks."

The Giant Rat realised his mistake and laughed. "That's OK, Leo. I'm not very good with them either. I'm trying to give them up, as a matter of fact, not just for my own good but for the safety of everyone else as well. You look very tired to me. Why don't I carry you home? Are you hungry?"

Leo nodded yes on both counts and Gilbert crouched down so that he could clamber aboard. "There you go, just climb up my front leg. Grab hold of my fur if you want to, you're so light I won't feel a thing."

The exhausted cat had barely enough strength left to pull himself onto the rat's shoulders.

"Now hang on tight, Leo."

The Giant Rat stood up slowly and headed off in the direction of his makeshift home.

Gilbert's always on the move as it isn't safe for him to stay in one place for very long. There always seems to be someone on his tail. The life of a large rat in a miniature world is very trying and fraught with difficulty.

Long before it was dark, Jock, Sandy and Jamie arrived in Sylvania. The crow was used to making the trip alone so he could be excused for not being thoroughly prepared.

Jock was right about one thing, they did all turn up at the same time, but the manner of their entrance was far from perfect. They came close to flattening the Royal Raven, who was standing proudly at the head of her squadrons of rooks, magpies, jays, hooded and carrion crows. Indigoletta staggered backwards in horror and set off a chain reaction. The ranks of birds were standing so stiffly to attention they fell over like rows of collapsing dominoes.

Crawford was apoplectic as he watched the ridiculous tableau unfold from his position in front of Kismet, the Royal Steed.

The immense Sylvanian Forest Cat was carrying an ornate gold howdah on his back which was occupied by Her Majesty Queen Celestina, her consort Hamish and their young daughter, Tabitha. They were accompanied by two ladies-in-waiting, the Queen's favourite poodle, Archie, and Moriarty, Crawford's bat. There was one other passenger, riding up front with Kismet, a rare lilac and blue fairy mouse. Wainscot is Kismet's best pal and they are virtually inseparable. The mouse was sitting on a fancy silk cushion by the cat's left ear.

Nine white-winged rooks circled above the Queen's head, making sure Her Majesty was protected at all times. These ferocious birds are Celestina's personal bodyguards.

A troop of elves carrying longbows and quivers of arrows fletched with the finest crow feathers formed a semi-circle to the right of the Royal Steed. On the left was a contingent of stocky, grim-faced goblins wielding stubby, formidable axes crafted from the strongest Sylvanian irongold.

There were standard-bearers and flag-carrying flunkies, groups of courtiers and officials dressed in bejewelled velvets and lace, servants carrying trays of refreshments and silver salvers groaning with tasty, exquisite morsels. Elegant pixies wearing studded leather gauntlets held exotic birds of prey on their slim wrists. They mingled with groups of purple liveried elves who were trying to restrain handfuls of boisterous dogs on fancy, beribboned leads.

A military band should have been playing the upbeat Sylvanian anthem but the conductor and musicians stood with stunned expressions and gaping mouths watching the calamity unfold.

Twitchett was at the head of the Impfantry choking in disbelief while colourfully dressed Crawdonian commoners roared their approval.

Sandy scrambled to her feet, bewildered but thrilled at the same time and, with the help of Jock, came to Jamie's aid. He lay in a horribly undignified position at Indigoletta's feet and was completely mortified.

The cat felt compelled to turn his back on everyone and wash himself in a none-too-convincing 'see if I care' sort of attitude. Jock and Sandy beckoned him towards them.

"Your M-a-a-j-j-esty, I'm so sorry, what can I say?" The crow clapped a wing-tip theatrically to his forehead and peeked through the splayed feathers in an attempt to ascertain the Queen's mood which was very hard to tell from where he was standing.

Indigoletta's state of mind was another matter. He could hear a hoarse, fizzing sound from the back of her throat, like the noise a keg of beer makes when it's about to explode.

The Royal Raven gave 'the one and only' a withering look and closed her eyes until she recovered her composure.

Her squadrons had sorted themselves back into perfect rows in a trice; they were top-flight professionals, after all.

Indigoletta stared disdainfully at Jock. She opened her beak to give him what for but was stopped in her tracks by a familiar sound.

Queen Celestina was helpless with laughter.

"Welcome to Sylvania! Thank you for the best display I've been treated to in years."

The Fairy Queen waved her wand, with Moriarty still clinging to it. Thousands of glittering gold and silver stars poured out from the tip in ever-increasing numbers. They danced and capered in the clear, warm air and drifted out over the throng.

The elf, the pixie and the dog were sitting in an open-topped, pony-drawn buggy watching the whole circus. Their anxious expressions were replaced with broad smiles. Pongo started barking and shouting in unconfined joy. He grinned at Alfie and scampered off to catch some magic stars for Pogo.

Sandy gazed at the celestial pageant. I suppose you could say she was star-struck. She wasn't dreaming; she was undeniably in Sylvania. There was no need to pinch herself, but she was tempted to do so all the same.

The dapper little conductor of the Queen's Own Musicians lifted his baton and the band of assorted fairy folk launched into a rousing rendition of the Sylvanian national anthem. Everyone sang lustily and when the song came to an end they roared their approval and stamped their feet in a joyous display of loyalty to the Royal Family.

Celestina bowed graciously to her subjects while her husband smiled and nodded at the crowd.

Prince Hamish is a gentle, well-read elf from Lotharion, a shire to the east of the Craggan Heights, between Crawdonia and Kelpien where Estella was staying with Pogo's brother Mervyn and his family.

"Let the festivities begin," commanded the Fairy Queen. She lifted her honey-coloured poodle over the side of the howdah. Sandy and Jamie exchanged puzzled looks. Celestina laughed heartily when she saw their startled faces. "They ain't seen nothing yet, have they Hamish?" He gave her delicate shoulder an affectionate squeeze. "You haven't even warmed up yet," he chuckled. "Just wait 'til they see your aerial flamenco."

When the Queen let go of Archie, his long, feathery tail began to rotate faster and faster and he rose into the air before flying down, helicopter style, to land at the astonished child's feet.

"Watcha," said the handsome poodle. "Queen Celestina gave me the power of flight for my last birthday. It was quite scary to start with, but I'm feeling more confident about solo flights now."

The poodle noticed Jamie staring up at the gargantuan long-haired cat. "The Royal Steed's impressive, isn't he? Kismet's a gentle giant, really. Sylvanian Forest Cats are renowned for their relaxed approach to life but they have an incredible turn of speed which can be very handy if you find yourself in a tight spot."

The benign beast nodded graciously from his exalted position. "Good to meet you, Jamie."

"Likewise," said the Siamese who was taking in every inch of Kismet's sumptuous maroon and silver coat. "I hope you don't think I'm being forward, but your colour scheme is most unusual and very becoming."

"I'm glad you approve."

"Sylvanian Forest Cats can be any colour or pattern they wish," said Archie enthusiastically.

"We simply choose a combination, say, black and purple stripes, or red and gold checks; whatever takes our fancy. It's great fun. I was shocking pink with blue and purple spots yesterday."

"Wow," said Jamie, "I'd love to be able to do that."

The Royal Party had already begun their descent. Queen Celestina could have flown down but chose to use the neat staircase that unfolds, at the press of a button, from its position underneath the howdah.

Alfie jumped out of the buggy in response to a gesture from his monarch. He bowed and doffed his hat.

The Queen smiled warmly. "Come and join us for refreshments in the Royal Pavilion." She waved Sandy and Jamie over. "You must be hungry, dears."

Celestina took her daughter by the hand and swished off in a dazzling array of iridescent silks and sequins. "Well, Tabby, do you think Cook might have prepared some of that chunky kibble the royal dogs and cats like so much? I know Pongo loves it. Do try some, Jamie, and let me know what you think."

Prince Hamish grinned mischievously. "We've organised some musical entertainment for you later on. Alfie's cousin is doing a turn."

The elf groaned. "How thoughtful of you, sir." He nudged his wife. "All we need now is Uncle Angus with an illustrated lecture on the rudiments of spell-weaving." Pogo burst out laughing and linked arms with her husband as they walked together into the fabulous royal pavilion.

Sandy and Jamie had a wonderful time getting to know everyone. Indigoletta was particularly welcoming. "I remember your father's visit as if it were yesterday."

"But that was nearly forty years ago," said a surprised Sandy.

Indigoletta was sitting on an ebony perch sipping a furry-fig sorbet through a long silver straw. "We have a very different system of time here, my dear. I'm three hundred and nine Sylvanian years old and I'm not yet in my prime."

Crawford had a ridiculous, lovelorn expression on his face. He waved a wing in the direction of Indigoletta. "Doesn't she look radiant?"

Sandy nodded vigorously, trying not to smirk.

The Royal Raven winked at her. "Why thank you, Crawf. I adore your polka dot tie. Violet is undoubtedly your colour."

"You think so? It's not too vivid with the emerald green spots?"

Indigoletta was in an indulgent mood. "Good heavens, no. It's absolutely divine." She spotted the recent addition to her household in his swanky new uniform standing uncertainly behind Sandy's chair. "Fetch Crawford some fingalberry wine, Will. He looks a little faint. It's a marvellous tonic." Then in a whispered aside to the lad, "Try a drop yourself, it's wonderful for calming the nerves."

Moriarty was reluctant to leave the Queen and return to Crawford. In fact, he was more than a bit crestfallen and had the demeanour of a damp flannel.

"Come and see me again soon, honey pie," Celestina called from her position at the head of the table. The bat gave a feeble flutter, rallying slightly at the sound of her voice.

"You've made your point, Moriarty," said Crawford through the crow equivalent of gritted teeth. He attempted to win the bat over with some scrumptious chuckleberries. Bullseye! Moriarty thrummed happily, demolished the sweet fruit then nipped into the pocket of Crawford's lavender silk waistcoat for a little nap.

The Siamese was purring up a storm on Sandy's lap. When she spoke there was a slight catch in her voice. "What a fantastic welcome. Everyone's so kind." She felt an arm slip round her shoulders and there was Pogo smiling reassuringly. The pixie tickled Jamie under the chin. "We'll find Leo, whatever it takes. I'm glad you're both here. Does it feel *very* strange?"

"Just a bit! I had long since stopped believing and now here you all are. I don't feel physically changed, not even smaller, but everything's completely different."

"It'll take time to adjust, but you'll soon settle in."

"Please don't think I'm unhappy, just overwhelmed, and I love it here already. Sylvania's miles better than I could ever have imagined. I can hardly wait for SSS and the Giant Rat to turn up."

"You'll meet Sammy soon." Pogo lowered her voice. "We'll talk about Gilbert later, he's been in a lot of trouble recently."

Sandy giggled. "Is that his name? It's not at all what I would have expected."

The music stopped and the jugglers, tumblers and performing poodles cleared the floor.

Prince Hamish rose from his chair. "We have a very special friend here this evening who is going to entertain us." He paused which added to the sense of anticipation. "None other than Wee Alfie Elf's cousin Fergus, better known to us all by his stage name, 'Bandolero'."

There were whoops and cat-calls, not the obvious reaction from such a grand gathering.

Sandy couldn't help noticing the fixed smile on Alfie's face; he clapped along with the others but his heart was not in it.

A troupe of sombrero-wearing musicians ran into the middle of the pavilion amid frenzied guitar strumming. An elf in full Mexican bandit regalia walked sedately into the spotlight which consisted of millions of fireflies in a controlled swarm. Fergus placed his sombrero on the ground in front of him and bowed first to the right and then to the left. "I veel now perform zee Mexican Hat Dance," he announced in a cod Spanish accent. With that, he leapt into the air, silver spurs jingling and jangling as he executed some nifty, complicated footwork while he systematically pounded his long-suffering sombrero into the ground.

When the dance finally came to an end, Bandolero strutted and pranced, soaking up the wild applause.

Alfie couldn't help joining in with the tumultuous ovation. "What a guy, you've got to hand it to him. He knows how to please a crowd. They *love* him."

Fergus, aka Bandolero, had almost disappeared beneath armfuls of floral tributes and the crowd showed no signs of letting up.

The trampled, dishevelled hat stood up on a pair of tiny feet, gave itself a half-hearted shake and trudged wearily backstage.

Pogo shouted over the rapturous clapping. "It's that poor sombrero I feel sorry for. Fergus has never been the same since he went on a package holiday to the Costa del Solvania."

Sandy grabbed some flowers from a floral display on the table and ran after the dejected hat. "Hang on a minute! These are for you. I thought you were fantastic. He couldn't have done it without you."

The sombrero stopped and raised its battered brim. "For me? How thoughtful, thank you so much."

She carefully placed the flowers around the crown of the hat.

"You really have made my day, Sandy. It's been a pleasure performing for you."

The hat shambled off through a tent-flap and she was glad when she heard it say, "I can't remember the last time I said that and genuinely meant it."

Sammy Slithering Snake sashayed in while Celestina was telling Sandy about her Fabulous Flying Flamenco. "SSS," she yelled as soon as she saw him. Her hand flew up to her mouth. "I'm sorry, Your Majesty, I didn't mean to shout."

"There's no need to be restrained around me. I'm all for informality. Even monarchs are allowed to have a sense of humour. Now why are you still here? Off you go and say hello."

Sandy scooted across the pavilion, weaving in and out of clusters of fabulously attired fairy folk. When she found herself in front of the Prince of Cobalt-Sibilance she suddenly felt shy and awkward.

Sammy gracefully coiled himself round her tentatively outstretched arm and briefly brushed his face against her cheek. "S-sandy, it's so good to meet you at last. You do look like your Dad, you know."

3

On the way home to 'Corbie Cottage', Alfie dropped Sammy off at the Cave of Sublime Spirit and the snake invited them all in.

Sandy and Jamie were introduced to the Giant Sapphire. The gemstone hummed and sparkled in response, turning a deep, glittering cobalt blue. They watched enthralled as the sapphire engaged its potent magic, creating an uplifting, regenerative spell to help Sandy and Jamie stay positive and centred during their quest for Leo.

The gem threw out beams of intense purple light that whizzed and zipped around the cave. Pongo dashed after the fleeting rays, but they dissolved before he could catch them. He's a smart dog and knows from experience it's a pointless game, but it still amuses him. Catching stars from Queen Celestina's wand is a far more rewarding exercise.

Sammy introduced Sandy to Spondoolicks who ran round in circles on the palm of her hand. "Capital," said the serpent, "he really likes you. He doesn't do that for just anyone."

"Too right, pal. Have ye got a moment, Sandy?" The spider nipped behind a vast pile of rubies that were waiting to be catalogued.

"Dear friends, I do believe you're in for a treat."

Alfie grinned at his wife. "You're not wrong, SSS."

Spondoolicks swung out on a thread from behind the heap of gems and made a perfectly controlled descent onto Alfie's outstretched hand where he burst into a quirky rendition of the Sylvanian national anthem on his jauntily striped woollen bagpipes.

The serpent leant towards Sandy. "He knitted them himself. A fascinating sound, don't you think?"

Everyone found the spider's antics hilarious, except for Jamie. Cats don't go in for that sort of thing, it's far too vulgar. When it comes down to it, they rarely see the funny side of things. All that fuss over a multiply dexterous, bagpipe-playing spider.

They were on the point of leaving when Sandy turned to the snake. Her face was pale and she looked small and tired. "What's happened to Jock? Come to think of it, I haven't seen him for hours."

Sammy flowed gracefully towards the child, his impressive crown sparkling in the half-light of the cave. He was wearing his serene, reassuring face. "Jock left the reception early for a chat with me, then he had some unfinished business to attend to in Irvine. He was set on telling your Dad you'd all arrived safely, something Ralph no doubt already knows if he's been following your progress through the Cauldron. However, Jock does prefer the personal touch."

Sandy wasn't ready to be pacified. "I didn't even notice he was missing until now. How completely selfish of me."

"It's hardly surprising after all you've been through today. Don't upset yourself. Jock isn't planning on being away for long, he'll be back before you know it. Now, it really is time you were all back at 'Corbie Cottage'."

60

Jock Craw had brought Sandy and Jamie safely to Sylvania and the arch was swallowed up again by the ever-vigilant hedge.

No one could move in either direction and Hosepipe Snout the Hairy Hedgehorn felt the weight of responsibility lift from his spiky shoulders. The search for Leo could be given greater priority and he felt confident the cat would be easier to track down with the child in Crawdonia.

Sandy had been so taken up with the spectacle of the elaborate reception she'd failed to notice Jock slip out of the royal pavilion.

An inconspicuous tent had been set aside for the rendez-vous within the general clutter of commoners' tents and other paraphernalia.

Sammy was nibbling a cherry and banana scone when the crow turned up. "Good to see you, Jock. I hear everything went more or less according to plan," he said with a wry smile. "I need to talk to you before I go off to meet Sandy. But first, do have one of these superb scones, you look famished."

Jock realised he hadn't eaten for ages and helped himself to a particularly chunky one which he scoffed with undisguised satisfaction. "I managed to have a brief word with Queen Celestina before I left the 'do'," he said through a shower of crumbs. "She's truly amazing. You'd never guess she's gravely concerned about recent developments. The Queen excels at playing the relaxed, frivolous monarch but we both know how shrewd she is underneath. Her Majesty's adamant we maintain an air of calm authority and don't spread panic throughout the land."

Sammy called for iced water from Cressmere spa on Moonglow Lake and he paused while a flunky filled their glasses. When the fellow was out of earshot he continued in an urgent whisper. "Recent intelligence suggests a conspiracy to free Maligna and reunite her with the anklet. Preposterous, but alarming all the same."

"I knew things were a bit dicey, my old string-bean, but I hadn't realised the extent of it."

"String-bean, eh? That's a first." The reptile allowed himself a restrained titter. "There's also the small matter of Leo. He could, through no fault of his own, prove to be a bit of a loose cannon. You know how it is with *uninvited* guests. They've come through the backdoor and the usual rules don't apply. Angus has introduced an extra complication with his jiggery-pokery. The old devil's finally given his wand to Alfie for safe keeping, but we still have to deal with his unfortunate legacy. Leo should not be here. I can't see him with my third eye and Sylvanian magic is limited in what it can do to help him. I've encouraged disgruntled mutterings that the whole cat business is a huge fuss about nothing in an attempt to keep folks off the scent. We know, however, it's not that simple."

Sammy paused for a swig of water. "Can you imagine what might happen if our enemies were to find Leo first? They wouldn't hesitate to use him to further their own cause. The Harpie is growing more confident with every day that passes. It's almost as if she knows what's going on, but how is that possible? Maligna's guarded round the clock in that loathsome sink-hole. None of the guards has anything significant to report, even after the recent earthquake which left her prison undamaged. She's a cunning opponent and irredeemably bad. I liked it better when she was depressed and despondent. Her upbeat mood is most disturbing."

The crow shook his head sadly. "It's extraordinary to think the cat could be so significant, potentially pivotal, in the current situation. I'll pick Ralph's brains when I go back to Irvine." He grimaced at his choice of words. "Metaphorically, you understand! I will have to cut my stay short now that I know the severity of the situation here. Ralph may well be able to help us and there's also the Craw Cauldron. Its magical powers are small, but it's still worth consideration."

Jock flexed his wings in preparation for the trip home. "It's such a shame Sandy's long-anticipated visit is overshadowed by all this uncertainty."

"It's most aggravating, but we're Crawdonians and we relish a challenge. We'll fight to retain our freedom whatever it takes. I'll make sure Queen Celestina and Prince Hamish have all the facts, Indigoletta and Crawford too. Your little cousin comes across as a posturing old fuss-pot but we both know Crawf's one hundred percent loyal and, furthermore, he's nobody's fool. I've already spoken to Alfie and Pogo about my concerns. I had supper with them the night before Estella left for Kelpien. Angus was there too. I was pretty severe with him and he now fully appreciates what we may be up against. He'll keep his counsel. After all, he was instrumental in thwarting Maligna last time around. In those days he was a brilliant young spell-weaver at the peak of his powers."

The serpent uncoiled, stretched and wove himself into his favourite figure of eight. "We can't afford to take too many others into our confidence. It's impossible to tell how far the corruption may have spread. I'll make arrangements with Hosepipe Snout for an early opening of the arch. Safe trip and, as they say in Scotland, 'Haste ye back'."

Alfie delivered his passengers to 'Corbie Cottage' and settled the pony into her stable at the back of the house. Later over mugs of choco-mead, they chatted about the amazing reception in Sandy and Jamie's honour. The gold and silver stars Pongo had collected hovered in the air above their heads, grouping and regrouping in ever-changing, complex patterns.

"How long will they last, WAE?"

"As long as we want them to, Sandy. We're hardly likely to tire of them, they're so beautiful and entertaining. Why don't you have them in your bedroom tonight? They're very therapeutic and they'll help you sleep."

Sandy was intrigued by the glittering display above Alfie's head. "Do they glow in the dark?"

The elf raised one eyebrow. "What do *you* think?"

She blushed. "I think that's the most stupid question I've ever asked!"

Alfie chuckled. "Maybe so."

Pogo wasn't letting that go unchallenged. "Don't pay any heed to Cheeky Chops the Elf. Your whole life has been turned topsy turvy overnight; you're in a world where a poodle can fly, so it's not unreasonable to ask if stars still glow in the dark."

Sandy sipped her hot drink, sitting cross-legged on the warm hearth rug. "It's very nice of you to say that, but it was a daft question all the same. This choco-mead's very tasty. Isn't mead a wine made from honey?"

Alfie grinned. "Yes it is, but it won't make you drunk if that's what you were thinking. Sylvanian wines and spirits are only alcoholic if you're over the lawful age to drink. The mead tailors itself to the age of the drinker which is extremely handy and saves us a lot of hassle. The pixies at the meadery don't have to brew two different strengths and we don't have any problems with under-aged drinking either. It's an excellent system."

Sandy nodded slowly. "This is an amazing place, full of surprises."

Pongo was sitting in his basket with the Siamese cat curled up next to him having a little snooze.

Alfie kicked off his boots and rocked back in his willow chair in front of the kitchen range. "Those two seem to be getting on well."

"Some cat," said Pongo admiringly. "He's very bonny, but don't tell him I said so. We wouldn't want him to get big-headed now, would we?"

"Surely you mean more big-headed," Sandy said with a snigger.

The cat lazily opened one azure eye. "I heard that, you little minx."

"Ooh, get him," said the dog, jumping out of the basket. "Can I fetch you anything, Your Royal Furriness? Would you like a collar studded with diamonds and sapphires to bring out the blue in your twinklies? I'm sure SSS will have something suitable." Pongo snickered when he saw Jamie's snooty expression.

"Sounds good to me," yawned the cat.

"Perhaps sir would like a few styles to choose from?"

"Whatever," said Jamie, feigning boredom as he dozed off again.

Pongo nipped over to Sandy and whispered in her ear. "Wait 'til you see his face tomorrow morning. Sammy has collected loads of collars over the years, I'm sure I can persuade him to part with one when he knows who it's for."

Maligna had worked out a way to feed and care for her new-found companion. It was simple. She had a limitless supply of water and a mug of milk with supper, so all she had to do was eat less herself and hide scraps for Cahoots.

The name had come to her when she lay awake that first night, her meticulous, distorted mind working unceasingly. They were going to be an invincible team. It would be the

Harpie and the dragon against her cruel tormentors. Cahoots was therefore the perfect name.

The young dragon understood he must never be discovered; Maligna had made sure of that. She scared him just enough, with frightful stories of what might befall them both, to ensure he never put a dragon foot wrong. In no time Cahoots was imprinted on her. The Harpie knew she had to work fast for small dragons rapidly turn into big dragons.

"We must escape from this hell-hole, darling one. This is living death for me and you deserve better; that apart, dragons grow at an alarming rate and then how will I hide you?"

Maligna spoke in an urgent whisper while Cahoots gazed adoringly into her black, featureless eyes from his den behind her pillows.

"I was very frightened the first time you sent me back through the crack in the rock, but I'm getting more confident. I'll try not to let you down again. Maybe I'll find a way out this time."

"I'm sure you will, treasure. Your mission is to deliver the message I've taught you, but first you must get away from the island before its malign atmosphere saps your strength. You're unlikely to be affected, being a dragon, but you're very young so don't take that chance. Be sure to leave a trail back here to me in case you get lost. I couldn't bear to lose you now."

She caressed his face with long, pallid fingers. "I have friends out there who will help you. Now you must rest so you're refreshed for your adventure tomorrow. I'll tell you everything else you need to know in the morning."

The Harpie lay down on her pallet under the threadbare blanket, her face level with his. Cahoots waited behind the pillows until she extinguished the candle. There was a faint light from above where the guards were playing yet another hand of cards. In the near darkness of the sink-hole the little

66

dragon wriggled towards Maligna and made a nest in her hair. Cahoots sighed happily and drifted off to sleep. The Harpie could hear his tiny heart beating as she lay awake plotting her next move. It was a curiously comforting sound and she placed a dry wisp of a kiss on his scaly forehead.

"Love you too..." murmured Cahoots from the edge of his dreams.

The Harpie was as old as time itself and beyond all redemption long before the island had first risen from the sea. She was disturbed and confused by her maternal feelings. This was not a good time to become emotionally attached to anything, least of all a dragon. Maligna the Harpie needed her formidable wits about her, now more than ever.

The Giant Rat arrived at his home by the River Pinkie after a very long trek. His primary concern had been to protect his exhausted little passenger.

It was a perfect, starry night and Gilbert knew he would stand out like a massive rat-shaped target in the moonlight. Stealth was not one of his strong points, but he had a new-found sense of responsibility. Leo needed looking after and the rodent had nominated himself for the job of Chief Protector.

The rat's accommodation was more than adequate for his needs and it was warm and dry.

He had stumbled upon his current abode while being hunted by a pack of rat hounds owned by a thoroughly obnoxious character who had placed Gilbert at the top of his 'Most Wanted' list. The rodent finally managed to give them the slip and dived into a massive bush to recover his composure.

Gilbert failed to look before he leapt, never a wise move, and found himself at the centre of a particularly nasty variety of Crawdonian holly which should never be approached without the protection of a full suit of armour.

He stumbled backwards, plunging through a gap in the tangled holly roots into a disused mine shaft which was hidden by the whopping shrub. Gilbert's size was to his advantage. The shaft was deep by Sylvanian standards but, from the Giant Rat's point of view, it had the makings of a perfectly decent new home, with a handy, built-in security system as well.

The rodent dug out a route beneath the holly bush that enabled him to reach his den without injury. He felt safer there than he had since he'd been transported from 'Woodburn'.

"We're nearly home, Leo, keep your head down."

The cat clung onto Gilbert though he was fast asleep and there was the unmistakeable sound of snoring.

The Giant Rat checked one last time to make sure he wasn't being followed and crept towards the carefully camouflaged entrance that led to his den. When he was satisfied he was alone and unobserved, he crouched down under the lower branches of the holly and wriggled along on his ample belly until he reached the edge of the shaft. Gilbert carefully lowered himself into the mine and stood motionless while he listened out for any unusual sounds before moving further into the old workings where he felt most secure.

A domed area formed by the ancient holly roots was Gilbert's sanctuary. It wasn't designer living but it fulfilled his undemanding requirements.

He stood on his hind legs and reached up to light one of the old miner's lamps he'd found at the foot of the shaft. Matches and lighters were second nature to the likes of Gilbert but he'd become more safety conscious since his birthday fireworks extravaganza blew up in his face. Rats, and for that matter, cats can see very well in the dark, but

Gilbert believed it was more civilised to use lamps, as long as the light wasn't visible from outside.

There was a cool, well-stocked larder. Gilbert loves his food and he's a skilful scavenger. Sections of the shored-up roof leak when it rains and he places battered tin mugs that once belonged to the miners underneath to catch the drips. The mugs are small and have to be emptied regularly but the water stays fresh if it's stored properly.

At the far end of the den were the Giant Rat's sleeping quarters.

Leo woke up with a start when he heard his name called out. He slid down Gilbert's fur and landed on the compacted earth floor.

"You'll be safe here with me."

The Abyssinian cat stood up on wobbly legs, stretched and promptly fell over. He was fuzzy with sleep and weighed down by suffocating layers of anxiety and exhaustion.

The rodent desperately wanted to raise Leo's spirits and would have turned somersaults while juggling Indian clubs on a monocycle if he'd thought it might do the trick. Somersaults were easy-peasy. Sadly, or possibly fortunately depending on your point of view, he was clean out of Indian clubs and monocycles. He had established earlier that sparklers and fireworks were definitely taboo. "...and a good thing, too," he told himself with studied conviction. That left the Giant Rat with a straightforward multiple choice question.

If you're not sure what to do next, but you're trying your best to help a scared cat who's had a very weird time, do you offer him: (a) food, (b) grub, (c) nosh, (d) chow, or (e) tucker?

Tick as appropriate.

Gilbert was famished as a result of his strenuous activity so, after careful consideration, he mentally ticked (a) and (c). It seemed churlish not to tick (b), (d) or (e), so he thought he might as well make it a full house/tummy (delete as appropriate).

He settled Leo in a cosy pile of fresh shavings he'd gnawed from old pit props and gave him some water before expertly preparing a tasty supper. The cat gobbled the delicious mix of stale cheese and fish heads sprinkled with sweetcorn kernels and slices of dried apricot.

Leo felt much better after he'd eaten. His features relaxed and he lost the anguished expression that had been with him since he arrived in Sylvania.

The Giant Rat had brashly entered his life a few hours earlier but Leo felt it was a fortuitous meeting for them both. It felt great to have a big guy like Gilbert as a pal in this strange world. Leo knew intuitively the rat was a lonely, well-meaning soul, very much in need of a chum and the little cat was more than happy to fill that gap in his life.

The Mischief Maker is a rundown, dilapidated tavern on the west bank of the River Pinkie. The pub is on the edge of Skerries, a village no more than a mile from Gilbert's gaff. It's little more than a boozer with an attached doss-house and it's the favoured haunt of hoodlums, ruffians and scoundrels. The inn belongs to Jem Slack, a shifty apology for a gnome, and his unfortunate wife, Gertie.

One supremely nasty piece-of-work has made The Mischief Maker his second home, self-styled 'Captain' Pestilence Grimshaw. When he's not looting ships on the high seas in his brigantine, 'The Cheeky Monkey', he's likely to be found slouched in a battered old lug-chair reserved for him in front of the inn's meagre fire. There he sits, quaffing ale by the quart, regaling everyone with stories of his brutal adventures.

His First Mate, Jedediah Malahyde, was sitting opposite Grimshaw, guzzling a bowl of herring-tail broth. Pestilence

was still waiting for his supper and was more than a little disgruntled.

"Landlord," bellowed the pirate, "where's my dinner? You wouldn't want me to come over and give you a smack on the head, would you?" The tall, wiry buccaneer made as if to get up from his chair. "It would be my pleasure to oblige you, Slack, you only have to say the word." His smile was a gash across his weather-beaten face. Violence is a way of life for Pestilence Grimshaw and his crew.

The landlord's left eyelid twitched nervously and he gave an uneasy laugh. "Now, now, Cap'n Grimshaw, your haddock and pilchard stew's on its way." He turned on the down-trodden, frumpy creature who had the misfortune to be his wife. "You're a lazy article, Gertie, and I won't put up with it. Fetch the stew right away." She didn't bother to acknowledge her husband and, with a sullen scowl, scuffed off in her grubby, down-at-heel slippers towards the kitchen.

Jem called after her, "Make sure you apologise to Cap'n Grimshaw for taking so long."

Gertie's voice was flat and toneless. "Whatever you say, Jem." She shoved her greasy hair out of her pale, watery eyes. "Nag, nag, nag. That's all I ever hear from you these days, Jem Slack. What happened to the cheerful young gnome I married?"

Pestilence Grimshaw couldn't resist poking fun at her. "He bought himself stronger glasses and saw what you really look like, Gertie. Isn't that right, Slack?"

Customers by the bar collapsed laughing and Jem joined in, relieved the awkward moment had passed. Grimshaw's cabin boy, Pigsblanket, was knocked from his stool by a sniggering goblin. He crashed to the floor, capsizing a quart of beer which the landlord had just placed on the counter.

The First Mate gave the lad a light cuff round the ear. "Pigsblanket, you oaf, get up and fetch the Cap'n another ale and be double quick about it."

The under-nourished boy was desperate to get back in Malahyde's good books. The First Mate was the only member of the crew who held any sway with Pestilence Grimshaw and he'd saved Pigsblanket's bacon on more than one occasion. "Yes, sir, Mr Malahyde. Would you like another ale yourself?"

"No thank you, lad."

Jedediah had a soft spot for young Pigsblanket and knew the lad could barely afford to pay for Grimshaw's ale, let alone one for anyone else. What Malahyde failed to realise was that the cabin boy had so little money he couldn't even afford a piece of stale bread for his supper.

Grimshaw is a man of his word when it comes to violent threats and Jem Slack gratefully swallowed the best part of a tankard of ale. If his luck held he might make it through the rest of the night without a beating.

The landlord was still recovering from a run-in with the buccaneer who had landed an all-too-accurate punch on his jaw only last week. Jem had tripped over Grimshaw's discarded boots when the tavern was filled to the rafters and, unhappily for him, had spilled some of the irascible pirate's beer. The pub was seething with folk who had come to hear Flip Flapper and the Snappers, an up-and-coming pixie band. They're fine musicians on the threshold of success and will soon never have to play disgusting dives like The Mischief Maker again. The group was supported by the tavern's resident ensemble, Pond Life, an especially apt name for this bunch of talentless no-hopers.

Jem's tavern has always been a serious drinking house, but recently it has become a magnet for the dregs of Sylvanian society. It's a dump and a disreputable one at that and, as such, is precisely the sort of place where you might expect to find supporters of a certain Harpie. Maligna may have been incarcerated for years but she's far from forgotten.

Pestilence Grimshaw is one of an increasing number of sympathisers who would like to revive her cause. He may be quick-tempered and violent, but he's nobody's fool. Maligna's wickedness appeals to him and he's sure there are great rewards to be had for anyone who can help her escape from the Island of Long Forgotten Dreams. Pestilence can see limitless possibilities for self-enhancement in befriending one such as her which is why he's aiming to make himself indispensable to her. They also happen to connect in another, less significant area of their lives. They both have the sea in their blood.

Grimshaw's mother is a formidable seawitch. His father was a foolish mortal who fell under her spell when, for a bit of fun, she decided to visit Irvine in the guise of a pretty young woman. You know how it is, callow youth has head turned by beautiful, heartless damsel. They were married and settled down together in a house near Seagate Castle in the centre of the town.

When the enchantress became bored with domestic life she returned to Sylvania with her newborn son, leaving her husband in a state of abject misery, never knowing what had become of them both. He died a few years later, a broken man.

A strange bed, in an unfamiliar cottage, in an enigmatic new world. The ideal recipe for a sleepless night? Most definitely not.

Pogo Pixie led them up the wooden stairs with the cluster of stars following on behind.

Pongo was sandwiched between Sandy and Jamie, determined not to be left out. "You'll be sleeping in Estella's room while she's away," he announced with an air of importance. "It's down the passageway to the left and the bathroom is straight ahead."

"Thank you boy, most informative. Make yourselves at home," Pogo said, ushering them into her daughter's bedroom.

It was surprisingly spacious and Sandy felt instantly relaxed in her new surroundings. The walls were decorated with pastel shades of luminous glitter paint depicting woodland scenes of unicorns and flying horses. Oil lamps and candles created a rosy glow and a log fire crackled in the hearth. Above the mantlepiece was an oil painting of two birds. The larger of them sported a clutch of white feathers on his broad, glossy chest and a suitably dignified expression on his noble face.

The smaller bird had a monocle and was kitted out in a flamboyant waistcoat and snazzy bow tie. He was sporting a pair of black patent shoes with bold silver buckles which he reserves for occasions of the greatest importance. Two distinguished characters with whom we're already well-acquainted.

The mass of stars drifted in and congregated in a desultory pattern above the bed.

There were new clothes on the chair by the window and a pair of boots behind the open door. Toiletries had been laid out on the dressing table, including a silver hairbrush with Sandy's initials inscribed on the back. Soft fluffy towels, a nightgown, a robe and a pair of exotic hairy slippers lay on the ottoman at the end of the bed which was covered with an elaborate quilt.

Jamie spotted a brush with his name engraved on it. "That's a nice touch, Pogo, thank you."

Sandy beckoned the cat. "Come and look at this quilt." The patchwork squares were moving vertically and horizontally in a constantly changing design. Jamie leapt onto the bedside table to take a closer look. "My word," he exclaimed. "I thought the stars were unbeatable, but this quilt might force me to revise my opinion."

The stars were not about to be shown up by an inflated, uppity coverlet. They formed a dazzling banner that read, "Match this, you over-stuffed show-off."

Pongo barked encouragement while Sandy and Jamie looked on appreciatively.

"That's enough, stars. You're behaving outrageously. That applies to you too, quilt." Pogo's attempt at a reprimand was unconvincing, she was clearly amused. The stars reluctantly returned to their random composition and the quilt stopped its mesmerising display. Its saggy demeanour indicated it was in a huff.

That gave Pongo an excuse to tease it. "That's all we need now, PP, a sulky quilt and on Sandy's first night here." The patchwork coverlet was distinctly unimpressed by the dog's remark but, without hesitation, reinflated itself and folded a corner back in a welcoming gesture.

"I hope you'll be comfortable in here, Jamie."

Pogo pulled back a chenille curtain to reveal a small turret that jutted out from the right-hand corner of the room. There were three lancet windows halfway up which overlooked the front garden and the path that led to the copse behind the cottage. Jamie inspected the cat-sized four-poster bed covered in turquoise silk cushions.

"What do you think? Will it do?"

"It's perfect," said the Siamese reverentially.

"I'm so glad you approve. We'll leave you both to settle in." Pogo embraced Sandy and blew a kiss to Jamie. "Ring this hand-bell if you need anything, even if it's the middle of the night. The slippers are a present from Queen Celestina and Prince Hamish. They're made from the finest quality struntie fleece."

Sandy removed her shoes and slipped her feet into the deliciously soft slippers. A blissful feeling of well-being washed over her. "Thank you for everything and that goes for Alfie and Pongo, too."

The pixie smiled indulgently. "Come out from under the bed, boy. I can see your tail wagging. You're not sleeping in here." The dog scrambled out with a 'well, it was worth a try' sort of look on his face. He decided the time was right to play his persistent card. "Why ever not, PP? The cat's allowed to, so why can't I?"

"I'm well aware of that, but Jamie does have his own bed in the turret and yours is waiting for you downstairs. Now, no more back-chat, you cheeky beast, it's time we were all in bed. Night, night. Sleep tight."

The dog padded across the room and, with one of his toothiest grins and a nonchalant "see ya", toddled off after Pogo. Sandy and Jamie listened to his toenails click-clacking on the wooden floorboards as he ran along the passageway.

"He's not at all bad, for a *dog*," said the cat, nudging the tasselled cushions around until they were just right. He yawned, displaying fangs worthy of Count Dracula himself, and settled down with one eye lazily watching the stars dancing to their own silent tune.

Sandy went off to the bathroom for what her Mum would have called 'a cat's lick and a promise'. A short while later she was tucked up in Estella's bed, watching the flames behind the wrought-iron fireguard. "Have you always been able to speak, Jamie?"

"Of course," said a sleepy voice from the turret, "but it wasn't appropriate until we came here. In our world it doesn't do to be caught talking if you're an animal. Most humans are emotionally unequipped to deal with that. They tend to feel threatened, in some way less special."

"I see what you mean, but they're missing such a lot." She blew out the candle on the bedside table. "Goodnight, Jamie. Maybe there will be news of Leo tomorrow."

Sandy sank into the fairygoose-down pillows and gazed at the dancing stars through unfocused eyes until she fell asleep.

When Jock Craw arrived back in the Hendersons' garden his first port of call was the rickety old bird table. He was not disappointed for it was groaning with tasty scraps and there were other titbits strewn on the grass underneath.

The crow was in need of fortification so he settled down for a good feed. He was halfway through a chunk of floury roll when he was pitched forward and found himself with his beak firmly planted in the ground.

Peg Leg had misjudged his landing and thumped Jock on the back of the neck. It's pretty tricky when you're being buffeted by a bracing south-westerly and you're short of a limb. The gull rolled over and cackled with laughter. "Great to see you, pal."

Jock's voice was muffled as he struggled to free himself. "You too, Peg," he spluttered, spitting out lumps of crummy turf, "but could you be slightly more restrained next time?"

"I did my best but it's a bit gusty."

The crow chuckled. "That was artistically choreographed compared with the way we arrived in Sylvania."

"Don't keep me in suspense. I'm *dying* to know how it went."

Jock looked doubtful. "I really need to catch up with Ralph…"

"I heard him talking to Tina just before you arrived," said the seagull helpfully. "He's popped down the town to buy something or other. You might as well fill me in while you're waiting."

Jock couldn't argue with that and was pleased to have the opportunity to talk to his old friend.

Lorimer was heading for one of the buckets on the dredger in Irvine harbour. The lobster wasn't relaxed. It would be fair to say he was a bit twitchy. His preferred bucket was the one just above water level, easy to get into and out of in a hurry, but the crustacean had been beaten to it by Yenka, a grey seal originally from the Faroe Islands who had decided Irvine was a good place to spend her retirement. Over the years the North Sea had become more of a challenge than a home for her. Generations of cubs had moved on and she had no other ties.

The seal loved the feel of the warm waters of the Gulf Stream off the west coast of Scotland and she'd always been made welcome on her occasional visits to the port.

Lorimer was forced to scramble up one of the ropes hanging down from the dredger and heave himself into the bucket above Yenka. He couldn't resist pinching her tail on the way past. The seal didn't flinch; she's a well-padded individual. The Irvine pilots and dockers have grown fond of her and make sure she wants for nothing.

"I'd know that claw anywhere Lorimer, how are you? " She rolled over and leant out of the bucket in time to see his tail disappear into the one above. She could hear him clattering about as he struggled to turn round. The lobster managed to hoist himself up over the edge and was about to answer her when Peg Leg skimmed in and landed on the rim of the bucket where the seal was basking.

"Good to see you, Yenka," Peg winked at her. "Thermidor, please tell me you're not sunbathing. You're a lobster, for goodness sake. I thought we'd established pink was not your best colour." The gull shook his head in amusement. "What do you make of him? He's unbelievable."

"I can't argue with that," replied the seal amiably. "Have you seen his posh new goggles? They're... em...strikingly different."

Peg groaned and rocked back on his leg. "Subtle is not the adjective that readily springs to mind."

"That about sums it up."

Lorimer couldn't stand it any longer, he just had to know what they were talking about. He checked to make sure his precious goggles were still hanging round his neck and flung himself over the side with the intention of gracefully swinging down to the bucket below, Tarzan style; the lobster in the loin cloth. He made an unsuccessful grab for the rope and Peg Leg and Yenka barely had time to think, let alone bail out, as Lorimer mistimed everything to perfection and joined them upside down but, thankfully, not quite inside out. The flustered lobster righted himself and donned his goggles. "Well, Peg, what do you think? Stylish, or what?"

The gull turned towards Yenka with an incredulous expression on his face. "You weren't kidding! My 'ghast' is well and truly 'flabbered'."

The lobster had been hoping for a more positive response. "Don't you like them?" he asked dejectedly.

Peg was dazzled by the excesses of the lobster's eye apparel but knew he had to make amends. "Of course I do. I wasn't expecting them to be so... magnificent. They're veritable show-stoppers."

Lorimer felt much happier. "Now you're talking."

The gull continued with as much enthusiasm as he could muster. "I particularly like the sea urchin shells and oyster pearls which in no way detract from the fossilised starfishes and seahorses in between."

"You don't think they're *too* much of a statement? I could have opted for something less showy, but as soon as I put them on I knew I had to have them."

"You'll certainly get noticed wearing those, Thermidor."

Not necessarily a good thing if you're regarded as a much sought after delicacy in local restaurants.

The lobster might make it onto the front page of *The Irvine Herald*, perhaps even *The Glasgow Herald* wearing such attention-seeking spectacles, but it was still odds on he'd be eaten after the photo call.

"Please tell me they help you see more clearly."

"Absolutely. The lenses are made of magnifying glass."

Peg looked relieved. "Where did you get the fancy frames, not from round here surely?"

"Hardly," Lorimer replied indignantly. "My cousin Kitt made them for me. He's great with his claws. He replaced the glass in a pair of doll's swimming goggles and made these fabulous modifications. Kitt's ever so creative. He's too talented to be a lobster and simply doesn't get the recognition he deserves."

The Harpie woke the baby dragon early to check he knew where to go and what to say before she sent him back through the crack in the rock behind her bed.

Cahoots repeated the message under his breath. He was word-perfect.

The dragon looked uncertainly at his mother. He was hoping for a reprieve. If he failed again, it might make her angry with him, which was something he couldn't bear to contemplate.

Cahoots was under a great deal of pressure. He desperately wanted to please Maligna but dreaded having to leave her. The early stages of separation anxiety were making him feel sick.

"It's time for you to go, darling one." The dragon was devastated, even though he had prepared himself for those words. "You'll be fine. I'll be with you in spirit and, if all goes well, we'll be reunited very soon." Her eyes were profoundly black and glittered like jet beads. "I *know* you won't fail me."

Cahoots smiled unconvincingly and Maligna saw a tear run down his cheek. She experienced another unfamiliar emotion; one of pity, triggered by the sadness the baby dragon was incapable of concealing. She knew not to prolong the moment. "Off you go, dearest."

The little beast slid down between the bed and the rock wall. The last thing she saw was the end of his tail disappearing behind the flimsy headboard.

Maligna strained to hear one final sound from him but there was nothing but oppressive silence. The dragon had gone and the Harpie felt acute loneliness of a kind she hadn't known since he'd come into her life.

Maligna should have been elated, he was potentially her ticket to freedom. Instead all she felt was fear, emptiness and a suffocating weight on her chest. Claustrophobia seemed determined to fill the void left by the dragon. The Harpie threw back her gaunt head and wailed in anguish.

The guards above her dungeon shuddered and exchanged nervous glances. The familiar shadows created by their flickering oil lamps deepened malevolently.

"I definitely preferred the wild laughter, didn't you?" said the older of the two with a hollow laugh.

Gilbert waited until he was sure Leo was dead to the Sylvanian world. It had been a nerve-racking day, full of new-found responsibilities and the Giant Rat was in need of something to calm his nerves. He was exhausted but unable to unwind and settle down for a much needed night's sleep.

He felt drawn to the last remaining packet of sparklers, like a child is to a comfort blanket, or a favourite teddy bear. Sparklers were not viable unless he ventured outside with them which would be seriously stupid.

The rodent's next thought was unsolicited and he should have known better than to act on it, but he was long past thinking clearly. "A relaxing drink and inconsequential chat, that's what I need. Just the one then straight back home to bed." Gilbert is in the habit of talking to himself since he is seldom in the company of others. Leo looked set to sleep for hours so the rat reckoned he could pop out and be back before he was missed.

There was only one place in these parts where the Giant Rat could go without fear of being set upon and that was a certain tavern frequented by rascals and rapscallions which was tantalisingly close to his den. He donned his Paisley patterned neckerchief and made for the shaft that led to the surface.

Gilbert sneaked out from underneath the holly bush and slipped into the shadows. In no time he was standing outside The Mischief Maker. He quietly opened the door and nipped in. He didn't feel he had particularly drawn attention to himself. The place was crowded and no one appeared to take any notice of him, something Gilbert should have been suspicious about from the moment he entered.

Considering how packed the place was, he managed to reach the bar surprisingly quickly. "What will it be, young sir?" asked the landlord with a sly, sideways look. "A pint's never going to be enough for a big lad like you now, is it?" That should have been Gilbert's cue to leave, but he was weary and beyond rational thought. "Shall I make it a quart?"

"Go on then," replied the rat reluctantly, "but I must be off after that, I can't stay long."

"Put that on my tab, Slack," called a voice from the lug chair nearest the fire. "This one's on me."

The Giant Rat turned to see who had spoken with such authority. Pestilence Grimshaw obligingly leant forward and raised his tankard in a silent toast to him. "Care to join us?"

Gilbert was confused. "Are you talking to me? I'm fairly certain we've never met before."

Pestilence gave a smug smile. "You're right, we haven't been formally introduced, but I have enormous admiration for you, Gilbert. You've managed to survive in a hostile world where you don't belong."

The rat was wary, he knew the buccaneer by reputation, but he was also flattered and found his legs propelling him towards Grimshaw's entourage by the fire.

"Pigsblanket!" yelled the buccaneer.

There was no response. Jedediah Malahyde gave the sleeping bundle at his feet a swift kick in the ribs.

The dishevelled cabin boy sat bolt upright. "Right away, Cap'n… Would you like a biscuit with your tea?"

Everyone round the lad, including Pestilence Grimshaw, fell about laughing. "No tea or biscuit, boy, just make room for my good friend, Gilbert."

Pigsblanket realised he'd said something foolish and tried to scramble behind the First Mate's chair.

"No need for that, there's space for us both," said the rat amiably. He noticed the boy was shivering. "Would you mind sitting by the fire? I'm too hot as it is."

Pigsblanket smiled gratefully.

The Giant Rat felt drawn to the puny cabin boy who was so desperately anxious to please, and wondered how he had become involved with the likes of Grimshaw. There was an indefinable quality about the boy that set him apart from the uncouth, nasty specimens that made up the crew of 'The Cheeky Monkey'.

Jamie woke first. He stretched and rolled over just in time to see Pongo tip-toeing out of the turret. The cat was intrigued and decided to lie doggo to find out what he was up to. Pongo glanced back at Jamie's bed. The cat feigned sleep and threw in a refined, rippling snore for good measure. He watched the rumpled little dog through slitted eyes. Pongo gave a satisfied snigger and jinked out of the room.

Three collars were laid out on the cushion next to the Siamese cat. They were all slightly different in design but each one was studded with various combinations of diamonds and sapphires. There was a little note which read: *'Sammy says you're to keep the one you like the most. Love Pongo.'* Then underneath. *'I didn't write this note, PP did. I'm smart, but not that smart.'*

Jamie was astonished and thrilled at the same time. "What a character, I honestly thought he was showing off."

It was impossible to tell whether Sandy was awake or not. All he could see was a bump in the patchwork quilt.

Jamie sprang from the bed, stretched languidly and padded across the room. He stood on his hind legs and gently placed a paw on the pillow. Sandy was still sound asleep.

The cat went off in search of Pongo. When he reached the foot of the stairs he was met by a mouth-watering smell wafting out of the kitchen. He ambled in to find Alfie and Pogo breakfasting on quail egg omelettes. They greeted him warmly.

Pongo bounced out of his basket with an innocent expression on his face. "Sleep well, Jamie?" he enquired airily.

"Wonderfully well, thanks for asking."

The dog wasn't about to be deflected that easily. "Notice anything different this morning?"

Jamie decided to play along with him. "I can't say I did."

"Then perhaps you ought to get your eyes checked."

"I can assure you there's nothing wrong with my vision."

"You could've fooled me," said an exasperated Pongo.

"Cut the cackle, boy," said Alfie. "Will you have some breakfast, Jamie?"

The Siamese responded to the offer of food enthusiastically. "I'll just pop outside for a…" He hesitated, choosing his next word carefully, "…reconnoitre."

"I've not heard it called that before," retorted the dog.

"Basket *now*, Pongo," chorused Alfie and Pogo.

Jamie made for the open door that led to the garden behind the cottage. The scent of fragrant herbs in the kitchen garden was glorious. He paused to sniff the air. "Catmint, if I'm not mistaken. How delightful."

Pongo was sitting in his basket attempting to look angelic when Jamie deigned to throw him a verbal scrap. "The collars are heavenly, but which one to choose…" The dog spun round eagerly. "You're the most extraordinary canine I've ever met."

Jamie stepped out into the warm sunshine wrapped in a blanket of well-being.

"Did you hear that, WAE? His nibs says I'm extraordinary and I couldn't detect the slightest hint of condescension in his voice."

Pongo whizzed round the table a couple of times, turned an untidy somersault and landed like a sack of spuds on the floor next to Pogo. The elf and the pixie clapped spontaneously.

The dog was panting after his exertions. "While he's still out of earshot," he puffed, "I'm glad he came with Sandy, aren't you?"

4

Cahoots squeezed through a narrow gap in the ancient limestone and found himself in a high-ceilinged cavern. The dragon didn't know how far he'd come since leaving the sink-hole, but it felt a very long way, most of which he'd covered wriggling on his belly with his wings flattened against his back. He scratched marks at intervals along the way which would be easy to find should he have to turn back. Maligna was depending on him and this time failure was not an option.

Instinct told him to keep moving upwards.

The dragon made a visual search of the cave but there was no suggestion of a way out other than the suffocating passageway he'd just come through.

Cahoots was scanning the rock formations above his head when he felt a slight draught on his face. He craned his neck and sniffed the air. The exact source of the draught was difficult to pin-point. The cavern roof was frighteningly high and covered in clusters of shiny stalactites. It was time to take a closer look but the rock walls were smooth and slippery.

"I may have to undertake my maiden flight sooner than I'd thought."

He tentatively unfurled his wings which felt ridiculously oversized and ungainly.

"These can't be mine, they're far too big. There must have been a mix-up somewhere along the way."

Cahoots had an instant mental picture of a huge dragon with tiny wings, shaking its head in similar disbelief.

"I suppose I'll just have to muddle along with this pair for now."

He had no inkling of what he was supposed to do to become airborne. Sadly, the wings came without an instruction manual.

Wild flapping and rushing about proved debilitating and resoundingly unsuccessful.

The dragon collapsed panting on the cave floor and a huge spurt of flames shot out of his nostrils. "I didn't know about that either!"

Life without Maligna was promising to be far from dull.

Cahoots was on a steep learning curve, not that he would have known what that meant.

"I need to calm down and take things at a gentler pace."

When he felt suitably rested, he decided to give it another go.

Sylvanian dragons, when they know how, can fly just as well inside caves as out in the open air.

Cahoots intuitively approached the problem from a different perspective; slow, measured breathing until he felt calm, centred and relaxed, while at the same time visualising himself flying serenely.

The dragon gradually reached a trance-like state and found himself floating above the cave floor. He engaged his wings and realised that he was actually flying. It seemed he had the right ones after all. He cautiously opened his eyes and found he was dangerously close to the roof.

Cahoots felt it was best not to look down until he was fully in control. Slowing the rhythm of his wing beats, he was able to hover just below the roof in front of a jagged fissure in the limestone. The draught was more of a breeze now which had to mean he was near the surface.

There was only one course of action and it would require split second timing. (1.) Fly towards gap in rock, straight as an arrow. (2.) Dive through gap while simultaneously closing wings. That was undoubtedly the tricky part. (3.) Land confidently no matter what you might find in there.

An ambitious sequence for a dragon with only the rudiments of flight.

"This one's for Mum," he said, flying at breakneck speed towards the opening in the rock.

"Oh no you don't! Not while I live and breathe," said a loud, imperious voice.

Cahoots was forced to apply his newly discovered airbrakes. He didn't stop quickly enough and had an altercation with the rock wall before falling backwards towards the floor of the cavern.

"Flap your wings," called the same insistent voice from the opening in the limestone. "What's up with you? Have you no sense of self preservation, you daft eedjit?"

Cahoots forced his wings to co-operate in time to break his fall. It was a clumsy landing but he wasn't taking part in an aerial display. He peered up into the gloom to see who had spoken to him so unexpectedly and in such a bossy manner.

"I'm up here. Use your big blue eyes, that's what they're for. What sort of a dragon are you, anyway? You seem to be unfamiliar with the basic skills that set you apart from the rest of us."

Cahoots was still trying to see who or what was berating him.

"Don't tell me your keekers are a bit iffy, too. Stay where you are, I'll be right down."

The tiny creature with the commanding voice emerged from the rockface and gracefully flew down to join him. It was covered in short grey fur and bore a striking resemblance to a cat but for a pair of feathery wings sprouting from its shoulder-blades. "I'm Minxie and I'm a wazwatt."

The dragon gaped foolishly at the strange apparition.

"Not familiar with wazwatts, eh?" She narrowed her eyes. "Or are you just stupid?

This was one shoot-from-the-hip little beast.

"Can you understand what I'm saying?" She drummed her paw impatiently. "Say something… anything." Still not a peep from the dragon. "Can you not speak? One nod for yes, two nods for no." The dragon nodded once. "Was that one nod for yes, I can't speak or yes, I can?" she enquired tersely.

Cahoots was by now nodding and shaking his head and the wazwatt was as perplexed as he was.

"That's it, I can't stand any more of this nonsense."

"I'm sorry," he said, finally finding his voice, "but you gave me a dreadful fright."

"And you call yourself a dragon, you big jessie!"

"That was your choice of word," Cahoots replied smugly.

"Whatever…" retorted the wazwatt. She shook her dainty head and exhaled in disgust. "Didn't your mum teach you anything?"

The dragon wasn't about to stand for criticism of Maligna. "I'd rather you weren't rude about my mother," he said darkly. Then with mock innocence, "What's a wotnot, anyway?"

"I'll give you wotnot, you cheeky article. I'm a wazwatt and don't think you can trifle with me." She fixed him with her jade green eyes. "Oh, I get it, you're teasing me." Minxie took a step backwards. "You're brighter than I thought. First impressions can be deceiving." A note of formality crept into her voice, "Good to make your acquaintance…" She waited for him to complete the sentence.

"…Cahoots," he replied obligingly.

The wazwatt snorted with contempt. "What sort of a name is that?"

The dragon assumed a vaguely menacing pose. "I like my name, do you have a problem with that?"

Minxie spotted a trickle of smoke coming from his left nostril which made her more conciliatory. It was time to quit while she was still ahead. "Absolutely not. Cahoots is a splendid name for a dragon."

Ralph and Jock were reunited shortly after Peg Leg caught up with Yenka and Lorimer in their respective buckets on the dredger.

Captain Henderson's understanding of the situation was limited to the jumble of images provided by the Craw Cauldron. He'd filled it with pure spring water from the sunken pond in the orchard and patiently scrutinised events in Sylvania as they swam in and out of focus on the mirror-like surface.

Ralph observed Sandy's inelegant arrival with wry amusement, caught a glimpse of the Giant Rat on the banks of the Sprinting River and briefly witnessed the Royal Party's descent from the lofty howdah on the shoulders of the spectacular Sylvanian Forest Cat.

Jock was dismayed to hear that Ralph was experiencing problems with the Cauldron. The crow had been hoping to use it in the search for Leo, but that seemed pretty unlikely now. The scenes it offered were disjointed and confusing.

On the rare occasions Ralph had tapped into its magic, there had always been a certain logic and recognisable chronology to the pictures it offered up, but the Cauldron had long been divorced from the source of its power in the Cave of Sublime Spirit and its magic had diminished relatively. It was overdue the equivalent of a 10,000 mile service, something that was not going to happen during turbulent times like these. Sammy had far more pressing matters to deal with and the Craw Cauldron was way down on his list of priorities.

Jock fleshed out the details of Sandy and Jamie's arrival and they puzzled over Leo's vanishing act and the lack of information as to his whereabouts. The crow expressed his mounting anxiety about the worsening situation in Sylvania. "If only that evil relic could have been destroyed."

Ralph was sitting on a paint-chipped wicker chair under the laburnum tree smoking a cigar while Jock paced back and forth on the Victorian summerhouse steps. If crows smoked cigars then Jock's would have been the finest Cuba had to offer.

The evening air was still and warm and there was no trace of the gusting south-westerly that had blown up during the afternoon. The leafy tumble and careless disorder of the old orchard was spread out behind them.

Jock toyed with his imaginary Havana. "There was potent dark magic at work when that anklet was forged. The Harpie is immortal, the anklet is indestructible. Together they're virtually invincible. It's a lethal combination. The best we can do is to continue to keep them apart."

The crow hopped down onto the grass. "The Mischief Maker is the rallying point for dissenters and supporters of Maligna. It's always been a dive, frequented by ruffians and ne'er-do-wells, but it now extends a welcome to pirates and the very toe-nail clippings of Sylvanian society. The Royal Raven has sent an undercover agent to stake out the place.

He's very discreet and, being a member of the crow family, is spectacularly good at his job." Jock never misses a chance for self-promotion.

"Don't sell yourself short now," Ralph said indulgently.

Jock responded with an exaggerated bow. "The bird in question is a chough called Redshanks. He has a chestful of medals for his services to the Sylvanian Royal Family and is likely to be made a Flight of the Realm any day now. Redshanks is the best there is and loyal right down to the last feather. It pays to watch your back these days and to be ultra careful about whom you take into your confidence."

"Have you discussed this with anyone else since you came back?"

"Absolutely not," Jock said vehemently.

Ralph rolled the cigar between his fingers, watching the smoke rise in quickening spirals from the tip. "I think it might be a good idea if you did. Peg Leg is resourceful and intelligent."

Jock's eyes brightened. "You're right, he's in a class by himself. I bumped into him earlier but I kept the conversation light and didn't touch on any of the serious stuff."

"Perhaps you should confide in him." Ralph stretched to ease the tension in his shoulders and rose from the chair.

He gazed fondly at 'Woodburn'. The sun was reflected in the long bay windows of the bedroom which projected from the second storey, its weight supported by two strong metal pillars. The outer walls were exposed to the elements and it was only occupied during the spring and summer months, proving impossible to heat when the temperature dropped. There was no central heating in the old house and electric blankets were the only concession to the cold on freezing winter nights when Jack Frost drew extravagant ice pictures on the windows.

They were submerged in their own concerns and Ralph broke the silence first. It was time to inject a humorous note.

"You mentioned pirates, didn't you? It's just conceivable Peg Leg may have crossed swords with buccaneers on the high seas around Irvine. He may even have some useful tips."

They allowed themselves a moment of frivolity, but Jock knew exactly where he was headed next. On a lovely night like this the seagull was likely to be dining at The Anchor Bar.

"I'll nip down to the harbour for a chat with him right away."

The crow felt for his friend the harbourmaster. "Sandy's fine, you know. She's in good hands. Sometimes being human is not as limiting as it might seem. Sylvania's kind to mortals as a rule."

"Right enough, but it's the Siamese cat I'm worried about."

Jock's feathered brows came together in a frown until he noticed the twinkle in Ralph's eyes. "I've known you all these years and I still fall for it every time. You're so plausible and I'm so gullible."

Ralph's shoulders took on their customary stoop as he ambled up the garden with the crow beside him. They paused by the greenhouse where the last of the tomato crop was patiently waiting to be eaten. "Joking aside, Jock, I'm not sure how safe either of the cats is. I don't believe the immunity extends to animals."

"The fairy folk are tenacious fighters. While we're waffling on, Queen Celestina and Sammy are most likely casting *ferocious* spells of protection for all their loyal friends and subjects. There's no way they'll have overlooked the kitties."

They took leave of each other with warm affection.

Jock Craw rose smoothly into the air above 'Woodburn'. His habitual victory roll was replaced by a series of rotations reminiscent of a carwash brush. When he levelled out his parting words drifted back to Ralph with a touch of the local vernacular thrown in. "Dinnae worry aboot a thing. Just remember, I'm Double-O-One, the-one-and-only."

Uplifting words to raise a glass to, if you were so inclined.

When we were last in the company of the dear old Giant Rat, he was getting acquainted with Pestilence Grimshaw and his never to-be-approached-without-a-loaded-blunderbuss crew of 'The Cheeky Monkey'. The emaciated cabin boy was huddled close to the meagre fire, thanks to Gilbert's generous gesture.

If Pigsblanket could have climbed into the hearth, without receiving the unavoidable slap on the head, he would have done so.

Grimshaw had long given up abusing the landlord for the lack of a decent fire to warm his tootsies in front of. No matter how much fuel is heaped upon it, the fire at The Mischief Maker gives out exactly the same amount of heat. Never enough.

The landlord's wife makes a point of serving Gilbert if she manages to escape the feeble but draining clutches of her husband. Gertie likes the harmless big beast, he's unassuming and courteous, and she usually finds a way to fetch him a pint, just the one, before he slips out again into the night.

Moderation is essential if you're living on the edge of your nerves and need to keep your wits as sharp as your incisors.

However, one of Gilbert's weaknesses is beer, he loves his ale but if he despatches more than a pint or two it goes straight to his head, rendering him very silly indeed. In a matter of minutes, his brain is performing about as well as a pile of whiffy raw mince. There is a brief window in time before this metamorphosis takes place when Gilbert is everybody's friend and the original party animal. The policy of alcohol tailored to the age of the drinker does not extend to a rodent from Scotland.

[Enter rat, stage right, wearing jester's cap and bells. He playfully capers about the stage, skilfully juggling riddles, songs and jokes while leaping and prancing wildly. The tavern echoes to appreciative laughter, punctuated with raucous shouts for more.]

Well, not exactly... but Gilbert is the centre of attention and he's having a fine time. Popularity is lifeblood to a creature who's been starved of the company of others, be they rats or, in this case, prats and dangerous ones at that. We must forgive his errors of judgement after years as the lonely outcast but, for a basically intelligent creature, Gilbert really should have known better.

The Giant Rat is a sucker for sea shanties, they bring out the romantic in him. The image of rats leaving sinking ships has no place in Gilbert's consciousness. Swash-buckling swordsman, or in his case, swordsrat, who snatches the ship from the clutches of disaster is more his style.

Pigsblanket had a blissful, faraway look on his pinched little face as he accompanied the Captain and the rest of the crew on his battered concertina. Grimshaw led the singing in a fine baritone with Gilbert humming along until he'd picked up the chorus well enough to join in. The song came to an end amid claps and cheers. The cabin boy winced but managed a weak smile when he received a hearty slap from the pirate. "Well played, boy!"

"Let's have another shanty, but first more ale. Gilbert, what will it be?" Pestilence smiled the sly smile of a crocodile, but the rat was enjoying himself too much to notice. What a day! Two new friends in the space of a few hours was almost too good to be true but Gilbert chose to ignore the warning bells clanging in his head. "Killjoys, the lot of you," he muttered and threw the switch on his ignore-this-and-you'll-be-very-sorry early warning system.

The pirate cut in. "I didn't quite catch what you said there, Gilbie…"

"It's of no significance." The Giant Rat carelessly flung a paw round Grimshaw's powerful shoulders. "It's definitely my round now, you bought the last two." Gilbert beamed at the puny cabin boy. "A shandy before the shanty, lad?"

Pigsblanket's face lit up. "That'd be great, sir."

"Call me, Gilbert. I can't be doing with formality."

The rat tried to push his way through the throng at the bar but was getting nowhere fast, wading waist-high through wet concrete might well have proved less taxing.

"Make way, you ill-mannered wretches," roared Grimshaw. "Gilbert wants to buy us all a drink!"

The turbulent sea of bodies parted and the rodent strode proudly, if a little uncertainly, on his hind legs up to the bar where the landlord had placed the first two drinks. "I'll take that empty tankard, shall I?" Slack gestured at the beers on the counter. "One for you and one for the Cap'n. I'll sort out the other drinks and have Gertie bring 'em over. You can pay me later, all right?"

"Excellent, Jem, but make sure young Pigsblanket gets a shandy straight away. It's thirsty work bashing out tunes on that decrepit squeeze-box, and sling in one of your 'House Specials'. The lad looks like he could murder some decent nosh."

Gilbert was starting to feel like everyone's fairy godmother. "Make sure you have a snifter yourself, landlord, and don't forget your missus now, will you?"

"If only I could, sir," said Slack wistfully under his breath. The fawning landlord rubbed his hands together and smiled crookedly. "Most generous of you, sir. Most generous, indeed."

The Giant Rat grasped the tankards to his chest and made his way back through the grateful throng amid shouts of "Cheers, mate", "You're one of the best" and other genuinely meant but soon forgotten remarks.

Jem Slack enjoyed a joke at the rat's expense with some of his regular punters. "If it's decent grub he's after, young Pigsblanket had better sling his hook. The Mischief Maker's not renowned for its five star cuisine."

Jedediah Malahyde left the pub shortly after Gilbert which meant Pigsblanket had lost his only protector.

The buccaneer couldn't fail to notice the developing friendship between the Giant Rat and 'the ship's rat' and was quick to exploit the situation.

The cabin boy shivered nervously inside his threadbare clothes.

"Now mind, find out where ratty's going and what he's up to and come straight back here with all the gen." Grimshaw's brows knitted together in an impressive scowl and he grabbed the boy by the ear. "Don't mess this up, Pigsbreath."

"I'll do my best, Cap'n."

"I should bally well say so!" The pirate's rage was violently unleashed. "WHY ARE YOU STILL HERE, YOU SNIVELLING LITTLE CRETIN?"

Pigsblanket cringed and hated himself for doing so. "I can't leave without my ear, Cap'n."

The buccaneer was incandescent. "YOUR EAR?"

"Aye, sir," said the boy in a meek, apologetic voice. "I can't very well leave without it." He immediately regretted his words. The pirate captain wouldn't think twice about tearing his ear off if he felt so inclined.

Grimshaw's mood changed abruptly, as it invariably did. He guffawed and slapped his thigh theatrically with his free hand. "Right enough, but get a move on, you mindless little grub." He caught the boy by the shoulders, spun him round and, placing his heavy sea-boot in the small of Pigsblanket's back, hurled him towards the door. "You know what you'll get if you let me down, don't you?"

The cabin boy smacked into the wall by the door, splitting his lower lip. A matelot dragged him to his feet amid raucous laughter. Pigsblanket wiped the blood from his mouth with his cuff and managed a breathless response. "Laldie, sir."

"And the rest, boy."

Anyone who knows Grimshaw's proclivity for violent behaviour won't be surprised to learn that 'laldie' translates as 'a beating'.

Pigsblanket stumbled through the door in Gilbert's weaving wake and paused for a second or two to let his eyes adjust to the darkness. There was a strong scent of wild garlic and the boy gulped in a lungful of night air.

It was a huge relief to be away from the mouldering atmosphere of The Mischief Maker. A brief respite from the reign of terror inflicted upon him by 'Captain' Pestilence Grimshaw was heartening, even for a boy with no chance of a better life.

It had been daft of Gilbert to leave Leo alone on his first night in Sylvania and downright stupid to head for the pub. He'd taken leave of his new friends at The Mischief Maker with the rat equivalent of a bear-hug here and a hail-fellow-well-met slap on the back there.

He staggered off towards his den talking in what he believed to be a hushed tone. Not so, he was jibbering at the top of his voice.

"What a splendid evening. I must do this sort of thing more often. I simply don't get out enough. They're an excellent bunch of...hickety-hic...chaps. Happy, happy day. My luck's changed at last. First Leo and now Pestilence, a true gentleman and, what's more, much maligned."

The sky was clear, the moon intensely bright. The trees and shrubs lining the road stood out against the starry backdrop of the late summer sky. Gilbert was alternately whistling and singing as he cheerfully barrelled along without a care in the world. He'd had a rip-snorter of an evening. Life was a brimming bowl of cherries and for the very first time since he'd tipped up in Crawdonia he felt that it wasn't such a bad place after all.

The night air was humid but there was a whisper of a breeze.

Pigsblanket staunched the blood from his split lip with a clean rag that served as a handkerchief.

The boy kept a good distance between himself and the rodent. When Gilbert stopped to catch his breath, bounced off a bush or toppled into a shrub, Pigsblanket moved quickly into the shadow of the trees that lined the road.

The cabin boy could have been dancing a Highland Fling in a dazzlingly loud kilt, accompanied by a full pipe band, and the rat might still have been unaware of his presence. Gilbert was in a delightful world of his own, divorced from everything going on around him.

The exhausted cabin boy unwittingly disturbed a family of hooties who rose into the air above his head. "Sorry!" he mumbled urgently under his breath.

"I should say so," screeched the mother owl as she settled on a gnarled branch, her brood clamouring for attention all around her. "First that drunken rat, and now a disreputable boy," she said sniffily. "What's this wood coming to?" The owl fanned out her feathers in a gesture of annoyance, looking as if she'd been on the receiving end of a frenzied hairdryer.

Gilbert hadn't a clue he'd upset the hooties, or that the boy had disturbed them shortly afterwards.

Presently the Giant Rat burst into a chorus of one of Pigsblanket's favourite sea shanties. Naturally Gilbert couldn't remember the correct words, so he made up some of his own. By now the hiccups were master of the rat.

"Hey ho, hey…hic… ho. Jolly jam tarts and a bottle of rum. In my tum. Twiddle-diddle-dum. In my tum. Twiddle-hickety-diddle dum."

Pigsblanket smiled, something he rarely did. His lip was not amused and made its feelings perfectly plain, but to no avail; the big beast was so endearing, cavorting about in front of the holly bush. The boy's stomach contracted with guilt at the thought of having to betray Gilbert to Pestilence Grimshaw. Still, so far so good. There was nothing significant to report.

It came as no surprise to Pigsblanket when the rat pitched backwards into the fiendish shrub and disappeared; Gilbert had fallen over more than once since he'd tottered out of the pub the worse for wear. The cabin boy guessed from the sound effects that the rodent had dropped a fair distance. Self-preservation and good common sense urged him to leave right away before he discovered more than he wanted to know, but what if the silly beast was seriously injured?

The yowls and howls didn't bode well. Perhaps he ought to make sure the rat was OK. Just one peek and then straight back to The Mischief Maker.

Pigsblanket braced himself and moved reluctantly towards the devilish shrub. He crouched down on all fours, flattening himself as much as he could, not difficult when you're wafer thin, and scrambled warily towards the centre of the holly.

Leo woke with a start. His mind was numb with exhaustion. The den was dimly lit and there was no sign of the Giant Rat. Leo called his name but it was still and quiet and his voice echoed eerily. Where was Gilbert?

The cat had been lost in a wilderness of menacing dreams while Gilbert carried him back to his den and hadn't a clue where he was, but he was sure of one thing; he had no intention of sending out a search party of one, namely himself. No, siree. Gilbert must have had good reason to leave him alone like this. In their short acquaintance the cat had formed the opinion that the rat was one of the good guys in this new world.

Leo steeled himself to leave his bed of shavings and padded quietly towards the tunnel that led to the shaft. Inky darkness wrapped around him when he ventured out of the den. Cats don't need to eat carrots to see in the dark, but the ground was cracked and uneven, so he chose his route with care. He stepped from the tunnel into a shaft of intensely pink moonlight and stood motionless, staring up at the stars through the tangled holly branches. There was neither sight nor sound of the rodent.

A drawn-out series of wails caused the hairs the length of the cat's spine to stand on end. Perhaps it might be prudent to wait for Gilbert back in his den. A nerve-jangling howl right overhead had Leo rooted to the spot, claws extended, his breathing shallow with fear. His legs were jelly wobbly but he had to get out of the moonlight before he came face-to-face with the monster that was making those terrifying sounds. In a flowing movement, worthy of SSS himself, Leo slipped back into the darkness of the tunnel.

One final plaintive yowl was followed by a whoosh of air and the sound a sack of coal might make if it were dropped from a great height down a mineshaft. Leo was caught unawares and found himself covered in dust and rubble dislodged by whatever it was that had dropped in so gracelessly.

"Dearie me," said a throaty voice to the left of the heap of debris which contained Leo. "What *does* he think he's playing at, Puddock?"

The cat didn't move although he was desperately uncomfortable. He was in liquid form, boneless with fear.

"That rat needs to take a firmer grip on reality, Natterjack," said a husky voice. At the mention of 'rat' Leo gave an involuntary gasp. He choked on some dust and sneezed.

"Did you hear that, Puddock? A sneeze if I'm not mistaken. We appear to have company."

"Aye, indeed we do, Natterjack. It'll be Gilbert's new friend, the one everyone's looking for."

"You may well be right, Puddock. I wonder if there's a reward for information leading to his apprehension."

These two guys can keep up their own brand of verbal tennis for hours and if Gilbert hadn't let out a series of heartfelt groans when he did, who knows when they would have run out of steam. Not soon enough, that's for sure.

Sylvanian toads specialise in long-winded conversations. They don't go out much, preferring dank, dismal corners unfrequented by other creatures, but they do know what's going on outside their immediate circle. News travels in Sylvania, even among reclusive amphibians.

The toads hopped towards the prostrate rat who had winded himself when he'd lost his footing and plunged down the shaft. His groans were punctuated with loud hiccups.

"He's had a run-in with that cantankerous holly again," said Puddock, the smaller of the two. "Presumably that's what all the fuss was about."

"Running the gauntlet of that shrub is bad enough when you're sober and have all your faculties about you. Put it this way, you'd have to be incredibly stupid or irredeemably drunk like ratty here not to show it due respect."

"You're darn tootin', Natterjack."

The loquacious toads were off again.

Leo wriggled free and watched them wide-eyed, practically hypnotised by their soporific exchange.

Gilbert struggled to his feet through a monstrous cloud of dust. The fall had sobered him up slightly but he had a long way to go before he would be accepted as a member of the Sylvanian Sobriety Society.

"What a fool I've been, Leo. I should never have left you alone and on your first night here. Please tell me you're all right." Gilbert hiccuped violently and dissolved into tears of remorse. "Where are you, my wee pal? I'll never touch another drop of ale as long as I live. I've…hic…learned my lesson, honest I…hic…have."

Natterjack and Puddock exchanged knowing looks; they'd heard this sort of twaddle from Gilbert before. "Put him out of his drunken misery, Puddock."

"If you insist, NJ."

The green and puce spotted toad sprang into the air and landed with a satisfying splunk in front of Gilbert who was by now crying like a baby.

"Leo's over there, you big soft twit. He's fine, no thanks to you, but he doesn't have much to say for himself."

Gilbert caught sight of the cat who was coming out of the shadows towards him. "You're a sight for sore eyes, wee chum." The Giant Rat snatched the neckerchief from round his scruffy neck, sniffed and hastily wiped his eyes. "Will you ever forgive me?"

"There's nothing to forgive, Gilbert," said Leo happily. "I'm so relieved you're OK, apart from the sore head you're going to have in the morning."

Puddock and Natterjack liked what they were hearing. Leo was shaping up to be their kind of cat. Natterjack's voice oozed self-satisfaction. "You're right on the buzzer there, puss, unless Gilbert has the sense to eat some alebane before he turns in."

"And where would I find that?" Leo asked haughtily.

The toads laughed conspiratorially. "Gilbert always keeps some in his larder in case he gets sloshed. It's in a jar marked…"

"Don't spoil it for me, let me guess." Leo scowled at the toads. "There's no need to be so smug. We all make mistakes unless, of course, we're perfect like you two. Now, if you'll excuse us, it's time Gilbert and I got some shut-eye. It's been a long, trying day and I don't imagine tomorrow's likely to be any less challenging. Shall we go, Gilb?"

The Giant Rat was agog with admiration. "That would be just great, wee pal. I'm more than ready for my bed."

I know you'll find this hard to believe but Puddock and Natterjack were speechless, without words, stunned into silence.

Leo helped Gilbert down the tunnel that led to his den. "Lean on me, if you need to."

"Thanks ever so but I wouldn't want to flatten you and I'm feeling much better now. You didn't half put those know-alls in their place." The rat chortled with pleasure. "I do believe my hiccups have gone, how heavenly."

"I'm so pleased, Gilbert."

"So am I, Leo. Hiccups can be a real pain in the …… hic … neck."

Natterjack found his tongue first. "That rat's one lucky chap, don't you think? Leo's a very special cat, Puddock."

"Without question, Natterjack, a veritable diamond."

"They don't make 'em like that any more, do they, Puddock?"

"Indubitably not, NJ."

It seemed the toads still had a lot to get off their warty chests.

The Royal Raven greeted the chough cordially when he emerged from the furry-fig trees concealing the entrance to the passageway from Indigoletta's private quarters to the cliffs above the Whiteraven Sea. This tunnel connects the Palace with the headquarters of the Sylvanian Secret Service. Queen Celestina, Hamish and a handful of others know of its existence and they privately refer to it as the 'backdoor'.

Indigoletta invited her special agent into the imposing mulberry tree which takes centre stage in her roof-top glasshouse. The tree was smothered in succulent fruit and its leaves were heavy with battalions of grazing silkworms. Redshanks settled on a branch a few feet from Indigoletta and waited for her to open the conversation.

The charismatic raven exuded warmth. "You *must* have some of these mulberries. I swear they've never been so sweet and delicious. It's such a boon having a cultivar that satisfies our desire for berries and the silkworms' demand for bigger and better leaves."

"Quite so, ma'am," said the chough, trying to look as if he knew what she was talking about.

The raven pushed a branch thick with smudged pink fruit towards him. The whopping amethyst and diamond ring on her foreclaw sparkled in the sunlight.

Redshanks responded appreciatively. "They certainly do look tempting, ma'am."

"Well then, dig in, but mind you don't scoff the caterpillars. They're furiously spinning the last batch of silk for Her Majesty's 'Fabulous Fairymass Frock'. These silkworms are out of the top drawer and there aren't any others up to the task."

The dazzling raven moved along the branch until she was directly in front of the chough. She spoke in a stage whisper. "These wee souls will be rewarded for their industry. They will be allowed to develop into fully fledged moths who in time will produce the next generation of elite silkworms. It's only right, you know." Indigoletta gazed benevolently at the relentlessly chomping caterpillars on the leaves around her. "I'm rather attached to them myself. They don't have time to say much, but it's exceedingly pleasant to have them around."

When the raven and chough had finished dining on the luscious berries, Indigoletta summoned Will who was standing in for her butler Ravenscroft. The old elf was spending a few days with his sister who lives in the tiny hamlet of Skirl where Estella was staying with Pogo's brother.

The imp had taken to palace life like a piglet tasting its first truffles. Indigoletta made sure her protégé was well looked after and Will did everything he could to make her busy life easier. She'd created a special position in her household for him, that of 'First Imp to the Royal Raven'. It had a grand ring to it and Will was still in a spin over the rapid change in his fortunes. Ear-to-ear smiles and Cheshire cat grins were the order of the day, especially when the bumptious Captain of the Impfantry happened to be in the vicinity.

The imp's rapid promotion might well have put many noses and beaks out of joint had it not been for Will himself. He's friendly, without affectation, and few can hold a grudge against him for more than a millisecond. His cheerful, freckled face, topped with its distinctive shock of scarlet curls is irresistible. Even Martha Snowberry, the redoubtable royal cook, takes time out from her hectic schedule to make Will his favourite furry-fig and fingalberry biscuits.

Will marched in at precisely the right moment with a crystal bowl of warm scented water and two soft purple towels.

"Just the job, m'dear. We'll come down to you. I need to freshen up after all that scrumptious fruit, the pulp plays havoc with my feathers."

Redshanks looked sheepishly at the Royal Raven. His coral red beak was stained with juice. "I'm afraid I took you at your word, ma'am. It appears I was somewhat unrestrained. Just look at the state of me; I'm fairly sure I'm stuck to this branch."

"Perhaps you'd like a bigger bowl, sir? Something to bathe in."

The chough raised a heavily feathered eyebrow.

Will gave a deep bow and smiled engagingly. "I'm not really being a cheeky imp, sir, just a practical one."

Indigoletta was thrilled at his charm and precocious intelligence. "So, Redshanks, what's it to be?"

"A bath it is, ma'am. Thank you."

"Don't thank me, thank..." But Will had already vanished behind the plum velvet curtains that were drawn across the entrance to the conservatory.

The Royal Raven had a faraway expression on her fine-featured face. "That imp is remarkable. To think his gifts might have been squandered by that insufferable nincompoop, Twitchett."

Redshanks studiously picked the last mulberry seeds from his claws. This is not considered bad manners where birds are concerned. "I see Twitchett remains out of favour, ma'am."

Indigoletta shuddered in mock horror. "What puts my feathers in a furious flutter is his apparent lack of respect for birds, particularly when it comes to me. He does his job well enough, which is all that matters, I suppose, but he's supremely aggravating."

When Redshanks had finished freshening up, they settled down to discuss the problems facing Sylvania.

"You confirm The Mischief Maker to be the focal point of a possible uprising?"

"Uprising is too strong a word, ma'am, but I'd rather we were prepared."

The raven lowered her eyes. "You're right, of course. I knew in my heart that it was time to take decisive action but I was still harbouring a fragile hope that we were not yet staring into the abyss. Queen Celestina plans to hold a meeting of the Clandestine Council. Once you've briefed me, I'll set the necessary wheels in motion."

"To cut to the heart of the matter, ma'am, everything my agents have unearthed so far seems to point to a certain pirate."

"Ah ha!" Indigoletta hopped from branch to branch like a boxer dancing round his opponent. She threw a confident verbal punch. "It's Pestilence Grimshaw, isn't it?"

"Very astute of you, ma'am. The blackguard's practically taken up residence at The Mischief Maker after countless years terrorising hapless mariners beyond our protection and jurisdiction. He's fly, mind you. Pestilence knows we can't touch him unless he puts a foot wrong which naturally he's at pains to avoid. 'The Cheeky Monkey' is at anchor in Corvine Harbour, right under our very beaks and Grimshaw couldn't have been more accommodating when I caught up with him. It was nauseating, ma'am. He was dripping charm and offered to help *us*. The bare-faced cheek of the knave."

Indigoletta rustled her feathers in agitation. "That's Pestilence Grimshaw for you. He can be infuriatingly smarmy. He's a crafty devil who will stop at nothing to increase his already substantial fortune. There's also the matter of his controlling personality which has to be topped up with regular injections of bullying and beastliness. Greed and violence are a thoroughly nasty pair of bedfellows, Redshanks."

"Without a doubt, ma'am." The chough raised his next concern. "You'll never believe who was cavorting with Grimshaw and his crew at The Mischief Maker; thick as thieves they were." Redshanks paused for maximum dramatic effect. "None other than the Giant Rat."

The Royal Raven was by now practically beside herself but decided one of her was more than enough. "Blow me out of a tree! How *very* weird. Gilbert's a reclusive beast by nature and, since his recent pyrotechnical capers, he's kept his head well below the parapet." Indigoletta shot the chough a fierce look. "My feathers are positively thrumming. Why is Gilbert behaving so out of character and, moreover, with that bounder Grimshaw?"

The raven recoiled as if she'd received a resounding slap on the face with a kipper long past its sell-by date. "Crikey, dear boy, I'm in danger of losing m'grip. I simply couldn't see the cliff for the rocks, and me a raven."

Redshanks edged towards her, concern showing in his bright eyes. "What is it, ma'am?"

"Gilbert's ridiculous attention-seeking behaviour leads me to believe he's got himself into a serious pickle. If I were a raven who enjoyed a flutter, in the non-feathered sense of the word, I'd bet good money the Giant Rat knows the whereabouts of young Leo."

After much deliberation and lots of pacing back and forth in front of the rose-tinted bedroom mirror, the Siamese cat finally decided which collar he wished to keep. To describe it as a 'collar' was a gross misrepresentation of the artefact. The craftsmanship involved was of the finest quality usually reserved for royalty and a certain snake of our acquaintance.

J.MILNE

Pongo happened to pop in as Jamie was returning the other two collars to the box they'd come in. The cat stopped what he was doing and gave him a suspicious look. The dog watched Jamie through narrowed eyes, his curly head over to one side. "So, you've made your selection. It looks very nice."

"*Nice*? Is that the best you can come up with?" The Siamese was hugely unimpressed. "Next you'll be telling me you've seen worse."

Pongo was delighted with Jamie's reaction. "Are you quite sure you've made the right choice? It's an important decision and I wouldn't want you to rush it."

The cat adopted a witheringly superior air. "You really don't know me very well if you think I would rush a decision of this magnitude. I've given the matter due consideration and this exquisite collar is the one for me."

"As long as you're happy. Might I venture to say it has your name on it?"

"If you feel you must, Pongo."

The dog gave a little twirl. "Shall I take the two that weren't up to scratch back to the snake? His nibs is downstairs, you know."

"Don't let 'the snake', as you have the temerity to call him, hear you being so disrespectful. He is a prince while you remain a mere dog."

Pongo dropped to the floor, placing his chin on his outstretched paws. "Pardon me, Exalted One, I'll just grovel here at your feet until you see fit to toss me a morsel of benevolence."

The cat snorted disdainfully. "I can assure you, you'll need to do better than that."

Pongo's hazel eyes sparkled wickedly. "You won't take too long though, will you? They're waiting for us."

The cat tore himself away from his unquestionably beautiful reflection in the floor-length Fairy-Baroque mirror.

"Why didn't you say so, Pongo? We'd better stop mucking around and get down there right away."

"Whatever you say, Your Feline Loftiness. May I get to my unworthy feet now?"

"Away with you, dog!" It was only then the Sylvanian penny dropped and Jamie realised the apparently random design of jewels on his fetching neck attire spelt his name backwards in the mirror, in perfect copperplate handwriting.

Pongo was ahead of the game yet again. The Prince of Cobalt-Sibilance was no slouch and neither was the dog. Jamie was quietly impressed. He enjoyed seeing Pongo prostrate at his feet, even though they both knew they were engaged in a mutually satisfying game.

The dog made a mad dash for the door, with the velvet box gripped between his teeth. His speech was uncannily snake-like. "Lassht one on Shammy's lap issh a bag of cold chipssh."

Jamie's reactions were flawless. He sprinted after Pongo and overtook him at the top of the stairs, his paws barely touching the treads on the way down. The cat applied the brakes at the last minute and skidded to a halt in front of Alfie and Sandy. Pogo was pouring tea from an antique Lotharian samovar.

Jamie turned his elegant head towards an unperturbed Sammy who was slurping tea from a generously proportioned china bowl. "Thank you so much for the collar. It wasn't an easy choice. I hope you don't think I'm being over-familiar but would you mind if I sat on your lap?"

The enigmatic blue and gold snake responded cordially. "Pleas-s-se do. That's the very collar I had in mind for you. I'm ecstatic you like it, old fruit."

The cat settled into Sammy's coils and found himself in a blanket of security and well-being, the likes of which he hadn't experienced since he was a carefree kitten nuzzling his mum. He felt the weight of responsibility slip from his silken shoulders. By the time Jamie remembered where he was and what he was there to do, his concerns had been s-sent packing with a s-stern warning from You Know Who.

Pongo strutted back and forth in front of Sandy attempting to look sweet and innocent. "That cat of yours is full of surprises," he said, trying not to appear too out of breath. "I'll tell you something for nothing. It would take more than a fancy collar to entice me to sit on Sammy's lap, but Jamie's no shrinking violet, is he?"

"You've noticed, have you? He's one beast who's not afraid to step into the spotlight."

Sandy slid from her chair onto the rug by the stove and put her arms round the dog's invitingly curly neck. "You really are incorrigible."

"That's the nicest thing anyone's said to me all day," he replied, enthusiastically licking her face.

"Steady on, Pongo. I've already had a bath."

"Anyone for another slice of chuckleberry and damson tart?" Alfie asked, during a gap in the laughter.

"Capital, WAE, and most appropriate under the circumstances," said the snake. "But perhaps Pongo would prefer a bag of cold chips."

The dog knew when it was time to throw in the towel. "Touché, SSS. I was definitely asking for that." Pongo turned towards Alfie. "Just a wee slice," he tittered coyly. "I really ought to watch my waistline."

Jock Craw set down outside the Anchor Bar and found Peg Leg demolishing the remains of a perfectly cooked scampi in a light coating of breadcrumbs. Said scampi had been left by a replete diner in a small nest of chips, worthy of Pongo's 'Last one…' challenge. The weather was glorious, warmer than is customary for the time of year, and the sun had thrown a shimmering, golden carpet across Irvine Bay.

The two birds settled down to pick over the remains of the meals around them before the plates were gathered up by the staff. When they'd finished eating they flew down to the Pilot Station at the mouth of the harbour and settled on the adjacent wharf where they could speak freely. Jock followed Ralph's advice and took his friend into his confidence.

The gull wobbled extravagantly. "What a carry-on. It's ridiculous that the whole balance of Sylvanian life could be threatened by a well-intentioned old spell-weaver. Alfie must have been spitting chips!"

The crow nodded vehemently.

Peg Leg fell silent and when he spoke again it was in an urgent whisper. "I'm probably being fanciful, but it's almost as if Leo's arrival in Sylvania, and Angus's part in that, were the last moves in a complex game." The seagull bounced unsteadily towards Jock who was preparing to dive out of his way should it become necessary. "We don't know what the game is and won't ever have access to the rule book. There has to be something I can do to help. Leave it with me, I'll sleep on it."

"I'm not sure there's time for that. I fear we're in danger of being out-manoeuvered, Jim, perhaps even overwhelmed."

The gull was surprised to hear the crow use his real name. Things must be very serious.

Jock picked at the white feathers on his chest in a distracted manner. "It's not just Sylvania that's threatened; what goes on there can influence events here." The crow's eyes were magnetic in their intensity. "I don't suppose you'd consider coming back with me?"

The gull was caught on the wrong foot, in his case the only foot, but he didn't even hesitate. "Try leaving without me, you silver-tongued wazzock; but won't you need special clearance?"

"Under the current circumstances, my salty, sea-faring chum, no prior permission will be required. It'll be tickety-boo with platinum knobs on."

In the murky water lapping against the old timbers of the wharf, a lobster languorously lurked. Not just any lobster, but one wearing preposterous eye-wear and a racy checked swimming costume, courtesy of his cousin Kitt.

Lorimer was living life to the limit since his narrow escape from the Swim Reaper, and there was no way whatsoever he was going to allow his best friend to go anywhere without him, certainly not while he was wearing his confidence-building whizz-banger of a bathing-suit.

Minxie, being the wazwatt she waswatt made certain the infant dragon reached the surface of the Island of Long Forgotten Dreams with his new-found confidence and fragile self-belief still intact. That doesn't mean to say she gave up teasing him or was any the less cheeky; both these traits are too much part of her nature.

Cahoots stepped out from under the brooding limestone overhang into the milky grey half-light of the cursed island. Minxie was treading air in front of him, her wings working busily. "It's pretty bleak," she said sympathetically when she saw the mounting confusion and despair in the dragon's eyes. Then added briskly, "If I were you, kiddo, I'd get away from here fast. Wazwatts are unaffected by the negative atmosphere of the island, as are dragons, but you're very young so don't push your luck."

The dragon's breathing was laboured and his distress clearly visible.

"Now then, my wee flame-thrower," Minxie said with forced cheerfulness. "I've let you take up too much of my precious time already."

Cahoots rallied and thrust his chin out. "I don't need a babysitter, thank you very much. I'm on an important mission, and I won't be spending more time here than is absolutely necessary."

Minxie adopted an annoying, sing-song voice and began to circle his head, slowly at first then increasingly faster and faster. "And what might that mission be, Your Scaliness?"

"Never you mind," replied the dragon who was starting to feel dizzy.

"Have it your own way," she called out, by now whizzing round him. "It's no skin off my cute little nose."

"Off mine, more likely," muttered the dazed dragon, "if you don't slow down."

The wazwatt stopped abruptly in mid-air and hovered above him. "Don't be daft. It's worth remembering us wazwatts are designed to be perfect at everything we do. Your smouldering nostrils have nothing to fear from me unless you see fit to provoke me."

Minxie knew she had to leave him and didn't find it easy. She flew east, spiralling down beneath the desolate undercliff, and shouted back at him. "See ya later, babe."

The dragon wasn't expecting that.

The wind buffeted his scaly body and screamed angrily in his ears. Cahoots called after her, his teeth chattering, but his words were snatched away on the wind like torn strips of ribbon.

Minxie dived through a small opening in the barren rockface.

The waves crashed against the cliffs below, falling back in a churning mass of foam before regrouping, with ever-increasing violence, and resuming their onslaught on the ancient infrastructure of the damned island.

The dragon didn't know it then but Minxie had done him an enormous favour by abandoning him for his greater good. The wazwatt knew he was all too likely to become dependent on her. By leaving him in the abrupt way she did, Cahoots was forced to think for himself and carry out his mother's instructions.

He carefully unfurled his wings and felt the strengthening updrafts lift him up and away from the Island of Long Forgotten Dreams.

The dragon tentatively circled the deadly reef and, when he felt a little more in control of his extremities, flew south towards the port of Corvine to face his next challenge.

5

Lorimer was bustling about in his new abode among the creaking timbers under the wharf at Irvine Harbour. The sheltered port on Scotland's south-west coast was a better bet than Dublin Bay where lobsters were routinely at the top of 'Today's Catch' notices. His best pal Peg Leg had made the harbour his base and Lorimer's cousin Kitt ran a lucrative recycling business out in the bay.

His nearest neighbour was Yenka the seal, an agreeable soul who never kept him awake with wild parties into the wee, small hours; not that the lobster would have minded if she had. He'd have been delighted to let off some steam, *without* being chucked into boiling water, had Yenka opted for one of those trendy parties with a different theme in each of the dredger buckets. Lorimer would happily cut a rug, dance a hornpipe or jitterbug the night away with the best of them and Kitt was bound to have some snazzy outfits for a 'bash' like that. Had Lorimer not been preparing for his trip to Sylvania he might well have thrown a bunfight himself.

The lobster had come across a battered old tin bath lodged in a cross-section of beams at the back of the wharf which he'd enterprisingly adapted to his needs. It was the lobster equivalent of a junk-room and Lorimer, not being the tidiest of creatures, had crammed it to capacity.

"I mustn't go unprepared, but I don't know where I'm going or what I should be prepared for." The lobster rummaged about, tossing what he deemed unnecessary to the back of the bathtub. "Why do I need an umbrella? I love being wet, it's my natural habitat, but here I am with three of them." He shook his head in disbelief. "Perhaps I ought to get rid of them, at least the broken one..." He continued in this indecisive manner for several minutes, unaware that he was being observed.

The pile of items to be discarded grew in size and rapidly dwindled again when he was overpowered by his irrational need to hang on to everything.

"What are you up to, Thermidor? Planning a holiday, perhaps?"

The lobster spun round like a child caught with his hand in the biscuit tin. He shuffled awkwardly along the beam towards the seagull.

"No," he said, turning a guilty shade of pink. "I'm just having a bit of a sort out."

"More like a sort in from where I'm standing."

Before the flustered crustacean could stop himself he blurted out, "When are you leaving?"

"What do you mean by that?" The seagull managed to appear unruffled. Give him enough rope... and then with feigned innocence, "What makes you think I'm planning a trip?"

"Oh, you know..."

"No, Thermidor, I don't know."

"Yes you do," insisted the crustacean in a blur of feelers. "I heard you discussing the details with Jock last night." He clapped his huge claw to his mouth but it was too late. "It appears I've let the lobster out of the creel."

"I think you'll find I was responsible for that, something I may well live to regret."

Lorimer was eager to please. "There's no need to say another word, it would be my unbridled pleasure to accompany you." He gave a satisfied nod. "There, I've said it!"

His warm, enthusiastic words were greeted with a prolonged silence, but the seagull felt a rush of affection for the eccentric creature he'd saved from certain death.

Something exceptional passed between them and there was no doubt that Peg Leg *and* Lorimer were going to Sylvania with Jock Craw whether he liked it or not.

Queen Celestina was troubled by the disturbing turn of events in her world but she is no stranger to anxiety. By fairy standards she's young, fit and strong and she's more than capable of taking fear by the throat and wrestling it into submission. She raised her platinum and diamond wand and deftly drew her name and password in stars before the unrelenting projection of limestone. The rock dissolved in a shimmering, grey mist and Celestina stepped through with Hamish to join the other members of the Clandestine Council before the rock silently returned to its former, impregnable state.

The barrel-vaulted chamber is situated deep within the limestone outcrop beneath the castle and is only accessible to those who know its exact location and the powerful combination of magic that enables them to enter. The room was washed in rosy light from torches on the walls and a log fire crackled in the open hearth. A hunched, shaggy figure was silhouetted against the flames and the torchlight glittered in its soulful yellow eyes.

Celestina crouched down in front of the wolf and stroked his silvery mane. "Thank you for coming. I know you'd rather be at your post."

She greeted the others in a relaxed, informal manner, taking time to exchange a few words with each of them.

The Queen and the Prince sat at either end of the ocean jasper table. "Will you join us, Grimpen?" The wolf took his place next to Celestina. Sammy sat in a precise coil on a large cushion to the right of the Queen with Alfie beside him. Indigoletta was sitting on an ornamental perch opposite the snake with a distinctly uneasy Crawford teetering beside her.

The Royal Raven requires plenty of space, being an expansive, demonstrative creature. She gestures extravagantly and Crawford knew before long he'd have to duck out of her way or be dashed to the floor. Jock, not being a perch sort of guy, was pacing around on the table in front of Prince Hamish.

Before the meeting got underway, the First Imp to the Royal Raven was sworn in as 'Attendant to the Clandestine Council'. Will was deeply honoured by this further promotion which had to be kept under wraps; but to know he was trusted so completely was beyond rewarding. He experienced a pang that he couldn't share his good fortune with the Captain of the Impfantry. The look of disgust on Twitchett's florid face would have been a joy to behold, not that the Captain would have known about the Clandestine Council in the first place, something even more thrilling.

The newly-appointed Attendant nipped off to fetch trays of food and refreshments which he placed at intervals along the highly polished table. He put a dish in front of Grimpen. "Martha Snowberry prepared this specially for you, sir." The wolf inspected the juicy slices of pie with quiet satisfaction.

Will gave a deep bow, laced with a cheeky grin. "As my Grannie would say, 'Get tore in!'"

Indigoletta smiled maternally. "Have no fear, we certainly won't be backwards about coming forwards." She cast an appreciative eye over the spread. "What a feast."

Hamish caught the young elf gently by the arm. "Don't

123

go, Will. You're a member of the council now."

The imp gaped at him. "I'm your new attendant, sir. No more, no less."

Hamish smiled warmly at his wife. "Dearest, would you care to explain?"

Celestina rose in a fragrant cloud of oyster silk and lace, the firelight glinting on her long dark hair. She moved gracefully towards the imp who was standing beside the raven. Indigoletta beamed at him, pride radiating from her magnificent feathers.

"Right from the start the Royal Raven recognised rare and highly-prized qualities in you, not least of all, those of loyalty and trust. You are one of the inner circle now, so sit down and tuck in. We have a long night ahead of us."

"Thank you, Your Majesty, but where am I to sit?"

Celestina flicked her wand and a perfectly proportioned chair materialised out of a swirling spiral of stars.

Alfie patted the pea-green velvet cushion. "There you go, Will, sit here next to me."

The imp relaxed into the soft contours of the cushions. "It fits like a…"

"Chair?" Indigoletta offered helpfully.

"Aye, ma'am." The imp stretched his legs and wriggled his toes inside his boots. "And the most comfortable there ever was."

Will realised everyone's eyes were on him. He sat up at once. "I didn't mean to be flippant, Your Majesty." He felt awkward and shy, two feelings which are not part of his usual repertoire. What he said next was clearly heartfelt. "I'm your devoted subject and I'll serve you 'til the end of my days."

Celestina responded with quiet conviction. "I know that, Will, and it's profoundly comforting. Indigoletta's instinct is *never* wrong. Now it's time we got down to business. There's much to discuss, not least the arrival of two more uninvited guests from Irvine, friends of yours, I believe, Jock."

If a crow could be described as sheepish, then that's how he looked. "In my own defence I'm obliged to say it's really only *one* uninvited guest. I did ask the seagull to accompany me."

"If you want him here, that's good enough for me," said the Queen emphatically. "But are you sure he'll be able to cope with just the one leg?"

That was too much for the Royal Raven, who jumped down from her perch and stamped her foot in irritation. "Seagull! One leg! What's all this about, Jock Craw?"

In the kerfuffle Crawford found himself hanging upside down from the perch.

Jock was losing patience. "If only you'd stop flapping around, ma'am, I'd be able to tell you."

"Well I never! Nobody talks to the Royal Raven like that, not even you." Indigoletta was seriously put out and completely unaware of Crawford's predicament.

Grimpen watched the ridiculous scene unfolding in front of him, wondering if there was anything he could do to bring the situation under control.

Hamish had seen and heard enough. He thumped his fist on the table. "This is a meeting of the Clandestine Council, not a rehearsal for the palace pantomime."

"I couldn't have put it better myself, sir," said Sammy, catching hold of the reins of the runaway council. "Peg Leg, that's the seagull, Indigoletta…"

"I've managed to grasp that much, I'm not a blithering idiot."

The Prince of Cobalt-Sibilance ignored her outburst and continued. "The gull arrived here with what can only be described as a flashily attired lobster."

Alfie scrutinized the snake's formidable face. "Very witty, SSS."

Sammy narrowed his eyes and his forked tongue flicked in and out impatiently.

"Staggering pixies! You're serious, aren't you?"

"Never more so."

"Where are they now?" asked the astounded elf.

"They're waiting for you at the palace."

"Waiting for *me*; how come?"

"I thought that would be for the best," said Celestina. "I've decided they ought to be in your care, at least for the time being. You'll have to keep a sharp eye on that lobster; he's one of a kind."

"So it would appear," Jock said under his breath. "I can't imagine why Peg Leg allowed him to tag along."

"I don't think he had much choice in the matter. In my brief experience of Lorimer it's pretty clear he's one determined crustacean."

The crow plucked irritably at his white feathers. "How on earth did they manage to tip up at the palace?"

The Queen's smile was slow and catlike. "That was entirely down to Hosepipe Snout. He happened upon the unlikely duo wandering around on the shores of Moonglow Lake. The hedgehorn was flabbergasted when he saw the lobster, understandable in view of Lorimer's stupendous apparel. The one-legged gull didn't go unremarked upon either. The warden sent word to Crawford and your cousin, brave soul that he is, interrupted Moriarty's afternoon snooze to send him here with the distinctly sound suggestion that Peg Leg and Lorimer be brought to the palace for safe keeping."

Crawford was proud enough to burst the seams of his fashionable dove-grey waistcoat, but he was also anxious for news of Moriarty, something Celestina had anticipated.

"Our guests have made themselves very much at home in the palace and seem totally at ease in their unfamiliar surroundings. Moriarty saw to that, he's so thoughtful. He even introduced them to Kismet and Wainscot. When I looked in before I came down here, Lorimer was taking a dip in the saltwater spa and Peg Leg was nibbling devilled shrimps, washed down with vintage kelp and bladderwrack tonic."

"And what of Moriarty, Your Majesty?"

"Kismet, Wainscot and your dear little friend were entertaining our visitors with some of the most exceptional music I've ever heard. Why didn't you tell us Moriarty is an accomplished harmonica player?" Crawford's face was a picture of incredulity. "You didn't know?"

The little crow was starting to feel giddy but he forced himself to respond cheerfully. "It's joyous news to me, Your Majesty. Here was I thinking he could only play a highly-strung haggis."

The words had escaped before he could stop them.

The Queen was laughing so much that she had to take a turn around the room to calm herself. Even Hamish was struggling to keep a straight face.

"What's wrong with us all tonight?" cried Celestina. "It's most peculiar. The more we try to discuss the problems facing us, the more we seem to digress. What must you think of us, Grimpen? Clandestine Council meetings are not usually occasions for unbridled mirth."

The Fairy Queen found herself on the receiving end of Sammy's level gaze. "I think there might be reasons why we're losing our focus and fragmenting at such a terrifying rate. I'm pretty sure we're under assault from the growing negativity that's pressing in on us from the dark side. It's time to bring the power of the Giant Sapphire directly into this chamber. Before we leave here tonight, we shall all feel a lot less frivolous and a great deal stronger, physically and spiritually, something I'm sure you'll be gratified to hear, Grimpen."

Maligna lay on her wretched pallet in the sinkhole on the Island of Long Forgotten Dreams, her right arm draped listlessly over dead eyes that reflected the dark side of the soul. The curled, yellow fingernails on her left hand scratched idly against the damp rock floor by her bed.

"Psst!" No response. "I *said*, 'PSST!'"

Time had abandoned her and the Harpie could barely summon enough energy to lift her head. A decrepit snail could have stopped for a cup of dandelion tea and a lettuce sandwich, pottered about among the cabbages and sprouts, and still have arrived home before time had managed to struggle out of bed. To cap it all, Maligna's own self-serving actions meant she no longer had Cahoots. The Harpie was lost in loneliness and had anyone said - "Your anklet or the dragon?" - she might very well have chosen the latter.

An exasperated, short-fused wazwatt whispered angrily, "What's wrong with you? Don't just lie there. My time's precious, I'll have you know."

Maligna stirred, but it was barely more than a flicker.

"Don't put yourself out on my account," hissed Minxie. "I've only battled raging seas and whirlpools, struggled across that spiteful, vicious reef in a force-ten-with-knobs-on gale, scaled the hateful undercliff and, as if that weren't enough, plunged valiantly into the uncharted horrors of the tortuous caves on this miserable lost cause of an island. And, when I finally get here, all you can do is lie there like a deflated beachball." The wazwatt paused to catch her breath. "Honestly! I'd heard you were seriously scary..."

Maligna turned her gaunt head slowly towards Minxie who was subjected to the full impact of her blank, indifferent eyes. "And I'd heard wazwatts could fly, so what's all the fuss about?"

"Fair point, dearie," replied the dainty creature without appearing to flinch before the Harpie's chilling stare.

In spite of her lethargy, Maligna was interested enough to sit up. "Who are you and why are you here?"

"Charming! When was the last time you had a visitor? I'd be more grateful if I were you, but since you asked, I'm Minxie."

The wazwatt flew towards the heavy iron grating high above them. The light filtering down was thin and grey like watery gruel and the only sound from above was that of the two guards snoring after a heavy lunch. A wazwatt could go mad in a place like this. She hastily descended and settled on the pallet next to Maligna. She moved closer to the Harpie and asked in a hushed voice, "Are there...em... no facilities?"

"Facilities?" Maligna smiled icily through chapped, bone-dry lips. "Does it look like there are *facilities*?"

Minxie grimaced. "I'm sorry I raised the subject but it was the first thing that struck me about your predicament."

"Don't bother your furry wee head, Minxie. Being a Harpie, I have no need for, as you so quaintly call them, 'facilities', but a curly kelp bath with a whirlpool of seahorses would be most acceptable. Perhaps you'd like to arrange that for me? Could that be the purpose of your visit?"

"I'm sorry to disappoint you, but that's not the porpoise of my visit."

Maligna scowled at Minxie who carried on unabashed. The wazwatt gave a fetching mid-air twirl, delighted by her own wordplay. "By the way, you don't have anything to do with that gormless dragon, do you?"

The Harpie sprang from the bed like a broken marionette miraculously restored.

Minxie laughed triumphantly. "Oh-ho, it seems I've pressed the right button or, more accurately, pulled the right string! So, you do know the little twit. I met him on my way here and, by my calculations, he should be well on his way to Corvine by now. That is where he's headed, is it not?"

Maligna recovered her composure but she had a wary, closed-off look about her. She didn't know whether this insolent article was friend or foe.

"You're wondering why I'm here which is fair enough. The reason's pretty mundane," she drawled, studiously inspecting the claws on her right paw. "I have a message from 'Captain' Self Importance himself... dah-dee-dah, dah dah... your friend and mine, that wily old sea-dog and pirate par excellence, Pestilence Grimshaw." The wazwatt had the Harpie's undivided attention. "I hope his cryptic message makes sense to you. I can't make head nor tail of it myself."

Maligna's jaw was so tightly clenched that Minxie was bolstering herself against a possible barrage of shattered teeth. "I take it those guards are likely to be out for the count for some time." Maligna nodded. "Well then, here goes: 'The plump partridge is on the wobbly wicket'."

Maligna's eyes became coal-black slits. "You can't be serious," she growled. "That's not code, that's gibberish."

Minxie giggled. "I'm so sorry, I don't know what came over me there. What I meant to say was..."

When Pigsblanket arrived back at The Mischief Maker he was informed by the landlord that the pirate captain had already left, something which surprised the lad. This was a departure from Grimshaw's usual routine when he was in port. The boy felt uneasy and knew he was likely to be in serious trouble, as ever through no fault of his own.

"Was there any message, Mr Slack?" He crossed his fingers, desperately hoping the answer would be 'no'.

"Yes, lad, there was."

The boy's narrow shoulders slumped and he couldn't bear to look the landlord in the face.

"His precise words were: 'Tell that feckless, cowardly, snivelling, shiftless...'" Jem donned his smeary spectacles and scrutinised the pad on the bar. "I wrote it down somewhere. Cap'n Grimshaw was most partic'lar. Let me see... yes, here it is: 'Tell that feckless, cowardly, snivelling, shiftless, rattling bag of - hang on a minute, I can't read m'own handwriting, oh aye, that's it - 'rattling bag of soon-to-be-broken bones that I want to see him in my cabin this side of midnight'."

Slack glanced up at the clock behind him and back at Pigsblanket's face which was draining of what little colour it had to start with. The boy's haunted eyes sunk further back into his skull.

"You've blown that then. It's already a quarter after midnight." The landlord felt a twinge of sympathy for Pigsblanket. He'd been on the receiving end of Grimshaw's anger more times than he cared to remember. "You're late as it is, lad, and you look fair done in. I'll have Gertie bring you some soup, shall I? On the house, that is..."

But Pigsblanket was already on his way out of the tavern.

The landlord's dumpy wife was framed in the kitchen doorway and she had the saddest expression on her careworn face. "Oh, Jem, I wish we'd had children. We'd have cherished them, wouldn't we?"

Jem gave his wife's arm a quick squeeze. "Aye, lass. I'd like to think we would've."

Gertie twisted the filthy dishcloth in her calloused hands. "Poor Pigsblanket."

Less than two hours later the cabin boy lay bruised and battered in his hammock. His spirit was little more than the dying flicker of flame from a sputtering candle. Tears of futile rage ran down his face. How had it come to this and why did that monster Grimshaw hate him so much?

Pigsblanket's earliest memory was of the buccaneer tormenting him. Grimshaw thrived on it and didn't mind who knew about it either. He treated his crew with undisguised contempt and was happy to provide a punch on the nose or a smack in the mouth when the fancy took him, but with the cabin boy it was much more personal.

What upset Pigsblanket even more than the savage beating was that he'd finally broken down and told Grimshaw everything he'd witnessed. Anyone with a half-decent brain and the teensiest bit of common sense would have walked away, long before they saw too much, but not him, he just had to make sure the rat was alive and well which naturally Gilbert was, being as he was relaxed and full of ale when he hurtled down the mineshaft.

Had Pigsblanket followed his instinct, and not been such a caring soul, he would not have seen Leo stagger out from under the rubble into the moonlight and thereby discover that the cat and rodent were on first-name terms, something else he'd been forced to tell Grimshaw.

The cabin boy felt thoroughly wretched. What would Gilbert think when he realised who had betrayed him? The Giant Rat had shown him such kindness and this was how he repaid him. The boy slipped into a wintry wilderness of despair.

Not even Jedediah Malahyde had dared to come to his aid, fearing Grimshaw would turn his white-hot anger on him instead. The First Mate had never seen the buccaneer in such a rage and knew he'd best keep his trap shut. It seemed there was much more at stake than Malahyde had realised.

Having been put to bed by Leo after his drunken escapade, Gilbert woke the following morning long before he was able to cope with the situation unfolding in front of his bleary, bloodshot eyes. He was emerging from one of those disorientating nightmares that are terrifyingly lucid but diminish in their potency as the dream gives way to reassuring but all-too-familiar grey reality.

The Giant Rat attempted to raise his pounding head but was immediately overcome by the searing pain which held his brain in an ever-tightening, vice-like grip. Gilbert fell back limply on the shavings. The scoreboard read: Nasty alcohol-related headache - 'l'. Well-intentioned rat with hangover - 'Nil'.

"Ooh-er," he groaned. "It appears I've let Leo down again. If I'm not mistaken, that's him being bundled unceremoniously into a sack while I'm lying here hoping the alebane fairy will put in an unscheduled appearance."

Leo couldn't believe what was happening to him but managed one snatched sentence before he was consumed by the coarse, itchy sack. The cat's voice became increasingly muffled, but his exasperation was manifest. "There's alebane right beside you, you great lummock."

The Abyssinian cat knew it was pointless to struggle, but he put up a fight nonetheless. He could hear Gilbert's indistinct ranting as they were manhandled out of the mineshaft.

The gossipy toads exchanged too many words on the terrible state of affairs the Giant Rat had brought upon himself.

"Dear oh dear, Natterjack. I knew Gilbert was sailing close to the wind, but I didn't think it would come to this."

"How were we to know he was such a waste of space? On the subject of sailing close to the wind, I reckon the big poultice might just be heading for a life on the ocean waves."

Puddock chuckled gleefully. "The voice of reason, as ever, NJ. It's a crying shame I'm the only one privy to your pearls of wisdom. Sadly, us toads are not regarded as having anything worthwhile to contribute to society."

A harrumph came from the smaller of the two sacks which was being winched up the shaft. "I don't think I can bear to listen to another word from those two smart-alecs. I've no idea where we're being carted off to, but *please* tell me Puddock and Natterjack won't be joining us."

Gilbert belly-laughed inside his potato sack. "And so say I, Leo. You're taking this terribly well. I can scarcely believe you're the same timid little cat I met so recently."

"That's because I'm no longer that 'timid little cat', as you so tactfully put it. How could I be in view of all the ridiculous things that have happened to me since I arrived here? Let's face it, one of us had to take control of the situation."

Gilbert tittered. "So that's what you've been doing, Leo, and here was me thinking we'd just been kidnapped."

They were brought up short by a voice from above. "One more word out of either sack and we'll keelhaul the pair of you."

The two toads were right again.

The Giant Rat and the Hendersons' cat were slung across the saddle of a stocky skewbald pony that was tethered near, but not too near, the dastardly holly. The pony received a sharp slap on the rump and lurched forward.

The final indignity was the sound of Puddock and Natterjack singing sea shanties at the bottom of the mineshaft.

A wearying amount of time later the two sacks were emptied onto the gun deck of 'The Cheeky Monkey' where a reception committee was waiting to welcome the contents.

Gilbert and Leo sprawled in front of a pair of elegant boots sporting a broad cuff of contrasting leather below the knee.

"How nice to see you again, Gilbert, and so much sooner than I'd expected."

For a fleeting moment the rat thought things might be looking up for them both. He raised his hopeful pink eyes towards the owner of the boots. "Pestilence, my dear chum. Thank goodness…"

"Now don't get your hopes up. I'm not your port in a storm nor your treasure chest stuffed with doubloons."

The rat blinked at Grimshaw in a state of increasing confusion but the pirate continued to smile infuriatingly. "I've been less than honest with you, dear chap, in fact I've been a downright scoundrel. I knew you were up to something and I had you followed when you left the tavern last night."

Gilbert gulped in dismay. "I thought you were my friend, Pestilence."

"'fraid not, Gilb, and from now on you'll address me as Captain Grimshaw."

The Giant Rat was well and truly flummoxed when, out of the blue, Leo piped up. "Aren't you going to introduce us, you great pudding?"

Before the rat could begin to form a response, the Bosun drew his cutlass, rushed forward and flung his arm round the cat's neck, lifting him clean off the deck. "Apologise to the Cap'n at once or I'll slit your scrawny throat, you mangy little twerp."

"For crying out loud, man. He meant the rat not me. Unhand him at once." Grimshaw rolled his eyes heavenwards. "Preserve me from fools and idiots."

The Bosun leapt forward again. "Just point me at the fools and idiots, Cap'n, and I'll toss 'em overboard."

The buccaneer could hear sailors in the ranks sniggering and his extremely limited patience snapped. He grabbed the man by the lapels of his serge jacket and pulled him roughly towards him. Grimshaw spoke slowly, giving due emphasis to every syllable. "You're going to have a very busy afternoon, Mr Leitzoff, and I'm going to be left with virtually no crew."

All the Bosun could muster was a silly, gap-toothed grin. The pungent smell of cheap rum on his breath fuelled Grimshaw's rage. "...AND NO BOSUN EITHER, BEING AS YOU'RE DAFTER THAN ANYONE ELSE ON THIS SHIP!"

Grimshaw dropped Leitzoff in bored disgust. The Bosun cowered at the buccaneer's feet, his heavily tattooed arms wrapped protectively round his bristly pate, waiting for the punch that never materialised.

The captain of the pirates decided restraint was the order of the day. His two guests needed a gentle introduction to life on 'The Cheeky Monkey'.

Leitzoff could hardly believe his luck.

"Trust you to get him in a good mood, you jammy devil," mumbled a matelot behind him.

Pigsblanket was watching the scene unfold from what he deemed to be a safe distance. The Captain clocked some of the crew peering over his left shoulder and whipped round just in time to see the cabin boy making his escape below deck.

"Oh no you don't, Pigsblanket. Come over here and greet our guests."

Gilbert and Leo exchanged nervous looks. The boy was in a terrible state.

"Move it, my little sea-slug. We haven't got all day."

The boy limped towards the buccaneer, his eyes cast down in shameful self-loathing.

"Gentlemen," exclaimed Grimshaw rakishly, toying with the jewelled hilt of his impressive sword, "it's Pigsblanket who arranged for you to be here today. It could not have happened without his freely given co-operation and undying loyalty to me."

The Giant Rat's small, sharp eyes flicked over the boy, missing nothing. He spoke directly to him, bypassing Grimshaw, which only added to the tension that was sending tendrils of fear to the farthest corners of the ship.

"Freely given, is that a fact? So why does he resemble a reluctantly tenderised steak?"

A nervous titter ran through the ranks.

Gilbert scuttled towards the miserable, dishevelled boy. "You were in better shape when we met last night. Please don't insult me by saying you came by those injuries in pursuit of a ridiculous, tipsy old rodent."

Pigsblanket remained silent throughout Gilbert's short speech but he was watching the rat closely, his breathing shallow with concern for the beast. He shot Grimshaw a covert look to find that the captain had Gilbert directly in his sights.

The buccaneer was privately amazed by the Giant Rat's bravery and disregard for his own safety. Gilbert wasn't just a bumbling misfit after all. When Grimshaw finally responded there was a hint of grudging admiration in his rebuke. "By jove, ratty, you're pushing your luck!"

Pogo Pixie sat in the kitchen at 'Corbie Cottage' with Jamie curled up next to Sandy on Alfie's rocking chair. The child was almost asleep but was fighting to stay awake so that she could greet the elf when he returned. She had no idea where he was but it was pretty clear from the mood in the cottage he was on serious business. Her eyes grew heavy and she drifted into a light, fitful sleep.

The day had been hot and humid but that had changed abruptly at sunset. There was a chill in the air which no amount of fuel in the stove was able to shift.

Pogo fetched a blanket from the cupboard in the hall which she wrapped around Sandy and the cat.

Jamie murmured his thanks. Cats are never fully asleep, something you'll know if you share your life with one or more of these remarkable beasts.

Pongo reacted to an unfamiliar noise in the front garden and reluctantly got to his feet. He was desperate to cut through the mounting tension with a barrage of confidence-building barks but he knew that was not on.

The pixie beckoned him to her and ruffled the top of his head. "I think we ought to investigate, don't you?"

The dog nodded but his eyes told a different story. Pogo recognised fear when she saw it and realised her own feelings of unease were more than justified.

In spite of his boisterous approach to life, Pongo has an indefinable sixth sense which told him evil was on the prowl in Old Rook Wood. He steeled himself to look braver than he felt. "There's no need for us both to…"

"That's OK, I could do with some fresh air." The dog appeared doubtful and grateful at the same time. "It might even be Alfie," she added unconvincingly.

They both knew that was rubbish.

Pogo walked out of the kitchen into the hall. "Right then, let's have a shufti."

She turned the wrought-iron handle as quietly as she could, something she would never have worried about under normal circumstances. The door to 'Corbie Cottage' is rarely closed at this time of year and never locked. It was only shut now because of the unseasonably cool weather.

Pongo nudged it open with his nose and sniffed the night air. At first he couldn't detect anything out of the ordinary as he crept onto the verandah and down the steps.

In the moonlight huddled clumps of shrubs and spires of hollyhocks stood out against the dark swathe of trees facing the cottage.

As Pogo stepped onto the path she felt something brush against her ankle. She was frozen to the spot until a familiar voice brought her back from the edge of fear.

Jamie slunk past in one long, fluid movement. "I didn't mean to scare you," he said, taking his place beside Pongo.

When she moved away from the cottage Pogo was overwhelmed by a brooding presence in the garden. The air was thick as lentil broth and she could scarcely breathe.

A feral growl made her break out in goose-pimples. The guttural sound was coming from Pongo who was crouched on the path snarling, his teeth bared, his ears flat. The once sleek Siamese resembled a short-haired bottle-brush.

A shadow passed in front of the moon and, in those few seconds of inky blackness, Pogo saw pairs of malevolent eyes all around them. The sickly smell of sulphur told her they were in the presence of pure evil. She called out but her voice was thin and reedy. Each syllable was stretched until it was unrecognisable. She tried to attract the animals' attention but her movements were slow and heavy. There was a dreamlike quality to everything.

The pixie felt herself being sucked down under 'Corbie Cottage' to a dark, suffocating world from which there was no escape.

Pogo uttered a high-pitched, near silent scream which the dog responded to at once. He moved towards her protectively and, as he did so, spotted Sandy coming towards them. Before he could do anything to stop her she ran down the steps into the garden.

"So that's where you all are," she exclaimed happily, rubbing the sleep from her eyes. "Are you waiting for Alfie?"

The dark spell was shattered. The fearsome eyes receded into the trees and the silent wood was once more alive with chirruping crickets and scurrying woodland creatures going about their nightly business. The smell of sulphur melted away and was replaced with the perfume of night-scented stock.

"Those vile eyes were spying on us," Sandy said calmly.

"Indeed they were," was all Pogo could muster before she bundled the child back up the steps.

When they were all safely inside the cottage again Pogo slammed the door and stood with her back against it, arms outstretched. "Quickly now, fetch the key!"

The dog rushed across the hall to where the key hung idly on its hook. He had to execute a series of jumps and half-turns before he managed to reach it. He grabbed it between his teeth and belted back to Pogo who snatched it from him. She secured the front door and engaged the stiff bolts top and bottom then ran through to the kitchen and bolted the backdoor as well.

"I'll check upstairs," said Sandy and, before Pogo could say "absolutely not", she was off at the double, taking the stairs two at a time. Jamie kept pace with her as she dashed from room to room closing windows where necessary.

One of the casements in the turret was ajar. The room was in semi-darkness, the furniture hunched and forbidding. She sang a made-up, nonsensical song at the top of her voice to keep her anxiety at bay and reached for the handle on the window.

A winged creature with gangling limbs and hideous yellow eyes let out a terrifying screech and lunged towards her, grabbing her wrist in its twisted, clammy fingers. In one desperate move it sank two razor-sharp incisors into her outstretched hand before she recovered herself enough to hurl it out into the night from whence it came.

"You have no business in this house. Get away from here at once," she bellowed, banging the window shut. She was stunned by the commanding tone of her own voice. Jamie and Pongo watched in silent admiration.

Pogo lit the oil lamp on the mantlepiece with trembling hands. The furniture shrank back to its usual unthreatening proportions and the painted unicorns and flying horses on the wallpaper once more glittered as they danced forever in their enchanted wood.

Pongo followed the pixie round the room, no more than a fairy inch from her left boot. He had no intention of letting her out of his sight again.

"Let me see your hand," she said in an uncharacteristically grim voice. Sandy obediently stretched out her right arm. There were two small puncture marks above her index finger which were already beginning to fade. Jamie's intelligent blue eyes were full of concern.

Pongo was so dismayed by the evening's turn of events that for once he had nothing to contribute. This was not how things were supposed to be at all.

The pixie's voice echoed eerily. "You're very lucky, Sandy. If you were Sylvanian you'd be in a critical state right now. A bite from a scrogwit is usually fatal. Don't be so headstrong again, even if you're only trying to be helpful. There's a vast amount you don't know about our world."

Back in the kitchen Sandy started to tremble. The stupidity of what she'd done hit home. "I'm sorry, I got carried away. I didn't think anything could actually harm me here in Sylvania."

Pogo laughed unexpectedly, cutting through the tension. "No one's invincible, not even you. The way things are these days it's best not to take risks, especially with scrogwits." Three pairs of solemn eyes were trained on her. "What say we have some tea to steady our nerves?"

Pongo liked the sound of that; business as usual. Perhaps not a cup of tea, but that bowl of leftover chops he'd seen in the larder earlier would be most acceptable.

"You surprise me, Pongo, I can't imagine you preferring chops when there's tea on offer. What a strange dog you are."

"Very funny, PP."

"What about you, Jamie?"

The cat inclined his head towards her. "I'll join Pongo on the chop front, if that's all right with you."

This exchange raised Sandy's spirits but the dog couldn't fail to notice she was still shivering. He picked up the discarded blanket and tugged it across the floor. "There you go," he said gently, draping it over her knees.

Jamie jumped onto her lap and embarked on a rich sequence of mellow, comforting purrs.

"Would you look at that," said Pongo, "she's got her very own living hot-water bottle. How about a nice cosy footwarmer as well?" He snuggled up under Sandy's dangling feet. "You can use my fur to keep your tootsies warm until I feel brave enough to nip upstairs for your slippers."

"I've heard that chops are good for the nerves."

"Is that so, PP? I'd better get stuck into them at once to see if you're right."

Jamie winked at Pogo. "Chops are most restorative. I'm sure I've heard Captain H. say as much on more than one occasion."

"Well then, that settles it. Ralph's no dim-wit."

Jamie stretched lazily. "How very nice of you to say so, Pongo. I'll be sure to tell him what you've just said when I arrive back in Irvine."

Pongo looked uncomfortable. "Those very words?"

"Absolutely," simpered the Siamese, "he'll be flattered to know you hold him in such high regard."

The meeting of the Clandestine Council finally came to an end some five hours after it began.

Prince Hamish had a quick word in the Royal Raven's ear which resulted in Indigoletta tactfully suggesting that

Crawford might like to fly her home. She wasn't one for effusive apologies but she knew it was the right thing to do. She was mortified that she'd flipped him upside down on their shared perch without even realising she'd done so. These were trying times and her nerves were shot to pieces but that was still no excuse. It was time to pull herself together. A long-overdue visit to the Cave of Sublime Spirit was what she needed to smooth out her emotional wrinkles and she told Crawford as much on the way to her quarters.

"That would be most efficacious, ma'am. Perhaps I ought to do the same myself?"

"Indeed you should, Crawf," she said good-naturedly. "You could do worse than follow that up with a visit to Cressmere spa. The Prince of Cobalt-Sibilance is likely to find himself very busy in the next day or two in view of the state we were all in tonight. I've arranged for Will to spend some time with him in the morning. A bit of meditation with the snake will do wonders for him."

On a whim they decided to fly out over the mighty crags that shelter the royal palace from the full might of the Whiteraven Sea. The massive cliffs rose up before them in all their glory and the wind beneath their wings was invigorating.

"I know I have an enormous sense of my own importance, Crawford," called the raven above the roar of the waves, "but we really must endeavour to maintain standards and dignity must prevail."

They landed on the balcony outside Indigoletta's aerial conservatory.

"Dignity must prevail, ma'am? I can't say I felt particularly dignified hanging from that perch."

Indigoletta made no response and Crawford thought he'd gone too far. He needn't have worried, the Royal Raven might be proud and pernickety but she's far from humourless.

"Fair comment, Crawf. Do join me for a swift glass of mulberry wine. I'm forever telling anyone who will listen about its wonderful properties. You might feel fortified enough to spin me round m'favourite branch before you leave."

Crawford was too shocked to reply which amused Indigoletta no end.

"On reflection that would take at least half a bottle and time's not exactly on our side."

Kismet moved through Old Rook Wood with his mixed bag of passengers in the howdah. They had just parted company with Grimpen and were beginning to pick up speed again.

The lilac and blue fairy mouse was in her usual position up front on a tasselled cushion. She tugged the huge cat's left ear to attract his attention.

"Is there a problem, Wainscot?"

"The lobster's just fallen out of the howdah."

The Sylvanian Forest Cat came to a halt.

Alfie called from his seat at the back. "What's up, Kismet?"

"Lobster overboard," affirmed the cat calmly.

"For pity's sake," cried the vexed crow, "this is the absolute limit! Honestly, Peg, why did you let him come here with you?"

The seagull shrugged. "It's hard to explain, but my instincts told me it was the right thing to do; so here we both are, like it or lump it."

The Prince of Cobalt-Sibilance had woven himself into a splendid crown and was sitting beside Wainscot on Kismet's head. It was a case of the crown with the crown on top. "S-sort it out would you, Will?"

The imp jumped over the side and slid down the Forest Cat's furry flanks. He landed on the ground to discover Lorimer clambering up the cat's copiously hairy tail. The lobster was making remarkably good progress. "When we swung round that last corner I was tossed out of the bucket of spa water Her Majesty insisted I should have. Thank you for coming to my aid but I seem to be getting on rather well."

"Aye aye, sir," said Will clutching at chunks of fur as he scrambled after the ungainly creature. There was more to the lobster than designer clothes and state-of-the-art eye gear.

With Lorimer reinstated in his silver bucket they continued through the wood towards 'Corbie Cottage'.

Sammy had been so taken up with affairs of the Clandestine Council that he'd ceased to pay proper attention to fleeting images from his third eye which swept in and out of his consciousness.

The snake centred his thoughts and slipped easily into a trance-like state. What he saw made him reel with shock. No wonder the council members were finding it hard to concentrate. The dark side was gaining in confidence to such an extent that it now threatened boundaries which had been in place for more years than there were hairs on Grimpen's head.

Sammy gently hissed in Kismet's ear. "I don't want to alarm anyone, but could you step on it without decanting the lobster? I've received some very disturbing pictures and I need to assure myself that Pogo and the others are all right."

The sleek, midnight-blue hare stood at the foot of a wind-blasted Sylvanian pine, one of a group of three high above Corvine harbour. The tree in the middle is a landmark used by sailors to navigate safely through the hazardous reef into the calm waters of the harbour within.

The beautiful creature was staring intently at a garishly painted vessel anchored below.

'The Cheeky Monkey', resplendent in bubblegum pink, turquoise and canary yellow, swung ostentatiously on her moorings as the tide swept in over the sandbar.

Sullen storm clouds were forming above Fractal Reef and a north-easterly intensified as the sky grew dark and threatening. That in itself was strange enough at this time of year but Cassandra was not concerned with matters meteorological. She was watching her arch-enemy Pestilence Grimshaw prancing around like the cat who'd stolen a scrumptious roast chicken and scoffed the lot before anyone noticed it was missing from the table. Had it not been beneath his dignity, the buccaneer would have been dancing a sailor's hornpipe. Instead he was laughing his head off and repeatedly slapping his thigh in a 'who's a clever boy then' kind of fashion.

The hare had been paying particular attention to his movements since he arrived in Corvine, something she never failed to do when he was in port, for Grimshaw had committed the worst sin against any mother. He had killed her children and eaten them in a game pie.

The hare had lain awake night after night until the months turned into years while she schemed and plotted her revenge and his downfall. The hatred she felt for Grimshaw consumed her, something she was ashamed to acknowledge, but then she had nothing else to live for.

Tonight was different and Cassandra was struck by the intensity of her conviction. For the first time since the cruel murder of her babies, she felt relief from the burden of her own despair.

The buccaneer was distinctly pleased with himself. It was as if Grimshaw had been given a treasure chest full of rubies, only to discover that his benefactor wanted him to have a chest crammed with emeralds as well.

He strode towards his cabin calling Pigsblanket's name at the top of his powerful voice. The boy ran on deck, clutching his bandaged ribs which ached from the beating.

"Mr Malahyde will be joining me and my guests for dinner tonight. I don't want Gilbert and Leo thinking we're barbarians, so dust off the best china and glasses, my little sea 'cumber. And fetch the cutlery inlaid with pearls and diamonds that puts me in mind of mermaids' tears."

The hare could clearly hear Grimshaw's words above the wind and she felt light-headed and reckless at the mention of Gilbert and Leo. The word hare-brained came to mind.

Cassandra knew she had stumbled upon something major. The whole of Crawdonia was looking for the little cat and, thanks to her obsession with Grimshaw, she'd found him without even trying.

She turned away from the harbour wondering what to do next, but there was only one course of action. It was imperative to get word to Queen Celestina.

She followed the crumbling cliff path, nimble as a mountain goat, then jinked under some scrubby gorse bushes that conceal the entrance to a disused tunnel which winds down through the hillside in the direction of the royal palace.

Cahoots flew low over Fractal Reef.

The dragon had managed the first part of his journey without incident; his next task was to find Pestilence Grimshaw and deliver his mother's message.

Maligna had furnished him with a good description of 'The Cheeky Monkey', including its gaudy colour scheme, something she had assured him Pestilence never altered. The pirate wanted everyone to know exactly whose ship she was and what better way was there than to make her eye-catchingly memorable.

Had the dragon been able to read he would have seen the ship's name painted boldly across her bows and stern but, as he couldn't, Cahoots wanted to be absolutely sure it was the right vessel. Maybe the tall man on the gun deck, who was consumed with mirth, might be able to help. The dragon felt sure the laughing buccaneer had to be one of the good guys, but then Cahoots was young and inexperienced with a huge amount to learn about life.

He banked sharply over the palace and, having scared himself silly in a near collision with a flagpole flying the royal standard, managed to recover himself in time to persuade his trembling wings to carry him down to the harbour.

6

The Royal Steed cantered through Old Rook Wood in the relaxed, effortless manner that is a distinctive feature of the Sylvanian Forest Cat.

Kismet galloped without making the slightest sound, not even the snap of a twig, nor the crackle of dead leaves. His fur constantly changed pattern to match his surroundings, giving him the ultimate disguise. This facility extends to howdah and passengers alike, although they are unaware of any change in their appearance.

Lorimer was careful to anchor himself firmly in his bucket to avoid being ejected for the second time. Peg had settled in a nest of eiderdowns with his chin on his chest, very nearly asleep after the rollercoaster ride he and Lorimer had been on since leaving Irvine.

Alfie joined the snake who was sitting in a slack coil among the embroidered cushions. "I've never travelled at speed with Kismet before, but it's totally brilliant." His voice had the breathless excitement of a child.

"Indeed it is, WAE, and quite astonishing in view of his size. The Queen chose well."

"There's only one thing that puzzles me."

"And what's that?" asked the snake with feigned innocence.

"Why the sudden change of pace?"

The snake tipped his crown forward at a studiously carefree angle and yawned. "It's been a long, exhausting day, and I mentioned to Kismet the possibility of a bowl of choco-mead when we reach 'Corbie Cottage'."

"But there's nothing exceptional about that."

The Prince of Cobalt-Sibilance closed his eyes, indicating he had no more to say on the matter, and Alfie stared in fascination as the snake slipped into a trance.

Will was standing up front on the steps which run round the inside of the howdah. He could barely see over the top.

"Who're you?" said an imperious voice.

The imp craned his neck but couldn't see who had spoken to him.

"I'm up here!"

Will blinked in happy surprise. "Bless me, so you are. You'll have to forgive me, I've never seen a fairy mouse in the fur before, not even one sitting on a cushion on a giant cat's head. You're an endangered species, are you not, particularly those in the rare lilac and blue livery like yourself."

"So, what's it to you if we are? You haven't introduced yourself and I'm not in the habit of talking to strangers, not even a smarty-pants imp who can see in the dark."

Will laughed out loud. "A wise decision if you're an endangered species. Is that why you stay so close to the big guy?"

The fairy mouse tried to hide her amusement. "That's one of the reasons. Now, who are you?"

"I'm Will, Attendant to the Royal Raven."

"And I'm Wainscot, Attendant to the Royal Steed."

"Is that a fact?"

The fairy mouse giggled and fell back on the cushion. "Aren't we an important pair?"

Kismet slowed down to a trot when they emerged from the darkest part of the wood and joined the track that led to Alfie's cottage. He stopped smoothly by the garden gate.

Sammy's eyes snapped open and he whizzed over the side of the howdah.

"Hey, wait for me!" shouted the elf. He made a grab for his Lincoln green hat and stumbled after the snake who could scarcely be seen for fairy dust. SSS had already slithered between two of the vertical slats in the gate and was motoring up the path. He needed to assure himself that all was well before Alfie came anywhere near the cottage.

The house was unnaturally silent and the front door was shut fast. Most concerning of all was the lack of cheerful, 'I'm-so-glad-you're-here' barks from Pongo.

Pogo heard voices outside and made for the parlour where she opened the curtains a chink. At first she couldn't see anything other than the moonlit garden and the wood beyond but she was pretty sure she could hear her husband's voice and Sammy's as well.

Kismet realised he was still in full camouflage mode and switched himself back to one of his preferred colour combinations, in this instance luminous lemon with tangerine tiger stripes.

The pixie jumped back from the window when the Sylvanian Forest Cat materialised out of the night.

Sammy called Pogo's name and thumped the door with his tail. Relief washed over her and she ran into the hall to let him in. Pongo peered round the kitchen door with his hackles on full alert.

"It's all right, boy, the cavalry's arrived."

She flung the door open and, in her agitation, grabbed Sammy by the neck. "Am I glad to see you, SSS."

The snake gulped politely. "The feeling's more than mutual, PP, but would you consider loosening your grip on my throat?"

Alfie bounded up the path to be met by the sight of his wife apparently throttling the Prince of Cobalt-Sibilance. Pogo let go of the snake, with a hasty apology, and hugged her husband instead. "I'm so glad you're home. What a time we've had of it."

Sammy nudged Alfie into the house. "I'll see to the others. You're going to have a pretty full house tonight, Pogo. We mustn't take advantage of your hospitality, shall I have the Royal Steed wait by the gate?"

"Absolutely not. He can stretch out along the path and have his supper in the front garden with Wainscot."

Pongo buzzed around making sure everyone was being taken care of. "More choco-mead, Will? Pogo's just made a fresh pot. Queen Celestina's certainly done us proud, that hamper's jam-packed with tasty treats."

The dog stopped in front of Sammy. "What a to-do. We were scared witless. And then to crown it all, platinum and sapphire crown, *of course*, SSS, we were visited by a scrogwit. You should have seen Sandy. She gave that disgusting creep what for!"

Pongo took a step backwards and fell over Jamie.

"So nice of you to drop in, I'll have some squid if there's any left, failing that there's always the lobster."

When the full impact of the cat's words hit the target with the lobster's face on it, Lorimer began thrashing and flailing around in a state of panic. He donned his fabulous goggles in a defiant gesture but why he thought they might be of assistance was anyone's guess.

"Excellent eye gear," said the dog with genuine admiration. "Those goggles set your cozzie off a treat. Now please don't distress yourself, Jamie wouldn't dream of eating you."

The lobster appeared to relax slightly, until the Siamese added mischievously, "Not unless there really isn't any more squid."

Sandy saw how distressed Lorimer was and tiptoed towards him through the sprawl of bodies.

The lobster scrambled out of his silver bucket and wedged himself under the rocking chair.

She knelt down beside him. "Pay no attention to Jamie," she said, trying to coax the beast out before a preoccupied Alfie cracked him open when he swung back on his chair.

"There's no need to flip your lid, the cat's only teasing you," Peg said sleepily, "and, if he's not, I'll try to save you yet again."

Lorimer scooted towards his bucket. "Why is it with me that everything comes back to pots, lids and hot water? It's most disturbing."

Alfie was so distracted he'd failed to notice what was going on around him. Sammy finally managed to attract his attention. "Where's Jock?"

The crow stepped into the kitchen when he heard his name. "I've been trying to get in touch with Ralph. The Craw Cauldron's right up the creek and I can't keep rattling back and forth either; the security implications are far too serious. We'll just have to find another way to communicate."

The lobster settled back into his spacious bucket and playfully squeaked the rubber duck which had found its way down from the bathroom courtesy of Sandy. "Are you sure Estella won't mind if I play with Mildred?"

The question was met with a perplexed silence. How did he know the duck's name, or about the absent child called Estella?

Lorimer bobbed up and down contentedly. Sylvania was frighteningly strange but at the same time strangely familiar. The crustacean was starting to feel at home.

Pogo was particularly puzzled by Lorimer's apparent knowledge of her daughter but decided to pursue the subject later. It was time to adjourn to the parlour.

Sammy stopped beside Sandy on his way out of the kitchen. "Keep an eye on things and call if you need us. No more heroics, particularly when it comes to scrogwits." The serpent fixed the Siamese with a stern look. "As for you, stop teasing the lobster, and don't go getting any ideas either, Pongo."

"Whatever you say, Your Princeliness." The dog narrowed his close-set, intelligent eyes. "Why don't you try using Pogo's seashell to contact Ralph, the magic one you gave her when she and Alfie were married."

The snake was clearly impressed. "What a very good idea, but how did you know about the shell in the first place? You weren't even born then."

The dog was tickled pink. He tapped the side of his nose with his paw. "That's for me to know and you to find out."

Pogo stepped back into the room. "I heard that, Pongo. You're getting far too lippy for my liking."

"Maybe so," said the snake drily, "but you have to admit it's a splendid suggestion."

Storm clouds gathered out beyond Corvine Harbour.

The sunset was an open wound trailing bloodclots of dark red clouds in its wake. The sky had the intensity and desperation of a doctor who is unable to save his dying patient, not through lack of skill on his part, but because fate in the shape of some meddlesome gremlin has made off with all the bandages.

Grim blankets of mist gathered at the harbour mouth and spectres of jaundiced sea fog floated in over the lower stories of the palace like restless wraiths, condemned to drift round and round for eternity.

The Fairy Queen stood on the highest balcony, her eyes fixed on a distant point to the northwest and the Island of Long Forgotten Dreams.

Celestina was gripped by flutters of fear round her heart. An unknown yet all-too-familiar terror tugged at the coat-tails of her consciousness. When she tried to bring the fragmented memory to the front of her mind it slipped further away.

The young queen sensed potent evil radiating from Long Forgotten Dreams. The Harpie's anklet was deep in the vaults under Moonglow Lake but Celestina had been acutely aware of Maligna's mood change long before the first reports ever reached her. The Harpie's star was rising and it terrified her.

Rolls of thunder rumbled out in the bay and jagged streaks of lightning mutilated the sky above dense fog banks over Fractal Reef.

Celestina wanted to rush from the balcony down through the vast palace to make sure her precious daughter was safe and sound in the nursery.

It was ridiculous to give way to fears worthy of a mere mortal when she could engage the unique magic and awesome power that is the preserve of the Fairy Queen.

She gazed inward through her mind's eye and saw Tabby sleeping peacefully. Sarah, her governess, was embroidering a cushion cover by fairy starlight beside the child's bed. She heard Sarah politely ask the stars to come closer and form a constellation over the detail of needlepoint she was working on.

Tabitha was in good hands but Celestina sent a spell of protection to the nursery all the same. The magic was transported in a small chariot of sapphire stars drawn by a pair of tiny unicorns. She watched the dainty beasts trot through the air into the solarium before they broke into a canter by the spiral staircase leading to the main part of the palace. The enchanted carriage disappeared in a dissolving galaxy of spiralling stars. Perhaps Tabby might surface from her dreams just long enough to see the spell delivered.

The deluge came unexpectedly and Celestina found herself a captive audience of one. The water fell in torrents quickly turning the balcony into a fast-running stream. The drains struggled to dispose of the rain which was forming deep, swirling pools at her feet but she remained where she was, mesmerised by a sky the unappetising colour of raw liver. Angry clouds churned and boiled as they were ripped apart by malicious bolts of sulphur yellow lightning.

The Queen's bodyguard of white-winged rooks cawed raucously and took to the air from the glass roof above the balcony. They flew in well-practiced formations above her head. The leader of the squadron restlessly scanned the horizon, searching for any danger that might threaten his sovereign before he swept down onto the balustrade in front of her.

Celestina was frozen in time, oblivious to the presence of the black and white bird or the torrents of rain that soaked her hair and seeped through her clothes. The rook inched towards her only to find she was no longer there. Her physical form was standing on the palace balcony high above Corvine but her spirit was far away on the deadly island where Maligna the Harpie schemed and plotted her downfall.

The dark blue hare sped through the tunnel that winds its way from the top of the cliffs above the palace through a labyrinth of small caves. It eventually emerges at the foot of a cataract which cascades from the rock high above the floor of a small cavern. The tunnel shadows the river as it rushes over limestone boulders worn smooth by its unending quest for a quieter life.

The fast-moving water was clear and cold and Cassandra stopped for a refreshing drink.

The hare knew all the disused mines and tunnels around Corvine intimately and something felt very wrong with this one. She couldn't work out what it was but her instinct told her she was in danger. She sniffed the air and listened hard for anything out of the ordinary which was when she became aware of a slight but persistent vibration beneath her feet.

Cassandra had experienced earth tremors before but this felt far more sinister. She frowned in confusion, not knowing whether to press on or retrace her steps. The decision was abruptly taken for her when she was knocked to the ground by the unrestrained force of an earthquake. The tunnel was blocked in less than the blink of an eye.

The hare lay stunned under a mass of shattered limestone choking on clouds of billowing dust. She was too weak and scared to move at first and lay panting for what seemed like an age before she finally summoned up the courage to crawl through a gap in the rubble.

The course of the river had been altered by the quake and not for the first time in its long life. Rivers are adaptable, free spirits; when it comes down to it, one route's as good as any other and perhaps this one would lead to that dreamed of, tranquil retirement. Its days of being a carefree, babbling brook were long gone.

Cassandra plunged gratefully into the churning water. When she touched the bottom she pushed up with her strong back legs and paddled to the surface again.

The hare dragged herself out onto a large rock to rest and recover. Her fur was slicked to her body and she was practically indiscernible against the dark, shiny boulder, which proved just as well in view of what happened next.

A harsh, rasping voice, no more than a few feet from where she lay, spat out five gloating words. "We're on our way home!"

The hare willed herself invisible and slowed her breathing down until it was lighter than a dandelion seed floating on the breeze. Cassandra opened one eye no more than a slit and immediately wished she hadn't done so. The brute she found herself so perilously close to was the stuff of fevered nightmares and wild imaginings. It was draped in bloodied animal skins and carried a blazing torch.

The snaglip began to growl like a demented bear. When it flung its head from side to side droplets of saliva flew from its mouth, hissing horribly as they hit the water. The beast cursed and shrank away, pulling anxiously at tufts of matted hair on its chin. "We must move away from this horrid river. Come now, my little scrablings, we've much to do."

The brute shambled towards the boulders blocking the tunnel and threw them aside as if they were made of candy floss.

Cassandra could hear excited, gabbling voices coming from the tunnel behind her.

"Wait for us, Balebreath," called the scrabling at the head of the horde with a flash of razor-sharp teeth, "our little leggies aren't as long as yoursies."

Hundreds of small furry creatures poured out of the tunnel like swarming termites. They flowed over every available bit of ground, including the rock where Cassandra lay. Nasty little claws dug into her skin but she kept still and silent throughout her ordeal. When she could no longer hear their incessant, mindless chatter, the hare furtively opened her eyes. She found herself alone again and sighed with gratitude. All she could hear was the sound of the river and the pounding of her own heart.

Gilbert lay on his back in a large hammock, hands clasped round his ample tummy, tail dangling carelessly over the side. He hummed a little tune under his breath, contemplating his fate with customary cheerfulness.

Since his arrival in Sylvania he'd lurched from one disaster to another, without actually coming to any real harm, so the chances were he'd come through this one unscathed too. "Ho hum, Pestilence is a strange one," he said, nodding his head thoughtfully. "One minute it's 'Make way for Gilbert, you ill-mannered wretches' and the next it's 'Clap him in irons, Mr Leitzoff'."

"Hardly," said the voice from the other hammock. "You're not even tied up, Gilb, and I don't hear the sound of chains rattling either."

The rat gave a hearty laugh. "That's me, I'm afraid, prone to exaggeration. I've always had this melodramatic streak; it's the frustrated actor in me, you know."

"So that's why you wear a neckerchief. Here was I thinking it was the Romany in your soul."

Gilbert continued loftily, "It's a bit of both really. I'm a complex creature with many dimensions to my personality."

Leo tittered. "You wouldn't be taking yourself too seriously now, would you? From where I'm swinging in this hammock it was your complex approach to matters that got us into this predicament; that combined with your inability, after an ale or six, to keep your gob shut or tell the good guys from the bad guys."

Gilbert struggled to sit up but he was very much the novice when it came to hammocks. He hung over the side with a mournful expression on his big face. "How right you are, my wee pal. I can be a right idiot when I get a drinking head on and, at my age, I really should know better. I've made a complete bish of things. I'm supposed to be looking after you and, when it comes down to it, you've been doing your best to keep me out of trouble. It's too shaming, it really is."

"Och now, Gilbert, I was only teasing you, and neither one of us belongs in Sylvania so we're bound to muck things up now and again."

The Giant Rat's whiskers twitched furiously. "It's kind of you to make allowances for me, Leo, but I've been here long enough and I ought to know what's what." He stretched a paw towards the cat with the intention of giving him a reassuring pat. The weight of his substantial rear end launched him over the side and he landed chin down on the wooden floor with a resounding thump.

"There I go again," he exclaimed with a merry chuckle, "but in my own defence these things are rather tricky when you're not used to them." The rat stood up and gave himself a good shake. "This floor's grubby, not exactly ship-shape..."

He was cut short by a knock on the door of their stuffy little cabin. A key turned in the lock and the door opened just enough to reveal Pigsblanket's head and right arm. "May I come in?" he asked tentatively.

Gilbert called out in his usual cheery manner. "Be our guest, dear boy, it's jolly good to see a friendly face, I can tell you."

Pigsblanket gave a nervous smile which made him wince. His lip had healed over but his face was a mass of bruises. "Your presence is requested for pre-dinner drinks in the Captain's cabin. I'm to escort you there."

"Preprandial refreshments, how very civilised."

Leo loudly cleared his throat. "You won't forget what we were just talking about, will you?"

"Have no fear, chumlet, I won't make that mistake again."

The cat was unconvinced but he jumped confidently out of his hammock and padded towards the door.

Gilbert adjusted his neckerchief and followed on behind. "Perhaps just the one to be sociable..."

Leo glanced at him suspiciously. "What was that?"

The Giant Rat waved his paw airily. "Nothing of any significance, just me blethering on as per usual."

Pigsblanket walked along the narrow passageway with the easy grace of an experienced sailor. "Mind your step, gentlemen. There's an almighty swell in the harbour tonight."

The cabin door closed behind them and the Bosun playfully swung the large key round on the end of its chain before heading off in the opposite direction to join other members of the crew for supper.

"There's no need to be formal with us. We're not used to being called 'gentlemen', are we Leo?"

The boy looked over his shoulder and a shadow of fear flicked across his pale blue eyes. "Captain Grimshaw will have me flogged if he catches me being disrespectful." He saw the concern on their faces and tried to make light of his remark with a rueful shrug.

The cat felt a shiver run through him for it was clear Pigsblanket meant exactly what he'd said.

Confirmation that Pestilence Grimshaw really was responsible for the injuries to the cabin boy sent a stab of fear to Leo's stomach and he was ashamed of his cowardly self-interest. Grimshaw wasn't about to harm him. The Captain of the Pirates had indicated almost as soon as they'd met that he planned to demand an enormous ransom from Queen Celestina for Leo's safe return. But what of Gilbert? No one would care about the rat and they definitely wouldn't pay anything to get *him* back. The Giant Rat was an enemy of the state with a catalogue of crimes to his name. Surely everyone would be glad to see the back of the hapless beast?

Pestilence eagerly awaited the arrival of Gilbert and Leo. He'd sent for a bottle of his finest sloeberry rum with which he planned to toast the health of his two 'guests'. He responded to a rat-a-tat-tat on the cabin door.

"Come in," he called in his friendliest tone; there was no need to scare the prisoners unnecessarily.

The heavy wooden door swung open and the buccaneer was surprised to see Jedediah Malahyde earlier than expected. The First Mate had a most peculiar expression on his face.

"Don't just stand there, man," Grimshaw barked impatiently.

Malahyde shifted from foot to foot in the doorway, casting around for the right words. "I have a small dragon with me who wants to see you at once. He says he has a message for you from his...er... mother."

Grimshaw looked blankly at the First Mate and then an idea popped into his head. "Ask him where he's come from?"

Malahyde turned towards the dragon who had heard the question loud and clear.

"The Island of Long Forgotten Dreams," he called out obligingly.

"Scampering seahorses and frolicking flounders! What a spectacular day this is turning out to be. Send him in at once, Mr Malahyde. You're dismissed for the time being, but this shouldn't take long. Tell cook there will be one more for dinner and that it's a dragon." Pestilence doubled up with laughter. "I wish I could be there to see his face."

Captain Henderson had returned to the harbour in the early evening to accompany the pilot who was bringing a large Russian tanker over the sandbar at the entrance to the port. With the vessel safely in dock, Ralph felt in need of a walk to clear his head before going home for a late supper with Tina. He'd confided in his wife before he left the house and she'd taken the news of Sandy and Jamie's quest for Leo with remarkable equanimity. She knew only too well that her daughter was a determined individual who wouldn't rest until she found her precious cat.

They had no secrets and Tina knew all about Ralph's adventures in Sylvania as a boy. Despite her own fascination with the parallel world of fairy folk, she had never been keen on her daughter going there and was hugely relieved when Sandy finally stopped pestering her Dad about meeting Alfie and Pogo.

Ralph stood on the shore beyond the Pilot Station watching the sun set over the island of Arran. So much had happened since he'd arrived at work on his younger daughter's 11th birthday. Sandy, Jock and Jamie were in Crawdonia and he was desperate for more news. He was also curious to find out whether Jock had persuaded Peg Leg to go back with him.

The harbourmaster thought he was alone until he heard the crackle of a transistor radio. He was mildly irritated by the intrusion and walked further along the beach.

The sound moved with him and he decided it was time to confront the annoying pest with the radio. When he discovered there was no one around he was forced to look closer to home for the answer. A distorted voice was coming from the inside pocket of his jacket where he kept a cowrie shell he'd had since he was a lad. These shells are considered to be very lucky and are reputed to bring their custodian much good fortune. The idea that the shell might have special qualities had always appealed to him and he rarely went anywhere without it.

"Ralph, can you hear me? It's no good, I'm shouting my head off but there's no response. I'll give it one more go." There was a slight pause. "It's Jock, Captain... I'm practically hoarse, SSS, why don't you give it a whirl?"

Ralph could scarcely believe what he was hearing when he held the shell to his ear. "It's SSS, Captain. If you're receiving me please speak clearly into the shell." Then in a faint but audible aside to Jock, "That's if he still keeps it with him…"

Ralph put the shell to his mouth. If anyone were to see him they'd think he was a haggis short of a Burns' Supper, but that was a chance he simply had to take. "Sammy, it's Ralph. Boy oh boy is it good to hear your voice again after all these years."

7

Pestilence Grimshaw, resplendent in a turquoise and emerald frock coat, opened his cabin door with a bow and a flourish.

"You can come in now," Cahoots said chirpily.

The sight of the baby dragon smiling up at him tickled Gilbert pink. "Would you look at that, Leo, a violet dragon, if that doesn't take the biscuit, I don't know what does."

"Biscuit, what biscuit?" Cahoots asked eagerly. "I'd love a biscuit, and I'm not violent, you know."

The First Mate ushered his little group into the cabin and propelled Pigsblanket towards the decanters on the sideboard.

Pestilence smiled benevolently and patted Cahoots on his scaly head. "Fetch a plate of biscuits for the dragon at once, Pigsblanket. Leave the drinks for now. Perhaps you'd care to do the honours, Mr Malahyde?"

"My pleasure. Would that be a sloeberry rum, Cap'n?"

"Ten out of ten, Jedediah, go straight to the top of the class, and I insist you join me; it's a veritable belter."

Pestilence called after the retreating cabin boy. "Tell cook we need some non-alcoholic beverages. The dragon's a bit young for wines and spirits and I don't imagine you're much of a tippler either, Leo."

"No, sir," replied the cat politely, "but may I have some water?" Leo was finding Grimshaw's ebullient mood disturbing and was treading carefully.

"Bring a chilled pitcher of Cressmere spa water, Pigsblanket. Still or fizzy, Leo?"

"Still would be nice."

The buccaneer sat down in his large leather chair by the stove and patted his knee encouragingly. "Sit up here with me, Cahoots. This has all the makings of a mighty enjoyable evening, by jove."

The dragon clambered onto Grimshaw's lap and scriggled around to make himself comfortable. Zipidee-doohdah, he'd landed on his feet and no mistake!

Pestilence cleared his throat and thumped the arm of the chair. "Gilbert and Leo, welcome to 'The Cheeky Monkey'." His eyes twinkled wickedly. "I'd like you to meet [pause for the drumroll] my nephew, Cahoots."

The dragon's face lit up with a radiant, toothy smile and the teensiest trickle of smoke escaped from his nostrils.

Gilbert smiled nervously. "Steady on, laddie, where I come from there's no smoke without fire."

"And you should know, being an expert on that particular subject," Leo added quietly.

The rat carried on regardless. "It's a pleasure and a privilege to meet your nephew, Captain Grimshaw." Gilbert was making jolly sure he addressed the pirate formally this time. No more 'Pestilence, my dear chum' for him after the ticking off he received earlier. "I take it he's your adopted nephew as I don't see any real likeness."

Leo clapped his paws over his eyes in disbelief. The Giant Rat had put all four feet in it this time, but Grimshaw was having a whale of a time. He took a long, slow pull on his cigar and blew a plume of smoke in Gilbert's face. "Now do you see a resemblance, ratty?"

Gilbert didn't know what to say and opted for silence instead, but Pestilence was having none of that. "Well, do you?"

"Yes indeedy, Captain," said the flummoxed beast. "How silly of me not to have noticed before. It's *glaringly* obvious now." Never one for understatement, our Gilbert.

Pestilence was playing him like a skilled fisherman reeling in a massive salmon.

Leo stared imploringly at his friend and mimed a zip-fastener being pulled across his mouth. Gilbert smiled foolishly.

The buccaneer was not to be deflected. "So you think I look like a dragon, do you?"

Pigsblanket moved between them with a bowl of water for Leo, hoping to take the heat off Gilbert at the same time.

"No, not exactly, it's just that…"

Grimshaw had grown bored. His short attention span had kicked in and he waved his hand dismissively at the rat. "It's of no consequence to me what you think, but I'd be happy to adopt Cahoots should his charming mother wish me to do so."

The dragon became misty-eyed at the mention of Mum. "I'm missing her so much, Uncle Pestilence."

Pigsblanket and Malahyde reacted as if they'd slapped each other on the face with a cold, wet haddock. The words 'Uncle' and 'Pestilence' did not sit together happily in the same sentence.

"There there, lad. I'll take care of you until it's time to go back to Mumsy. Have another biscuit to cheer yourself up. The one with the jam in the middle's very good."

The dragon held the biscuit reverentially in his claws, examining it crumb by crumb. He tentatively nibbled the outer edge. "Mother told me about biscuits but I've never had one until tonight. They're absolutely brilliant, aren't they?"

Grimshaw's teeth were startlingly white when he flashed his infamous crocodile smile. At that instant everyone in the cabin was willing to believe the buccaneer might indeed be related to the dragon.

They took their places round the table and Pestilence raised a silver goblet studded with moonstones and black opals. "May our wildest dreams come true," he said with an enigmatic smirk. "I don't know about yours but mine are well on their way to being realised. Now then, let's get stuck into some grub. Serve dinner right away, Pigsblanket, and no helping yourself when my back's turned. This fancy cuisine is not for toe-rags like you. It's far too rich for your delicate stomach."

The cabin boy kept his eyes firmly fixed on the floor and said nothing. He knew from past experience that any answer would be the wrong answer.

"What has the cook come up with for my nephew?"

Pigsblanket placed a salver of seafood and local cheeses in the middle of the table. In the centre of the platter was a bowl crammed with unidentifiable blobs of raw flesh.

Grimshaw choked on his vintage claret, spraying copious amounts over the table and onto those unfortunate enough to be within range. "What's that foul mess in the bowl?"

The boy wanted to run for cover but stood his ground. "I'm not sure, Captain, but the cook said it was the best he could come up with for a dragon at short notice."

Grimshaw jumped up from the table, knocking his chair flying. "He did, did he?"

Everyone's eyes were on him and Cahoots' jaw dropped open at the sight of his uncle's fury.

"Bring the imbecile here to me at once. No nephew of mine's eating that muck."

Pestilence saw fear in the dragon's eyes and reined in his anger. By the time the cook knocked on the cabin door Grimshaw had his temper pretty much under control.

Trencher Halibut, rotund in a blue and white striped apron, approached the table wishing he'd had the courage to throw himself into the harbour rather than face the Captain's wrath.

"Well, man, what's this disgusting plate of entrails doing in my cabin?"

"That's top quality bat guts and rat spleen, Cap'n."

Gilbert spluttered. "Did he say rat spleen?"

Cahoots glanced nervously at the Giant Rat then back at his uncle.

"No dragon on my brigantine is eating guts or spleen, and you owe Gilbert an apology, Halibut. In case you've failed to notice, he's a bally big rat."

The cook's cheeks turned crimson and he mumbled a hasty apology.

Pestilence spoke quietly to reassure the dragon. "What do you fancy, lad?"

Cahoots rolled his eyes while he gave the matter his consideration. "Mum and I only ever shared stale bread and milk so I don't know what I'd like. She said something about dragons eating vegetarians so perhaps I could have some of them."

The buccaneer laughed heartily. "I don't imagine cook has any freshly caught vegetarians but a selection of fruit and veg should do the trick."

"If you say so, Uncle Pestilence."

"I'll be back in a jiffy, Cap'n, with the best the Sapphire Valley has to offer."

Halibut fled the Captain's cabin for the sanctuary of the ship's galley and returned a short while later with a sumptuous array. Cahoots eyes grew large at the sight of the wonderful spread. "May I, Uncle P?"

"Of course, m'boy. This little lot will put a shine on your scales." Grimshaw rose from the table and tied a folded triangle of linen round the dragon's neck. Cahoots murmured his thanks and grabbed a handful of cherries.

171

"Steady! They have stones in them."

The dragon shot his uncle a sidelong glance. "Stones, inside these? How peculiar."

"Just spit 'em out, lad. That's the way it is with cherries. It's not worth filling your noddle with inconsequential trivia."

Cahoots had stopped listening to Pestilence the minute he sank his teeth into the delicious fruit. The blood-red juice dribbled from his mouth and spread out across the white napkin.

The meal passed pleasantly enough and Grimshaw's guests of honour found themselves nursing comfortably full bellies. The Giant Rat proposed a toast to the pirate captain which was readily taken up by Jedediah Malahyde. Leo was suspicious that Gilbert might be more than a little tipsy, but he joined in all the same.

Cahoots declined the toast, declaring he was too full and fit to burst.

While the cabin boy was pouring Grimshaw a cup of chicory and kelp coffee, a wave hit 'The Cheeky Monkey' amidships, causing her to lurch violently to starboard. Crockery and cutlery flew all over the cabin and Pestilence ended up with a lapful of hot coffee.

"Pigsblanket! What do you think you're playing at?"

The lad struggled to his feet from behind the buccaneer's chair. He'd been floored by the powerful surge of water against the timbers of the old sailing ship.

Grimshaw's irritation was teetering on the brink of full-blown anger. "Bring me a cloth, then sort this mess out."

The buccaneer noticed Gilbert gaping at a fabulous display of fruit on the sideboard. Leo was spreadeagled on a small cantaloupe melon that topped the pyramid.

"While you're at it, fetch kitty back to the table. It's very tempting to leave him up there. He does set that fruit off a treat."

Pigsblanket gently lifted the shocked cat and set him down next to Gilbert who fussed over him like a mother hen.

"We're in for a batterin' tonight, Cap'n. I reckon we won't be sailing on the late tide after all. That reef'll be un-navigable in these conditions."

Grimshaw was disenchanted to hear this from his right-hand man but he was smart enough to realise Malahyde was likely to be right. "Damn and blast, Jedediah, this is not the time to be kicking our heels in Corvine Harbour, but I suppose I must defer to your better judgement. Let's hope the storm blows itself out before it's too late for us to sail off into the sunset with our little prisoners."

"Prisoners, what prisoners?"

Grimshaw gave the dragon a reassuring cuddle. "Shoosh now, that's our secret."

"Righty-oh, Uncle P, I love secrets. Mother and I have lots of secrets."

I'll bet you do, thought the pirate, mentally rubbing his hands together, and wouldn't I like to know what they are.

Back at 'Corbie Cottage', at the end of his first day in Crawdonia, Lorimer slept in his silver bucket by the pot-bellied stove. He dreamed of a magical child wearing a dazzling kilt and sporran who danced with dashing lions and graceful unicorns in an enchanted glade. The child laughed and sang as she spun and twirled in a kaleidoscope of fluorescent plaid, weaving her way in and out of the exotic creatures. She bore more than a passing resemblance to Wee Alfie Elf and Pogo Pixie.

"Lorimer, Lorimer, can you hear me? This is no time to sleep. I'm sending a very important package home and I want you to make sure it fulfils its destiny. Don't let me down."

As the images dissolved the lobster heard a voice from the outer limits of his dream.

"Mervyn, dearest, come in for a bite of supper and bring Estella with you. In my experience, wild dancing always makes a child hungry."

The residents of Crawdonia were dazed and bewildered by the drastic change in their lives in the space of one night. The focus of the main quake was deep in the earth below Moonglow Lake.

The foreshocks had started around midnight in villages and hamlets scattered across the southern slopes of the Sapphire Valley. They grew in intensity throughout the early hours as the pressure built up along the fault line. The earthquakes struck suddenly, with unrestrained ferocity.

Whole sections of farmland and clusters of houses slipped into dizzyingly deep chasms that opened mighty jaws to receive their helpless victims. The lucky ones were thrown from their beds with no time to look out of windows to see the terrible fate that awaited them.

Others watched in fascinated horror as their neighbours' homes shifted sickeningly on their foundations and slid into scorching pits of ash and molten rock.

The aftershocks were equally swift and deadly, sending uprooted trees through twisted roofs and hurling already damaged structures onto those who were dragging chunks of masonry from the maimed and injured.

The shire had been dealt a crushing blow and shocked fairy folk were to be found wandering around the ruins of their lives in a state of emotional paralysis.

The steady, repetitive pattern of daily life had been blown to pieces in a matter of seconds, leaving a trail of chaos in its wake and disbelieving, traumatised families desperately searching through the debris for missing loved ones and pets.

The royal household was quick to respond, but they too were dumbfounded by the extent of the destruction.

The vaults beneath Moonglow Lake had sustained major damage while the nearby spa resort of Cressmere was unaffected, that being the unpredictably random nature of earthquakes.

A detachment of the National Guard was despatched to the vaults, as soon as it was deemed safe, to assess the damage and help the injured.

Battalions of elves, goblins and imps set out from Corvine once they'd been briefed by the Royal Raven whose airborne divisions had returned with news of the worst affected areas.

Pestilence Grimshaw's plan to sail on the late evening tide had indeed been scuppered by the appalling weather and he'd been forced to leave his brigantine at anchor in Corvine harbour. He was livid at being thwarted by unforeseen developments. Leo should have been on his way to a secret hideout beyond Sylvanian jurisdiction, from where the buccaneer planned to make his outrageous ransom demand for the cat's safe return. Grimshaw remained undecided about the fate of the Giant Rat but Gilbert's long-term prospects were likely to be grim.

The very last thing he wanted was to be a sitting duck in Corvine harbour if word should get out of his abduction of the unlikely pair. The catastrophe had temporarily taken attention away from 'The Cheeky Monkey', but Pestilence knew it was only a matter of time before his ship was boarded by the Queen's troops and searched on some pretext or other. Unless the violent storms subsided his vessel could not sail;

to attempt anything rash was foolhardy at the very least with the likely outcome of the ship foundering on Fractal Reef.

The buccaneer was in a cold fury that his plans had come to nothing and was very drunk by the time he finally crashed into his bunk, ranting and raving about lost opportunities.

Jedediah Malahyde went ashore at dawn to establish the extent of the damage caused by the quakes in the early hours.

The First Mate knew Pigsblanket would be the target for the Captain's frustration from the moment he opened his eyes. The lad was in dreadful condition and Jedediah was pretty sure he would not survive another vicious attack.

He slipped a hastily scribbled note under the door of the Captain's cabin, explaining where he was headed and why, with humble apologies for having taken Pigsblanket away from his usual duties to row him ashore. The best Malahyde could hope for was that Grimshaw would be far too hungover to realise Jedediah was perfectly capable of making the short trip himself.

He ordered Pigsblanket to stay with the rowing boat. To leave it unattended in the current climate would be folly.

There was panic everywhere and Malahyde found himself in the middle of a chaotic throng as soon as he stepped ashore. Conflicting stories were being bandied about and it was hard to determine what had actually happened.

The telling and re-telling of events had distorted the true picture so much that any sense of reality had been gobbled up by voracious, wild speculation.

Tales of hideous monsters with three heads and twice as many mouths, spewed up by the earthquakes and now roaming the erstwhile tranquil shires of Sylvania, were turning usually sensible fairy folk into silly, mince-for-brains hysterics.

"My brother told me one of them snittersnods tore his head off and left 'im for dead."

"Well I never," said a dumpy gnome wife, clutching her terrified infant closer to her chest.

A husky-voiced goblin piped up. "He's lucky to be alive."

"That's nothing, my scampi-hound was eaten by a slavering bladdysnort whose stomach was well out of sorts from all the strunties and hedgehorns he'd eaten. Jackyscamp was vomited up only to be guzzled by a passing werepig."

"Queen Snooty-nose'll be very upset," snarled a goblin behind Malahyde. "That'll put a spoke in the wheels of her Fabulous Flyin' Flamenco, and not before time if you ask me. That flibbertigibbet needs puttin' in her place."

The first goblin continued unabashed. "It's an absolute tragedy. Jackyscamp was the best scampi-hound I've ever had."

A shrill female voice rang out. "Ain't that your mutt scavenging around in them rubbish bins over there? She's in pretty good nick for a dog what's been eaten twice before most of us've had one breakfast."

These preposterous exchanges continued unabated, but it would take more than a bunch of imaginary beasts to threaten Her Majesty's Personal Project, Hosepipe Snout's battalions or, for that matter, a ferocious scampi-hound.

Jedediah felt drained by the feverish nonsense being spouted all around him and realised how hungry he was. He was also in need of something to calm his nerves before he reported back to his boss, so he made his way towards The Mischief Maker.

It was this single decision, insignificant in isolation, which unleashed a whole series of events that might never have taken place had the First Mate headed straight back to the ship instead.

The wind tore at his clothes and chilled his ears as he struggled through the rain towards the door of the tavern, his collar pulled up and his tricorn hat down over his face in an attempt to keep himself warm and dry. Somehow he'd managed to part company with his cloak as he made his way through the crowds.

The pub was buzzing with talk of the earthquakes and the atmosphere in the tavern was charged with a heightened, spiky excitement verging on hysteria.

The Mischief Maker was unaffected by the quakes. There were many fairy folk who would have been delighted had it been reduced to a heap of rubble, forcing the worst kind of rogues and scoundrels to congregate elsewhere.

Jem and Gertie found themselves rushed off their feet with the sudden upturn in daytime trade. The Flighty Fairy, the only other tavern in the area, was unable to open due to extensive flooding in the cellars.

Malahyde discovered his preferred chair occupied so he pushed his way back through the crush and sat down on a rickety stool in a dark corner at the far end of the bar. A mangy, stuffed eagle gazed at him from a dusty alcove. The raptor held a wizened vole-like creature in its beak and Malahyde, brave seafarer that he was, felt a slight shiver run through him. He turned his back on the bird of prey and settled down to his flagon of beer.

The First Mate found himself listening to idle chatter around him while he waited for his food. His attention was caught by a discussion between a shady-looking character and his disreputable sidekick. Their dialect was harsh and guttural and Malahyde had to listen closely to make sense of what they were saying over the general noise.

They were waiting for someone called Jimlet who was hoping to join them within the hour.

Malahyde wolfed down his breakfast of fried pigeon eggs, kippers and soused herring and raised his tankard to quaff the last of the ale. He took a swig and stopped abruptly when he realised what they were saying.

"Trus' Jimlet to find summin' val'able, Smidge."

"Don't be so soft! Izz juss some worthless ol' bangle."

Filch was undeterred. "It could've bin washed ashore after quakes, m'be from them vaults what got damaged."

"You're mad as a fox in a box, you are. Who'd want an 'orrid black bracelet like that? My missus'd skelp me round noggin if I give her that ugly trinket. She'd say, 'You've lost yer marbles again, Smidge Numpty', and she'd be right an' all!"

They both laughed themselves from silly to stupid and back again then robustly clinked their tankards together.

"Watch it, mate," Smidge exclaimed when Jedediah suddenly barged past him. "You spilt me beer, you big galoot."

Filch grabbed his pal to restrain him, his eyes bulging out of his head. "Don' you know who that is? Heez yon pirate captain's henchman. You don' wanna go upsettin' that un."

Malahyde grunted something unintelligible and wove his way towards the door. He accosted a tousle-haired ragamuffin sheltering in the porch. "Want to earn yourself some money, lad?" he asked, producing a shiny doubloon from his pocket.

"You bet, mister, but I'm not a lad, I'm a lassie."

The grubby-faced urchin with arresting green eyes jumped up and down trying to catch the coin which Malahyde held just out of reach. He hesitated while he considered whether a mere girl was up to the task. She knew exactly what he was thinking and gave him a mischievous, freckly smile from under a thatch of unruly yellow hair.

"And I'm smarter and faster than any lout from these parts."

Jedediah wasn't inclined to contradict her. He bent forward level with her ear. "Get down to the harbour as fast as you can and tell the skinny lad in the rowing boat next to the crab-catcher's skiff to fetch Captain Grimshaw here at once. Say Mr Malahyde sent you and that I'll be blazin' mad if he doesn't obey my orders. Report back to me and, as soon as Captain Grimshaw gets here, this coin is yours."

The imp took a step backwards and looked up at him doubtfully. "You mean that, mister?"

The First Mate stood up, doffed his hat and gave a deep bow. "On my word, as a sailor and a..."

"...pirate! That's the word you're after, isn't it?" Mabel danced back and forth, throwing mock punches and, seeing he was knocked for six, stamped her foot gleefully. "Everyone knows who you are, but I reckon I can trust you. You wouldn't cheat a lassie; it would be bad for your image, pirate or no pirate." She threw him an impudent grin and scurried off into the crowd, slicing her way through the jumble of legs like an energetic terrier in pursuit of an appetising rabbit.

Jedediah couldn't deny the truth of what she'd said and admired her for having the guts to say it to his face. He slipped back into the tavern to keep an eye on Smidge and Filch while they waited for Jimlet.

Indigoletta's undercover agent, Redshanks, witnessed the exchange between Jedediah and Mabel and decided he best follow Miss Mince to see where she was going in such an all-fired hurry.

"Another ale, Mr Malahyde?" Slack asked eagerly when Jedediah finally made it back to the bar. The landlord wiped his brow with a soiled dishtowel. "What a mess everything's in. Who can say how long it'll be afore we're back to normal?"

Malahyde removed his hat and ran his fingers through his thick, greying hair. "It seems to me it's in your best interest if things stay exactly as they are. I've never seen this dump so busy. Line one up for me, and make sure you give the Captain's tankard a good polish with a *clean* cloth. He'll be here directly."

The landlord nudged his wife who was rinsing glasses in the cracked porcelain sink behind the counter. "I'll have old Gert take care of it right away."

"A 'please' wouldn't go amiss, Jem Slack, and less of the 'old'."

"Don't get hoity-toity with me, missus." The landlord scowled at his wife's receding back and made a corkscrew gesture with his forefinger against his temple.

"I saw that!"

"So you've got eyes in the back of your head now, have you?"

"No, but I cleaned the mirror this morning so as I knows what you're up to. You can shine Cap'n Grimshaw's tankard yourself. He's not interested in me. You're the one who needs to keep in his good books."

Slack was embarrassed by his wife's outburst. He hated being shown up in front of his customers, but the landlord had done more than his fair share of blustering in his time. "It's always a privilege and a pleasure to see Cap'n Grimshaw, Mr Malahyde. I'll have that ruffian removed from his chair in a jiffy and stoke up the fire."

"Try usin' some decent coal furra change," said Smidge in a stage whisper.

Filch sniggered appreciatively but Jem studiously ignored them. "I wasn't expectin' the Captain. I thought he'd be busy with other matters after all that's 'appened. "

"Not when he hears what I have to tell him, Slack."

"What a night," said Pogo, pouring a strong brew of lavender and lettuce tea from the samovar. "I've never experienced the likes of that. The foundations of 'Corbie

Cottage' were rattling like ill-fitting false teeth in an ice storm.'"

Alfie smiled at his wife's quirky choice of imagery, but her amber eyes had a disturbing intensity about them. She placed a mug of tea in front of him, half expecting a late tremor to send it skittering across the table. "Foul weather is one thing, but those quakes were way out of the ordinary. What I'm about to say may sound far-fetched, even daft."

The elf scrutinised her face while he savoured his first spoonful of fingalberry porridge.

"An ill-tempered, slumbering giant woke last night and went on the rampage. Call it pixie intuition if you like, but I'm certain those earthquakes are not part of the natural order. They're just the beginning and there's worse to come."

Alfie felt a sliver of fear shimmy down his spine. "Steady on. We've had earthquakes before but I grant you these were on an unprecedented scale." His unease increased with each word he uttered and the porridge lay like a poultice on his flutteringly queasy stomach.

Pogo was pierced by darts of anxiety flying out from her husband.

Alfie's hand trembled as he smoothed the plume of feathers on his hat which lay comfortingly close to him. "Try not to let your imagination run away with you. Scrogwits, storms and earthquakes are a heady combination."

Pogo's closed-off expression surprised Alfie and he found himself excluded from her innermost thoughts. He gulped down a mouthful of tea and the calming blend of leaves took the edge off his nausea. Alfie shifted the conversation away from the uncharted waters of his wife's instinct and intuition.

"Indigoletta sent one of her most trusted magspies here at daybreak. The vaults have taken the brunt of the quakes, and Maligna's anklet is unaccounted for."

"Never! That's not possible." Pogo had the urge to tuck her feet underneath her on the chair for fear a scrogwit or something far worse might grasp them and drag her down to that dreaded, stifling darkness from which there was no escape.

Alfie squeezed her hand which was ice cold. "Until yesterday I'd have agreed with that."

"What about the palace?"

"It's absolutely fine. The promontory is protected by strong magic, as is the Cave of Sublime Spirit."

Pogo seized her husband's arm, making him jump. "I don't know why we've come out of this unscathed but it's significant."

Alfie nodded and pushed the bowl of uneaten porridge away from him. "That's my feeling too. Old Rook Wood has survived, but there's a contrived randomness about all of this. We have our parts to play and that probably extends to everyone under our roof. We haven't received any scripts and probably never will. Let's hope we know when we're on stage and what we're supposed to do."

The elf was brought up short by a series of insistent knocks on the front door of the cottage.

Lorimer called out from his bucket by the kitchen sink. "That'll be the parcel from Estella."

Alfie and Pogo whirled round to face him.

"How *do* you know about Estella? I meant to ask you last night but there was so much going on it slipped my mind."

Lorimer squeaked the rubber duck and toyed with a miniature sailing ship, not unlike 'The Cheeky Monkey'. "I don't understand that either, Pogo. I just seem to know and then up she popped in my dream last night and I recognised her at once. This is a crucial parcel and Estella's counting on me to make sure it fulfils its destiny."

Alfie threw him a sceptical look and went out to see who was threatening to break the door down with their fists and every other fist they could lay their hands on.

Pogo squatted on the rug beside the lobster in his five-star accommodation. "So, tell me Lorimer, what's in this parcel?"

The crustacean propelled the little ship across the water towards a wide-eyed Mildred. "I haven't the foggiest idea but hopefully the contents will enlighten us."

The rumpus had woken Peg Leg. "What's all this about, Thermidor? A delivery from Cousin Kitt perchance?"

Lorimer waved his claws irritably. "It's far more serious than that. I'm guilty of being ridiculously frivolous on many occasions but this is not one of them. I'm not *just* bravado and bathing costumes."

Alfie came back into the kitchen carrying a slim, neatly wrapped package which he placed on the table. Pongo gave the parcel a good sniff. "Lorimer's no slouch, it's from Estella right enough. What are we waiting for, let's have a dekko."

Sandy and Jamie walked in, having also been roused by the disturbance. The child had dark circles under her eyes. She looked small and fragile, but she brightened up when everyone greeted her with obvious pleasure.

Alfie untied the string and opened the parcel. Inside the softest tissue paper was a neatly folded kilt with a sporran lying on top of it. There was a label attached to the kilt which read: 'Think before you act'. The sporran also sported a wee tag which was more provocative: 'Who wears wins'.

"Is there a letter with it?"

"Yes, there is, Pongo."

"What does it say?"

The note was short and written in Estella's neat script.

'Dear Mum and Dad, MacGregor told me to be sure and send these to you. And, no, I don't know who they're for.'

"Who's MacGregor when he's at home?"

Alfie continued reading out loud. 'Tell Pongo I don't know that either but he's a very beautiful, long-haired cat, a bit like the Royal Steed. He came to see me while I was asleep and when I woke up the kilt and sporran were on the end of my bed. I couldn't resist trying them on but MacGregor was most insistent their destiny lies elsewhere. Must get some practice in on my pogo stick now. I'm coming on in leaps and bounds. Love, Estella.'

Lorimer was hanging out of his bucket. "Let's have a look, perhaps they're meant for me. After all, I was the only one who knew the parcel was on its way."

Alfie put the sporran to one side and shook out the kilt.

Lorimer's boot-button eyes gazed longingly at it. "My my, that *is* a bobby-dazzler. Bring it here so I can try it on."

The lobster was a windmill of anticipation.

"No fear! You'll make it wet. In any case it's several sizes too big."

Pongo was panting extravagantly. "It'd be a laugh to see him in it though, WAE. I'm confident we could sell bookfuls of tickets for 'The Lobster's Narrow Escape from the Giant, Marauding Kilt Extravaganza'. The dog was revelling in his own cleverness. He nudged Jamie in the ribs to provoke a reaction, but the cat was scornfully dismissive and faked a bored yawn.

Lorimer sank back into his bucket dejectedly. He felt positive he'd have cut a dash in a kilt and determined there and then to have Kitt run one up for him, in a fittingly raucous tartan, on his return to Irvine. Blue and green with yellow and white stripes was far too subdued for a lobster like him.

Sandy studied the woven material. "I think that's Henderson tartan," she exclaimed.

Jamie landed light as a snowflake on the table in front of her. "There's no doubt about it. Your Mum wears a skirt in that pattern regularly. I've curled up on it many a cold winter's night in draughty old 'Woodburn'." Jamie's blue eyes grew large. "Would you look at the size of that topaz in the kilt pin? It's positively gigantic."

Pogo picked up the kilt and handed it to Sandy. "Why don't you nip upstairs and try it on."

"Do you think I should?"

"You'd be daft not to," said Pongo. "It's a real corker."

Sandy made an enthusiastic grab for the kilt and headed for the door.

"Exc-u-u-u-se me," said a gruff voice nobody recognised. "Ye've forgotten something."

They looked round to see who had spoken.

"Ah'm right here on the table in front of youz. Have ye no got eyes in yer heids?"

Pongo twigged first. "Jings, a nebbie wee talking sporran, and so early in the day too!"

Sandy squealed in surprise when the material in her hand quivered with irritation.

"Take no notice of that silly nyaff," said the kilt in a serious tone befitting one of the more sedate tartans. "What good's a sporran without a kilt to hang it on?"

The sporran flapped on the kitchen table like a beached flounder. "I'll remind you of that the next time you ask me to pay for the drinks."

The kilt sighed the sigh of one who's used to sighing a lot. "Och, you'd best bring that wee nuisance along too. We'll never hear the end of it otherwise. I'm like royalty, you understand. I never carry money."

8

Maligna lay on her pallet in a state of excited stillness. The pent-up, stifling tension which was always with her gradually slipped away from her bony neck and shoulders and the bed beneath her floated off leaving her suspended on a sea of healing waves. Minxie had not provided the curly kelp nor the whirlpool of seahorses, but the Harpie wasn't about to complain. She was closer to a state of pure happiness than she could ever have imagined. Minxie's message from Pestilence had raised her spirits after endless years languishing in an arid landscape of her own despair.

Though they had never met, Maligna understood Pestilence Grimshaw. The buccaneer's formidable reputation had made him the subject of many an exchange between her guards and she'd built up an accurate mental file on the pirate. What else had she to do but listen? Most of the time to trivial rubbish and mind-numbing, idle chit-chat, but there was a gem or a nugget once in a while.

The Harpie saw the pirate for what he was; a rare breed, a veritable thoroughbred in terms of scheming and self-serving opportunism, and that was before she considered his appetite for cruelty and ruthlessness.

His mother was a feared and respected seawitch and, although Grimshaw was half mortal, there was nothing to suggest he had taken after his father in any way.

She was certain Pestilence wouldn't open his eyelids of a morning, let alone get out of bed, unless it was to his advantage. More significantly, he wasn't the type to align himself with lost causes. In essence, he was a supreme asset and someone she was more than capable of dealing with once she was back in business.

The dragon's departure had underlined her state of isolation, several times in angry red ink, but Minxie had kindled a long-extinguished fire and raised the Harpie's expectations with her coded message.

Maligna was far from forgotten, perhaps even revered, and she couldn't fail to notice her powers returning. When she sighed with satisfaction, she inadvertently scorched the hem of her blanket with a red-hot breath worthy of Cahoots.

With the inhabitants of Corvine in a state of barely controlled hysteria, Pestilence Grimshaw wasn't about to take any chances. He slammed through the door of The Mischief Maker with his hand poised above the hilt of his sword and smacked into a burly goblin who howled in anger and spun round shaking his fist. The pirate cursed and the goblin shrank back into the crowd with an apologetic grin and a mumbled "All right, Cap'n? Clumsy old me!"

When the buccaneer saw how packed the tavern was he grabbed Pigsblanket by the collar. "Get cracking, sea-slug, clear the way for your lord and master."

The cabin boy braced himself and pressed forward but he was unable to move more than a couple of feet. Pestilence kicked him repeatedly in the shins to urge him on. In his desperation to get away, the lad ducked down through the jumble of legs, leaving an irate Grimshaw in his wake.

"Come back here! I'll have you boiled alive for desertion!"

But Pigsblanket had been swallowed up by the throng and was slowly making his way towards the bar. He was reduced to crawling on his hands and knees and only recognised the First Mate by his distinctive seaboots which were trimmed with strips of mackerel skin. The boy fetched up beside him, ashen faced and panting.

"Crivens, lad, you look fair done in." Pigsblanket's eyes were dim and expressionless and he suddenly slumped forward. Jedediah caught him under the arms and heaved him onto the stool he'd just vacated. "Get your breath back," he said, scanning the tavern. "You did bring Captain Grimshaw, didn't you?"

"Aye, sir. I left him by the door." The boy was seized by a fit of coughing and clutched his ribs in agony.

Malahyde pushed his beer towards him but Pigsblanket was too weak to lift the tankard. He lapped the liquid like a dog drinking from its water bowl.

"I'll see to the Captain. You stay where you are and order yourself some breakfast."

"I've no money, Mr Malahyde."

"Put it on my tab while I keep Grimshaw at bay. What I've got to tell him'll take his attention away from you, and that's a promise."

Pigsblanket had never heard the First Mate refer to the Skipper disrespectfully. The omission of one word was very significant.

Jedediah moved through the crowd easily. He had an air of quiet authority which his height reinforced. No one was going to impede his progress, unless it happened to be an imp by the name of Mabel Mince. She tugged repeatedly at his sleeve until he acknowledged her.

"I did what you asked and I was quick."

"Yes, you did and yes, you were," he said with the faintest smile.

"So where's ma doubloon?"

"You mean this doubloon?" Malahyde produced the coin from behind her ear.

Mabel laughed before she could stop herself. Then added scornfully, "Not that old trick!" She held out her hand palm upwards and Jedediah let go of the coin. Her fingers closed round it like a steel trap.

With a swift "thanks, mister" Mabel headed for the door.

The First Mate caught up with Pestilence in time to see him throw a spectacular punch which would have floored its target had there been any available floor. The dazed gnome's response made it abundantly clear he was from out of town. "I tried to get out of your way, matey, but I'd nowhere to go."

Malahyde pulled the buccaneer away before he had time to react to the slur. "He's not worth the trouble, Cap'n. Just another daft galoot. It seems there's no shortage of them these days."

Jem Slack came towards them out of the gloom. He was sweating profusely and smelt of stale dishcloths. His worn leather apron was a map of cracks caked with years of accumulated grease and slops. If he'd had a forelock to tug, he'd have been tugging his forelock. As it happened, his hair was on the skimpy side.

"I've reserved your usual chairs, gentlemen, and I've chucked an extra log on the fire."

Grimshaw sneered lavishly. "Oh my, Jedediah, what have we done to deserve this? A measly handful of coal is what we're used to. Though to call it coal is to dignify nutty slack." The buccaneer's face crumpled with mirth at his unintended joke. "How appropriate in a dump run by Mr Nutty Slack himself!"

The landlord's watery smile evaporated and the wretched wolf that was once an energetic young cub looked out of Jem's bloodshot eyes and recalled wistfully what it was like to be bold and fearless.

Grimshaw whooped and, capitalising on his superiority, went in for the kill. "Are you sure you can afford to burn a log on that meagre fire of yours? Come into an unexpected inheritance, eh Slack? Or perhaps you've sold that ugly wife of yours. Mind you, that's unlikely. I doubt you could give her away."

Slack's subservient mask slipped and the old wolf's yellow eyes flashed defiantly before Jem snatched the mask back into place. "Gertie's still here with me and she'll be along with your drinks directly. Will you be wanting some victuals?"

The buccaneer's mouth was a thin, quivering line. "What do you think, bone-brain?"

"It's just that Mr Malahyde's already eaten."

Pestilence was in danger of upstaging himself. "So it's 'Mr Malahyde's already eaten', is it?" The buccaneer waggled his head from side to side in a perfect imitation of the landlord. "I'm delirious with joy to discover my First Mate's had his breakfast, but I bally well haven't had mine, you cretin, so jump to it."

"Yes, sir, Cap'n. One 'Full House' on its way." Slack's heart was thumping and his head ached from the tension of his encounter with the pirate. He stumbled off towards the kitchen, vowing to stay well out of Grimshaw's way for the rest of the day. The wolf slunk to the back of Jem's mind again where it curled up and drifted off into a dreamworld where wolves never grow old and decrepit.

Pestilence flung himself into his chair by the fire which was still little more than a damp squib in spite of the addition of a skinny branch of green oak. He was starting to feel the effects of his over-indulgence the night before and there was only one target for his displeasure. "Where's that disreputable sea-slug? I'll give him *two* fat ears for abandoning me like that."

Malahyde lowered his voice. "I know you're vexed with the lad, but what I'm about to tell you is for our ears only."

Grimshaw narrowed his eyes in anticipation. "Don't keep me in suspense, Jedediah. I'm not in a mind to be trifled with. This'd better be good news you got me out of bed so early for."

Malahyde checked Smidge and Filch were where he'd left them. "I reckon it's that and more."

The Royal Steed had dropped Sammy and Will at the Cave of Sublime Spirit just before the first earthquake hit Crawdonia.

Kismet and Wainscot found themselves in the thick of the action as the huge cat galloped along the eastern shore of Moonglow Lake. The forest cat and fairy mouse were under assault from rocks and loose stones raining down from the escarpment that shadows the lake south of Cressmere until it reaches the Flighty Fairy Falls.

Kismet was forced to lengthen his stride as he navigated ever-widening cracks in the ground that spread like frenzied forks of lightning in front of him. He took to the water to escape the worst of the landslide, creating a churning, frothy wake as he hurtled along.

The fairy mouse clung tightly to the cat's left ear while he swerved and jinked his way out of trouble.

When they were clear of danger Kismet stopped to compose himself. Wainscot loosened her grip and the cat started to purr. "That was a wee bit scary," she said, straightening her bejewelled collar. "I'm glad I wasn't making the trip on my own."

Kismet gave a low growl. "Let's hope we get home to our beds without any more mishaps."

The Attendant to the Royal Raven floated above his body which was lying comfortably on a mound of midnight-blue cushions beneath the Giant Sapphire. Will couldn't fail to notice how dashing he looked in his plush velvet and gold uniform which set off his scarlet curls a treat. The imp had been a member of the Royal Raven's household for a trifling amount of time, but he was already displaying characteristics worthy of the great bird herself.

The fact that he was disembodied and could see himself from every angle, even though he was floating on his back, didn't bother Will in the slightest. He'd slipped into another dimension as easily as he might a favourite old cardigan, not that the imp is the cardigan type, you understand. His Grannie would have been mortified if she'd known about the drawerfuls of striped, checked and diamond-patterned cardies she's knitted for him that have never been worn.

Spondoolicks had set aside his homemade bagpipes in favour of a small set of quartz crystal bowls. The spider hung on a platinum thread above the circular formation and was playing increasingly complex sequences of notes. The strange music filled the cave with warm, nurturing sounds.

Morgana stood on the Sentinel, an uncut amethyst crystal which sits near the entrance to the cave. The magpie had been assured her husband and fledglings were safe but she couldn't rid herself of persistent, niggling worries.

The Prince of Cobalt-Sibilance rotated gently in a clockwise spiral above the glittering gemstone. There was potent magic in the making and the serpent's third eye was as keen as ever but, try as he might, he was unable to find any trace of the Harpie's black gold and clovenstone anklet.

Morgana reacted to a noise behind her. Indigoletta had entered the cave and was picking her way through piles of treasure. She inclined her regal head towards the magpie who dropped a half curtsey. Crawford was right behind her and his eyes were taking in every inch of the cavern.

Indigoletta spoke in a whisper. "Do you feel the powerful magic emanating from the Sapphire? My head feels clearer than it has for days. I thought the mulberry wine was a good tonic, but this puts it well and truly in the shade."

"Indeed it does, ma'am." Crawford undid his bow tie and inhaled deeply. "I've never seen the Sapphire radiate so many colours before."

"Nor I. It's staggeringly beautiful and no mistake."

The raven was drawn to the ethereal sounds coming from the tiny bowls. "How delightful. I had no idea Spondoolicks was such a talented musician."

"It's far from obvious when he's belting out a tune on his knitted bagpipes."

Indigoletta acknowledged Crawford with a wink and he turned a soft shade of pink under his feathers.

The snake came to rest on the Giant Sapphire and the instant he opened his startling yellow eyes Will snapped back into his body. The imp got to his feet smartly when he realised his boss was standing over him.

"My dear boy, you look wonderful. This rich blend of magic obviously agrees with you."

"So it seems, ma'am. The lightshow's not bad either; spell-binding even."

"In more ways than one, if I'm doing my job properly." The blue and yellow diamonds on the snake's skin were almost luminous and he looked magnificent framed by the shimmering light radiating from the gemstone. "Indigoletta, Crawford, a word with you, please."

Before they had time to respond Spondoolicks swung across the cave to join them. He looked around eagerly and fixed Indigoletta with his bright, beady eyes. "What do you reckon, Your Majestic Featheriness? Am I not the bee's knees on those bowls, or even the spider beside her?"

Spondoolicks changed tack before Indigoletta had time to respond. "Your aura's showing again, SSS."

The snake's eyes were half closed and he was showing signs of irritation. "I'm enchanted to hear that, dear one."

"You're enchanted, full stop," said the smug arachnid.

"Very clever, Spondoolicks."

"Nothing goes by me!"

Sammy's expression was cold enough to freeze a lake in high summer.

"Perhaps I ought to leave you to it. You obviously have things to discuss. I'll be meditating in the casket of rubies."

"Sleeping more like," said the snake as he watched the nimble spider spin his way back across the cavern.

"You do look the business in that kilt," Pongo said with conviction. "It's a real humdinger. The sporran's not bad either."

"Come over here and say that to ma face, ye cheeky wee dug."

Pongo shook his head in amused disbelief. "I still can't get over the fact that you two can talk."

"For what it's worth, neither can I," replied the kilt soberly. "We were just like any other kilt and sporran until MacGregor turned up. That was when I found my voice and, unfortunately, so did the purse."

"Purse, indeed. See what ah've got tae put up with!"

"I wish you were a dress sporran. I can't imagine one of them being so lippy."

"Leather's what I am, and proud of it. I can't abide those stuck-up posh jobs."

The skirt and purse had their audience enthralled and Pongo was desperately thinking of ways to fan the flames. He enjoyed nothing better than a good ding-dong and this one was shaping up very nicely.

Sandy was fraying round the edges. "I don't know if I can cope with this latest development. I prefer my clothes to keep their own counsel. I can hardly think with them chattering on." The kilt and sporran fell into a respectful silence. "I didn't mean to be rude, it's just that I'm having trouble keeping up. Please don't take offence."

"None taken, Sandy. We're here to help you and to look after you," said the kilt. "Those were MacGregor's express wishes."

Pongo was bursting with curiosity. "Who is this guy? I'd really like to meet him; he sounds intriguing."

"Meeting him's the easy part, ye hairy midden. As to who he is, we don't have a clue. Isn't that right, kilt?"

"Aye, sporran, that's about the gist of it." At last, something they were agreed upon. "I could introduce you to him now if you like."

"Oh I don't know," Sandy said doubtfully. "I'm a bit overwhelmed, but he does sound lovely."

The overall consensus was that they were keen to find out more about the mysterious cat and the kilt suggested they make their way to the nearest pond or stream. "Those were his instructions, you understand."

Alfie ushered them out into the garden behind the cottage. "There's the burn that separates the garden from the copse. Will that suffice?"

Pogo shrugged. "But what do we do when we get there?"

"Don't ask me, ask them," he said, laughing at the absurdity of the situation.

Sandy gently tugged the kilt. "I haven't a clue," it replied. "Let's just wait and see what happens. After you, m'dear."

"And after me, too," said the sporran who liked to have the last word on most subjects.

The Siamese adopted his customary superior tone. "It seems to me Sandy has no choice in the matter; you lead and she follows."

"*Au contraire*," said the sporran triumphantly, "we can't go anywhere without Sandy. We're as good as useless on our own."

"Surely not," said the cat, moderating his tone and trying to salvage a morsel of dignity. He felt like kicking himself for being so silly.

Pongo was too preoccupied to notice Jamie's predicament. "That sporran's all talk and no action, just as I thought," he said under his breath. Then with grudging admiration, "The French was unexpected though."

Peg Leg and Lorimer were following on behind, something no one else had noticed. The gull hopped along beside the lobster who was dressed to thrill in yet another zingy bathing costume.

The crustacean had persuaded a splinter group of stars to form a shimmering cluster above his head which spelt his name. Not very diverting, he had to admit, but it gave them something to do. The poor wee souls were getting bored hanging around.

Peg had no trouble persuading the mischievous stars to rearrange themselves into a banner that proclaimed 'Dish of the Day: Lobster Thermidor'.

Sandy led this unlikely lot along the narrow, winding path. She paused in front of a bed of aubergines and peppers, stepping back in amazement at the sight of four colossal marrows. Corkscrew-like tendrils spiralled out across the path, their sinuous fingers curling round unsuspecting tomatoes in the bed opposite.

She stopped to wait for the stragglers by the arched stone bridge over the stream which separated the garden from the copse behind. It brought to mind the bridge not far from her school in Ayr which inspired Burns' poem, 'Tam o' Shanter'. Prior to her unheralded departure, she had been working on a tricky essay entitled 'Robert Burns: His Contribution to Scottish Culture', in no more than five hundred words. An impossible task in less than twenty thousand, at the very least.

Sandy suddenly found herself gripped by an all-consuming desire to be back at 'Woodburn' in the secure daily routine of family life and not in this unfathomable world where she didn't belong.

There was no doubt she'd handled herself well in her encounter with the scrogwit but she'd been plagued by horrible nightmares in which her family were under attack from hordes of demons who'd found their way to Irvine. She'd woken in a lather of perspiration with the strong conviction that she would never see any of them again. The continued separation from Leo had provoked a gloom-laden anxiety which was briefly alleviated by the arrival of the kilt and sporran.

For years Sandy had longed to visit Sylvania and she was ashamed of her emotional wobbliness when it actually became a reality. She tried to maintain an upbeat, cheerful exterior but, as ever, the pixie sensed her mood.

Pogo's eyes were dark with concern. "You're homesick, aren't you?"

Sandy nodded but was too upset to say anything.

"Please don't be sad, we're here to take care of you and, by their own words, so are the kilt and sporran. Do you think those two have names?"

Sandy's face brightened a little.

"You mean us two?" offered the kilt. She couldn't fail to notice their reaction; she was wearing them after all. "I haven't had time to think about anything like that. I'm still coming to terms with being able to speak."

"Come on now, you big jessie, tighten your buckles and pull yourself together." The sporran gave an impatient flutter. "Ah've got a name."

"Why doesn't that surprise me?"

"The name's Florin. Florin the Sporran."

"But you only have a few coppers."

"Which is more than you've got. And, before ye say it, I know you don't carry money."

"That's not even a proper rhyme," said the kilt indignantly.

Pongo nibbled at its hem eagerly. "What's it to be? Surely you can come up with something better than that?"

"Hmm… something dignified but modest. Not *too* modest though." The Henderson tartan kilt grew thoughtful. "Why, of course, 'Invincible', that's the name for me. It has just the right amount of confident authority."

Pongo sniggered. "Don't undersell yourself, will you?"

"Vince, it is then," Florin said gleefully.

And try as the kilt might to persuade him otherwise, Vince it was.

Redshanks' instinct to follow Mabel Mince had paid off and he returned to The Mischief Maker at a discreet distance behind the buccaneer and his cabin boy.

Indigoletta's secret agent entered the tavern on the brim of a particularly fancy hat worn by a young goblin. These extravagantly feathered affairs were currently the height of fashion and provided excellent camouflage.

Once inside he picked his way along the worn timber beams below the roof until he was directly above the alcove where the stuffed eagle crouched, forever flexing its wings in preparation for a flight it would never make. Ensuring he was unobserved, the chough darted down and stationed himself on a branch below the raptor. In one slick movement he had become part of the tableau. The cobwebs picked up along the way only served to complete the illusion.

It was a good vantage point and Redshanks was able to see most of the tavern. The mirror behind the counter ran the length of the bar which was to prove extremely useful as it also reflected images from the one above the fireplace.

When Pestilence realised the possible significance of Jedediah's words, he sat forward and roared his approval. Malahyde pushed him back into his chair. "Wheesht, Cap'n. Easy now. You don't want to draw undue attention to yourself today."

The buccaneer was livid at being manhandled. Had it been anyone other than the First Mate who'd dared lay a finger on him, there would have been hell to pay. Grimshaw adjusted his jacket and brushed imaginary specks of dust from his wide velvet cuffs but he was not deaf to sound common sense when he heard it.

"That's damned fine advice, Jedediah. It'll be softly, softly from here on. We wouldn't want anyone else to get in on the act." The buccaneer felt skittish and fidgety, two adjectives rarely used to describe Pestilence Grimshaw.

"It may yet turn out to be nothing more than a trinket but there's only one way to find out."

Malahyde noticed that Smidge and Filch were having a lively conversation with someone who had just joined them. Might this be the long-awaited Jimlet?

"Wait here, Cap'n. I'll do a quick recce."

Sandy and Jamie stood on the bridge over the stream at the back of 'Corbie Cottage'. The rest of the party were gathered on the bank nearest the house. The child's sadness was almost tangible. Her concern for Leo and the feelings of loss associated with that only served to bolster her increasing anxiety. The kilt and sporran had stopped bickering, caught up as they were in her sombre mood.

Florin broke the silence. "This is awful. For pity's sake, Vince, get a grip and help her out."

The kilt was consumed with the desire to pull the tassels off the over-familiar, insolent purse but didn't have the wherewithal to do so. At a time like this a pair of hands would have been very useful.

"My dear," said the kilt solicitously, "it's time you met MacGregor."

Sandy's face was ghostly pale. "Do you think that's a good idea?" The question wasn't directed at anyone in particular. "It's just that I feel a bit faint, I don't know why."

"Take a deep breath and try to relax," said Vince kindly. "Concentrate on the water. Look behind it if you can."

The stream shimmered with dappled sunlight and flickering reflections from the willows on the opposite bank.

At first all she could see was a shift in the patterns on the surface of the water which gradually formed outward moving circles. Sandy felt apprehensive but never once had the desire to look away. She didn't even blink.

Alfie was struck by the silence. The wind had dropped and there was neither birdsong nor insect noise. When the stillness was complete, at the very moment when everyone collectively held their breath, it happened.

The eyes appeared first and then a longish nose and serious mouth. The ears were tufted like those on a lynx, and the fur was rich shades of gold, brown and sable. A lump formed at the back of Sandy's throat and she longed to touch the magical beast, to hug him to her. The silence was replaced by a deep, rhythmic rumbling which filled the wood.

Jamie realised what it was straight away and moved closer to the stream in the hope that he might catch a glimpse of the beast that was purring so loudly. The Siamese stared at the beautiful face in the water. The magnificent cat glanced at Jamie then his eyes came to rest on Sandy.

"It's good to meet you, my dear. I'm MacGregor but I expect you've worked that out for yourself." The cat's mouth curled upwards in a smile. "Our paths were not meant to cross just yet. We won't meet properly for at least another thirty years."

"But I know you, don't I? You're so familiar."

"That's lovely to hear. What's time between friends anyway?"

"I'm not sure I understand what you're saying."

"I'm always with you and always will be. That's all you need to know. You could say I'm the feline equivalent of a guardian angel."

"Are you really? You don't know how glad I am to hear that." Sandy pulled a hanky out of her tunic pocket and swiped at her eyes. "That's wonderful, isn't it, Jamie?" Her hand flew to her mouth when she realised she might have given her own dear cat cause for offence.

"You're not offended, are you, Jamie?"

"Not in the slightest, MacGregor. I'm pleased she has someone special looking after her."

"Don't underestimate your part in her life. You're doing a grand job."

MacGregor turned his attention back to the child. "How are you feeling now, any better? Homesickness is such a bleak emotion."

"How did you know I was homesick?" she asked in astonishment.

"You can't hide your inner feelings from me, there's an unbreakable bond between us. It's little wonder you're in a state. Your life's taken an extraordinary detour in the last few days and the situation here is far from good. An encounter with a scrogwit is enough to give anyone the creeps and, in view of last night's events, I decided to pay you a visit. I also wanted to make sure the kilt and sporran were behaving themselves. Good choice of names, by the way, boys."

There were disgruntled mutterings from the kilt about having no choice in the matter whatsoever.

The cat was already starting to fade and Sandy leant out over the bridge. "Can't you stay a little longer?"

"I'm afraid not. I bent the rules to come here today. You're happier now, I am pleased."

"I feel much better thanks to you."

"Well, bye for now. Be strong and remember what I said, Sandy. You're never alone. See you in due course. Just one more thing, I'll be a lot younger than I am now, so you may not recognise me at first."

Jamie rubbed against her arm affectionately and she hugged him to her. "I wish I could touch his fur, it looked so beautiful." But MacGregor had already vanished and the wood was once more filled with vibrant birdsong and the steady hum of insects.

Sandy opened her right hand and found she was clutching a chunk of soft, silky fur. She called after him, "I'll keep it with me always."

Cassandra's knowledge of the tunnels through the cliffs above Corvine was second to none and she realised there was no option but to follow Balebreath and his army of scrablings. She left the main tunnel as soon as she could through a small passageway that wound down to the ancient wine cellars underneath the palace.

The hare made her way slowly along the narrow first section and was dismayed to discover the tunnel blocked at the point where it should have opened out. She set about clearing the stones away though her head ached and she felt feverish. Her need to find Queen Celestina kept her going even though she was on the verge of collapse.

In spite of her rapidly deteriorating condition Cassandra managed to dig her way through; she entered the wine cellars on her belly, too weak to walk and barely able to crawl. Squeezing her way through a gap between two vats, the hare collapsed on the damp flagstone floor. Her breathing was laboured and she was wracked with stomach cramps.

The beast knew there was something horribly wrong with her. It was as if she'd swallowed a draft of hemlock, and it was a welcome release when she finally lost consciousness

Indigoletta's old retainer, Ravenscroft, was making his way through the cellar that housed, among other treasures, the best fingalberry claret. The butler held a blazing torch before him to light the way.

"Are you all right, Mr Ravenscroft? I can go on ahead if you'd rather." The voice belonged to Perkin Rawclaw, Keeper of the Royal Wine Cellars. He was one of the youngest Rawclaws ever to hold such an important post in royal service and the elf was proud of his position.

The aged butler was more than happy to take Perkin up on his offer and stood back to let him pass.

The elf wore a leather jerkin over a red and black striped tunic and saffron breeches. He carried a storm lantern he'd been given by a seafaring cousin. The glass was engraved with spouting whales and exotic sea creatures set against a background of palm-fringed islands. Their distorted reflections flickered on the limewashed vaulting of the cellar roof.

Rawclaw stopped by the vintage claret and waited for Ravenscroft to make his selection.

Suddenly his eye was caught by a shadowy mass at the foot of an old sherry cask. At first he thought it was a hessian sack but something about the shape made him take a closer look.

The butler came up behind Perkin and peered over his shoulder.

The imp crouched down and placed a hand gently on the bundle. "What do you suppose a hare's doing down here, and a very sick hare at that?"

9

Jimlet was basking in the warmth of his unexpected popularity. Not only were Smidge and Filch giving him their undivided attention, something hardly worth boasting about, but the gaunt figure by the bar was also watching him closely. Jimlet was flattered and tried to draw Malahyde into the conversation but the First Mate wouldn't be drawn. This caused the young gnome to double his efforts; he was full of himself and wanted to be noticed.

Pigsblanket sat in grateful silence beside Malahyde, pleased to be out of the Skipper's unrelenting spotlight. The boy was tired - soul, brain and bone tired - and he couldn't deny how grim he felt.

He was jolted out of his weariness by a squawk from Smidge. "Go awn then, Jimlet, give us a proper look at this 'ere bracelet if izz that speshul."

The gnome gave an annoying smirk while he savoured the hold he had over his stupid pals. He thrust his hand deep into his waistcoat pocket and fished out an object wrapped in a large spotted handkerchief which he proceeded to taunt them with. "Want a peek then, do you, lads?" He waved the bundle in front of them and lifted a flap of cloth enticingly.

Jedediah was impaled on a stiletto of light which escaped from the darkness. The searing pain brought him to his knees, and he knew there was no mistake; that ridiculous, posturing oaf held the Harpie's anklet in his pudgy hand.

The cabin boy's paper-thin voice faltered. "Mr M-malahyde, what's wrong?"

Jedediah's forehead was laced with beads of perspiration and his usually intense, hawkish eyes were dull and unresponsive. He spoke in a whisper. "I'm blind, lad, I can't see a thing, but never mind that now, just get that fool over there to shut up." Malahyde anticipated the unasked question. "The idiot with the spotted handkerchief, is he still waving it around?"

"Aye, sir, but what shall I say?"

Malahyde's vision was beginning to clear and he was flooded with profound relief when the boy's features swam towards him out of the mist. "Don't worry, I'll sort him out myself. My sight's returning, thank heavens, but I don't mind telling you that was damned frightening."

Pigsblanket was close to fainting; the situation had gone beyond bizarre into the realms of nightmarish unreality.

The First Mate stepped forward and, slipping his hand under Jimlet's elbow, swung him round. "There you are. I've been trying to find you for ages. My boss wants a word with you, pronto."

Malahyde's commanding figure was daunting, particularly to someone less than half his size with a brain smaller than Jedediah's clenched fist.

"Who's your gaffer and what does he want with me?" The gnome's confidence was draining away and his bravado had already legged it out the door.

Filch nudged Smidge in his well-padded ribs. Things were shaping up very nicely and he couldn't wait to see how Jimlet was going to pull this one off without getting a bloody nose, and serve him right if he did.

Malahyde maintained his calm exterior. "Captain Pestilence Grimshaw, that's who, and he doesn't like to be kept waiting. Get your skates on. He's over there by the fire."

Jimlet gaped at the First Mate, amazed and impressed at the same time. "You work for that nutter?"

Smidge and Filch doubled up with laughter and made to follow their chum but Malahyde raised his hand to stop them. "You two stay right where you are. Take my word for it, you're better off here."

In spite of his well-practised, fearless demeanour, Jedediah's heart was thumping in his chest and he was deeply affected by his horrifying introduction to the anklet. His eyes burned and his throat ached and he was having difficulty keeping his breakfast down. The pirate was genuinely frightened for the first time in his life.

Malahyde is not an evil person. Misguided, drunken, harsh; these are all charges that might be laid against him, but of far greater significance is his state of isolation. He's one of life's misfits who lives in a world where violence is the key to survival and a cosy fire, enjoyed in the convivial company of a few trusted friends, is inconceivable. Grimshaw needs the First Mate, and his subordinates fear him, but Jedediah walks alone, wrapped in a cloak of solitary seclusion.

Malahyde had experienced first-hand the sinister power of the anklet and the anklet had recognised Malahyde and the part he might play in its destiny. The pirate was consumed by the desire to keep everything exactly as it was, to carry on his day-to-day existence as a buccaneer. It wasn't such a bad life, with treasure to be had and more than his fair share of adventures. Why rock the boat now?

Jedediah teetered on the edge of the endless void and tasted the fear. He had to tread carefully, keep his thoughts under wraps and, more than anything, give the anklet a wide berth. He tapped Jimlet as casually as he could on the shoulder. "I'm sorry, lad. I thought you were someone else. My mistake. Go back and join your pals."

But it was too late and there was no going back. Pestilence Grimshaw was already getting to his feet. The captain of the pirates extended a hand towards the young gnome. "Good to meet you, boy. What's your poison?"

Hamish stopped by at first light to check on his daughter while she slept in the royal nursery. Her governess, Sarah, was asleep in the room between the nursery and Tabitha's bedroom, her embroidery set aside until the morning. Tabitha's elven guardians stepped forward to greet the Prince and usher him into his daughter's suite of rooms.

The elves were dressed in grey velvet stitched with pearls from the freshwater oyster beds of the Sprinting River. Coralie had a quiver of arrows slung over her shoulder and held a light-weight titanium bow. Meriel carried no conventional weapon but her hand loosely encircled a staff of petrified wood from the sacred site of the Twisted Oak. Thousands of years earlier this tree had occupied the spot where 'Corbie Cottage' now stands. Wood from the oak is prized for its benign magical properties and is greatly valued for its powers of protection.

"Was all well here during the night?"

"Not even the atrocious weather caused the princess any distress, sir," Meriel replied. "She didn't wake once. Her Majesty's spell saw to that."

Hamish nodded thoughtfully. "I heard about that charming bit of magic. Is the Queen here? I haven't seen her these past few hours."

"Her Majesty's with Princess Tabitha," said Coralie.

The Prince gave no outer signs of the relief he felt. He thanked them both, then gently applied pressure to a carved rose on the linen-fold panelling. The concealed door slid open to reveal a small passageway that led directly to the nursery, bypassing the governess's room.

Hamish stepped through into his daughter's bedroom to find her sleeping soundly. Her long hair was spread out on the pillow and she lay with her hand tucked underneath her chin.

He wasn't in the least perturbed to see a lioness curled up on the end of his daughter's bed for his wife took many forms. The tawny beast was breathing lightly and there was the faintest sound of snoring, but her body was taut as a coiled spring. Visual signs of the spell of protection had all but vanished, leaving the merest trace of sapphire stars above Tabitha's head.

The little unicorns stood on the table beside the bed, their elegant heads bowed, their eyes closed. They were not asleep, just resting, and when they became aware of the Prince they trotted towards him. Hamish patted first one, then the other with the tip of his forefinger; he was pleased to see a tiny manger of hay with a pail of water nearby.

His dark, soulful eyes took in the peaceful scene and he stooped to kiss Tabitha lightly on the cheek. Hamish chose not to disturb the lioness. His wife was very much in need of sleep and this mighty incarnation enabled her to rest and protect her daughter at the same time. Besides, Tabby had told him many times over that she slept resoundingly well when one of the royal cats was allowed to sleep on the end of her bed.

"My word, Leo, what a commotion. If I was hurled out of my hammock once in the early hours I was hurled out a dozen times. It's just as well I had my sea-legs on." The giant rat's pink eyes were bright with excitement. "The sea's in my blood and that's an exciting discovery."

Leo yawned and stretched in the neighbouring hammock. "But we haven't even shipped anchor, Gilb, and I can't say I'm sorry. It was cutting up rough in the harbour last night and I don't fancy my chances out there on the open sea. I'm definitely more of a landlubber."

Gilbert's tummy rumbled and he gave it a friendly pat. "Each to his own, dear wee chum. It would be a dull old world if we all liked the same things." The rodent rolled out of his hammock and gave himself a thorough shake. "D'you reckon we might be able to scare up some breakfast? I'm fair famished. I wouldn't want PG to think I was ungrateful for that was a veritable slap-up feast last night but the sea air has increased my appetite."

Leo experienced yet another rush of affection for the rat. His ability to make the best of any situation and his cheerful optimism continued to amaze the cat, as did Gilbert's capacity for food, but then he wasn't called the Giant Rat for nothing.

"I expect we're locked in again, but I might as well find out." He rattled the handle on the cabin door which was immediately thrown open. Leitzoff greeted him with a slack-jawed smile. "Mornin' ratty. What can I do for you?"

"I must say the service is jolly good on this brigantine. We'd like a spot of breakfast, Bosun. Scrambled eggs with cheese, mushrooms, tomatoes, fried bread, sausages and two rounds of toast and marmalade, please." Gilbert looked over his shoulder. "Would you like a little smoked salmon with that?"

Leo couldn't even begin to respond, his sense of the ridiculous had reduced him to silent laughter but he managed to nod his head and squeeze out a few words. "Easy on the mushrooms and tomatoes, I'm not sure if I like them or not." He collapsed back in his hammock, struggling for breath.

The Bosun didn't know what to make of them and wasn't sure whether to tell them to get knotted or rush off and organise their grub. They were the Captain's guests after all, so he reckoned he'd better have Trencher Halibut pull out all the stops. "Right, gentlemen, I'll get onto that right away.

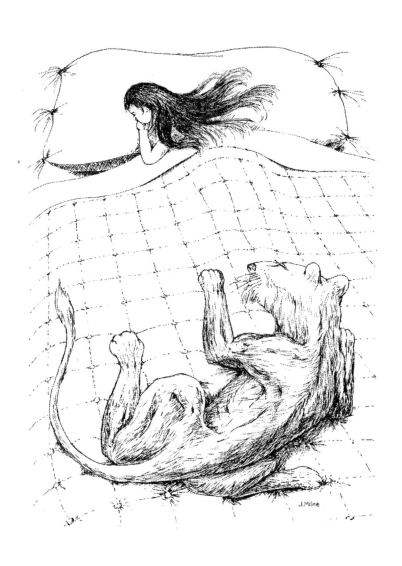

Would you like something to wash it down with?"

Leo was beyond help and was biting on the side of the hammock. Gilbert didn't dare make eye contact with his friend for fear of braying like a donkey. "A pot of tea for two would be nice," he squeaked, in a voice most unlike his own.

"Right you are, gents." Leitzoff closed the door and they heard the key turn in the lock. His footsteps receded and when they felt he was out of earshot they exploded.

"Crikey," said Leo, "this is all getting out of hand. I'm virtually hysterical. What's going on?"

Gilbert was dancing the rat equivalent of a sailor's hornpipe, nimble and dainty on his neat little feet. "I'm feeling a wee bit lightheaded myself. I might think it was something we ate, but a morsel hasn't passed our lips for at least six hours!"

There was a thump on the door. "Gilbert, Leo, it's me."

"I'd know that tail thump anywhere," said the Abyssinian. He called out to the dragon. "Come on in but you'll need the key."

"Key?"

"We're locked in."

"How odd. So is Mother, but I intend to change that."

"We've been meaning to ask you about your mother. Perhaps you'd care to join us for breakfast? Mr Leitzoff has the key and he'll be back any minute."

"I don't need to wait for him. Stand back, chaps." They could hear Cahoots sucking in a phenomenal amount of breath and a blast of smoke-tinged flames squirted through the keyhole. Leo flung himself against the wall. "Stand by your hammock, Gilb. He means business."

There was a kerfuffle outside the cabin which culminated in a roar, a screech and an angry retort. "You've singed me eyebrows, burnt the sausages and stripped the varnish off the walls, you daft flame-thrower. The smoked salmon's not looking too hot either."

"What are you talking about? That salmon's roasting," said the dragon, trying to appear blasé. He'd given himself the collywobbles with the unexpected upturn in his smoke and fire-related abilities. These were only outmatched by the hourly increase in his size which he hadn't noticed at all. It isn't obvious unless you grow out of your clothes at an alarming rate and dragons don't wear outer garments as a rule.

Leitzoff continued peevishly. "You only had to ask if you waz wantin' to visit Cap'n Grimshaw's guests. What's wrong with the youff of today? No patience, that's what's wrong with 'em." The Bosun squinted at the dragon through the gloom and scratched his head. "Blimey, is it me, or have you grown some since last night?"

Cahoots wasn't listening but he was nodding politely. It was a case of blah, blah, blah-dee-blah. The aroma from the mushrooms had caught his attention. They smelt delicious. "Breakfast would be nice," he simpered.

"Wouldn't you know?" said an impudent voice behind the Bosun which made him jump. "That dragon's about to stuff its face and here's me run ragged trying to keep tabs on things!"

Leitzoff nearly dropped the breakfast platter when Minxie whizzed past him. "Where's Captain Self-Importance anyway? I'm not in the mood for hanging around waiting for him." The wazwatt began circling the Bosun's head in a whirr of wings.

Cahoots was transported with joy. "You're back. Hooray!"

"I'll give you 'hooray', you daft eedjit."

Gilbert was hopping about on the other side of the door, his ears cocked and his whiskers twitching. "What's going on out there? Who's back? Don't keep us in suspense."

217

"My goodness," said Minxie, genuinely taken aback. "That almost sounds like the Giant Rat."

"It *is* the Giant Rat,' exclaimed the Giant Rat indignantly. "Who are you?"

"Don't start 'who are you-ing' me." The wazwatt inclined her neat little head. "Next thing you'll be telling me Leo's in there with you."

"But he is!"

"Nice try, you big chump." Minxie executed a half turn. "On the subject of big, you're growing at an alarming rate, tinderbox."

"So what. I'm a dragon, aren't I? And, for your information, Leo really is in there, I had supper with them both last night. With Uncle Pestilence and Mr Malahyde."

Minxie applied her air-brakes and drifted down until she was level with the dragon's face. She fixed him with her piercing green eyes. "Honest," he added emphatically.

"Good grief. This is an unexpected development. PG must be cock-a-hoop. Well done him."

The Bosun angled the tray towards the wazwatt.

"Crumbs, that breakfast looks appetising."

Leitzoff favoured her with a lopsided smile. "Do you mind eatin' with the Captain's guests and this 'ere purple dragon?"

"Far from it, Mr L. I've always wanted to meet Gilbert and I hear the much-sought-after cat from 'Woodburn' is with him as well. What a lucky break."

"Cap'n Grimshaw's well chuffed, he is. Mind you, he's blazing mad that we haven't been able to leave port."

"I can see why, Bosun, he's a veritable sitting duck."

"His very words, miss."

"So where is he then?"

"Gone ashore on some very hush-hush business. Taking a risk, if you ask me. The Queen's imps-at-arms are swarmin' all over Corvine."

Minxie looped the loop. "Jings, if they only had a sniff of who was here, they'd board this brigantine at the double by the dozen."

Gilbert and Leo had been listening to the conversation with acute interest when the rodent's stomach rumbled and once more took centre stage. "Don't let that breakfast get cold. We're ravenous."

The Bosun produced the key on the end of its long chain. "Keep yer fur on, ratty. I'm on me way."

Minxie flew into the cabin behind the Bosun with a delighted Cahoots in her wake.

Ravenscroft made his way to Indigoletta's quarters and found the great bird poring over ancient manuscripts in her study. "Madam! Madam! We found a hare in the cellars and she's very sick." The old butler had lost his customary reserve. He was agitated and his hands trembled. "Perkin Rawclaw's taken her up to the infirmary and has sent for Her Majesty."

"He's done what? The Queen's far to busy to be disturbed, as indeed am I. The palace vets will take care of the creature. Have her taken to them at once."

"She's too far gone for that, ma'am. I doubt she'd survive the move."

Indigoletta put down the magnifying glass she held in her claw and gazed indignantly at her loyal retainer.

"Rawclaw thinks she's been poisoned. The poor beast's delirious and she's covered in tiny cuts."

The raven grew pale under her feathers. "Were the wounds crimson as a freshly cut pomegranate and was there a sweet, sickly smell about them?"

"Come to think of it, they were and there was a very strong odour, like aniseed tinged with almonds."

Indigoletta launched herself from the desk in a flurry of feathers and Ravenscroft's mane of white hair fell forward as she connected with his chest, frantically beating her wings. "Do you realise what this means?" The raven was met with blank incomprehension. "Scrablings, is what it means." She hastily smoothed the old elf's hair back into place with her wing-tips.

"I'm sorry, madam, you've lost me."

"You're too young to know what I'm talking about."

"But I'm positively antiquated," protested the butler.

"Comparatively speaking, y'understand." Indigoletta returned to her perch in front of the desk. "Scrablings were long ago confined to the history books, or so I'd thought. This is grave news, and Perkin's right. Queen Celestina's the only one who might be able to help the hare. Was it Cassandra?"

"I can't say, madam, but if it's of any use she was the most unusual colour, an intense shade of midnight blue."

"That's her, right enough."

Indigoletta was airborne in an instant. She flew through a series of hatches in the walls which enable her to move from room to room without having to consider whether the doors are open or not. She made a dramatic swoop to collect the huge emerald on its chain from the perch beside her bed. She called to the startled butler. "Brief Will at once. I'll send for him as soon as I can."

"That was like taking a lollipop from a kiddy, Jedediah. It's as well that nosey bird in the alcove was flushed out, otherwise he might have seen too much. His cover was good, I'll give him that. It was damned handy a fight broke out when it did. That's one of the good things about this dump, there's always a punch-up when you need one."

"If that lunk-head hadn't made a grab for the stuffed eagle and whacked Slack over the head we'd 'ave been none the wiser. Gertie sent that chough packing and no mistake. I didn't realise she could move so fast."

Grimshaw chuckled at the memory. "The way she wielded that broom was a sight to behold. I'd watch my step if I were Jem. That missus of his has a temper on her these days. Now, Jed, I want you to stay here and make sure Jimlet and his cronies get completely plastered. Drop-dead drunk, if you get my drift. We don't want them blabbing about my little transaction, that'd never do."

Malahyde tried to mask his increasing sense of unease. "That won't be difficult. They're well on the way already, at least two sheets to the wind."

Grimshaw ignored the joke. His eyes were cold and empty of emotion. "Mind now, *dead* drunk." The Captain winked but his eyes didn't soften. "I'm heading back to the ship with a charming present for Cahoots' dear mother. Something that'll put the roses back in her cheeks." He patted his greatcoat pocket. "What a stroke of fortune. Talk about things dropping right into your lap. Leo's no longer of any real importance but we'll take him with us when we sail. I don't want him falling into the wrong hands and he may still prove useful later on. When we hit the open sea the rat will be disembarking. Now then, where's that wretch Pigsblanket?"

Malahyde snatched a look at the bar. "He'll never hear me over this racket. I'll fetch him myself."

Grimshaw tapped his foot impatiently. "Don't be long about it, man, and that applies to the other business too. We must be ready to leave Corvine at the earliest opportunity."

Malahyde gave a terse nod and shouldered his way towards the counter, wishing there was something he could do to alleviate his sense of foreboding.

Cassandra lay on a sterilised trolley in the palace infirmary, drifting in and out of consciousness. Her wounds had been angry red slits to start with but fast became hideous, gaping mouths. Perkin Rawclaw, Keeper of the Royal Wine Cellars, stood behind the nurse who was holding a damp towel against the hare's forehead in an attempt to comfort her.

Rawclaw reacted to a low, anguished growl. A shadow spread across the limewashed wall that put him in mind of a large, crouching cat and he turned nervously to see what was there.

The Fairy Queen stood behind him, dressed in fawn taffeta trimmed with dark brown lace. Her face was etched with concern. Perkin recovered himself enough to execute a well-practised bow.

"Your Majesty, thank you for coming. I know everything's gone haywire, but this poor creature needs your help."

She lightly touched the elf's arm and stepped round him to study the limp hare. "The situation is critical, but I must make time for this." The nurse moved aside and the Queen removed the towel and placed her hands on Cassandra's head. "Poor dear, as if you haven't suffered enough and scrabling wounds are so very difficult to treat."

There were anxious mutterings from the hospital staff.

"I'm afraid those little demons are back with us and we're moving into the shadows once more but, be assured, I'm ready for whatever I have to face." Her voice was like ice cracking on a lonely pond and her eyes burned with determination.

The silence was so deep, it was almost audible.

"I'm taking you into my confidence but the situation with the hare must be kept out of the public domain. There's enough panic and civil disorder already after last night's catastrophe. The fewer who know about this the better. I want your word on this matter." The staff nodded solemnly. There were mutterings of "I swear" and "On my life".

"I need to stay with Cassandra but first I must get word to Wee Alfie Elf. The Royal Steed has only just returned from his hazardous journey but he must go straight back to 'Corbie Cottage'. Will you accompany him, Perkin, and see that Alfie gets this message?" She handed over a folded letter that bore the royal seal.

"I'll get right onto it."

"Tell Kismet I'm sorry but needs must. I've made all the other arrangements and this will complete the circle."

Perkin paused by the door. "There is one more thing, Your Majesty. It's something the hare said. She was rambling, not making any sense at all, but there was a moment when she opened her eyes and stared right at me. I asked her if there was anything I could do to help but all she did was repeat the word 'ship' over and over again and then the word 'cat'."

Sandy had been transformed by her meeting with MacGregor and all traces of homesickness had gone. Her eyes were shining and her confidence was fully restored.

"I'd like you to have this locket. It's been in our family for generations."

"It's lovely, Pogo, but are you sure you want to part with it?"

"Of course she is," said Pongo adamantly. "We can't have Jamie being the only glamour-puss round here. He's ever so toffee-nosed since SSS gave him that swanky collar. If I wasn't such a laid-back beast, his posing might get on my nerves."

"You have to admit Jamie's collar is spectacular and takes some beating in the sparkly stakes."

"Maybe so, PP, but your locket is a bonnie piece. Those are rubies in the owl's eyes, are they not?"

The Siamese strolled in from the garden. "You're not a teensy bit put out that His Hissyness gave me a jewelled collar and not you?"

"Course not. What does a dog like me need with a jewel-encrusted collar? Totally impractical and altogether too flashy."

"Indeed so," replied the cat, his nose firmly in the air. "You're far too rough and ready for that sort of adornment."

"Quite," Pongo said bluffly, "but take a look at Sandy's locket from PP. Pretty, isn't it? Discreet but striking in its simplicity."

Alfie was working his way through a heap of documents that chronicled the Harpie's first attempt to take control of Sylvania. He was completely engrossed and nearly hit the ceiling when Pongo fired off a round of ear-splitting barks and pelted out into the hall. For the benefit of those who don't speak dog he provided an on-the-spot translation. "Bless my soul, it's the Royal Steed. What's he doing back here so soon?"

Alfie rose from his chair. "Something's amiss. Kismet should be curled up in his bed after last night's shenanigans."

Pongo was bouncing up and down by the front door, barking at the top of his lungs. "What are you waiting for? Let me out and I'll ask him what's going on."

The inevitable "you'll do no such thing" came back at him from Pogo.

"I'll go out to meet him," Alfie said with quiet authority. "If you stop horsing around, I might let you come with me."

The dog landed neatly on all four feet, silent as the grave.

Kismet stood by the gate waiting for Rawclaw to swing down the emergency rope ladder. Alfie stepped forward to greet the elf who was related to him on his mother's side of the family. They embraced and Perkin handed over the letter. "Queen Celestina asked me to deliver this personally."

"It must be very important. A messenger rook is what I would normally expect." He broke the seal and his eyebrows shot up as he read the contents. "This is most unexpected; you'd better come in."

Pongo scratched Alfie's leg, demanding attention. "Not now, boy. I need to talk to Pogo." He turned on his heel and walked briskly up the path. The dog trailed along behind, his usually pert tail uncurled and droopy.

Pogo was waiting on the doorstep with Sandy and Jamie.

Peg flew out to join them and Lorimer called after him. "Wait for me. I'm useless by myself."

The lobster flung himself out of his bucket and crossed the wooden floorboards at a rate of knots. He rounded the corner into the hall in time to meet everyone coming back into the cottage. Lorimer dodged out of the way, flattening himself against the skirting board, something not to be scoffed at when you're a seriously large crustacean with multiple appendages.

Pongo stopped beside the frazzled lobster and gave him a quick sniff. The creature was showing his vulnerability and the dog felt for him. Lorimer watched him uncertainly from behind his goggles. "I'll give you a lift back to your luxury accommodation, if you like, and I promise I won't drop you."

Pongo carried the flailing beast into the kitchen. He lowered him into the bucket of spa water.

"Things are a bit thrang round here," he said. "Put your feet up for a while, *mi amigo carapacho*. That's Spanish for 'my carapaced friend', you know."

Alfie's train of thought was derailed and his amusement was plain to see. "Your Spanish is coming on a treat, boy."

"*Gracias*, WAE." The dog started to snigger. "I'll have to try it out on 'Bandolero'."

"Don't waste your breath. Fergus wouldn't know genuine Spanish if it jumped out of a book and wrapped him in a floured tortilla. The Mexican hatdance is as far as it goes. On a more serious note…" The elf cleared his throat and checked to make sure he had everyone's attention. Several pairs of very different eyes were trained on him. "Queen Celestina wants all those from Irvine to move into the palace for reasons of security. Kismet told Her Majesty about the incident with the scrogwit which may well have influenced her decision."

Pongo's face fell. In Scottish parlance 'his face was tripping him'. "Does this mean it'll be just us three at 'Corbie Cottage'?"

"It does, I'm afraid." Alfie moved towards his wife. "Unless you would consider staying at the palace. I have a lot to do myself and won't be able to spend much time here. It might be for the best if you and Pongo were to go with the Irvine contingent."

The dog sloped over to Pogo and sat down at her feet, placing his head on her knees. He'd gone beyond clever wordplay and quick retorts. His hazel eyes were compelling in their intensity. "I've never been inside the palace. Please say we can go, PP. I'll have no one to play with otherwise. Besides, I don't want to be parted from my new chums."

Pogo tickled him under his curly chin. "How can I refuse when my husband and my dog have put their case so eloquently? We'd better start packing right away."

"That takes a huge weight off my shoulders. Kismet has instructions to take the others straight to the palace. I'll let him know you're going as well."

The relief showed in Sandy's face. "I'm so pleased you're coming with us." Pongo looked up at her expectantly and she dropped to her knees and put her arms round his neck. "And you, too, boy."

Jamie sighed. "Here was me thinking we were about to give that fleabag the slip."

"Oh, ha ha!" Pongo strutted off towards his basket. He shoved his blanket around with his nose and, when he was satisfied, flopped down in front of his bed. "That's my packing done. I expect the palace will provide everything we need. It's silly, I know, but I don't sleep well unless I'm in my own basket. Will you be taking your bed with you, Jamie?'

The Siamese sought Pogo's advice. "Why not? There's plenty of room in the howdah but let's get cracking. We mustn't keep Kizz waiting."

"You won't leave us behind, will you, Sandy?"

"Of course not, you daft gowk," Florin sniped dismissively. "A fat lot of use we'd be hanging in a cupboard here."

Vince bristled. "Why do you always have to be so confrontational?"

Sandy ran out into the hall and took the stairs two at a time. "You're both coming as long as you stop bickering." Florin's voice drifted back into the kitchen. "Jings! That took the wind out ma sails."

Alfie put his arm round his wife's shoulders. "I hope they don't prove too much of a handful."

"Their hearts are in the right place." Pogo grinned self-consciously. "Listen to me, hearts indeed!"

They hugged each other.

"I'll contact Ralph and let him know what's going on. That cowrie shell's our only way of communicating for now. I'll join you when I can. The missing anklet has to be the main concern but that doesn't mean anyone's forgotten about Leo. Make sure Sandy knows he's still a priority."

Pogo stepped back from her husband and her eyes were dark with concern. "The loss of the anklet is terrifying. I have such a bad feeling about all of this."

"I know you do, my love, and it chills me to the bone."

"Let's hope I'm wrong this time. I best go up and fling a few things into a case."

Alfie listened to his wife trudging up the stairs and felt a stab of anxiety in the pit of his stomach.

Lorimer was dangling over the side of his bucket. "I'll do my best to look after her."

The elf squatted in front of the lobster. "Thank you, Lorimer. You're a good beast. I'll see you into the howdah, bucket and all. There's no sense leaving Mildred here on her own. Estella wouldn't want that. You might as well take the model ship too."

"Thanks, WAE. The rest of my stuff's in the kitbag by the front door. Pongo carried it out there for me. He's all right when you get to know him, isn't he?"

"You couldn't wish for a better friend unless there happened to be a one-legged seagull in the area." Alfie checked round to make sure no one had forgotten anything. When he was satisfied he picked up the lobster complete with container. "Shall we go, Lorimer?"

The crustacean nodded vigorously. "I'll try not to make waves."

10

The Harpie sprang from her miserable bed in the sinkhole on the Island of Long Forgotten Dreams, screeching and shrieking with unconfined joy. The anklet was on its way home. She could feel its unleashed power.

Maligna howled and bayed like a wolf. She danced like a dervish and jigged like a jester.

She taunted the guards above. "Hello, my lovelies! Why don't you join me? I'm having an impromptu party but you'll have to supply the liquor. The wine cellars in this dungeon leave much to be desired and I'm fresh out of party frocks. I'll have to wear this old rag again." She stood with her arms crossed defiantly over the wasted frame of her chest. "No takers, eh? Don't you know it's churlish to refuse a lady's invitation?"

Gone was the docile, listless creature who would lie with her face turned to the wall for days on end, barely showing signs of life.

Harpies are capable of slowing their breathing and heart-rate right down so that, to the inexperienced eye, they display all the outer signs of death. A mirror placed in front of Maligna's mouth during one of those prolonged periods of inactivity might well have suggested she'd expired, but harpies don't make a habit of dying; immortality is more their style.

In an instant they can switch from a passive state to one of frenzied, skull-crushing mania without resorting to sorcery or magic. It's wise to keep your distance from a harpie and to avert your gaze from those soulless black eyes which are capable of inducing a form of mental paralysis that turns its victims into brainless zombies.

Maligna's jailers believed she'd finally slipped over the cliff of reason into a chasm of madness. They tried to keep their spirits up with silly jokes at her expense which they swapped in whispers.

The Harpie's mood changed abruptly and she slumped on her pallet, crying hot tears of angry relief. Years of wretched, pent-up emotion poured out in a torrent of unstoppable grief. "Come home soon, precious anklet." She cradled her gaunt head in bone-white arms, tugging at her lank hair with sinuous fingers while she fretfully rocked back and forth. "We'll show them, dear one."

Maligna repeated these five words until she finally fell into a deep, dreamless sleep.

Ralph called to his wife as he picked up the car-keys from the tallboy next to the grandfather clock. There was no response and he shouted again. "That's me off then."

Tina was upstairs rummaging about in the spare bedroom cupboard where she kept her posh frocks. They were due to attend a function and she wanted to air the dress she had in mind. She lifted the gown from the rail and hung it on the outside of the walnut wardrobe that dominated the room.

Trixie, the Hendersons' brindle boxer, was snuffling around by the open cupboard door when her hackles rose and she started to growl. Tina was surprised and placed her hand on the dog's shoulders to reassure her.

The dog sank to the floor snarling through bared teeth and Tina steeled herself to take a closer look. She crouched down and parted the clothes hanging on the rail. The cupboard was in deep shadow and there was no overhead light but she could make out a mouse-like shape in the corner right at the back.

"What a fuss about nothing. You're a grown dog; don't tell me you're scared of a teeny wee rodent."

Ralph was watching the scene unfold from the bedroom doorway. The boxer had put as much space between herself and the cupboard as she could without actually deserting Tina. She was uttering dark-side-of-the-dog noises that gave Ralph the creeps. "Trixie's in a bit of a state, isn't she? What's up with her?"

"It's only a mouse, but she's carrying on as if Old Nick himself is in that cupboard."

Their exchange was cut short when the phone rang, startling them both. Tina rushed down the stairs to answer it, leaving Ralph alone with the jibbering heap that was the family dog.

Trixie was going nowhere in a hurry and nothing would induce her to approach that cupboard again.

Ralph's eyes took a moment or two to adjust to the gloom. In the farthest corner sat a small bundle of fur with its back to the door. The creature reacted to his voice and he was treated to the full impact of its oversized mouth crammed with unnervingly sharp teeth. These were matched by clusters of long, curved claws on its spindly feet. Ralph staggered back from the cupboard but had the presence of mind to lock the beast inside.

He could hear his wife coming up the stairs. "I'm off to see Jessie about next week's fund-raiser for Guide Dogs for the Blind." Then, almost as an after-thought. "Did you find Trixie's mouse?"

Tina didn't wait for an answer, she was already running late.

Ralph's mind was racing. Thoughts tumbled over each other anxious to claim his attention. How was it possible that a scrabling could be here in Irvine? The situation in Crawdonia must have deteriorated drastically.

Donning the leather gloves he kept in his overcoat pocket, he crept towards the cupboard and slowly turned the key in the lock. The door creaked open on its ageing hinges and Ralph knelt down, hoping to grab the scrabling should it decide to make a run for it. What he was going to do with the creature then was anyone's guess.

In all his years in the Merchant Navy, even on the dangerous North Atlantic Convoys during the Second World War, he had always known what to do in any given situation, but this time it was different. A being from another dimension was something he'd never had to deal with before, particularly one with such a nasty disposition.

He was dismayed to discover the original scrabling was no longer alone. He could hear a sound like the high-pitched screech of a owl. Ralph felt for the right-hand drawer of the dressing table, never taking his eyes off the the creatures. He fished out a small torch and shone the beam into the corner. Two pairs of yellow eyes glared at him and the screeching intensified. He kept his nerve and flashed the torch round, moving the dresses aside until he was sure he'd checked every inch of the cupboard. There wasn't even a mousehole to be seen. The light from the torch revealed a further pair of eyes. He banged the door shut and, having locked it, shoved the key in the inside pocket of his jacket. His fingers brushed against the magic cowrie shell.

Tina had taken Sandy's unscheduled trip to Sylvania remarkably well but were she to discover the nasty little critters in the cupboard she might not be quite so rational or understanding.

It was time to contact Sammy and bring Sandy and Jamie home, with or without Leo. There was also the pressing matter of sending those scrablings packing.

Everyone, with the exception of Wainscot, was at the back of the howdah and those who had arms to wave did so. Sandy and Pogo held a gesticulating Lorimer aloft while the pixie blew heavy-hearted kisses to her husband with her free hand.

Peg Leg was flying along behind Kismet, emitting the stark, eerie cries gulls specialise in; the ones that conjure up images of drowned sailors and ships lost at sea. To those of a melancholy disposition they epitomise the sadness and cruelty at the heart of the world. The irony is that seagulls are just saying "hi", "bye" or "get off, I saw that fish first", unless they happen to be cut from the same cloth as our one-legged friend who is set apart from his peers by supreme intelligence and his ability to speak the language of humans.

The sun reflected off Lorimer's goggles and glittered on the rows of blue and white sequins which made up the Scottish flag on his lavish bathing costume. He's very patriotic, which is not something lobsters tend to concern themselves with on an average day in the Firth of Clyde. They're too busy swimming with or, as often as not, against the ever-shifting currents without the BBC Shipping Forecast to help them on their way.

Alfie remained where he was long after the Royal Steed and his precious cargo had disappeared into the wood. He experienced a wave of abject loneliness which brought a lump to his throat. The elf gave himself a thoroughly good talking-to and headed for the stable to saddle the pony.

Pigsblanket shoved his few belongings into his coat pockets. Apart from his concertina and an old diary, he had little more than he stood up in. He scanned the tiny cabin, trying to avoid eye contact with the parrot who was watching him reproachfully from a makeshift perch beside his hammock. Technically the bird belonged to the Skipper who believed her to be dead.

The cabin boy had managed to revive the bird after Grimshaw, in an alcohol-fuelled rage, attempted to throttle her. The reason: she wouldn't talk, virtually unheard of for a bird in this saga.

The buccaneer had purloined the parrot during a raid and revelled in her badinage and clever retorts but, after a few days in the company of Grimshaw, the bird was traumatised to the point where she'd stopped talking altogether.

Pigsblanket gave her refuge, safe in the knowledge that the Skipper never visited the crew's quarters, not even his cabin which was slap bang next to Grimshaw's own. That apart, a mute parrot was unlikely to draw attention to herself.

The cabin boy often went hungry but he always made sure he squirrelled something away for the bird. Trencher Halibut baked bread twice a week and the boy would slip into the galley and collect any spilt grains or seeds. No one noticed when a few fusty grapes or a rotten apple disappeared and he always shared what he had with her. Late at night, when all was quiet on the brigantine, Pigsblanket would go up on deck so the parrot could take some aerial exercise without being detected.

The boy and the bird had grown close. He wanted to go it alone and not draw attention to himself. She sensed the turmoil he was experiencing but couldn't bear the prospect of life without him. The parrot determined that, whatever he decided, she would be leaving 'The Cheeky Monkey' with him. She needn't have worried. Pigsblanket was unable to contemplate life without her either.

"Come on then, Conchita." He opened his jacket and pointed at the capacious inside pocket. The parrot flew towards him and tucked herself safely out of sight. "Make yourself as small as you can, I don't want anyone wondering why I've suddenly filled out a bit."

The cabin boy had one last look round the miserable space where he'd been so unhappy. "If I have anything to do with it, Chita, we'll never have to spend another night in this hole."

Pigsblanket jumped out of the boat into the shallow water by the crab-catcher's skiff and made fast the rope on a nearby bollard. He placed a folded piece of paper, addressed to Jedediah Malahyde, by one of the oars where the First Mate couldn't fail to see it.

The boy had purposely arrived early to give himself time to make good his escape. He hated leaving Gilbert and Leo behind but what else could he do?

He set off along the docks with his hat pulled down over his eyes and a moth-eaten apology for a scarf covering his mouth. The weather was closing in again and the wind had strengthened. He pushed his way through groups of overexcited, chattering folk, keeping an arm protectively round Conchita, and climbed the worn stone steps that lead up from the docks onto the High Road.

The cabin boy had never been close to the palace before and saw how difficult it would be to breach its security systems. The massive watergates protecting the promontory from the might of the sea were shut fast and the formidable locks and bolts were firmly in place on the Great Daria

Gate which separates the royal complex from the rest of Corvine.

His attention was caught by a distinctive shape out beyond the harbour mouth. Pigsblanket raised an ancient but serviceable telescope to his eye and a smile of recognition touched his bruised lips. It seemed he wasn't the only one leaving 'The Cheeky Monkey'.

A purple dragon, with a package strapped to his right foreleg, flew against the prevailing wind high above the jagged rocks of Fractal Reef. Cahoots steadied his wings and banked in a north westerly direction, his heart thumping with excitement at the prospect of being reunited with his mother.

Cassandra moaned and muttered in her fevered state. The air in the infirmary was polluted with the sickly smell rising from her diseased wounds.

On the rail behind her head sat the Royal Raven, her radiant cowl of feathers bowed low over the flawless emerald cradled between her feet. The room was washed with light from the gemstone.

Will sat on a stool by the bed with a bowl on his lap. He fed the hare tiny amounts of water from a dropper to prevent her from becoming too dehydrated.

The Queen of the Fairies stood at the foot of the bed, her shoulders relaxed, her arms loose by her sides. Celestina's eyes were fixed on the light at the heart of the emerald. Green vapour floated out over the hare and the anguished expression melted away until Cassandra's face took on a more tranquil appearance. The Queen crossed the room and opened the casement window. "Come, my little Corncobbers. We're in need of your help."

There was a faint tinkling of bells which heralded the arrival of a host of tiny fairies who flew in through the window. They were dressed in yellow gossamer and wore coronets studded with topaz. On their ankles were garlands of dainty flowers intertwined with ribbons and bells and they flew in formations of furious intensity to a faultless choreography.

Throughout these lightning-fast manoeuvres, the Corncobbers played on fiddles and lyres while they sang songs of rebirth and regeneration in twittering, birdlike harmonies. The notes swirled out around them in shining cascades of minims, crochets, quavers and semibreves.

The leader landed on the pillow by the hare's head. She held her fiddle and bow in one hand and conducted the floating notes with the other.

The Queen drew a wand from the folds of her flowing gown. She murmured an incantation and focussed on the wand which she held in front of her. The fairies stopped playing but continued their mesmerising flying display. The notes finally came to rest on the hare and she was soon covered in a healing blanket of music. The leader of the fairy orchestra was joined by the others who formed a circle round the patient.

Celestina bowed to the conductor then addressed the throng. "Thank you all. Cassandra might not have survived without your music. May I keep these notes in case she has need of them again?"

The Corncobbers nodded in unison and the leader pointed to the bedside cabinet. The top drawer opened silently.

The fairies took a collective deep breath and exhaled gently. The notes rose from the bed and swirled into the drawer which closed smoothly behind them.

They curtsied to the Queen and, in a whirr of wings, flew out of the window back to their homes in the maize fields of the Sapphire Valley.

The cuts on the hare's body had healed and there wasn't a scar to be seen. Cassandra's coat was shiny and healthy again and rhythmic snores indicated she was sleeping soundly.

"Whatever she has to tell us will have to wait," said Celestina. "She needs complete rest to recover from the trauma."

Indigoletta flexed her wings. "A job well done, Your Majesty. Do you think the music may help ease her sorrow over the loss of her children?"

"I think we'll find a gradual improvement. Their music works on many levels. Look at young Will."

The Attendant to the Royal Raven sat with his eyes closed and a blissful expression on his face. "I've never heard anything so beautiful," he said dreamily.

"So you've not come across Corncobbers before," said the raven. "Sightings of them are rare. They're reclusive, private souls. You'll never hear more accomplished musicians and they hardly ever perform for anyone who isn't one of their own."

"Aye, Indigoletta, and I'm most grateful they always come when I need them. I'll leave orders for Cassandra to be protected round the clock. I've had the cellars searched and the tunnels sealed. The last thing any of us needs is a horde of scrablings finding their way into the palace. I must go now for there's much to be done." Celestina paused on her way out. "Ask Martha Snowberry to prepare one of her special vegetable broths, Will. The dear beast will be ravenously hungry when she wakes, and make sure the nurses know about our glittery friends in the drawer."

Alfie dismounted and tied the pony's reins to a tree by the entrance to Sammy's cave. There was a pail of fresh water, a tidy heap of hay and a neat stack of apples and carrots. Jock flew down from the upper branches where he'd been watching out for the elf in his distinctive Lincoln green.

"Courtesy of SSS. He thought Celia might appreciate some refreshments."

"How typically thoughtful and when he's so busy." The elf gave the pony a friendly slap on the withers. Celia took a mouthful of hay and whinnied her appreciation.

"How's it going, WAE? Did you manage to persuade Pogo to move into the palace with the others?"

"She didn't take much convincing, I'm pleased to say, and Pongo was delirious with joy to be going as well. He's fair taken with his new friends and I dread his reaction when it's time for them all to go home again. Kismet tells me security at the Palace is tighter than ever."

Jock tidied the white feathers on his chest. "That's as it should be with scrablings on the loose. Wherever those little pests are, you can be sure there's a snaglip not far behind. Great blundering oafs, but they can't half do some damage when they get going."

Their attention was caught by loud cawing above their heads. A squadron of magpies and jays wheeled in tight formation and flew out over Moonglow Lake.

"Let's get on in. Sammy's waiting for us. You've brought the cowrie shell?"

"It never leaves my side these days."

The Royal Steed came to a halt before the Great Daria Gate and Wainscot raised a paw in greeting. The sentry imp looked down from the watchtower and back at a scroll of paper containing a list of names. There was none of that self-important, overblown nonsense, those exchanges that go something like:

"Who goes there?"

"The Royal Steed."

"Password?"

"McGillicuddy's jodhpurs."

"That was last week's."

"I'm losing my patience."

"Oh, it's you, Kismet, why didn't you say so?"

"I *did* say so."

Instead, the sentry greeted the Royal Steed politely and read the roll-call loud and clear, ending with "One gaudily attired crustacean in a silver receptacle bearing the royal seal and I don't mean a water-dwelling mammal with flippers and a tiara."

Kismet chuckled. "I have two others with me who won't need clearance."

"That'll be Pogo Pixie and Pongo the dog."

"You're no slouch," declared 'the dog'. "You're not by any chance related to a certain imp?"

Malcolm laughed, doffing his feathered hat to reveal an explosion of scarlet hair. "Will's my cousin. Welcome to the Palace."

Pigsblanket was concealed in a dense patch of scrub, keeping a safe distance between himself and the ferocious gorse bushes which grow in abundance on the rocky outcrops around the palace.

The arrival of the Royal Steed with his mixed cargo of passengers offered the lad an opportunity too good to pass up. Here was his entry ticket to the palace if ever there was one, but could he pull it off? The direct approach was not an option; there were too many variables which were likely to result in failure. His ragged clothes and battered, punchbag of a face were two obvious stumbling blocks.

He listened attentively to the exchange between Kismet and Malcolm and decided his best option would be to stow

away on the Sylvanian Forest Cat. Not such a ridiculous plan since he wasn't much heavier than a mound of marshmallows and the cat was large, well-nourished and extremely hairy.

The decision was made for him when the iron door within the Great Daria Gate swung open and Kismet broke into a trot. Pigsblanket hurled himself out of the bushes, with Conchita pressed against his injured ribs. He made a desperate grab for Kismet's mane and slipped behind a curtain of soft fur.

Will was waiting by the fountain in the inner courtyard. "Brilliant," he declared, rubbing his hands together. "I couldn't believe you were here already when my cousin sent word. You made very good time, Kismet."

The fairy mouse laughed. "And we picked up an extra passenger along the way."

"What extra passenger?"

"That ragamuffin hiding in your chest wig, Kizz." Wainscot was delighted with herself. "The cheeky article hitched a lift outside the gate. Us fairy mice never miss a trick. You might as well come out now."

Will peered up at the cat's furry chest.

Pigsblanket willed himself invisible which was a pretty pointless exercise. He reluctantly lowered himself hand over hand and landed in front of the imp.

"What have you got to say for yourself?" The boy didn't flinch before Will's steady gaze. "You're likely to spend the rest of your life behind bars unless you have a very good reason for sneaking in here like this."

The others were already disembarking with the help of a small deputation from Twitchett's Impfantry and Pigsblanket couldn't help staring at Lorimer in his spangled bathing suit as he was carried past shoulder-high. The lobster anxiously clung to the rim of his silver bucket while Pongo bustled around underneath. "Steady now. Don't drop him. You're spilling water all over the place."

The foot soldiers weren't used to receiving instructions from a dog and grumbled their disapproval.

Pigsblanket decided to leap straight in before the situation became any more bizarre. "I know where Leo is."

"That's a pretty good reason," said the irrepressible pooch. "You may escape the slammer after all."

Will stood his ground. "Why should I listen to a load of old flannel from a rag-bag like you?"

"That's a fair point, sir. In your position I wouldn't believe me either."

The imp's face softened. "So where exactly is Leo?"

"He's being held prisoner on 'The Cheeky Monkey'. The Giant Rat's there too. Grimshaw's aiming to sail as soon as there's a window in the weather. I jumped ship to come here for help. If you won't believe me, I'm as good as dead. The Captain doesn't take kindly to desertion and betrayal, particularly when it's his own cabin boy stabbing him in the back."

Pogo approached the wretched lad and looked him over with the experienced eye of a mother. "If we don't rally round you'll be dead before he notices you've gone. I take it Grimshaw's responsible for the state you're in." Pigsblanket mouthed an emotional 'yes'. "Let's get you inside. Food, a hot bath and someone to take a look at those wounds is what you need. I'll take full responsibility. I reckon we can trust…" She smiled encouragingly.

"Pigsblanket," he said with tangible embarrassment.

"That's some name," said Pongo. "I don't imagine you get many of them to the pound."

"At his weight you probably do," said Jamie, sniffing the air. "Is that a parrot you have in your pocket, Pigsblanket?"

The boy's hand went instinctively towards Conchita who was sitting patiently inside his coat.

"Don't worry. I'm not in the habit of eating parrots. They're too tough and stringy in my experience."

Pongo wasn't the only one holding his breath to see what the cat would come up with next.

Jamie paused just long enough to enjoy the effect of his words but didn't overcook it. "I simply can't resist alliteration after an anxious altercation and I've never had so much as a morsel of parrot."

The impact of Pigsblanket's disclosure finally hit home and Sandy clapped her hands impatiently. "What are we waiting for? We must rescue Leo and Gilbert at once."

"Hold your horses," Kismet said with calm authority. "Nobody's going anywhere without special clearance from the Royal Raven. Let's get you settled and feed this poor wretch before there's no longer any need. You'll let Indigoletta know about Leo, won't you, Will?"

The imp was already out of earshot, halfway up the spiral staircase that led to the Royal Raven's eyrie. Indigoletta was as good as on her way.

11

The old pixie sat by her daughter's grave. She often came to visit the spot and tend the flowers she'd planted all those long years before. Strictly speaking it wasn't a grave, for Feya had drowned and her body was never recovered but Kedda needed a focus for her grief and this was one of the child's favourite places. Feya's silver baby-bangle and a few of her toys were buried in a little casket under the Sylvanian pine where her mother would sit staring out to sea, sometimes for hours at a time.

The timber-framed cottage she shared with her husband Creel wasn't part of any hamlet but sat on a lonely stretch of beach below the cliffs north of Corvine. They were a solitary couple by choice and the child did not mix with others her own age. It would be fair to say they did everything they could to prevent it without her becoming too suspicious. Feya had never gone to school. Folks might have asked too many questions, not least of all how two pixies came to have a fairy child.

Creel rarely spent time by the grave and Kedda envied her husband's detachment although deep down she resented his contained, unemotional response to their daughter's death. It was as if he'd buried his grief with the casket containing Feya's treasures.

Their daughter was not a blood relative but that shouldn't have mattered. For years they'd longed for a baby and at last Kedda had provided one, not her own, but that had never mattered to her and she couldn't see why it should have bothered her spouse.

Creel had welcomed the arrival of the baby. Feya was bonny enough and filled the gaping hole in their lives. His wife was the most senior midwife in the royal household and had all the skills necessary for bringing up an infant. The provenance of the baby was not for discussion and Kedda wouldn't be drawn. "The less you know, the less you'll tell," she chided. "I don't want you blathering after a pint too many at The Staggering Parrot. Anyway, I swore to the baby's mother that her secret was safe with me and I'll not go back on my word." Creel was hurt by her lack of trust. He wasn't a drinker and rarely, if ever, frequented taverns.

In the end he stopped asking. What was the use of causing rows when they were glad to have the child? She brightened up their days and, like him, she loved the sea. He was an old-style fisherman, not part of any fleet, and he worked the inshore waters in a rowing boat with his own hand-crafted rods and nets. When Feya took her first wobbly steps they were towards Creel's boat; the child went fishing with him long before she formed her first words.

There's good money to be made in row-boating if you have the skill and the family always had a full larder and a cellar of top-quality coal, none of that cheap rubbish bought by the Jem Slacks of this world. His wife's position at the palace gave them respect from their peers, not that they cared about that. They were self-contained people but always polite in their dealings with others.

Creel couldn't remember when he first noticed the change in Feya. It was very gradual and Kedda always made excuses for the child and accused her husband of being overly strict. Perhaps he was too much of a disciplinarian

J.Milne

247

but he truly believed it was for the good of them all. In their isolation it was desirable they live in harmony and Feya's deteriorating behaviour was causing friction. What made it really difficult for Creel was that she rarely put a foot wrong in front of Kedda. When he and his wife were locked in bitter disagreement about how to deal with her, Feya often as not had a sly expression on her pretty face which instantly turned to tearful distress when her mother turned to look at her. Kedda would rush over to comfort the child and berate her husband for his intolerance and lack of compassion.

On their daily fishing trips Feya worked as before but she withdrew into herself and the easy camaraderie they'd shared gradually slipped away until Creel wished he could think of reasons why she should stay at home.

As the child grew up, the gap widened between Feya and her father and she became increasingly close to Kedda. When he walked into a room unexpectedly or came across them in the garden they would fall silent and he felt as if he had intruded in their private world. Feya had a furtive look about her and Creel could feel hostility radiating from her, something his wife never seemed to be aware of.

That precious hour at night when he sat on the verandah after supper reflecting on the day's activities was ruined for him when Feya regularly refused to go to bed at the appointed time. She threw tantrums that resulted in her mother siding with the child against Creel. What did it matter when she went to bed? She was at an awkward age. It was just a passing phase. Why was he so rigid and unyielding? Throughout these tirades Feya would stand behind her mother smiling with smug satisfaction.

Time passed but the child's behaviour didn't improve. She grew more and more difficult with the onset of adolescence and resorted to vicious kicking and biting when anything upset her. She rarely went row-boating which was a blessed relief to Creel who stayed out later because he hated coming home.

The balance of power in the household shifted too. More and more Feya took charge and Kedda slipped into the background. His wife laughed scornfully and accused him of being paranoid when he pointed this out to her. She was glad of her daughter's help after a busy day at the palace.

When Kedda fell ill, he was forced to take on extra responsibilities. Feya refused to do anything round the house which didn't involve looking after her mother. Her possessiveness towards Kedda reached the point where she suggested Creel move into the small bedroom so that she could take care of her properly.

There was something in Feya's cold, dark eyes which made it impossible for her father to stand his ground. When he managed to snatch a brief moment alone with his wife, Kedda urged him not to fret. It was for the best that Feya stayed with her at night. He needed proper rest if he were to cope with his work and the extra chores around the house. Besides, ill health caused her to sleep fitfully. When she did drop off she was plagued by nightmares and kept Feya awake talking in her sleep.

Creel felt guilty being caught in his own bedroom when Feya walked in unannounced with a tray of supper for Kedda. She pushed past her father before brusquely suggesting he ought to go and make his own meal. He wanted to slap her when she added that he had no right to tire Kedda out with his selfish demands. His wife smiled weakly but said nothing to contradict their daughter.

Life continued in this miserable way for Creel and with no improvement in his wife's health either. If he did manage to snatch a moment alone with her she seemed not to recognise him any more. When he suggested they call in a doctor Feya flew into a fury and locked herself in with

Kedda, refusing to come out until he swore on his wife's life that he'd do no such thing.

Kedda's disturbed nights became more frequent and he could hear her fearful sobbing through the walls in the early hours.

Creel's nerves were stretched to the limit and there came a point one dreadful night when he couldn't stand it any longer. Kedda was howling like an animal in pain. He could hear her begging Feya to make the monster go away. It was a close night when sleep was elusive even in the happiest households. Creel rose from his rumpled bed and went out onto the verandah to clear his head. He knew it was time to act. He'd been weak long enough and he resolved to fetch the doctor the following morning. The first Feya would know about it was when the physician stepped into the house.

He stood outside his wife's room listening to the waves breaking on the shore. There was always comfort to be had from the sound of the sea. Feya's voice drifted out through the open window. The words were reassuring and comforting but the tone made his flesh crawl. He crept closer and noticed a small gap in the curtain. The room was lit by two oil lamps although it was the middle of the night.

What Creel saw practically destroyed his sanity. Kedda was propped up on pillows with her head turned towards the wall. Her anguished cries were chilling. At the foot of the bed, shrouded in darkness, was a hunched, predatory shape. Feya was nowhere to be seen but he could hear her soothing words distinctly.

The monstrosity sprang onto the bed and scuttled towards Kedda on all fours. She begged for delivery from the ghastly apparition and called for her daughter in mounting distress. The hideous entity squatted beside Kedda and stroked her hair with long curled nails. "Feya's here mother, just like I always am. Don't fret now. Let me brush your hair, that will soothe your nerves."

250

The full horror of the situation struck Creel when the foul creature leapt off the bed and snatched the hairbrush from its usual place on the dressing table. It bounded back across the room and up onto the bed again.

Kedda begged to be left alone but to no avail.

"You wouldn't want me to break your neck now, would you? I thought not. Maybe that is a bit drastic. Perhaps I'll pull your fingernails out instead? What an ungrateful wretch you are when all I do is wait on you hand and foot. I've squandered my youth attending to your trivial needs." Kedda whimpered piteously. "What would you do without me? That swine of a husband won't take care of you. He'll turn you out on your ear and install a pretty young wife. You'll be left begging for fish heads at Corvine docks if he has his way."

Creel staggered back from the window and slumped onto the porch swing. He was appalled by what he'd seen and felt sick to death. The shock brought on acute paralysis. His mind raced but he was imprisoned in his own petrified body.

The grievous discovery pitched the fisherman to the edge of reason and, mercifully, he passed out shortly afterwards. At dawn he came to and found he could move again. Creel forced himself to look through the chink in the curtains, hoping to find that he'd been sleepwalking and the whole episode was nothing more than a particularly horrific nightmare.

Kedda lay staring at the ceiling, her eyes wide with fear while Feya sat calmly in the chair by her bed with a sweet smile on her lips. "There there, mother, have a little snooze. People can go mad if they're deprived of sleep and we wouldn't want that to happen. Next thing you know, you'll be seeing monsters at the end of the bed." She stretched lethargically and ran her fingers through waist-length dark hair. Feya closed her eyes and her head fell forward onto her chest.

251

In that instant Creel knew he must rid them of the curse that was their daughter. They were living in the presence of pure evil.

He crept back inside and crawled into bed to think.

Creel needed time to forge a plan that was flawless. Feya's suspicions must not be aroused by a change in his daily routine but time was not on his side. Somehow he had to get her away from the house. He knew Feya would insist on staying with Kedda unless he could come up with an irresistible reason why she should accompany him.

He rose at the usual time and washed. Throwing on some clothes, he forced down a bowl of mackerel porridge and went to collect his tackle from the outhouse.

The fisherman set off down the path to the beach with his customary shouted 'goodbye' but stopped halfway. If Feya was spying on him it would look as if he'd forgotten something. He turned and walked back to the cottage where he found his daughter in the kitchen decanting her home-brewed tonic for Kedda. She rounded on him. "What do you want? I thought you'd gone fishing. I don't need you under my feet today."

"I came back to let you know I'll be staying out tonight."

Feya was genuinely surprised. "Why would you want to do that?"

"I have my reasons."

"What will I tell mother?"

"She doesn't even know who I am these days, so why should you have to tell her anything?" Creel was apprehensive but he managed to keep his voice steady. "Right then, I'll see you tomorrow morning."

Feya grasped his arm and her fingers bit into his flesh. "Tell me what you're up to." Kedda's malevolent tormentor was watching him with undisguised loathing from behind her eyes. "You're sneaking off to fetch a doctor from Corvine, aren't you?"

"Of course not," he said, forcing himself to look away. "If you must know I'm mermaid watching."

His daughter laughed cynically. "What utter nonsense. Surely you can come up with a better story than that?"

Creel sensed she was wondering whether to believe him or not and might just be persuaded to take the bait. His daughter had been fascinated by tales of mermaids from an early age and had once come across one sitting on the Skellid rocks near the cove where he kept his boat. The mermaid dived into the sea when she saw Feya staring at her.

"I'm deadly serious. I spotted three of them yesterday when I was fishing off Cormorant Point. They were asleep on the rocks. I'm off to investigate and if they're still in the area I'll go back at dusk. Mermaids are always more active at night."

There was excitement in her voice when she spoke. "You wouldn't lie about something like that, would you?"

Creel strode off towards his boat and Feya called after him. "I'm coming with you."

"You can't do that, your mother needs you." It pained him to say those words after what he'd witnessed.

"She'll be fine. I'll leave her some food on a tray and give her a light sleeping draught. Wait for me down at the cove." Feya turned on her heel and ran back to the house.

Creel couldn't believe how easy it had been to get her away from Kedda. His legs were like jelly as he made his way towards the boat. He knew he had one chance only to get rid of her and he did have that vital element of surprise on his side. There must be no bungling when it came to the final act. The monster within would retaliate and take great pleasure in snapping his neck like a twig.

A short time later they were on the land side of the Skellids and Cormorant Point was clearly visible in the distance. He stopped rowing and shipped the oars. Feya, who hadn't said a word since they set out, demanded to know why they had come to a halt.

"I've fishing to do and queen shrimp are plentiful round here. We'll reach the point soon enough. It's a good place to have lunch and we can keep an eye out for mermaids at the same time."

She was angry and scowled her disapproval. "Why can't we go there straight away?" she asked peevishly. "You can fish any time."

"With Kedda indisposed we need to keep cash coming into the house."

"She's still on full pay."

"It's best not to rely entirely on the generosity of the Palace."

Feya shaded her eyes while she squinted at Cormorant Point. "Give me your telescope. I'll see if I can spot any mermaids."

Creel had deliberately left it behind but made a pretence of searching for the telescope among his kit. She grew angry when she realised it was nowhere to be found. He ignored her and cast his nets off the port side of the boat. Starved of any response without Kedda there to take her part, Feya sat in a childish huff staring at her feet.

The fisherman was buying time to crystallise the final details of his premeditated act of murder. The reality of what he was about to do disgusted him and Creel was barely able to control his body's desire to rid itself of that breakfast of mackerel porridge.

Feya's regressive, childlike demeanour disconcerted him. Could the pretty, sulking creature sitting opposite him really be so monstrous? Creel concentrated his mind on the demon he'd seen tormenting his wife to strengthen his resolve. Feya was nothing more than the outer shell that cloaked the foul being within. The grim reality was that Creel and Kedda had no daughter.

He'd laced his flask of tea with a stronger dose of the sedative Feya had given Kedda. It was undetectable but he planned to drink some too so as not to arouse her suspicions. He was banking on the fact that she'd be thirsty by the time they reached Cormorant Point. It was a hot, sunny day and she'd forgotten to bring a sunhat in her rush to join him.

Creel would sip his tea and tip it out when he had the opportunity. The longer they spent in the unrelenting heat the thirstier she would become which is exactly what happened and sooner than he'd hoped. Feya demanded something to drink when he was hauling the first netful of shrimp into the boat.

"Help yourself, can't you see I'm busy?"

She unscrewed the outer cup on the flask and placed it beside her, then took out the smaller, inner one. "I suppose you want some?" she asked ungraciously.

"I'll have half a cup," he said, "but I don't want us to run out."

"You begrudge me a cup of tea, do you?" Unwittingly Feya was playing into her father's hands.

He sighed. "Of course not. Take as much as you want."

Creel pretended not to notice the change in her and, pulling the last net onboard, set off for Cormorant Point.

He watched Feya gradually succumbing to the effects of the sedative. When he judged the time to be right he slowed the rhythm of his rowing right down until he'd stopped altogether.

"We're off Cormorant Point. Will you have some lunch?"

"Don't bother me now," she replied drowsily. "Maybe later."

Creel never once took his eyes from her in case the being within was still awake. How could he tell? It might well be toying with him for all he knew.

He carefully positioned one of the oars across his lap and bowed his head sorrowfully at what he was about to do if he were courageous enough to go through with it.

Feya lay with her head resting on the side of the boat, her long, dark hair spread out over her shoulder. In repose, she was lovely and Creel's heart ached at the sight of her. The parental love he'd felt for her surfaced violently. The curve of her mouth and the delicate thrust of her chin conjured up unwanted images of the young child when the monster inside was in its infancy.

He shook Feya to try to rouse her. "Leave me be," she moaned.

"You must wake up. There are mermaids over on the rocks."

Feya forced herself to sit up. "Whereabouts? I can't see them."

Creel stood over her with the oar resting across his arm. "They're up on the crags."

Feya yawned and struggled to her feet. "I don't know what's wrong with me, I'm so tired."

"Here, let me help you."

"I don't need your help," she said, pushing him away.

Creel seized the moment. He swung the oar with tremendous force and struck her across the temple. Feya didn't stand a chance in her drugged state and, with a howl of rage, fell backwards into the sea.

She was a strong swimmer but the blow to the head, in combination with the sedative and her wet clothes, caused her to panic. Incredulity at Creel's deliberate act only added to her state of angry confusion. "Don't you leave me here to drown, you murderer," she screamed, spitting out mouthfuls of water.

Creel rowed away from her and the adrenaline rush caused by what he'd done gave him extra strength. The evil entity devoured him with its foul, yellow eyes and the fisherman knew it would steal his sanity were it able to hold his gaze.

He kept rowing and didn't lift his head again for some time. When he did what he saw consumed him with horror. Feya's arms were raised above her head and her hands were clawlike.

With one final string of curses, in a snarling, savage voice from the pit of the damned, she sank beneath the waves. He continued rowing with his eyes fixed on the spot until he was sure she had drowned.

The bile rose in Creel's throat and he vomited until his ribs ached. Tears coursed down his face and he howled for the loss of the daughter he'd once loved so dearly.

12

"Mr Malahyde, where the devil are you and what have you done with the sea slug? Send him in here at once. You've monopolised him long enough."

The First Mate steadied himself with a belt from his hipflask and stepped into the cabin. "Don't get yourself in a state, Cap'n. Sit down and I'll fetch you a sloeberry rum."

Grimshaw smelt a rat and it wasn't Gilbert. "Is there something you want to tell me, Jedediah? Might it involve that brat Pigsblanket?"

Malahyde's hands were unsteady when he poured the liquor from the decanter. "Get this down you," he said, holding a brimming rummer towards the buccaneer.

Pestilence inspected the contents. "What you're about to tell me must be horrendous, judging by your generosity with my booze."

"Pigsblanket's gone missing. I waited as long as I could. It's murder on shore and the whole of Corvine's gone nuts, so anything could have happened to him."

The cabin boy's note was burning a hole in his pocket.

"Jedediah, what do you take me for? I didn't sail into Corvine on a giant cabbage leaf. Pigsblanket's jumped ship."

"I wouldn't say that..."

"He didn't leave a note, then?" Malahyde twitched guiltily. "Of course he bally well didn't! Deserters don't as a rule."

"He may yet turn up."

"We can't hang around to see if he does and he'd have to be a pretty good swimmer unless he commandeers someone else's rowing boat. The little blighter's likely to betray me. I should have silenced him when I had the chance."

"Who'll listen to the lad? He's not in the best shape."

Grimshaw had a dangerous glint in his eye. "Meaning what, Mr Malahyde?"

"I reckon he was sickening for something's all I meant."

"When I catch up with Pigsblanket, he'll wish he'd died a slow death of the plague. It would be preferable to what I'll do to him." Grimshaw drummed his fingers on the table. "We've got to leg it. Leo might yet be a valuable asset. Once we're clear of the harbour, chuck ratty overboard and, being as rats are renowned for their swimming abilities, make sure you wrap him in anchor chain. We don't want the old devil blabbing about the time he spent with puss on my brigantine."

Malahyde felt a stab of anxiety for Gilbert which mortified him. Somehow the galumphing great beast had managed to get under his skin. Was he getting soft? That didn't sit well with his self-image.

Jedediah crossed his fingers behind his back. "I'll see to it myself. We've some stout chain that'd sink a rat twice his weight."

"Make sure I have the best view on the ship. I can't think of anything more entertaining unless it were Pigsblanket and Gilbert going into the drink together."

The dragon was fast discovering how much he'd grown since leaving Maligna. With the increase in size came greater strength and a distinct improvement in his flame-throwing abilities. When he found obstacles blocking his way through the caves he was able to remove them easily with a slap of his tail or a thrust of his shoulder. In places he burned his way through old tree roots that impeded his progress. Cahoots could scarcely believe he'd been so small so recently.

The dragon reached the crack in the limestone that opened into the sinkhole and put his ear to the gap. He could hear his mother breathing rhythmically. He managed to dislodge some stones and squeeze his head through the opening.

"I'm back, Mother," he hissed. "I've something for you from Uncle Pestilence."

The Harpie was instantly awake. She eased herself onto the rock floor and ducked under the bed. Maligna lit a candle stub and found herself nose to nose with Cahoots. "Look at the size of you," she exclaimed.

The dragon was clearly agitated. "How am I going to get back into the sinkhole? I could blast my way through."

"There's no need for that. If you've brought what I think you have I'll be able to leave this dungeon. I'll take the parcel and you must wait for me at the northernmost tip of the island. I'll join you as soon as I can, darling one."

Cahoots was overjoyed to hear this and his head was swiftly replaced by the leg with the package attached to it.

The Harpie and the anklet were about to be reunited and she was shocked by the strength of its power. She carefully removed the package and crawled out from under the pallet.

Maligna shivered with anticipation as she unfolded the black velvet cloth. Spears of light shot out from the anklet and lit up the sinkhole. She hastily wrapped it up again and the dungeon returned to its former gloomy state.

The guards were too scared to investigate and huddled together over their game of peggity.

The Harpie experienced a surge in her depleted powers. It was time to take control of the anklet once more and bend it to her will. The long separation had increased its confidence and the roles of servant and master were dangerously blurred.

Maligna willed it inconspicuous and, removing the cloth, clasped it round her left ankle. It thrummed gently against her leg, indicating its acceptance of her control and then grew still.

The force of the volcano tore the dark heart out of the Island of Long Forgotten Dreams and spewed it into the sea. The sinkhole collapsed in on itself killing the two guards.

Cahoots flew out over the reef dodging rocky debris as it plunged through the waves which churned and boiled with molten lava. The dragon was in a desperate state as regards the fate of his mother. He was sure Maligna could not have survived the volcano and facing life without her was a bleak prospect indeed. So much for Uncle Pestilence's present.

When it was safe to do so he searched the island from the air and was distressed by the extent of the destruction above the dungeon. He made several circuits hoping to find Maligna miraculously unscathed.

Exhausted, Cahoots landed at the appointed meeting-place and gave himself up to unfettered grief. Tears poured down his scaly face and splashed into the sea.

"That's no way to behave," said an old grey seal lying on the rock opposite. "Come and give your mother a kiss."

The seal faded from view and in its place stood Maligna. She was taller than he remembered but the ragged dress was the same as before and she was still pale and gaunt.

Cahoots was overwhelmed and his sobbing increased.

His relief at finding her alive emphasised the enormity of his attachment to her and the horror of what he had so recently faced.

The dragon finally calmed down enough to ask how she'd managed to survive the volcano. He was also curious about her shape-shifting abilities but that could wait.

"I *was* the volcano. That present you brought helped me to escape. She pointed at the anklet and Cahoots sniffed it suspiciously.

"It's just a piece of jewellery, isn't it?"

"Don't ever be disrespectful. The anklet's a relentless, unforgiving enemy. You're only young so it will make allowances for you."

The dragon's face grew serious. "I meant no offence. Please tell it I'm sorry."

"The anklet understands everything anyone says or thinks in its presence. It senses your fear at this very moment."

Cahoots tried to banish dangerous thoughts to the back of his head and replace them with mindless trivia.

"Don't distress yourself. It can't harm you without my permission. Now let's take our leave of this sorry place. They'll think I was destroyed by the volcano which gives me a huge advantage over my enemies." She clapped her hands together and Cahoots noticed the jaundiced talons had gone. Her fingers were slim and elegant. "I'd like you to fly me to Corvine. I have urgent business with Pestilence Grimshaw."

"Jock Craw delivered it personally," said Will, handing Pogo the letter from Alfie. "There have been some new developments we could well do without, and who booked the volcano?"

"The roaring sound earlier was a volcano?"

"There's been an eruption on the Island of Long Forgotten Dreams of all places."

Pogo sank back into the cushions on the couch. Her face was grey as watery porridge. "I've been worried about something like this happening. I've had this unshakeable sense of dread." She fingered the letter nervously. "Where are the others?"

"I left them settling into their new accommodation. Lorimer and Pongo were off for a dip in the guest spa with Peg Leg. Sandy plans to join them when she's finished unpacking."

The pixie settled down to read the letter but her concentration was broken by a kerfuffle outside. Indigoletta flew in through the open window with Jock and Crawford. She settled on the back of a chair with the two crows flanking her.

"Dire news, I'm afraid, but then you know that already." The raven inclined her head towards the letter in Pogo's hand. "Scrablings in a cupboard at 'Woodburn'. That portal has been sealed off for an age of ages. I'm ashamed to say most of us had forgotten it even existed. Ralph wants Sandy and Jamie home immediately and Her Majesty is of the same mind."

The pixie gazed at a distant point on the intricately patterned rug, trying to make sense of what was unfolding in front of her. She raised her head and looked right into Indigoletta's fearsome eyes. "The Harpie's escaped, hasn't she?"

The air was sucked out of the room, right down to the very last gasp, and Pogo's words echoed eerily in the vacuum.

The Royal Raven had grown in stature and exuded an awesome, formidable power. The purest white light flowed out from her and enveloped Jock and Crawford, turning the trio into one phenomenal entity.

Indigoletta's impassioned response rattled the windowpanes and the crystal in the chandeliers. "Maligna will *never* prevail!"

Pongo had nipped back to the bathroom to fetch a towel for Sandy who was enjoying a swim in the spa. He'd promised to enquire about Leo and Gilbert's imminent rescue and was on the point of doing so when he caught a snatch of the Royal Raven's words which stopped him in his tracks. Sandy and Jamie were to return to 'Woodburn' at once. The dog sank to the floor in an agony of disbelief but there was no mistaking what he'd heard. White light was streaming out of the main living area and he baulked at the sight and sound of Indigoletta.

The dog grabbed a fluffy towel from the pile in the bathroom and bounded back to the spa taking care not to trip over it as he ran along.

Sandy dried herself and followed Pongo to the rest area where Jamie was curled up on one of the loungers.

"There's nothing for it, we'll have to go back," said the cat matter-of-factly and, registering the dog's stunned expression, swiftly added, "I'd rather we didn't have to, of course."

"We have no other choice," Sandy said miserably. "If that's what Dad wants, and the others agree, then what else can we do?"

Pongo rubbed his nose against her leg sympathetically. "What about Leo? You said you'd never leave without him."

"I meant that."

"And there's Gilbert, too."

"I know, but I can't defy everyone."

"You won't have to defy anyone if you get a move on."

Sandy's eyes lit up like sparklers and common sense was sent to the back of the queue. "If we do a bunk *before* they tell us we have to go home then, technically, we haven't defied anyone."

"Now you're talking, let's burn rubber."

"Give me a minute, boy. I can't go like this." She dashed off towards the changing rooms.

Jamie was far from happy. "I'm here to take care of Sandy and help her find Leo, but this really does smack of irresponsibility on my part if I go along with your hare-brained scheme."

"She'll only go without you," said the dog in a 'so there' sort of tone.

The Siamese cat's tail twitched angrily. "Don't threaten me with that."

"It's not a threat. It's a fact."

"I know that," said the cat with resignation. "But you shouldn't have egged her on."

Sandy rushed back to join them, brimful of derring-do.

"I'm not sure whether I'm glad you're wearing Vince and Florin or not. I hope they haven't given you a false sense of security."

"Be fair, Jamie," said the kilt. "We're here to protect her and that's what we'll do."

"Vince is right," said Florin emphatically. "Now then, what's the plan?"

Pongo gave one of his endearing, trademark grins. "I forgot that little detail in all the excitement."

Creel watched billowing plumes of ash rise over Long Forgotten Dreams from the headland above the beach. The island was a grey shape against the horizon but he could clearly see the unfolding disaster against the darkening sky.

The old fisherman had been there most of the day, lost in memories, his mind taken up with long-suppressed thoughts of Feya. He was sitting under the Sylvanian pine by the carpet of flowers that marked her grave.

Kedda didn't understand her husband's closed-off emotions. In her freely-given opinion a burden of grief was something to be shared and she couldn't make sense of his quiet detachment.

He was a reluctant visitor to the spot, usually when his wife's carping got the better of him. Creel would snatch up his hat, slam out of the cottage and trudge off up the cliff path to get away from her constant reminders of what had been.

Today was different. He had chosen to be there, hoping to rid himself of his increasing preoccupation with Feya by confronting his guilt.

Depression and ill-health had chipped away at Kedda and she rarely felt strong enough to take on the steep, winding path, something for which Creel was profoundly grateful. The terrible secret he'd kept from her weighed him down and the shadows lengthened in his heart with the passing years.

Kedda's mind had been wiped clean of the sinister side of life with Feya and the months of mental torture were nothing more than fragments of barely remembered nightmares. Hardly a day passed without her recounting some anecdote or other about their beautiful, headstrong daughter.

Creel pulled his hat down over his ears. He wiped his eyes with his sleeve and reached for the binoculars on the bench beside him. He trained them on an object above the reef which slowly swam into focus.

He was amazed to see a dragon flying towards him from the north west. The fisherman watched fascinated as the beast drew nearer. It flew over his head, briefly obliterating the sun. Creel's heart lurched when the hunched creature on its back turned and looked straight at him. The binoculars fell to the ground and he covered his face with his hands.

Minxie stood on the gun deck of 'The Cheeky Monkey' watching Cahoots circle over the brigantine. His landing was faultless, considering he was carrying his first passenger.

Maligna stepped down from the dragon's shoulders.

The buccaneer rushed forward, his arm extended, but she merely gazed at him impassively, refusing to take the proffered hand.

Undeterred by the snub, he bowed extravagantly. "Captain Pestilence Grimshaw, at your service, now and forever more, dear lady. I've waited a very long time for this pleasure."

"*No one* has waited for anything longer than I have." The Harpie's black, featureless eyes slipped past him and settled on the wazwatt. "Minxie, it's good to see you outside the confines of that stinking prison."

"Likewise," said the grey furry one. "You're in better shape than you were but that frock doesn't do anything for you. To be honest, it makes you look dowdy."

Grimshaw aimed his boot at the wazwatt but Maligna restrained him so violently he almost fell over. The buccaneer laughed uncertainly. No one had dared take him on before.

"Don't ever do anything like that again," she hissed through gritted teeth.

Minxie could sense the pirate's confusion and thought she detected the first signs of fear.

The dragon was so pleased to see the wazwatt he missed the incident altogether. Minxie struggled to free herself

269

from his scaly embrace. "Steady on, furnace face, you're suffocating me."

"No need for introductions there then," said Maligna with a thin-lipped smile.

"Minxie helped me find my way out of the caves," he said eagerly. "I couldn't have done it without her, Mum."

The wazwatt stared at Cahoots. "There's something wrong with my ears, I could swear you just called Maligna 'Mum'."

"He did and I am, is that a problem?"

Minxie realised frostbite was an option if she persisted on that tack. "Absolutely not. Why don't we go below deck and see if we can find you something to wear? It'll be a challenge in this all-male establishment."

"Don't trouble yourself. I'd forgotten I was wearing this disgusting rag." The Harpie snapped her fingers and the torn frock was exchanged for white, flowing robes trimmed with grey mink-like fur.

"Wow, you look fabulous!" said the dragon with an appreciative puff of smoke.

Minxie was furiously comparing her own fur to that on the Harpie's ensemble. "I'd have thought black was more your style."

"Too predictable. In any case, I've spent enough time deprived of light. I see you're interested in the trim, Minxie. You'll be relieved to hear it's fake wazwatt. Very realistic and an identical colour match."

The little beast took to the air and flew round the Harpie to see for herself. "That is good and in better condition than mine. I'm a bit rough round the edges just now, what with one thing and another."

Pestilence Grimshaw found himself in a supporting role on the ship where he was usually centre stage and couldn't think of a single line to give himself. He had expected gratitude at the very least from Maligna;

instead he was treated to contempt bordering on outright loathing.

Drooling, dribbling spectres of evil shuffled towards the palace. Crouched on the slates, wriggling along the gutters, lurking in dark corners on the battlements. Celestina could feel them closing in. They couldn't harm her, but their gloating presence was a distraction. The Fairy Queen knew she had to fight, possibly to the death, to save her people.

Long Forgotten Dreams was not a volcanic island. Maligna had most likely caused the eruption to mask her escape so it was fair to assume the Harpie and the anklet were back together again.

In the silence of her private chambers the Queen faced the full implications of defeat at the hands of this powerful adversary and what it would mean for her subjects should she fail them. Daria, her mother, had been the ultimate force for good and she'd barely managed to defeat Maligna before dying of the wounds inflicted upon her by the Harpie.

Celestina was half the age her mother had been when she took on the creature and half as experienced. She sat by the mullioned windows overlooking Corvine harbour, knowing Maligna was out there somewhere preparing to unleash her wrath.

All non-essential members of the household had been sent home or were in the underground bunker accommodation. Tabitha and her nurse were there too. Hamish insisted on staying with his wife and she'd reluctantly agreed to this if he swore he would escape with their child should the Harpie look like winning.

The Queen's heart was aching at the thought of never seeing her daughter again. She rested her head on the back of the chair and, closing her eyes, indulged in a moment of self-pity.

Celestina wasn't sure when she first became aware of the scent of bluebells in the room. The perfume wrapped around her and she grew stronger with every inhalation. She rose from the chair and followed the fragrance across the room to its source on the dressing-table.

An unfamiliar glass bottle sat on its own in front of her other toiletries. The stopper lay beside it. The Queen lifted the bottle to her nose and breathed in the glorious aroma. She had a vision of herself as a child skipping along beside her mother who was gathering armfuls of bluebells. They were Daria's favourite flowers, something she'd long since forgotten.

The Fairy Queen was filled with a renewed determination and resolved there and then to take the fight to the Harpie and not wait for Maligna to make the first move.

Lorimer scuttled across the marble floor of the spa with Peg Leg flying sedately above him. The lobster was agitated which conveniently took the heat off Pongo who was fresh out of escape plans.

"Thermidor saw something nasty through that big grating at the far end of the pool where the water's pumped in. How many eyes did it have?"

"Too many," said the crustacean, nervously pinging a strap on his swimsuit. "Ooh, it was awful."

"One look at you and the poor thing couldn't get away quick enough," said the gull ruefully. "I expect it was those goggles of yours or that scary bathing costume you've got on."

"What's scary about a bathing suit with a three-dimensional picture of me on it?"

"You need to ask? Two for the price of one is way too much for most of us. Consider those poor souls who're meeting you *both* for the first time."

"Shoosh, you two," said Pongo, in full bustle mode. "I think you've just solved the problem of how we're going to get out of here."

"I don't want to leave. I love it here," said the lobster, scooping up his towel with the royal crest on it. "Besides we've only just arrived."

"Pongo overheard the grown-ups saying Sandy and I have to go back to 'Woodburn' right away and, despite my better judgment as 'chaircat', the assembled committee has decided we'll do the mature thing and run away."

"Not without us," said the gull, "We signed up for the total experience."

"No question about that," said Lorimer, chucking the towel over his shoulder. "Have I time to pack an overnight bag?" This was met with disbelieving looks, an angry accordion of pleats and sporran gestures best left to the imagination.

"That's a 'no', is it?" Lorimer tried to hide his disappointment. "I'll just fling on my St Andrew's flag cozzie. It's confidence-building and might come in handy if we find ourselves in difficulty. Solidarity of clothing and all that."

Peg Leg cackled with mirth. "The kilt, the sporran and the bathing-suit. I can see the headlines now."

Pongo herded the little group towards the deep-end of the pool. "Right, you lot, it's time we vamoosed."

Lorimer was still fazed from his scary eyes experience and was eventually flung in at the deep end when all other forms of persuasion failed.

Jamie stood at the edge of the pool. "What do you think? Is it feasible to go out that way?"

"I don't see any immediate problems, or eyes, thankfully."

Peg Leg joined the lobster and they both peered through the grating. There were sluice gates to control the flow of water in and out of the spa, and a raised walkway shadowed the culvert.

Queen Celestina's decree to seal the tunnels meant no one could come in. It didn't prevent anyone from trying to get out.

Sandy crouched down on the wet tiles and took hold of the top of the grating. She gave it a good rattle followed by a quick chug to see how secure it was. It came away easily and flew up in the air with Sandy still attached. She staggered backwards and knocked Pongo into the pool.

Jamie jumped clear. "For pity's sake, child, you nearly had my eye out."

"You don't know your own strength," said Florin. "Vince'll need counselling if you carry on like that. He can't bear being made to feel inadequate."

The kilt rustled with irritation and Sandy giggled. "I thought the grating was screwed onto the tiles but it just slots in."

"Makes cleaning and maintenance easier," said Pongo, treading water. "I don't suppose you fancy getting your tootsies wet, Jamie. You can sit on my head if you like."

"Don't be ridiculous. I'm not that precious. What you're doing doesn't look that difficult." The Siamese cat dived into the pool and, stifling a gasp, managed to pull the whole thing off pretty well considering he'd never had a swimming lesson in his life.

Pongo was a panting paddle-steamer, all froth and curls. "That's it, Jamie, keep those paws moving, doggy paddle's always served me well enough."

Sandy was last through. She clambered in feet first and reached for the grating which slotted back into place with a satisfying clunk.

She waded towards the others, who were waiting for her up on the walkway, wondering what on earth they were going to do next and wishing she'd not been quite so headstrong or impulsive.

The Attendant to the Royal Raven pushed his way through the swing doors that led to the guest spa. The imp was struck by the lack of noise; no yells, no splashing, in fact virtual silence.

Discarded towels lay in damp heaps on the tiles and the water in the pool was still agitated from recent activity.

Will called out and his words came back at him from the polished granite walls. The spa had been vacated so recently he almost convinced himself he could hear the dying echo of their voices. There was only one way in and one way out, and he hadn't passed anyone.

The imp headed back to the guest suites to see if they were there. Indigoletta would be hopping mad if she were kept waiting. Her temper wasn't at its best and Will knew she didn't relish having to break the news to Sandy and Jamie of their imminent departure.

"Well, where are they?" she asked briskly.

"I'm afraid I don't know, ma'am."

The raven's feathers were spiky with irritation. "What do you mean by that?" she snapped.

"I can't find any of them. Actually, that's not strictly true. Pigsblanket and Conchita are fast asleep in one of the bedrooms but other than that the guest wing's deserted."

"Impossible!" she barked. "Look again and this time more thoroughly."

Will was stung by her tone and the raven was immediately ashamed of herself for being so tetchy. "I'm sorry, that was rude of me."

The imp smiled warmly. "That's OK, ma'am. I'll give it another go but I'm pretty sure they're not here."

"No need, Will, I'm sorry I doubted you. Run and tell Twitchett I want the whole complex searched from top to bottom. They can't have gone very far."

13

"I want you to put to sea at once," said the Harpie. "You must take puss to a safe hideout until I need him. Meanwhile, I have unfinished business to take care of up at the palace."

The buccaneer looked doubtful. "There's another storm brewing. I hope we can make it through the reef. The weather's been crazy recently."

"You'll just have to risk it. There's a battalion of uniformed imps assembling on the docks. Most likely a boarding party heading your way."

"Pigsblanket must have squealed, I should have done for him long ago."

"You're a sham, Grimshaw. Where's that ruthlessness you've built your reputation upon? Believe you me, it's the only way."

Cahoots landed with a thump at Maligna's feet. "I've had a brilliant time flying with Minxie. She's taught me lots of tricks. Watch this." The dragon flipped upside down and zoomed round the Harpie at waist level. "Look out, here she comes now," he yelled, still the wrong way up but managing to put a safe distance between himself and the wazwatt.

Minxie smacked into the Harpie, catching her right between the shoulder blades. Maligna didn't flinch but the air whooshed out of Grimshaw like a burst balloon. Surely there could be no doubt the little pest had overstepped the mark this time?

"Crumbs!" said the wazwatt, righting herself. "I'm terribly sorry, I was blown off course at the last minute."

The Harpie was furious until she saw the dragon rolling around on the deck consumed with mirth, and Minxie's expression of impertinent horror dampened the flames of her anger.

The buccaneer had the temerity to take her on. "What was that you were saying about ruthlessness?"

Maligna's eyes narrowed until they were glittering, black slits. "Have a care, Pestilence, or I might show you what ruthless really means. You're dangerously close to being surplus to requirements."

The way she spat out his name made Grimshaw's flesh crawl.

Minxie flew past the pirate and hissed, "Not so self-important now." She landed beside Maligna. "If it's all right with you, I'd like to catch up with Gilbert and Leo."

"What a good idea. Send for them at once."

The wazwatt treated the buccaneer to a sly, sideways glance. "They're under lock and key as it happens."

Grimshaw wanted to strangle her, something not lost on the Harpie. "Lay one finger on Minxie and I'll tear your hand off." She called out to the Bosun who had just come on deck. "Release the prisoners at once."

Leitzoff quailed at the sight of the Harpie and looked to Grimshaw for guidance.

"Do as she says," snarled the buccaneer.

"You what, Cap'n?"

"Fetch the cat and the scabby rat," he bawled, lashing out at Leitzoff and biting a chunk out of his own tongue in the process.

Maligna snorted. "That's more like it! Will you issue the orders to sail or shall I?"

He did before she could.

The rodent arrived shortly afterwards with Leo following on.

Minxie grinned at Gilbert and waved a paw in the vague direction of the cat who was watching a dust devil whirl across the deck in front of him. "Have you two met Maligna?" Her feigned innocence was barely concealed. "She's a friend of Captain Grimshaw."

The tall figure in the flowing white robes had her back to the rodent. Gilbert rushed forward to greet her as she turned to look at him. The rat bowed and beckoned his pal towards him. "I'm Gilbert and this is my wee chum, Leo. That's an interesting name you have..." The rat was mid sentence when he saw her eyes for the first time. "Dear me, I quite forgot what I was saying, what an empty-headed ninny."

"Ninny?" The Harpie's voice was toneless.

The rat tittered nervously. "I meant me, of course."

"No change there then," said Minxie impudently.

Leo had never seen a living being with blank eyes like a Greek statue in an unremitting shade of black. The only way he could tell whether she was engaging with him or not was from the angle of her head.

"The infamous little cat from Irvine. You've caused quite a stir by all accounts. Don't you have anything to say for yourself?"

Leo didn't respond. The eyes had done for him.

"Don't tell me the cat's got the cat's tongue." The smile was glacial. "We'll just have to get acquainted some other time. I'll send for you when I need you, in the meantime Captain Grimshaw will take care of you. If there are any complaints, refer them to me." She nudged the buccaneer's arm. "Keep Leo under constant surveillance but no locking him up when my back's turned."

"I can't wait for her back to be turned," mumbled the rat.

"You find my eyes unsettling, Gilbert?"

Leo went to the aid of his bumbling sidekick. "Don't mind him. He often opens his mouth and lets his brains rattle."

The dust devil was growing in size behind the Harpie and had already taken on the characteristics of a mini tornado. Maligna's hair blew about in snakelike tendrils and her billowing robes flapped against her meagre frame.

Deckhands ran hither and thither as the Bosun issued orders. Matelots scampered up the rigging to unfurl the sails. They shrieked and hollered like over-excited cockatoos as they ran along the spars, nimble as circus tightrope walkers. The sails, dyed to match the ship's turquoise, pink and canary yellow paintwork, billowed and swelled in the wind. 'The Cheeky Monkey' swung to starboard and pulled against her moorings. The brigantine was ready to put to sea.

"We could do with a torch or something. I can't see my hand in front of my face."

Pongo snorted. "Don't you mean your sporran in front of your kilt?"

"It's a good thing your faithful stars decided to tag along," said Lorimer from his comfortable position on Sandy's back where he hung like a rucksack.

"They did?"

Jamie's voice came out of the dark. "Isn't that them forming a halo above your head?"

"Why so they are," she exclaimed. The stars quickly regrouped into a jaunty 'hello'.

"Clever wordplay," said the cat, acknowledging their collective intelligence.

The stars spelt out a neat 'thank you'.

"D'ye think you might make yerselves useful for a change and stop showing off? I cannae see too well in the dark and Sandy's already made her position plain."

The stars rushed ahead and formed themselves into the stellar equivalent of a strong torchbeam.

"Now yer talking. How's that for you, Vince? Do try tae keep up."

The kilt didn't dignify Florin's jibe with an answer.

Peg Leg returned from his sortie through the tunnel. "It doesn't look too bad up ahead. We can press on for now and, before you ask, Thermidor, I haven't seen any eyes."

Sandy reached behind her and gave the lobster's tail a reassuring tweak. "D'you think we've been missed yet? I've lost all track of time."

"You betcha," said Pongo. "Indigoletta wasn't about to waste a moment packing you off home. She had more than enough on her plate as it was and now some volcanic eruption's added itself to her list of problems."

Sandy was regretting her impetuous behaviour. "They're probably worried sick. I should have left a note telling them not to panic."

"A fat lot of good that would have done," said Pongo pragmatically. "They'd still be up to high doh."

"At least they'd realise we haven't been abducted."

"Let's hope they think that's exactly what's happened to us," said the Siamese, dodging a puddle. "If the Royal Raven knew we'd scarpered to avoid being sent home she'd be livid."

Pongo was loving every second of it. "We're in for a severe ticking-off when this is over. It'll be tail between legs and no mistake. I'm pretty good at grovelling."

"You've had a lot of practice no doubt."

"Shssh, I thought I heard something moving up ahead," hissed the kilt.

"Stay where ye are and I'll have a dekko," urged Florin in a stage whisper.

"How do you propose to do that unless Sandy and I come with you?"

"And we're not about to do that, are we, Vince?"

The gull took to the air and flew silently round the next corner, leaving them all frozen to the spot. The stars turned themselves off, plunging the little group into pitch darkness.

"Good plan, twinklies," whispered Pongo, "if a tad unnerving."

"At least you can see in the dark," said Sandy, crouching down to give him a cuddle.

"Trust me, that's not always a good thing."

Lorimer tightened his grip round Sandy's neck. She stifled a cough and struggled to loosen his claws.

The blackness pressed in on them and they moved closer together in the claustrophobic silence.

Cassandra listened to the conversation going on around her. The hare felt groggy and lay on her side with her eyes closed. The infirmary staff were discussing the disappearance of the girl from Irvine and her friends while they were cavorting in the guest spa.

"I ask you, where could they have gone?" said one of the nurses, smoothing the blanket of notes which was playing a soporific melody to comfort the beast. "There's such a to-do but no one's found a trace of them."

The other nurse leant across Cassandra and pulled her colleague towards her. "Have you heard the latest rumour? They say Maligna the Harpie has escaped."

"Never!"

The hare's eyes snapped open.

"Hello dear," said the first nurse, "how are you feeling? You've had a rough time."

"I'll warm up some broth for you," said the other. "You'll need to build up your strength."

Cassandra's voice was weak and reedy. "Has Maligna really managed to escape?"

"So they say, but don't you worry about that. You're safe here with us."

"I'm not worried for myself," said the hare quickly.

"Good for you," said the nurse, patting Cassandra's head. "You're a very special patient, you know. The Queen doesn't invite help from corncobbers for just anyone."

At the mention of Celestina, Cassandra grew agitated. "You must tell Her Majesty the cat from Irvine's on Grimshaw's brigantine, I saw him with my own eyes."

"Keep your hair on." The nurse chortled at her unintended pun. "That's old news, I'm afraid. Was there anything else, dearie?"

Cassandra slumped back on the bed. She'd nearly died conveying a message no one wanted to hear.

Pigsblanket woke feeling better than he could ever remember. He was used to sleeping in a hammock in the most squalid conditions. The cotton sheets on this bed were crisp and smelt of fresh herbs.

The lad lay on his back staring at the ornate plaster mouldings on the ceiling and laughed out loud at the sight of Conchita perched on the chandelier, cleaning her beak on the sparkling crystal centrepiece.

The parrot's feathers were vibrant shades of scarlet, mauve and emerald and the boy almost didn't recognise her. The Conchita he knew was the faded colours of a long-dead,

283

stuffed bird that would have been right at home on a dusty shelf at The Mischief Maker.

"Look at you!" he exclaimed, grinning all over his face.

Pigsblanket braced himself for the customary pain when he swung his legs out of bed but his ribs were cradled in a loosely woven bandage of struntie fleece and he was able to stand up without even a twinge of discomfort.

The boy caught sight of himself in the full-length mirror. He was wearing a striped nightshirt.

"That can't be me," he said, rubbing his eyes. "I'm in an awful state."

Pigsblanket waved his arms around to check the data being presented to him but the mirror continued to show a boy of his age waving his arms around. He moved closer and peered at his reflection. The swelling had gone down and the bruises were barely visible; even the split lip had healed.

There was a knock and Will popped his head round the door. "Would you like a spot of breakfast?"

"Yes, please."

"And the parrot? I see she's polished off the bowl of seed I left her. How about some fruit?"

"She'd like that, thanks."

"The bathroom's over there," said the imp, pointing to a panelled door. "I laid out some clothes for you while you were asleep. They ought to fit."

Will broached the subject of Sandy's departure when he returned with a large cooked breakfast and a generous pile of hot buttered toast. He was pretty sure the boy had slept through the whole thing which turned out to be the case.

"I bet they've gone off to rescue Leo."

"That would be my guess, too, but there's no sign of them between here and the harbour. Corvine's crawling with troops and there's a boarding party heading for the brigantine if the weather ever settles down. They're such a distinctive group. It ought to be hard to miss them. I'll take you down to the spa when you've scoffed that little lot. A fresh pair of eyes might pick up something I've missed."

"You're sure I can have the clothes?" Pigsblanket had never worn anything so splendid. Even Grimshaw's togs couldn't live up to these and the buccaneer always dressed to kill.

"Aquamarine suits you."

"You think so?" The boy tugged at the lace shirt-cuffs and straightened the collar on his silk frock coat.

"Without a doubt."

"You're teasing me."

"Of course I am but your new rigout is a distinct improvement on its predecessor. I binned your old clothes, that was the right thing to do, wasn't it?"

"I'd have torn them to pieces then chucked them in the bin."

"Thank you for the message, Cough," said the Prince of Cobalt-Sibilance. "Tell the Royal Raven I'll contact Ralph and report back."

The hooded crow withdrew, leaving Sammy, Alfie and Jock profoundly shocked. The Giant Sapphire poured out spirals of rosy light to soak up the negativity unleashed by the news of Sandy's disappearance.

"What on earth are we going to tell him?"

"The truth, WAE."

"Sammy's right," said Jock. "It's the only way."

"He asked us to send Sandy home and offer some advice on dispatching those little horrors in the cupboard. We've blown it on both counts."

"Not entirely, Alfie. I've sealed off the portal. No more scrablings can slip through but Ralph still has the problem of what to do with the ones that are already there. At least there's good news as regards Leo, as long as we manage to rescue him." The snake took a turn round the Giant Sapphire to focus his mind and stopped in front of his two friends. "I suggest we get this over with."

The elf reluctantly took the cowrie shell from his tunic pocket and placed it to his mouth. "Here's goes."

"Once you've made contact, I'll do the explaining," said the serpent. "I feel somehow responsible, although I truly believed they'd be safe at the palace."

Ralph stood outside the Harbour Office in a state of shock. He was severely shaken by Sammy's news and couldn't begin to imagine what he was going to say to Tina.

Nothing as yet.

He was sure their daughter hadn't been abducted and had said as much to SSS. The palace was armed to the teeth and why would anyone, whatever their motives, take the others as well? It simply didn't add up. The fact the whole shebang had vanished suggested they'd decided to take matters into their own hands and try to rescue Leo. He could well imagine his headstrong daughter adopting that course of action. There was no reason for him to assume they might have run off to avoid coming home.

The harbourmaster headed for 'Woodburn' to see what he could do about the scrablings. He was relieved the portal had been sealed off but the critters had to be dealt with. He had less than an hour before Tina was due back.

Trixie rushed towards him, her tail wagging furiously. He gave the boxer a pat and headed upstairs to the spare bedroom. She followed him but stopped when she realised where he was going.

"I don't blame you, lass. I'd rather stay out here on the landing too, but needs must." Ralph closed the door behind him and stood listening for a full minute before he heard the high-pitched whine coming from the cupboard. He tiptoed across the room, avoiding the boards that creaked, and put his ear to the door.

The scrablings were whispering to each other. The intensity of the whine indicated the extent of their distress and only stopped when they spoke.

"Ooh, what are we going to do? We can't go home. The nasty creeps have imprisoned us in this strange, horrid place."

"It's our own fault. Balebreath told us not to muck about when he stumbled on that old portal but we just had to find out where it went, didn't we?"

"And now we're stuck."

"At least it's dark in here."

"What if the human comes back again?"

"We'll just have to scare him off."

There was a crescendo of keening and whining, interspersed with nervous giggles. Ralph almost felt sorry for the little devils and, from the racket assaulting his ears, he realised there were more scrablings than he'd thought in the cupboard.

He slipped the key into the lock and turned it clockwise. The din stopped instantly. The scrablings were waiting to see what would happen next. The tension was unbearable and some of them started to snigger like naughty children.

Ralph gingerly opened the door and was met by layer upon layer of yellow eyes, interspersed with massive sharp teeth and claws as long as porcupine spines. The scrablings were stacked up on top of each other in a wobbly column. They screeched and howled in an attempt to sound frightening.

One voice rang out above the others. "The light's hurting me."

"Don't say that, silly!"

"It's too late now, stupid, he's already said it."

"I was wondering about that," Ralph muttered as, with a hefty pang of guilt, he swung the door wide and moved out of the way. The sun streamed in though the tall windows and the scrablings screamed as it touched them. The tottering tower fell apart and they spilled out onto the carpet at his feet. He leapt out of the way to avoid their ferocious weaponry.

They scuttled in all directions in an attempt to escape and Ralph was starting to regret his decision when he noticed they were changing into harmless house mice. What a stroke of luck!

The rodents rushed round the room in a frenzied pack, huddled together for security. They were eeking and squeaking hysterically, having lost the power of speech which was probably just as well.

Ralph decided to let them out onto the landing for want of a better idea. Trixie was waiting for him and was stunned by the sight of a horde of mice charging towards her. They flowed between the dog's legs in a river of fur and tumbled down the stairs into the hall just as Tina let herself in through the front door. Thirty or more mice galloped past her into the front garden and out onto Bank Street never to be seen again.

She was too surprised to say anything to start with and stood watching her husband who was doubled up with laughter at the top of the stairs with the family dog standing beside him wagging her tail uncertainly.

"If those mice are anything to go by, it's time Jamie and Leo came home," she said, heading for the kitchen and a strong cup of tea.

Pigsblanket and Will walked towards the pool while Conchita flew around enjoying her new-found freedom. There was no obvious source of natural light but tropical plants and trees grew in abundance and the parrot was swift to discover delicious berries and fruit.

The boy watched his feathered friend fondly, delighting in her changed circumstances. Conchita was still silent but he was positive she'd soon regain her confidence and start talking again.

"So, Pigsblanket, any thoughts?"

The lad's eyes followed the parrot as she swooped down and skimmed across the surface of the pool. "Easy, Chita, don't get too cocky!" She flapped wildly, trying to get herself out of trouble but her concentration was broken and she splashed into the water by the large grating. She struggled out using her beak and claws to haul herself up the spars which formed the drain cover.

Pigsblanket ran over to help the saturated bird. He reached down and prised open her beak. "You're lucky you didn't drown. If it hadn't been for that grating…"

Will pushed a towel into the boy's hand and he set about drying her off. "As a matter of fact I have had a thought," he said, finally answering the imp's question. "I've a strong suspicion they've gone out through the drain."

"Bless me," said Will as a light clicked on in his head. "Talk about not being able to see the wood for the trees. The Royal Raven reckons I'm frightfully intelligent; she'll change her mind when she hears about this."

"I'll go after them. I doubt I can persuade Sandy and her friends to come back but I may be able to help them."

"You're supposed to be recuperating. Indigoletta won't hear of it."

"Don't tell her."

"That's not how I operate."

"Make an exception this time, sir."

"You haven't called me 'sir' since we first met. You're

trying to get round me, aren't you?" The lad nodded ruefully. "Ach well, why not? It makes more sense than alerting Twitchett and his impfantry. They're stretched as it is. There's just one condition: you're never to call me 'sir' again."

Pigsblanket smiled self-consciously. "Fair enough, but I can't go in these fancy clothes. I'll stick out like a punched nose."

"And you should know. Stay right where you are. I saw a black cloak when I was rooting around for your new gear. You'll need something to sustain you, so I'll fling some grub in a bag as well."

The imp tore off before Pigsblanket had time to respond. He knelt down to remove the drain cover. "Well, Chita, here we go again, unless you'd rather stay behind." The parrot climbed up his silk breeches and slipped inside his coat. "All right, you've talked me into it. But you don't have to hide anymore."

Will slammed back through the swing doors, carrying a vast cloak and a bulging knapsack. "I hope you know what you're taking on, Pigsblanket. We've no idea what might be lurking through there."

"As long as it's not Pestilence Grimshaw I'll be just fine. The water doesn't look very deep. If I play my cards right I'll only get my boots wet."

The boy threw off the frock coat and, supporting his meagre weight on his arms, dropped over the edge of the pool and swung his legs into the drain. He landed in the culvert with a splash and whistled for the parrot.

Will's upside-down face peered at him through the hole. "Get ready to receive the cloak and knapsack."

"If I find out anything useful I'll send Conchita back with a message."

"But she's mute."

"We'll work something out. Bye for now and thanks, Will."

Peg Leg landed untidily in front of Sandy. "There's definitely something up ahead but I'm pretty sure it's moving away from us."

The child felt around in the dark until she found the gull and stroked his head. "What would we do without you? We wouldn't stand a chance."

"Is that so?"

The kilt swished with irritation causing a draught on Sandy's legs. "Shut up, you ignorant wee purse, you know she's right."

The stars formed themselves into a dim torch beam trained on the ground in front of them. "You can switch to full power again," said the gull.

"So we can press on then," said an unenthusiastic lobster.

"Absolutely, Thermidor. You do make an eye-catching backpack; that's definitely the way to travel. I'll come back when I've more to report."

Pongo scratched at the ground, raring to go. "Let's crack on. Leo and Gilbert need us." He trotted off along the tunnel, tail up. Jamie ran after him, proud to be his friend.

They kept up a good pace for a while and stopped for a breather and a drink from one of the waterfalls flowing from the rock.

Pongo glanced at the lobster. "I don't suppose anyone thought to bring some nosh."

The crustacean was quick to notice the dog's beady eyes on him. "You're not eating me!"

"Not unless we get really desperate," said the Siamese drily.

Sandy gave herself a mock punch in the jaw. "I'm rubbish at this sort of thing. I've come totally unprepared. Remind me not to lead an expedition again, I'm not up to the job."

Florin piped up eagerly, "I've some sweeties."

"That's a start," she said.

"I don't suppose you've a tin of sardines in there or some potted shrimps."

"Sorry, pal. No can do."

"I don't answer to 'pal'," replied the cat haughtily.

"You just did," said Pongo smugly.

"Thanks for pointing that out, Your Hairiness."

"Barley sugar or fruit gum, Vince?"

"I never eat sweets," said the kilt.

"You never eat anything," quipped the sporran. "That leaves more for everyone else."

Pongo opted for a barley sugar and Jamie a fruit gum.

"It gives you energy," said the dog, rattling the boiled sweet against his teeth.

"Yeff, I've heard that," said Jamie, finding speech awkward with a sweet in his mouth.

"What would you like, Lorimer?"

"I'll have a bash at a barley sugar. I don't much fancy a fruit gum being a scavenging crustacean with a preference for the smaller invertebrates."

14

Celia clearly enjoyed her food. She'd made short work of the apples and carrots and was eyeing up a nosebag of bran and sultana mash Sammy had laid on for the trek to Corvine. There was also a net of hay and a bunch of carrots behind the saddle.

Alfie jumped on the pony. "What about me, SSS?"

"You eat raw carrots, don't you?"

"If there's nothing else going."

"Then you'd better take this with you."

A rattan picnic hamper materialised in front of Alfie. He let go of the reins and caught hold of the basket. "There are some treats in there for you too, Jock, in case you find foraging too much of an effort."

They parted in high spirits but they each knew it was a pretence.

The journey to Corvine was likely to be difficult. The freak weather had created havoc and chaos was the order of the day. Pockets of evil were full to bursting and no longer confined to the shadows. They were multiplying at a terrifying rate throughout the land.

Sammy wanted Alfie reunited with Pogo. His place was with his wife since the situation in Crawdonia had gone so far wrong. It was comforting to know that Estella was safe in Skirl with Mervyn and his family.

The Prince of Cobalt-Sibilance watched his two friends from the ancient tree by the mouth of the cave. The snake was loosely coiled through the branches in a relaxed manner which belied his inner feelings.

Sammy felt lonely and crushed by the weight of his responsibilities. Queen Celestina was preparing to face the creature who had killed her mother and he had to come up with the right combination of magic to protect her. He wondered if he were up to such an onerous task.

The snake slithered down from the tree and entered the cave with a reluctance he'd not experienced before. He sent Morgana home to be with her family. The bird polished the Giant Sapphire before she left, talking quietly to it, like a mother reassuring a child facing its first day at school. There was a special bond between the jewel and the magpie and Sammy sensed the Sapphire's sadness and knew it was already pining for her.

"It's down to us now, my dear friend."

"And me," said Spondoolicks, dropping down on a thread level with the snake's eyes. "I'd play some rousing reels and jigs if I thought it would cheer you both up. Maybe later, eh? I can see you've work to do."

There was an explosion of light at the centre of the Sapphire. The gemstone was rocked by the force of the blast and the air round it hissed and crackled like a bonfire.

Spondoolicks sought refuge in a nearby chest of doubloons and Sammy flung himself round the base of the Sapphire to prevent it from flying across the cave. The jewel was numbingly cold but he had no time to dwell on that. The endgame had started.

Jedediah Malahyde wasn't about to jeopardise the crew's safety. He caught the Bosun by the scruff of the neck as he ran across the deck. "What going on, man? We can't leave the harbour in conditions like these. It's the worst storm for years. Have you taken leave of the little sense you had?"

Leitzoff wasn't the brightest penny in the pile but he'd had enough. "That's as maybe, Mr Malahyde, but I'm only obeying orders and they ain't from the Cap'n. In case you haven't noticed, the ship's no longer under his control."

Malahyde grabbed the Bosun and shook him vigorously. "So it's mutiny now, you miserable wretch."

The sailor's teeth should have been rattling but poor diet had seen most of them off years before. "Course not," he said indignantly. "But where waz you when I needed you? In yer cabin feelin' sorry for yerself, that's where. I knows you're upset about young Pigsblanket, but it's not on. Me and the rest of the crew's come to depend on you and things've got a might peculiar. Have you seen her in the white robes, Cap'n Grimshaw's squeeze? It's bad luck to allow womenfolk on board and this one's not backwards 'bout coming forwards, she's already callin' the shots."

Jedediah's nerves were frayed like worn elastic bands. They snapped and he clouted Leitzoff to shut him up. The Bosun rubbed his jaw and mumbled an apology but his defiant expression painted a different picture.

Malahyde was white with anger but Leitzoff persisted. "You'll be tellin' her we're not sailing after all, will you? Cap'n can't stand up to her so I doubt you'll be able to. It's them eyes of hers, they'd put a starved cat off a bowl of clam chowder."

"That's enough, man." The First Mate was weary but did his best to hide it. "What's wrong with her eyes?"

Leitzoff winced at the memory and his hand strayed to the charm he wore round his neck for protection. "They're the black eyes of the damned."

"Don't be ridiculous," said Malahyde, trying to keep the fear out of his voice. "Superstitious nonsense like that has no berth on this ship."

The Bosun remained boot-faced, Jedediah's words weren't about to float his boat. "I knows what I saw and I reckons we're done for. I don't mean to be disrespec'ful but Cap'n Grimshaw doesn't half pick 'em. He'd be dating yon Harpie if she wasn't rotting in that smelly old dungeon."

Jedediah's frustration boiled over. "Damn it, man, are you really such a lunk-head?" Leitzoff shrugged and shuffled his feet awkwardly. "Who do you think's at the helm of our beloved ship? The cat's auntie wearing a pair of striped pyjamas!" The Bosun blinked foolishly and looked hopeful. "Why didn't you bring this to my attention earlier?"

Leitzoff's eyes were glazing over. He'd done more than his fair share of thinking for one night and couldn't believe he was now being accused of dereliction of duty.

'The Cheeky Monkey' pitched heavily to port at the harbour mouth as the twister whipped across her bows. Malahyde stumbled and landed awkwardly on his right knee. The pain shot up into his hip and he let out a string of curses. By the time he'd recovered Leitzoff had melted away.

Maligna was outlined against the ruptured sky, her ghostly robes flapping in the wind.

"Jedediah, not before time. Someone I have respect for at long last. There's really no need to kneel, but I'm flattered all the same."

Peg Leg scanned the culvert from every conceivable angle. He listened out for sounds which might indicate what was happening further along the tunnel.

The gull neatly dodged a clutch of stalactites and, rounding a blind corner, found himself flying towards a multitude of scrablings who were blocking the tunnel. He swiftly concealed himself in a cranny before the preoccupied beasts caught sight of him.

"Now what?" said Snuck, the leader of the horde. "We've followed Balebreath's orders and what good's come of it? The big palooka's done a bunk and left us here to defend the drain."

"It all started to go wrong when we came across that portal," said Meesles, her second-in-command. "We've always been too nosey for our own good. I was biting chunksies out my nailsies when those ninnies decided to sample life on the other side. That snaglip's several ribs short of a rhino but he was right when it comes to dodgy portals. I doubt we'll see those foolish artichokes again."

The remaining scrablings swung from right to left in stacked rows, singing lustily. "Gone for ever, we'll not see them again, they're in clover with Rover and good luck to them."

Snuck spluttered with exasperation. "When you hear drivel like that, lieutenant, you know extinction is imminent."

"Indeed so, ma'am." Meesles rolled on his back and set about sharpening his incisors with his front claws.

The commander stared at him hoping he'd substituted 'artichokes' for 'articles' in the heat of the moment. She was unconvinced.

Meesles burbled on happily. "We've fine weapons for our size but brainsies bigger than apple pipsies would've been handy."

Snuck wished she had not been cursed with intelligence. What a miserable state of affairs to be in such glorious isolation.

The gull slipped out of the cleft in the rock and flew back along the tunnel wondering what he'd stumbled upon. Not the wisest critters in Sylvania, that was for sure.

Peg Leg was describing what he'd seen when Pongo's body suddenly stiffened. The dog cautiously looked back along the tunnel. His ears flicked forward and his tail dropped.

Something was closing in on them from behind. They were fast becoming the filling in a sandwich. Who was going to take the first bite and from which direction was more than a bit diverting. He sniffed the air, analysing the scent. It was not one of the familiar pongs stored in his nasal filing cabinet but it was one he recognised.

"Well," whispered Sandy, "any ideas?"

"Yes, as it happens. Back in a tick." The dog padded off into the tunnel with Jamie beside him.

Lorimer gave Sandy's ear a gentle tweak. "Who do you think it might be? It can't be someone who's angry with us for doing a runner. Pongo wouldn't be so chipper if that were the case."

"That's good to hear, barnacle chops, I'm not ready tae confront the bagpipes just yet."

"What are you bletherin' on about now, Florin?"

"...facing the music, Vince, in an unprepared state." The kilt scowled but not so you'd notice unless you happened to be a sporran. "Don't sulk, you big balloon, it makes your pleats saggy."

Pongo and Jamie burst out of the darkness into the starry spotlight. A small, lean figure was following on behind. The stars widened their beam to accommodate the new arrival.

"Pigsblanket, is that really you? You look so different, so well!" The lad nodded and smiled at Sandy, revealing a fine set of teeth. Her brief memory was of someone horribly disfigured.

Pongo grinned his toothiest grin. "The denture fairy paid him a visit while he was asleep."

"Surely they hurt your gums after the beating you took?"

Pigsblanket moved Conchita from his wrist to his shoulder. "He's pulling your leg, Sandy."

"That's better than pulling your teeth, I suppose," said the kilt, taking its first tentative step towards humour.

"You mean to say those are proper teeth? That's truly amazing."

"Not really, kiddo," said the dog. "This sort of thing's pretty run of the mill in fairyland. Gnashers are two a penny here. Easy come, easy go, easy come again."

"Not much work for dentists then?"

"Not if you have the right connections or are blessed with perfect teeth like mine which Pogo brushes regularly for me."

Pongo was interrupted by an ecstatic Peg Leg. "Conchita, you look gorgeous! I've seen less colourful rainbows." He flew towards the parrot who instinctively ducked, not that there was any need for concern; the gull landed neatly in the crook of Pigsblanket's arm.

Lorimer yanked himself further up Sandy's back to see what was going on. "You don't think Peg's got a crush on the parrot, do you? I wouldn't like to see him get hurt. You never know where you are with exotic flibbertigibbets. These flashy types can be very unpredictable."

"You should know," she replied with a smirk.

The lobster waved his feelers. "I'm not with you…"

"On the contrary," said Pongo. "I've never seen a lobster more with anyone."

Pigsblanket struggled to overcome his natural shyness. He cleared his throat. "Right then, you lot, what are you up to?"

"Would you like to field that question, Sandy?" The dog plonked himself sack-of-spuds style at her feet with his eyes fixed on the ground in front of him.

Alfie and Celia were making reasonable progress with Jock as their aerial scout. If there was trouble brewing, the crow might just spot something the elf was unaware of from the ground.

When they first set out they were determined to skirt Old Rook Wood. A shortcut through the ancient forest was tempting, it could save them time, but it was a risk neither wished to take. The wood was no longer a friendly place.

Debris from a landslide eventually forced them off the only remaining track which ran cross-country from Moonglow Lake towards Corvine. They picked their way through marsh and moorland, inhospitable terrain the elf wouldn't have dreamt of visiting unless he was being pursued by an angry wild boar who'd mistaken him for the hunter who'd put an arrow in its rump.

The crow directed operations from above, staying close enough to be heard over the rising wind. The weather was demanding attention again and rogue slivers of lightning flitted across the brooding sky, adding to Jock's sense of unease.

In places the marsh was so treacherous, Alfie had to dismount and lead the pony by the reins. Celia's distress was barely contained; she rolled her eyes fearfully as he coaxed her across narrow spits of peat bog. The pony's hoof prints filled up with brackish water with each reluctant step she took. When she lost her footing and sank into the mire Alfie tightened his grip on the reins and wrenched her forward.

Jock spiralled down and landed on a blackthorn bush. He tugged distractedly at his rosette of white feathers. The bird's demeanour was that of a general breaking bad news to his troops.

"Something weird's going on. You know how accurate my sense of direction is but we're being drawn towards Old Rook no matter what I do."

Alfie tried to keep the anxiety out of his voice but his laugh was hollow. "You'll have a bald spot if you don't pack that in."

The crow felt the first drops of rain on his head. He spat out a feather which was carried off on the wind. "You're not wrong, WAE, but I have to tell you I'm worried. Whether we like it or not, we're going to end up in the wood. I was considering turning back but I don't believe that's an option now."

Celia had picked up on their mood and Alfie tried to cheer her up with a handful of carrots. The pony didn't attack them with her usual enthusiasm; she ate one after the other, her eyes anxiously following his every move.

"I suggest we take the path of least resistance. That way we can shelter, not that I need to being one hundred percent waterproof."

"Show-off!" Alfie was relieved to hear Jock more like himself again. "Celia's coat's as good as a thatched roof and I did bring my struntie wool cloak. It's strictly a winter garment and took some finding without PP there to point me in the right direction. Let's face it, we both know the rain's the least of our worries but surely to goodness Old Rook hasn't been overwhelmed by a bunch of dodgy scrogwits? It's far too venerable and wise to let rabble like that get the better of it."

The crow frowned under his feathers. "Let's hope you're right. Age can have its limitations."

The decision to accept the inevitable removed all obstacles from their path and they entered the wood on the first stroke of dusk.

Jock flew into the tree canopy with the silent stealth of an owl, a smudge of shadow against the inky backdrop. Alfie quickly lost sight of him but the crow cawed now and then to let him know he wasn't far away.

They had hoped to leave the marsh mist behind but it drifted in through the trees just above ground level. Alfie soon lost sight of his feet and Celia appeared to be floating along beside him. She shied away when he tried to mount her. When it came to invisible feet, Celia didn't want hers to be the only four.

Sylvanian ponies, unlike their larger equine cousins, rarely talk and their understanding of other languages is extremely limited. Alfie dredged his memory and came up with a few words of reassurance in her own tongue to steady her. He thrust his foot in the stirrup and swung himself into the saddle.

The mist stretched out in all directions, covering everything beneath its ghostly shroud. The unnatural silence was eerie. This was the hour when the nightshift took over from the dayshift which invariably refused to go quietly. It was often as not a rowdy business undertaken with garrulous enthusiasm, but not on this occasion. Everyone had decided to have an early night.

When Jock flew towards roosting birds they shrank away from him into the leafy gloom. They didn't answer when he called out. They were clearly terrified and his presence increased their fear.

Where were the hooties and dusky hawkmoths, the silvery screech-bats and diamond-slippered fireflies? Even the twilight chorus of speckled salamanders was muted.

Old Rook's night patrol should have been tending the boundary hedge which dissects the wood, but there wasn't a hairy hedgehorn to be seen.

The Prince of Cobalt-Sibilance hung onto the Sapphire with all the strength he could muster. On every facet of the stone was a flickering image of 'The Cheeky Monkey' in the grip of a ferocious funnel-cloud. Sammy was in no doubt Celestina had made the first move in her deadly encounter with Maligna.

The temperature in the cave plummeted and the stone shrunk in on itself. The gem gave a sickly shudder and the light at its heart grew dim. Sammy cradled the Sapphire in his coils and rocked it like a baby.

Maligna looked out at him from inside the stone. "Save yourself the trouble, serpent. It's as good as useless. The anklet is the supreme source of magic in Sylvania now. Why should I waste time playing tiddlywinks with you when I can capture your precious little Queen in the ultimate game of four-dimensional chess? Your footling spell-weaving is no threat to me."

"I wouldn't bet on it," hissed the snake, "and Queen Celestina already has the upper hand, something she won't fail to capitalise on."

A huge lizard's tail coiled around Maligna's neck. Her enraged scream was cut off as it tightened and she was snatched from view.

The jewel was flooded with indigo light. "Welcome back, dear friend. It will take a great deal more than boastful words to defeat us."

Rays of light from the Giant Sapphire illuminated even the darkest corners of the cavern.

The spider crawled out from his hiding-place and scurried along the edge of the casket. "That put her gas at a peep, SSS."

"How right you are, Spondoolicks."

Sandy gave the dog a veiled look. "Thank you, Pongo, I didn't realise that question had my name on it. I can't blame you for wondering what this is all about. It's quite straightforward, Pigsblanket. We're off to rescue Leo, and Gilbert as well, if we can."

Jamie was studying his right front foot. He spread his toes like a fan and bit off a skliff of ragged nail. "Why does that put me in mind of the 'Wizard of Oz'? Something about the rhythm."

The boy's steady gaze made Sandy uncomfortable and the parrot's fiercely protective expression brought on a guilty squirm. The smile melted from her face. "You think we're running away, don't you?"

Pongo nibbled Sandy's ankle, trying to prevent her from blurting out the truth. "Pigsblanket hasn't accused us of running away," he said. The unspoken 'yet' hung in the air.

The cabin boy's confidence had grown since he'd escaped the clutches of Pestilence Grimshaw.

"You're settling in, haven't even finished unpacking when you decide to go for a swim. A short while later, Will comes to deliver the message that you're to return home and finds nothing but a pile of soggy towels. It's a reasonable conclusion. Who tipped you off?"

Pongo started to hum and began rooting around in some pebbles.

"I should have known the dog was responsible."

"There, you lot, did you hear that? At last, someone who appreciates my finer qualities. Good to have you onboard, lad." The boy couldn't help ruffling Pongo's mop of curls. "I thought the nautical reference would go down well, you being of the naval persuasion. What say we chuck a few anchors around and take it from there?"

Pigsblanket's amused 'yes' was met with joyful relief.

Sandy found herself dancing a Highland Fling, with a jubilant lobster on her back, thanks to the boisterous reactions of the kilt and sporran, united briefly in the unsurpassed joy of Scottish country dancing.

Peg Leg whisked Conchita into the air and whirled her round his head while Pongo bounded around barking at the top of his lungs. It was great just to be a dog sometimes. Jamie watched from the sidelines, controlled as ever.

Pigsblanket tried to shut them up with frantic hand gestures but they assumed he was joining in the celebration.

The penny dropped first with the purse. "That's torn it, Vince. We're supposed to be keeping a low profile. Talk about announcing our presence."

"Never mind that, you wee pain. What's torn? Are you trying to put the wind up me?"

"Kilts by their very design are prone tae turbulence. Surely you don't need me to tell you that but, dinnae panic, yer precious wee pleats are intact."

"This is not a game!" One by one they fell silent, chastened by Pigsblanket's angry words. "I think it would be for the best if I took you all back to the palace."

Pongo's world crashed around him. His miserable expression said it all.

"Don't look at me like that. You brought this on yourselves."

Gilbert trotted across the foredeck towards the bowsprit. "Why's Captain Grimshaw's ladylove turning somersaults out there over the reef?"

"It seems she got carried away."

"This is no time for larking about. I thought she was of a more serious disposition. Still, you never can tell."

The cat padded wearily towards his friend. "You're far too gullible to be a rat, sometimes verging on downright silly which is very unratlike indeed."

Gilbert tried to find a sustaining morsel of meat in a sentence full of dry bones. "Gullible I could learn to live with, but silly is altogether more wounding."

Leo regretted his choice of adjective. "What I mean, Gilb, is that your innocent approach to life may put you at a disadvantage sometimes. Take now, for instance. Maligna's in the grip of a twister and lucky for us that she is. And what made you think she was Captain Grimshaw's girlfriend, for goodness sake?"

"The way she treats him. He's henpecked. It's a dead giveaway."

Leo chortled. "I see what you mean, but it's much more complicated. There's some seriously scary stuff going on and it's down to that creature. She's very bad news."

"It's as well she likes you then, dear wee chum."

"There you go again, always seeing the good in everyone." Leo's exasperation was manifest. "The Harpie couldn't care less about me, Gilbert. I'm of use to her in some way or another. Her relationship with Minxie's a bit of a puzzle. I reckon we ought to watch our backs where that wazwatt's concerned and, as for Cahoots, how come he thinks Maligna's his Mum?"

"I'm not going to be the one to set him straight, are you?"

"Certainly not, we're in enough strife as it is."

The air behind them was ripped apart by an anguished scream from the dragon. Cahoots thumped past them, wings flailing furiously. "Hold on, mother. I'll save you." He was in such a flap he failed to take off and plunged straight into the harbour.

"Dearie me, what does that nincompoop think he's up to now?" The wazwatt flew off to assess the damage with a bewildered Gilbert and Leo in her wake. They hung out over the gunnel as Minxie zipped back the way she'd come. "Dragon in the drink!" she yelled. "Fetch a boathook!"

Jedediah Malahyde broke into a run and Leitzoff tossed him a hook with a long length of rope attached to it. Several members of the crew deserted their posts to take advantage of the free entertainment.

Cahoots was caught up in a vicious undertow and was likely to drown with the weight of water on his wings.

"Trust you to jump into the briny before you've learned how to swim. Grab hold of the boathook!" The wazwatt urged the exhausted dragon forward. "That's it, you can do it, you big daft fire-hazard."

Pestilence Grimshaw came up behind the First Mate and the Bosun as they reeled in a bedraggled Cahoots. "Great heavens, what's he doing out there? I assumed you were disposing of the Giant Rat somewhat prematurely. That bally tornado's preventing us from putting to sea but at least it's keeping 'Laughing Girl' out of my hair."

Gilbert's jaw almost hit the deck and he stared goggle-eyed at Leo. Malahyde gestured with a desperate flick of his head. The cat received the message loud and clear but Gilbert was rooted to the spot and Leo had to nudge him repeatedly before he so much as twitched. "It's time to make ourselves scarce," he whispered, "or you'll be dangling on a length of anchor chain on a one-way trip to the bottom."

Maligna had planned to launch her offensive against Celestina before the Fairy Queen discovered she was already in Corvine. The tornado had upstaged the Harpie but she wasn't going to let that stand in her way. She had to destroy the Sapphire and its Protector. Get rid of the gem and the snake, then dispose of Celestina and the rest of her clique one by one.

When the tail tightened around her neck Maligna knew some clever shape-shifting had given her enemy the upper hand. From tornado to flying lizard in the blink of an eye was impressive.

The reptile swung the Harpie out over Fractal Reef and dashed her on the malicious rocks at the northernmost point.

Maligna exploded with incandescent rage when the Lizard Queen, protected by her white winged rooks, made a dive for the anklet which tightened protectively around her leg. She gave an enraged scream. "You'll pay for that with your life, just like your wretched mother."

The Harpie hurled a fireball through the air which engulfed the birds but the lizard doused the flames with a torrent of seawater. The rooks were sucked under the waves and spewed out again in a fountain of foam, shocked, singed but very much alive.

The Prince and the Royal Raven watched the battle unfold from the balcony outside the solarium. Hamish was encouraged and said as much.

"The Harpie cannot be defeated so easily, sir. I've seen her in action before and, believe me, this is not typical. She hasn't even begun to show what she's capable of. Her Majesty is the only one who can stop Maligna now. The combined military might of Sylvania is as nothing before one such as her. The young Queen has a long, lonely night ahead of her and the outcome is by no means certain."

The grave expression on the Royal Raven's face tightened the knot in Hamish's stomach. "But surely my wife's tactics have disadvantaged the Harpie?"

Indigoletta's intelligent eyes rebuked him for his naivety. "I know it's hard for you to imagine the all-consuming evil we're facing. Those of us who witnessed Queen Daria's brutal death have never truly recovered. Such horror diminishes the soul."

"Sylvanians are a peace-loving folk. It's hard to imagine why anyone would wish to destroy us."

"Indeed, sir, and Maligna came so close to achieving her ambition. You cannot imagine how hard it was for us to defeat her. We were very nearly overwhelmed and have never regained our former strength. The damage she inflicted endures."

Hamish brushed his hand against her cowl of feathers, risking her annoyance should she find the gesture over-familiar. The huge bird moved closer and rested her head against his arm. "All we had to do was keep the Harpie and the anklet apart and we couldn't even manage that. It's disgraceful."

"No one can take the blame for what happened. The earthquake surprised us all and we've yet to discover how Maligna came by the anklet. It could have been a simple accident of fate."

Little did he know then how close he was to the truth.

The sky darkened ominously over the reef as the raven sank further into a pit of despair.

The fog round the castle was spreading out over the harbour and the capital was virtually deserted. There hadn't been time to put a curfew in place but fear had emptied the streets.

A stray dog mooched her way along the docks picking over scraps of fish the harbour cats had left in their hurry to get away. She was crunching a herring skull when she noticed a slight movement by the waste-bins behind the fish-packing sheds. The bins were no more than twenty paces from where she was foraging and they were in deep shadow. The dog slunk behind a crate and waited to see what would happen next.

She was on the point of giving up when a large mass detached itself from the darkness and passed right in front of her. She swallowed hard as it moved off towards the breakwater at the harbour entrance. Its progress was slow and surreptitious against a backdrop of shifting shadows. The creature slunk onto an exposed stretch of wharf as the moon burst through a gap in the clouds.

Now she ought to be able to make out what it was and from a safe distance. The dog shifted her weight onto her front paws in anxious anticipation, but the wharf remained exactly as it was, deserted. Nor was there a trace of the stealthy being that had captured her attention for so long.

The stray turned her back on the harbour and made straight for the town and the company of the other homeless dogs who lived alongside her in the sewers.

The air was damp and moisture from the trees dripped off the feathers on Alfie's hat and trickled down the back of his neck. He stuffed the hat in one of the saddle-bags and pulled the hood of his cloak up over his head.

Old Rook Wood was pin-drop silent. The only sounds came from the elf and his pony as they made their way through the trees. The crow continued his aerial surveillance but no longer called out his position to Alfie. Why risk playing into the hands of something that might wish them harm?

Jock dropped onto the pommel of the saddle, taking care not to scare Celia. "Have you an earthly clue where we are, WAE? You know this wood like the back of your hand."

"Not anymore. I don't profess to have a Sylvanian clue, never mind an earthly one. If I didn't know better I'd say we'd slipped into another dimension."

"Heaven forfend! Two dimensions are more than enough for me."

Alfie suggested they stop briefly to rest the pony. The mist showed no signs of dispersing so they chose somewhere open to avoid being ambushed. The rising moon filled the clearing with cool amethyst light. The elf dismounted and led Celia down to the stream for a drink. He unloaded the picnic basket and took out a large pie embellished with his initials in pastry. There was a bulging linen napkin with Jock's name embroidered on the corner which he opened on a tree stump.

The crow watched him attentively. "Would you look at that; a veritable mound of chuckleberry and haggis patties," he said, demolishing three in the blink of an eye.

"Impressive picnic, and no mistake. Trust old Sammy." The elf bit into an aubergine fritter before cutting himself a generous slice of pie. He savoured his first bite. "It's pumpkin and pineapple. What a treat."

"Did you say pumpkin and pineapple, dear boy? How yummy."

The words came from the opposite bank of the stream where an old elf sat cross-legged on a slab of rock. Alfie turned away from Jock. "Uncle Angus, is that you?"

"None other. Now how's about a nice slice of pie? There's far too much for you to manage on your own."

"What are you doing here when you're supposed to be at home staying out of trouble?"

"Pie first, talk later," replied Angus in a sing-song voice.

"Talk first or no pie," said Alfie irritably.

Jock was gripped with anxiety. He moved out of the moonlight and skirted the clearing until he was right behind Angus. He flew up into an oak tree and positioned himself in an overhanging branch.

"I've come to help you, nephew dear. It seems to me you're in a heap of trouble so show some respect, you ungrateful little creep."

"That's enough," said the elf, tightening his grip on the knife. "You've talked yourself out of a slice unless you come over here and apologise at once."

Angus smirked. "Make me!"

"Don't be silly. It's been a long day. Why don't you have some pie and we'll leave it at that."

"Not unless you bring it yourself."

"Fair enough," sighed the elf, playing for time. The second he took his eyes off Angus, all hell broke loose.

Celia was brought to the ground by a pair of wild-eyed wolverines who'd crept up on her under the low blanket of mist. She let out a very un-ponylike wail which alerted Alfie. He threw off his cloak and dived into the fray, knife blade glinting as he plunged it into the shoulders of the beast that was going for Celia's throat.

Jock began a frenzied attack on the other wolverine, ripping chunks out of its pelt with his diamond-hard beak. He'd had plenty of practice clearing up roadkill down the years but it was a bit more challenging when the target was still moving.

The pony's instinct for survival kicked in; she lashed out with her hooves and dealt one of her attackers a hefty blow in the ribs. The beast was winded and Celia managed to roll over and trap it underneath her belly. Jock tore at its exposed throat and it howled in agony.

The other wolverine let go of the pony's neck and went to the aid of its trapped partner. Alfie slashed at its hindquarters while Jock pecked holes in its shoulders like a demented sewing-machine.

Angus sat impassively throughout with a horrible grin on his face until he realised the wolverines were in serious trouble. He leapt down from the rock with an agility he hadn't displayed in years and, springing across the brook, jumped his nephew from behind.

"Get off me!" shouted the elf. "You're in the way." He could feel Angus's rasping breath on his cheek. His uncle let out a hideous shriek and Alfie found himself looking into the bloodshot eyes of a foul-smelling scrogwit. It screamed triumphantly and caught him in an armlock.

The wolverines limped off into the wood while Alfie was wrestling with the demon. They'd had more than enough for one night.

Celia staggered to her feet wondering what she could do to help. Her coat was slicked with blood but she had well and truly overcome her fear. She felt the satisfying crack of bone as her jaws closed round the scrogwit's ankle. The demon tried to kick her with its free leg but the pony jinked clear.

The fight between Alfie and the scrogwit was fast and furious, but Jock managed to inflict a series of wounds, one of which demolished the scrogwit's right eye. Still it showed no signs of giving up, if anything it was growing stronger and more persistent.

Jock was devastated when he realised it had bitten Alfie's neck. The poison quickly worked its mischief and the elf's eyes rolled back in their sockets as he slipped into unconsciousness.

The scrogwit whooped with delight, its job done.

The beast's triumph was short-lived. Jock was so distraught he went for its remaining eye and it lurched off into the trees clutching the bloody remains of its face. Its enraged cries were cut short in one grisly, strangulated howl.

Celia stood over Alfie sorrowfully. It was a distressing picture, the injured pony and the dying elf.

Jock was numb with despair. He stood helplessly waiting to see what was crashing towards them through the trees.

15

"Hang on, Pigsblanket. You don't really mean that."
Sandy was surrounded by shocked faces. Even Lorimer was
in her line of sight, dangling from her raised left arm where
he'd pitched up when their undisciplined dancing came to
an abrupt end.

"I'm afraid I do. You're all behaving irresponsibly."
Jamie coughed discreetly. "Excluding the cat, that is."

"And Conchita," Peg said soberly. "I shouldn't have
whisked her off like that."

The parrot was frantically tidying herself up after her
first dancing lesson.

Lorimer clambered onto Sandy's back again and Pongo
flopped at her feet trying to appear suitably humbled. His
instinct told him Pigsblanket wouldn't take them back
without first trying to rescue Leo. The boy was livid and
quite right too. They'd been very stupid and deserved to be
told off.

Jamie interceded on behalf of the others. "We've been
living on our nerves since we left the palace and then Peg
found the tunnel up ahead blocked by masses of horrid furry
things, all teeth and claws."

Pongo gave the Siamese a sly look. "You can't move
without tripping over cats these days."

"I'll let that pass for now," Jamie said snootily.

Pigsblanket looked surprised. He'd heard stories about the near destruction of Sylvania by the Harpie and her hosts of demons but he'd always assumed the tales had grown in the telling. "It sounds as if you came across a bunch of scrablings. By all accounts they're silly little squirts but very nasty collectively. Their claws are poisonous so it's probably best we steer clear of them. Was there an ugly brute with them?"

"I didn't realise you were there too, Pongo," Jamie said in a quick aside.

"Not that I could see," Peg supplied helpfully. "They were bemoaning the fact they'd been left to fend for themselves by someone called Balebreath."

"That sounds like a snaglip. Those big lunks are even dafter than scrablings."

"We were being followed and there was no means of escape," said Sandy vehemently. "When our stalker turned out to be you, we were so relieved we momentarily flipped our lids."

"Precisely," said Lorimer, over her right shoulder, "although I might not have chosen those exact words."

"If we behave ourselves from now on will you help us?"

"If you promise not to muck about."

"We'll toe the line."

The others nodded earnestly.

"That's good enough for me. It's not my place to tell you what to do, Sandy. I ran away myself."

"What you're saying is people in glass houses shouldn't throw stones." Pongo received a swift jab in the ribs from Jamie. "What's that for? It's a reasonable comment."

Pigsblanket swung the rucksack from his shoulder onto the ground. "Who's hungry then?"

"I could eat a rancid bloater stuffed with rotten anchovies," said the Siamese cheerfully.

"How about a crab and shrimp mousse instead?"

"That's a tough decision, but put me down for the mousse."

They discussed strategy while they ate. Pigsblanket consulted his compass and discovered the culvert was heading inland from the harbour. The spa water was being ferried underground from Moonglow Lake.

"It's just as well you turned up when you did," said Sandy, "we'd have carried on through the drain regardless. What now?"

"There must be access to the culvert for maintenance. Let's press on and see if we can get down to the harbour that way."

"What about the scrablings? Perhaps it was their eyes I saw through the pool grating." Lorimer shuddered at the memory.

"We'll deal with them if we have to, but I really ought to send Conchita back with a message. Have you paper and a pencil in there, Florin?"

"Help yourself."

The parrot crawled under the folded cloak by Pigsblanket's side.

"I don't think she's very keen and I don't blame her."

"I'm with the lobster," said the dog. "You never know what might be lurking between here and the spa."

"But I said I'd let Will know if I found you."

"That was before you realised the culvert was full of monsters."

"A slight exaggeration, Lorimer, but I wouldn't fancy going back *all by myself.*"

"There's no need to lay it on that thick, Pongo. I'm convinced. Now where is she?"

The dog started digging around in the folds of the cloak. "She's in here somewhere, honest."

With the parrot reassured, they set off again. Peg Leg continued to act as scout and the stars provided the minimum light necessary for them to find their way.

The gull reported back shortly afterwards. "The scrablings are still blocking the tunnel but they're in a right paddy. I'd say they were in full panic mode."

"How close are we?"

"Close enough to hear them if you listen hard enough."

"What's the plan, lad?" Vince asked solemnly. "Is there anything Florin and I can do to help?"

"Were you two responsible for Sandy's dancing display earlier?"

"Aye, we were," said Florin twitching with pride.

"I'd like you to perform again."

"But you said we were to behave ourselves."

"Yes, I did, but this is different. I think you might be able to scare off the scrablings."

"We weren't that bad, surely?"

"Of course not, Vince. You were very good as it happens."

"I get it," said Pongo. "You want them to entertain the scrablings."

"Perhaps you could holler and hooch, Sandy," suggested the sporran.

"Like we do when we're dancing at weddings?"

"The very same. Why don't we all get into the swing of it?"

And they did. The stars turned themselves to full beam and whizzed around like disco lights while the little gang got ready to dance up a storm.

Florin counted them in, "A-one, a-two, a-one, two, three, four…"

Off they danced with Sandy singing at the top of her voice, heeling and toeing as she went.

The scrablings didn't know what had hit them. It was a terrifying spectacle for creatures who'd never seen a human child, let alone one who was doing a war dance in an animated skirt with a lively purse attached.

Jamie yowled and Pongo howled while they jigged and capered. The parrot and the seagull performed a raucous, aerial sword-dance without the swords and Pigsblanket made a series of noises that passed for bagpipes.

Lorimer was jumping up and down behind Sandy's head but, unsurprisingly, that wasn't fulfilling enough for a lobster of his temperament. He flung himself into the air where he performed an unintentional double somersault and was caught by Pigsblanket before he hit the ground and cracked himself open.

The wall of scrablings dissolved amid shouted recriminations and they scuttled off through the culvert cursing the snaglip and calling each other names.

"Splendid result," declared Jamie. "Amazing what you can achieve with Scottish country dancing. It's most invigorating."

Crawford couldn't believe the change in the Royal Raven when he arrived in the solarium. Things were pretty grim admittedly but she wasn't responding the way he would have expected. It was as if she'd given up without a fight. Very un-Indigoletta.

Hamish excused himself and stepped through the curtains to join the little crow. They moved further into the room so they could talk without being overheard.

The Harpie was growing stronger and she had the Lizard Queen on the run. Celestina wanted to protect Corvine but

Maligna was doggedly edging her back towards the palace and the town.

The raven sat motionless on the balustrade. She could no longer bear to watch. All her suppressed doubts and fears had come to the surface. Her powerful shoulders drooped and she sat hunched over like a vulture. She was consumed by her belief that Celestina would soon be defeated. If fate was remotely kind the Harpie would kill the Fairy Queen. To live on in Sylvania under the tyranny of Maligna with her cohorts of demons would be unendurable. Death would be a welcome release and not just for Celestina.

A scrogwit crouched on the glass roof above the balcony watching the raven's decline with relish. To think this bird was feared and respected throughout the land. The so-called Royal Raven was little more than a parasite who leeched off those foolish enough to be taken in by her provocative posturing. The demon gestured to a figure squatting at the foot of a vast chimney. The creature moved across the roof on all fours to join its peer. There was no spoken exchange; they could read each other's thoughts.

"What's happened to Indigoletta, sir? I was with her earlier and she was positively formidable."

"When I found her out on the balcony she was her usual redoubtable self. I noticed a change in her when she was telling me about the first battle for control of Sylvania. It was odd really as Celestina had the upper hand at that stage."

"How are things now?"

"Not good. I made a promise to my wife that I'd take our daughter to a place of safety if…" Hamish faltered, unable to talk of defeat. "I can't believe this has happened so quickly. A few days ago we were celebrating Sandy's arrival and now we're on the brink of destruction."

A notion had presented itself to Crawford. He moved towards the balcony and peeked through the curtain. The

Royal Raven had shrunk in on herself and was trembling violently.

"Great heavens, I must do something about this at once. If we are to help Her Majesty we have to believe she can defeat the Harpie. That's imperative." He ran onto the balcony at the very moment the scrogwits pounced on Indigoletta.

Crawford was briefly frozen to the spot but he cawed for help and Hamish drew his sword and went to his aid. The smaller demon leapt at the Prince and had its arm chopped off for its trouble. It sprang back onto the roof in a fountain of blood and ran off across the slates jibbering with futile rage.

The other scrogwit snarled and bared its disgusting teeth as it lunged at the Royal Raven. This was more than Crawford would tolerate. He flew at the abomination, flapping his wings so desperately that it slipped over the balcony and was left hanging by one gangly arm. Hamish slashed at its fingers and it fell to its death on a buttress several stories below.

"You should have let them kill me. Death at the hands of the Harpie will not be so quick."

Crawford exploded with rage. "Snap out of it, you cowardly, self-pitying bag of old feathers!"

"What did you just say?"

Crawford squared up to her. "You heard me, you cantankerous old boiler!"

Hamish was unable to tear himself away from Crawford's mesmerising performance.

"Who do you think you're talking to?" said the raven with the first hint of anger in her voice. "You know how I feel about rudeness."

"I couldn't care less what you think anymore, you're a washed-up old has-been. Why don't you resign your position as Royal Raven and let someone else have a go? You're as good as useless."

Indigoletta's eyes grew large and she thrust her head towards him. "I'll give you old, you treacherous little skunk!"

A bright-eyed Crawford nodded at the Prince. "That's more like it."

"First you insult me and now you're after my job." Indigoletta poked him in the chest and pushed him back along the balustrade. "You're an ungrateful, conniving little worm. I wouldn't stuff a mattress with your mangy feathers. Listen carefully, pea brain. The position isn't vacant and, even if it were, crows need not apply."

"Welcome back, ma'am."

"Don't upset yourself, Cahoots, your mother's a tough old boot. She's not going to let a flying lizard get the better of her."

"Isn't there anything I can do, Minxie?"

"Look what happened before. You ended up having an early bath. With help like that, Maligna's better off on her own."

"If you really think it's for the best," said the dragon miserably. Then, "Why did Gilbert and Leo rush off?"

"They're avoiding Captain Grimshaw."

"Why would they want to do that?"

"Your Uncle Pestilence wanted Gilbert to go for a swim. He didn't fancy the idea in weather like this."

"The storm's moved out over the reef now, so maybe he'll change his mind."

"I wouldn't bet on it, scaly face. He may be the biggest rat in the pack but he's not the bravest."

"Did you hear that, Leo? What a cheek!"

The rat and the cat were hiding inside a huge coil of rope on the foredeck. It was a bit of a squash so Leo was sitting on Gilbert's shoulders. From time to time he'd sneak a peek to find out what was going on.

"Never mind what Minxie says, that's just the way she is. I'd like to be able to trust the wazwatt. She's no fan of Captain Grimshaw but she's a bit too chummy with Maligna for my liking."

"It's a pity Pigsblanket ran away."

"You can't blame him. He wouldn't have survived another run-in with Grimshaw."

"I wish he'd taken us with him."

"How could he? We were locked in our cabin."

"I'd forgotten that. What about the First Mate? Who'd have thought he'd save my skin?"

"We can't expect him to take us on. Can you imagine what would happen to Mr Malahyde if the Captain knew he'd helped us?"

Gilbert shivered as a series of horrible images flashed though his head. "Still, it's good to know we have one friend on this tub. We'll just have to fend for ourselves again which might prove a bit tricky. The two of us up against a bunch of dastardly cut-throats. How are your fencing skills?"

"About as good as yours, Gilb."

"So no cutting, thrusting and parrying for us then."

"A cut throat, perhaps."

"I'll oblige you if you don't shut up!"

Leo was so startled he sank his claws into Gilbert's head. A hand slammed over the rat's mouth before he had a chance to squeal. Jedediah put his finger to his own mouth and backed away from them. He picked up some discarded sailcloth and tossed it casually over the coil of rope.

"At the double, sailor. There's extra rum rations if you find the kitty and the big galoot. I've had a good poke around here and there's no sign of 'em. Have one of the topmastmen report to me at once. The best view of the ship's to be had from up there in the rigging."

When Jock saw Grimpen running towards him out of the trees he almost collapsed with relief. The wolf was dismayed by the scene that met his eyes but he kept his emotions in check and quickly assessed the situation.

The crow was in a wretched state but he was unharmed. The pony's condition was serious but by no means life-threatening. The same could not be said for the elf.

"I'm sorry I didn't get to you sooner, but the wood's teeming with scrogwits and other foul monstrosities. I dispatched the one that did this to Alfie. From the state of it, you must have put up a good fight."

"Not good enough," said Jock mournfully.

"You saw off a pair of wolverines and a scrogwit, that's no mean feat."

"When I saw Angus sitting on the rock, I had my suspicions that all was not as it seemed, but it never occurred to me a scrogwit might be impersonating Alfie's uncle. I didn't realise they were that clever."

"Don't be so hard on yourself, Jock. We've been plunged into a menacing world of shadow where reality has shifted and the usual rules no longer apply. Old Rook Wood has been polluted by the darkness that's spreading throughout Crawdonia. We must get away from here fast if we are to have any chance of saving Alfie."

Seven adolescent wolves entered the clearing and Grimpen set about issuing instructions. He crouched down and the others gently pulled the unconscious elf onto his back. Jock tugged the struntie wool cloak over Alfie's limp body to protect him from the relentless drizzle.

The young wolves acted as outriders and Grimpen set off with Celia stumbling along behind him. Jock flew alongside the pony urging her on even though she was completely exhausted.

Malevolent eyes watched their progress but they travelled through the wood unmolested. Scrogwits are terrified of wolves who are immune to their particular brand of poison.

Grimpen finally came to a halt in front of an ancient oak on the edge of a hazel copse. He gave one high-pitched howl. A short wail came from somewhere inside the tree then a bark-covered door in the trunk opened and a pale face peered out.

The wolf's tone was formal but friendly. "Wee Alfie Elf is in dire need of your skills if he is to survive a scrogwit bite."

"No one's sought my help in years," said the Banshee wistfully. "I thought everyone had forgotten I was once a healer."

"I have a long memory. Will you help us, Marta?"

"I'll do everything I can to save him. You'd better bring the pony round to the back entrance. There's an underground room where she can rest while I treat her wounds."

Contrary to popular belief Banshees are not always miserable souls wringing their hands while they rant about the latest death. Some have special gifts which can be put to good use. Their melancholic disposition does have a habit of taking over which is why Marta gradually turned into the wailing wet blanket everyone falls over backwards to avoid.

Here was her chance to turn her life around and what better way was there than by saving the life of a dying elf?

The Banshee was stronger than her meagre frame indicated. She lifted Alfie easily from Grimpen's back and carried him into her home inside the tree.

"Would you mind if I stay with him?"

"You're most welcome, crow."

Jock walked towards the old wolf. "Thank you for all you've done. Alfie would be dead had you not found us. I mustn't keep you from your flock any longer."

"The strunties are safe at Palace Farm. We moved them there after the first earthquakes. Now that my work is complete here, I'm going to Corvine to see if I can be of service to Her Majesty. I heard from one of Redshanks' agents that the battle for control of Sylvania is already underway. A battalion of the fiercest Kelpien dwarves has been deployed along Old Rook's boundary hedges to protect the hedgehorn patrols who were decimated by scrogwits. My wolves will patrol the area to keep those who wish you harm at bay."

"Go carefully, Grimpen. I'll join you as soon as I can."

The wolf had one last look round then loped off into the night.

Pongo had his nose pressed up against the grill. "What a lucky break! You were right, Pigsblanket. This must be the access for the maintenance team."

The grating connected the culvert to a small sea cave. There was debris caught in the crossbars indicating the cave was subject to the tides.

Pigsblanket gave the gull a detailed description of the port and its surroundings. "It'll be getting dark soon but 'The Cheeky Monkey' should be hard to miss, she's very colourful."

"Let me go with Peg," said Lorimer urgently. "Four eyes are better than two."

"So you're not scared anymore, Thermidor?"

"No way. I've put all that behind me. I'm as brave as the next lobster now."

"And how brave is that?"

"I can't really say. We're pretty solitary as a rule. To be honest, I'm itching to get back in the sea."

Pigsblanket unscrewed the grill and set it to one side. "Right then, who's first?"

The water glittered invitingly. Lorimer donned his goggles and scrambled down Sandy's arm. He landed with a joyful splash, the sequins glinting on his bathing suit as he rolled over and dived under the waves.

Peg flew after his pal and the others settled down to wait for their return.

Lorimer swam off, delighted to be back in a watery world, even one as unfamiliar as this.

Clusters of glowing barnacles in a rainbow of colours clung to the rocks and shoals of tiny silver rays swam along beside him. A school of phosphorescent seahorses wove in and out of the rays, their curiosity aroused by a lobster unlike any other in the Whiteraven Sea.

Lorimer bobbed out of the water by the cave mouth to get his bearings.

"Love the goggles," said a female voice behind him. "You're not from around these parts, are you?"

"Er... no, I'm not," said the bemused lobster, trying to ascertain where the words were coming from. He was scanning the rocks to his right when he saw her. "Well now, aren't you the daintiest mermaid I've ever seen?"

"So I should hope. I'm the rarest of the rare, you know. You're lucky I'm still here."

"I am?"

"Yes, you are," said the mermaid emphatically. Her pale blonde hair was threaded with pink sapphires and fire opals. "I was on the point of leaving. I've been mixing recreation with a spot of work but my holiday's been blighted by recent events. I'm gathering material for my next lecture tour. The caves around Corvine are inhabited by a rare species of

Papery Hawkmoth. They're white with black dots all over their wings and come in two varieties, the Tabloid and the Broadsheet. We're hoping to introduce them to a similar habitat back home. They're very beneficial to the marine environment."

"Where's home?" Lorimer asked eagerly.

"Can't you guess?" teased the mermaid. "If I were to say the clue is in the cozzie, would that help?"

Lorimer glanced at the flag on his bathing suit. "You don't mean to say you're from Scotland?"

"Where else?"

The gull circled the lobster's head impatiently. "Thermidor, for pity's sake, what are you playing at? I've been waiting outside for you."

"If it isn't Peg Leg," said the mermaid calmly.

"Samphire, long time no see."

Lorimer felt deflated. "You two know each other?"

"Mmm. But we'll have to catch up some other time. You and I have work to do."

The mermaid's interest had been aroused and she decided to stick around for a while to find out what they were up to.

"I don't know what came over me, Crawford, but thank you for bringing me to my senses in such an ingenious way."

"You fell victim to a spell of negativity which interfered with your natural optimism, and strong it was too, ma'am. The Harpie dined off your despair and grew stronger. Those scrogwits wouldn't have dared take you on had you been your usual self."

"We must protect ourselves and do what we can to sustain the Queen. Knowledge is power, Crawf. A united front of positivity."

"Quite, ma'am." Crawford sighed happily. Indigoletta wasn't just back, she was dynamite in feathers. "As you said, in fine window-rattling form, 'Maligna will never prevail'."

"And I meant it, in spite of that unfortunate lapse."

Celestina had managed to drive the Harpie away from the Palace but Maligna sensed she was tiring, the shape-shifting had drained her energy. She stepped up the attack on her adversary and flew at the Queen with the force of a battering ram. The hatred poured out of her in dark waves which Celestina repelled with her strongest white magic. The Queen channelled additional power from the Giant Sapphire and the Prince of Cobalt-Sibilance sent his most potent formula against evil through the night sky in a string of blue stars that wrapped themselves round her in a protective cloak.

Maligna screamed in frustration when she found she was unable to break through the starry shield which burned her skin horribly on contact. The Harpie flung herself into the Whiteraven Sea and sank beneath the waves.

Will's cousin Malcolm was still on duty when the wolf arrived at the Great Daria Gate. Grimpen was admitted immediately and the imp left a junior officer in charge so that he could escort the wolf himself.

"I'll take you straight to the Attendant to the Royal Raven. He's helping Pogo Pixie move from the guest accommodation into the main part of the palace. With the Irvine mob gone, she was rattling around there on her own."

"I need to see Will by myself first. Can you arrange that?"

"It won't be a problem."

Malcolm could tell from the wolf's eyes it was a matter of grave concern and, being a professional soldier, didn't ask questions. Instead, he broke into a trot which Grimpen matched.

An inner courtyard connected the guest wing to the ground floor of the palace. Malcolm called out a long list of letters and numbers which constituted the current password. A sentry leapt out from behind the shrubbery and gave a jaunty salute.

"I'm looking for the Attendant to the Royal Raven, is he around?"

"Your cousin's indoors, Malky. Shall I fetch him?"

"I wouldn't bother him but it is very important."

"Right you are."

Malcolm grinned. "There's just one thing, could you be a bit more formal? Less of the 'Wee Malky's here' sort of thing."

"Sorry, sir."

"Don't mention it. My promotion was only made official two days ago."

Will shook his head in disbelief when he heard about Alfie. "Several members of the Clandestine Council are with Prince Hamish in the solarium. I was on my way there when Malcolm intercepted me, so I'll take you up myself. Pogo's gone to visit Cassandra in the infirmary, caring soul that she is. Twitchett has assigned two of his most experienced soldiers to her protection and the hare is being cared for by a skeleton staff of medics." He smiled inwardly at his unfortunate choice of word.

They made their way along endless corridors, through elaborately furnished rooms, across ornate covered bridges linking one elegant wing of the palace to another. The wolf kept pace with the imp as he dived round corners and ran up tortuous flights of stairs.

"This is the most direct route, believe it or not. Her Majesty's been toying with the idea of installing the odd lift or two, for those of us who have to rely on our legs rather than fairy wands or wings. It won't happen, she's a traditionalist at heart and I'm with her on that. I can't get used to the palace being so deserted, it's usually like a going fair. Having said that, the security bunkers are crammed to capacity. Have you ever been down there? The facilities are brilliant, almost as good as the palace proper, but a lot more snug."

Grimpen said very little but he found Will's friendly commentary comforting. He hated being the bearer of bad news but the imp's irrepressible attitude lifted his spirits. There was something very special about Will and he understood why Indigoletta had singled him out.

The imp clattered up the narrow spiral staircase connecting the solarium to the rest of the palace and waited at the top for the wolf who'd never negotiated one before. Grimpen picked his way carefully to start with but his confidence increased as he climbed.

The Royal Raven's eyes burned with anger. "This terrible news about Alfie only strengthens my resolve to destroy the blight on our land. We must keep this from Pogo for now. The poor soul is worried enough as it is. Realistically, what chance does Alfie have, Grimpen?"

"I enlisted help from an unlikely source, ma'am, and I firmly believe he's in good hands. Marta the Banshee was a great healer in her day."

"Bless me, that's truly inspirational and she might just pull it off. To cure that miserable, mooching creature of her melancholia would be one in the eye for Maligna and a massive smack in the chops should she save Alfie's life as well." Indigoletta spun the emerald pendant once round her neck, indicating how pleased she felt. "We've made a useful discovery, Will, for which I can take no credit. It was entirely due to Crawford's nimble intelligence." She paused to acknowledge the crow who was so thrilled he bobbed a curtsey instead of his usual bow. "What it boils down to is believing we are invincible no matter what is thrown at us, even something as horrific as this."

"It's better than I thought," said Pigsblanket, smoothing the seagull's feathers. "We're actually in the harbour. The rowing boat you found in the next cave must belong to the maintenance team. I don't think they'll mind if we borrow it, do you?"

"The brigantine's going nowhere in a hurry," said Peg. "It's chaotic out there."

"You recognised her, then?"

"Without a doubt." Lorimer was breathless with admiration. "The fabulous paintwork with matching sails make their own statement. She's definitely my kind of ship."

"I'll swim round to the boat and come back for you all." Pigsblanket took off his boots and dived into the sea, still cushioned by his struntie wool bandage. He swam out into Corvine harbour, keeping to the calmer water at the foot of the palace promontory.

The lad swung himself into the rowing boat and took up the oars. He pulled away from the mooring in the cave and rowed back to pick up his friends. "Righty-oh, in you get. It's blowing a gale in the harbour so sit low in the boat and don't move around unless you want us to capsize. We mustn't attract attention so we're lucky there's a lot going on. Keep your head down, Sandy. With that ponytail, there's a good chance you'll be mistaken for a lad."

"You really know how to make a girl feel good," said Pongo drily.

"I didn't mean to imply..."

"Of course not, but I grew my hair to *stop* being mistaken for a boy."

"Different fashions in different worlds," said Jamie, teetering his way onto the boat.

Pigsblanket whirled the huge cloak round his shoulders. "The rest of you can hide in here with me. You'd better stay out of sight too, Chita." The parrot took up her usual place on his shoulder and he pulled the hood forward to cover their heads. "I can't have Grimshaw clocking me either, that would wreck our chances well and truly."

Pongo curled up in the bottom of the boat, with Jamie and Lorimer tucked in beside him. The cloak covered them easily with enough left over for Sandy's lap to hide Vince and Florin. "Folks in Sylvania don't go in for kilts and sporrans as a rule, so we'll keep you out of sight for now."

The ever-inventive stars clustered together as a small light at the front of the rowing boat and Peg stationed himself behind them, leg firmly planted beneath his centre of gravity. "I'll act as the eyes in the back of your hood, Pigsblanket. We don't want you colliding with something because you can't see where you're going."

Sandy crossed her fingers and touched the locket with MacGregor's fur in it for luck.

Corvine harbour was bigger than she'd expected and there were a good few ships at anchor. Schooners sat alongside tea clippers, and fishing boats lined the docks, unable to put to sea in the current conditions. The marina was dotted with sailing boats and cabin cruisers straining on their moorings in the high winds.

Pongo was desperate for information. "What's going on up there? Give us some idea or my curiosity might just get the better of me."

"I thought cats were supposed to be curious, not dogs," said the lobster from somewhere within the folds of the cloak.

"What makes you think I'm not? I can't wait to get an eyeful of the legendary brigantine."

Sandy whooped when she saw 'The Cheeky Monkey'. "She's absolutely beautiful, even in this light."

Pongo was keen to demonstrate his knowledge of nautical terms. "Is she to port or to starboard?"

"What difference does it make when you can't see her anyway?"

"Fair point, Jamie." The dog fell silent which is not something that happens very often.

Pigsblanket's hood fell back as he fought for control of the rowing boat when it was swept in front of a trawler. Conchita joined the others under the cloak.

"I'll try to keep my distance until I've some idea what's going on. Take the telescope, Sandy. Pestilence Grimshaw's unmistakeable. He has similar taste to Lorimer when it comes to clothes."

"You mean tastefully loud and garish." She held the telescope to her right eye. "There's men all over the rigging. I think they're trying to take in the sails. There's a tall figure in sombre clothes and a tricorn hat waving a lantern around."

"That'll be the First Mate. Mr Malahyde was the only friend I had on 'The Cheeky Monkey'. I think it's time to send in our scout. How about it, Peg Leg?"

"Sure thing. I can have a good poke around without anyone being suspicious. I expect one-legged gulls are not that rare here."

"Actually, they are. Sylvanian seagulls just grow a replacement."

"How very convenient. If anyone asks I'll say I'm between legs."

The lower section of cloak tittered. "Nice one, Peg."

"I aim to please, Pongo."

"Drink up," said the voice at the end of the tunnel. "I'm sorry it tastes disgusting but one more swig should empty the cup. This carefully blended beverage saved your life. You very nearly had your chips."

Wee Alfie Elf was lying under a blanket on a small cot; he was still very weak and woozy. His eyes swam into focus and he let out a yelp of surprise. "Pogo, what have they done to you? You look like death. That health spa's well and truly gone to the dogs. Talking of which, Pongo could have chewed your hair into a more becoming style. I hope you refused to pay. It's nothing short of criminal."

Alfie was suffering side effects from the antidote to the poison and was likely to carry on talking rubbish for some time to come. He was remarkably chipper for someone who should have been dead and Marta decided this drivel was a small price to pay. It almost brought a smile to her solemn face.

"That's some makeup they've slapped on your dial. I've rendered the walls at home with better quality plaster. And you've no lips, just a thin, squiggly line where your mouth should be. Come closer so that I can see the extent of the damage." The Banshee leant over Alfie to adjust his pillow and pressed a cool compress of leaves against his hot forehead. "Oh my, Pogo, it's worse than I thought. Your eyes are like two..."

"That's gratitude for you." Jock jumped up from the end of Alfie's bed, yawned and stretched his wings. "I apologise on his behalf, Marta. He's a discourteous wretch."

The elf's inane chatter subsided and he drifted back into a land of strange dreams.

"You look much better, crow."

"The name's Jock," he said, dispensing with his usual long-winded introduction. "And I have to tell you I feel like my old self. Raring to go."

"That'll be the passionflower and scrogwit cordial. It's good for the nerves and promotes restful sleep."

The crow's voice went up an octave. "Passionflower and *what*?"

"There's not much scrogwit in the cordial, if that's what's worrying you. The potion I gave Alfie was very concentrated, one tenth scrogwit to nine tenths flower essence of my own decoction."

Jock fell back on the blanket theatrically. "No wonder it tasted so foul. I can hardly bring myself to ask how you came by the aforementioned scrogwit."

"A couple of Grimpen's wolves brought me an arm. I didn't feel it was my place to enquire how they came by it."

"Very wise, some questions are best left unasked."

16

"The old fellow insists on talking to you, sir. No one else will do. He was most insistent otherwise I wouldn't have bothered you."

"Good grief, Will, doesn't he realise what's going on out there?"

"He appears to understand the situation only too well, that's what's so weird. He grew very agitated when I suggested he should come back some other time, insisting it would be too late by then."

The Royal Raven scrutinised Will's face which was unusually troubled. The imp's eyes flicked desperately from Hamish to Indigoletta and his voice grew more insistent. "I really think he wants to help us. I'm positive it's not some sort of trick, but we won't take any risks."

"There will be no question of that," said Indigoletta, fanning her cowl of feathers until she resembled a defiant owl. "Run on ahead, Will, and tell Twitchett the Royal Raven won't tolerate anything less than the highest level of security." She paused, then added. "And that goes for Crawford, too."

The little crow rippled with pleasure.

Grimpen moved protectively to the Prince's side. "I'll accompany you, sir, if I may."

Hamish let out a long sigh. "It seems the decision's been made for me. Where is he?"

"I left him in the small reception room under armed guard. He's tired and frail. It must have taken a lot out of him to get here."

The Prince turned to Indigoletta and Crawford and his features grew fierce and fox-like. "I must be kept informed. Regular bulletins, do you understand? If my wife is in difficulty, I wish to know at once. Come, Grimpen, let's get this over with."

The wolf trotted after Hamish, negotiating the narrow spiral staircase with new-found confidence.

Indigoletta contemplated the amethyst and diamond ring on her foreclaw. "So, Crawford, what are we facing now, I wonder?"

The crow removed his monocle and left it dangling on the silk ribbon round his neck. He edged towards the raven. "Who knows, ma'am, but we're facing it *together*."

A white-winged rook had broken away from the rest and was making its way towards the palace. The bird cawed a last-minute warning as it was carried towards the balcony on a sudden squall. The rook was battle-scarred but unbowed.

Indigoletta felt she could be more direct with the prince out of the way. "How bad is the situation out over Fractal?"

"It's pretty desperate, ma'am, but we will die before we surrender. Her Majesty is fearless in her cloak of Sublime Stars and it will take more than a fireball to destroy us."

The rook saluted and dropped from the balcony in a hair-raising manoeuvre which made it abundantly clear 'vertigo' was not a word in its vocabulary.

One of the marine wardens, a pipefish called Flute, witnessed Maligna's fall from the sky after her heated encounter with the Fairy Queen.

Flute belongs to an elite unit of Freckled Foghorns and she was monitoring the bladderwrack boundary hedge from a submerged cave when it happened. The squirming mass of seaweed moves restlessly on the volatile currents round Fractal Reef as it shifts with the ebb and flow of the tides.

The foghorn patrols were being supported by stealthy fighter rays brought in as an emergency measure to protect the protectors. These giants of the deep glide along with the slow grace of a stately galleon matching their surroundings if necessary but, when they launch an attack, it is swift and deadly.

The pipefish propelled herself towards a dense clump of kelp and hid among its fronds to observe Maligna. There was a fighter ray shadowing her which was good to know should she find herself in a tight spot.

The Harpie wasted no time. She took the form of a sea serpent and swam off towards Corvine, following the contours of the coral beds which give way to watery meadows of seagrass, a favourite habitat of queen shrimp.

When the serpent was no more than a trail of dwindling bubbles, Flute raised the alarm, a coded sequence of toots only audible to those equipped with sonar. The message included details of Maligna's changed appearance and the route she had taken.

The Fairy Queen flew back to the palace promontory to wait for the Harpie. She knew Maligna would force her back to Corvine sooner or later and she wanted to choose where she faced her enemy for the final showdown.

Celestina raised her solitary standard on the highest escarpment above the entrance to the harbour. She stood resolutely on the headland, a tiny beacon of midnight-blue stars, shining out to all four points of the compass.

"What's that lizard got against my mother?"

"Who knows," said Minxie. "They're tetchy beasts who are easily upset. Perhaps she gave it one black look too many." The wazwatt laughed at her own joke. "It pays not to cross a flying reptile."

"So don't wind me up," said Cahoots, puffing smoke rings from his nostrils.

"You're not a reptile, silly, you're a dragon."

"I look pretty similar."

"You're not as ugly."

"Thanks." Then he realised what she'd actually said. "So you think I'm hideous?"

"I didn't say that. Ugly was the word I used. Hideous is a bit strong."

Minxie whizzed up into the rigging.

"Come back here," shouted the exasperated dragon.

The wazwatt studiously ignored him and scanned the waters round Fractal Reef trying to discover what had happened to the Harpie. The flying lizard had vanished and in its place was an unfamiliar constellation of arresting blue stars.

Minxie was waving at the dragon down below when she noticed a bow wave crossing the harbour with nothing visible behind it. The wazwatt hadn't come across anything like that before and flew down to investigate.

Cahoots was seriously fed up without his sparring partner.

"What's up, lad?"

"Minxie's left me on my own, Uncle P."

"I'd be grateful if I were you. That wazwatt's trouble."

"Mum likes her."

"Odd, isn't it?" Grimshaw tried to sound unconcerned. "Seen anything of Mumsy recently?" Cahoots shook his head sadly. "Why don't you go and play with the kitty? Gilbert's about to leave us, so Leo will be glad of a new friend."

"Nobody knows where they are, and Gilbert wouldn't go anywhere without Leo."

Grimshaw addressed the dragon as if he were stupid, giving each word due emphasis. "I run a tight ship. Gilbert and Leo cannot have gone missing."

"But they have. Mr Malahyde's been searching for them for ages."

The buccaneer slapped the dragon hard across the face. "Don't you dare lie to me. I won't tolerate lies from anyone, not even you."

Cahoots was shocked but unhurt. The scales on his face were tough as armour and the buccaneer's hand throbbed. Undeterred, Grimshaw drew his sword and thrust the point under the dragon's chin, tilting his head back. Cahoots was frightened but didn't let on. He was starting to feel justifiably hard done by and would never refer to the buccaneer as his uncle again. "I'm not fibbing. I wouldn't ever."

"He's telling the truth, Cap'n."

Grimshaw spun round and lunged angrily at the First Mate. His sword caught in the frogging on Malahyde's coat. "Why don't I know about this, man? What were you thinking?"

Jedediah stood his ground and held Grimshaw's gaze. He didn't trust himself to speak and Pestilence mistook his silence for outright defiance.

There was something about the expression in Malahyde's hawklike eyes that gave him the heebie-jeebies. He backed off with a forced laugh and thrust his sword back in its jewelled scabbard. "You had your reasons, no doubt, but I'd be obliged to know what you're doing about finding them."

Pongo poked his head out from under the cloak. "So Gilbert and Leo have done a moonlight flit. That's a wee bit unfortunate seeing as the cavalry's just come over the hill."

Pigsblanket reacted to Sandy's wail of disappointment. "Leo's too sensible. He'd never let Gilbert do anything rash and where would they go? When I left they were locked in their cabin. They must have managed to escape. I expect they're hiding somewhere on the brigantine. There's no shortage of places, I should know, I've hidden in most of them."

Lorimer scrambled up onto Sandy's lap, apologising to Vince for digging his claws into him. "What if they were panicked into doing something daft?"

"Are you speaking from personal experience, Thermidor?"

The lobster turned to confront the seagull and fell on top of the sporran as a rogue wave caught the side of the boat.

"I've had just about enough of this carry-on," said the irascible purse. "What are we going to do now? I've nae intention of goin' back empty handed."

"Simmer down, Florin. You don't have hands."

"It's a figure of speech, Vince, and here's another one. Keep your hair on."

"That's enough, you two," said the gull sharply. "I'm going back to the brigantine to see what else I can discover."

Peg Leg swooped low over the foredeck and landed in the middle of the sailcloth covering the coil of rope. Whenever possible, he opted for a cushioned landing.

"What was that?" asked Gilbert.

"How should I know?"

"Why don't you have a quick look?"

"And come face to face with PG, no thanks."

"I can hear it moving about."

"It's rolling around on my head."

"So it's unlikely to be Captain Grimshaw then."

The gull pulled back the sailcloth and thrust his face through the gap. "Gilbert and Leo, pleased to meet you at long last. I'm Peg Leg and I'm the scout for the rescue party."

They were fizzing with excitement and he had to silence them on the spot. "Not a word," he hissed, "if you want to get out of this alive."

Peg had a quick look round to make sure he wasn't being watched. No one was paying him the slightest attention. The crew were far too busy trying to keep 'The Cheeky Monkey' out of trouble. Some of them had spotted the blue stars up on the headland and a vigorous debate had begun as to what they were.

"You must swear not to go bananas when you hear what I have to say." Gilbert and Leo nodded solemnly and crossed their hearts. "Sandy and Jamie are in a rowing boat nearby with Pigsblanket and the others who've come to rescue you. I'm going back to give them the good news."

Leo was snatched up in a suffocating hug by Gilbert who was choking back huge, gulping sobs. The cat's face was blank of all expression but he was purring so loudly Peg suggested he might like to turn down the volume.

"Back soon," whispered the gull, tugging the sailcloth over their heads.

The Fairy Queen was drawing a phenomenal amount of power from the Sublime Stars and the positive charge could be felt throughout Corvine. Folk opened curtains and peered through shutters to see what was going on. Their collective fear was diminishing and they began to venture out onto the streets again. Word was spreading about the beacon of stars above the palace and many gravitated towards the harbour.

The Prince of Cobalt-Sibilance placed an enchantment on the Harpie which would prevent her from shape-shifting. Celestina had exhausted that side of her magic and the snake wanted to even the odds. The next time she tried to change, Maligna would revert to her original state.

The Harpie's desire for revenge was all-consuming and she'd launched her offensive against the Queen before her powers had reached full maturity. The creature who killed Queen Daria had been virtually invincible but Sammy was sure Maligna was not the great sorceress of days gone by.

The Harpie was aware of Celestina's presence long before she surfaced by the watergates. The Fairy Queen exuded heat like a furnace and the temperature of the water around the sea serpent had gone beyond comfortable and was well on the way to unbearable. When Maligna tried to take to the air as a flying fish, she found herself back in female form, horribly encumbered by her robes which were saturated with saltwater.

The Harpie was furious at being thwarted right under the nose of her enemy, most probably by that irksome, meddling serpent. She looked forward to roasting the snake alive and cutting him into bite-sized pieces on top of his precious sapphire.

Maligna conjured up a wave from the deadly waters off the Island of Long Forgotten Dreams. It moved along the coastline from the northwest past Cormorant Point, sucking greedily at the waters off the Skellid Rocks on its way to Corvine. The wave was already showing its terrifying potential by the time it reached the strait of water between Fractal Reef and the port itself.

Queen Celestina was aware of the crowds gathering round the harbour and knew she had to do something to avert yet another disaster. The townsfolk were unaware of the approaching tidal wave, which was obscured by the promontory and cliff.

The watergates would divert the massive wave away from the palace right into the harbour instead. She had to act fast to prevent loss of life and destruction on a catastrophic scale.

A vast cheer went up when she raised her wand and sent a luminous shaft of ice crystals into the sea. This was followed by gasps of horror from those who could see the massive wave bearing down on them.

The water froze in an accelerating chain of particles until the whole wave was suspended in a shimmering arc over the entrance to the harbour.

Maligna had hoped to conceal herself within the curling plume of water as it swept up over the massive gates and so enter the palace grounds undetected. Instead she found herself running across the frozen sea in full view of the Queen.

Celestina didn't dare leave the spell in place for long as the whole Whiteraven Sea would gradually turn to ice, causing an environmental disaster. She pointed her wand at the crest of the frozen wave, splitting it into billions of droplets of water which were carried away on the wind and dispersed safely in the ocean far beyond Fractal Reef.

As the ice turned back to water the Harpie tried to dive under the waves. The Fairy Queen hurled a bolt of lightning at her while she still had the advantage but the anklet managed to wrench Maligna out of its path. The Harpie's hatred for Celestina was interfering with her ability to think clearly and plan strategically. By the time she realised what was happening, she was already seriously disadvantaged.

The Queen's bodyguards swooped down from the cliffs in an arrowhead formation and Maligna shrieked in horror as eight white-winged rooks began mobbing her.

Their leader sat on the Fairy Queen's shoulder watching his squadron with immense satisfaction. Revenge was not an emotion to be nurtured until it was all-consuming, as the Harpie was finding to her cost. Vengeance should be treated like a vintage wine; something to be sipped and savoured, not devoured greedily with no care for the consequences.

The birds' attack was ruthlessly precise and Maligna's hands and arms were quickly covered in lacerations sustained as she tried to protect her face from their savage beaks. When one of the birds became tangled in her hair it tore out lumps of scalp to free itself.

The weight of her garments finally dragged her down; she no longer had the strength to swim and her ability to breathe underwater was seriously impaired.

This was not how Maligna had envisaged things at all, quite the reverse. She had to rid herself of the robes, a simple spell was all it would take, mere childsplay, but her concentration was shot to pieces and she could feel herself beginning to panic.

The crowds pressed forward as their numbers were increased by other fairy folk rushing to support their monarch. The more they cheered and hollered the brighter the stars shone out from the clifftop.

The Harpie was quick to realise her powers were decreasing due to the positive energy radiating from

Celestina's supporters. She struggled out of the sea onto a small strip of beach tucked underneath the overhanging cliffs.

Maligna screamed her frustration at the anklet for letting her down when she needed it most. It retaliated with white-hot waves of pain that brought her to the ground. The anklet was no longer under her control. She howled in anguish and stumbled into a cave to salvage what was left of her fragmenting strategy.

The Harpie conjured up a set of dry clothes and was grovellingly grateful her sorcery had not abandoned her totally. She sat for what seemed like an age with her head in her hands wondering what she could do to turn the situation around.

The anklet suddenly tightened round her leg and she looked up. The Fairy Queen was silhouetted against the moon at the entrance to the cave.

"Hi," said the mermaid when she realised Pigsblanket had noticed her sitting beside the starry bow light. A ribbon of magic stars broke away from the rest and formed a bracelet round her dainty wrist. She smiled her thanks. "How's the rescue going? I thought I might be able to lend a hand." Samphire flicked her tail impatiently. "Pull yourself together, boy, and stop gawping. Surely you've seen a mermaid before?"

"Of course I have but never in miniature."

"Don't let my size fool you. I'm supremely intelligent and held in high esteem throughout the Whiteraven Sea and, for that matter, the Firth of Clyde. I don't suppose you've ever been to Scotland." He shook his head. "It's your loss."

Peg Leg landed beside the mermaid. "Hello again, Samphire. I thought your relentless curiosity might get the better of you."

Her smile was cool, verging on wintry. "Tact was never your strongest point, was it, Stumpy?"

"Nor yours," said Peg, swaying towards her dangerously. "I enjoy a bit of battered fish, so watch your tail."

Samphire shrank away from him in mock terror before she exploded with laughter. "They'll think we don't like each other if we keep this up."

"That would never do."

The mermaid waved her hand in Sandy's direction. "I've seen your father many a time at Irvine harbour. I would have introduced myself but there's never been the opportunity. How are you enjoying Crawdonia? Your timing could have been better but at least you have an excuse. I, on the other hand, should have cancelled my working holiday but I didn't want to disappoint my students who are eagerly awaiting the results of my research."

Pongo nosed his way out from under the cloak and scrabbled to the front of the boat to have a good look at the mermaid. He sniffed her thoroughly and backed off when she playfully whacked his nose with her tail. "Manners, Pongo."

"My name's a closely guarded secret," he teased. "You're well switched on."

"There's no one more so, not even you."

She wrinkled her nose at him.

"And delightfully modest."

Pongo was warming to Samphire already.

"There's far too much jawing for my liking," said Florin, shaking his tassels. "I'm fed up sitting here on Vince's lap. I'll go it alone if there isn't some action soon."

"There's no need," said Peg, "entertaining though that would be for the rest of us. But you're right, Florin, it is time we got cracking. I've made contact with Gilbert and Leo and they know what's afoot." Sandy punched the air and Jamie's excitement was equally unconfined; he gave a dignified nod. "The next part of the mission is a wee bit more tricky. I would suggest you come alongside to starboard, Pigsblanket. I doubt anyone will notice as they're flapping around like beached flounders. Getting the prisoners off will not be so easy. Gilbert is one seriously big beast."

"We'll just have to create a diversion then, won't we, Lorimer?" Samphire beckoned to the lobster and swung her tail over the side of the boat. "Let's boogie."

Lorimer flipped his goggles on and shimmied across the boat. He flourished his splendid claw and bowed. "After you, gorgeous."

"They make a lovely couple," said Pongo with an impudent grin. "Glitz meets glamour."

The Harpie stared at the Fairy Queen in utter amazement. Celestina looked small and fragile inside her cloak of stars.

The leader of the white-winged rooks watched Maligna closely from his position on Celestina's shoulder while the rest of the squadron circled outside.

"I suppose you've come to crow over me," she said with a bitter laugh.

"I need to know who you are and why you're doing this?"

"Your goody-two-shoes mother stood between me and everything I ever wanted, as you do now. I've always felt cheated watching your pathetic family squander all that power. It's a disgusting waste. I hate maudlin benevolence." Celestina's eyes followed the Harpie as she walked past her onto the beach. "And I always get what I want no matter how long it takes. You should have destroyed me when you had the chance."

The anklet engaged with the Harpie who grew in stature until she towered over the Fairy Queen in a roaring manifestation of incandescent evil which tore the air apart and scattered the Sublime Stars to the four winds. The black gold and clovenstone anklet glittered in the moonlight. Maligna raised her arms above her head and lightning bolts shot out from her fingertips across the night sky. Celestina collapsed on the beach as a shaft of darkness pierced her heart.

The frenzied rooks flew at the Harpie but they were no match for her now and she swatted them away as if they were nothing more than annoying flies.

Maligna had locked onto a split-second chink in Celestina's magic. One tiny lapse of concentration was all it had taken.

The Harpie stood over her. "Not so all-powerful now, Queenie. I'll take the wand and the hair ornament." She picked up the crown and placed it on her own head but when she tried to prise Celestina's fingers open she was struck by a lance of searing white light. "If you want the wand, you'll have to kill me first."

"I intend to, make no mistake about that."

A shadowy form broke away from the rocks behind Maligna and sprang silently into the air. It felled the Harpie with one almighty swipe and trapped her under its massive paws. She cursed and screamed in frustrated confusion as her attacker's features swam into focus. The beast hissed savagely as it opened its crushing jaws above her head.

"Got it!" yelled Minxie triumphantly as she shot up into the air with the anklet held firmly between her front paws. "I was hoping our surprise attack would force the little monster to relax its grip. Talk about team work. That demon cat impression had me scared, Kizz."

"And me," chimed Wainscot, loosening her hold on the cat's neck.

The wazwatt flew across to Celestina. "I think you ought to look after this, Your Majesty."

"Dearest Minxie and Kismet, I'm profoundly grateful. That was a close call." Her voice was heavy with emotion and her breathing harsh and laboured. "You came out of nowhere."

"Kismet's ability to match his surroundings was the key, ma'am."

The Queen stumbled towards the Harpie. As she leant over the prostrate figure a malevolent, predatory entity rose out of Maligna and passed through Celestina's body. She shivered with revulsion as the amorphous, spongy mass slithered down the beach and slunk off into the sea.

Celestina turned back towards her defeated adversary and found she was looking at her own face. The creature at her feet was the mirror image of herself.

"Salvation is at hand, Leo, how positively splendid. We'll be celebrating our liberation before the night's over. I can feel a fireworks party coming on."

"Let's hope your optimism is better placed than your previous form with explosives would indicate."

Gilbert smiled weakly. "There I go again, always getting carried away."

"Play our cards right and we'll both get carried away, hopefully to a peaceful place before fireworks were ever invented."

The gull landed on the sailcloth and surreptitiously slipped underneath.

"Right, Leo, here's the deal. Pigsblanket is the only one who can row, so he'll have to stay where he is. We're going to lower you to the boat in a lobster creel and then we'll come back for Gilbert. Sounds simple enough, doesn't it?"

The Giant Rat giggled nervously. "How big's the creel?"

"Not big enough to accommodate you."

"I'm a tolerable swimmer."

"You could be Olympic class before the night's out."

"Who's doing the lowering?"

"Sandy's the only one with the required amount of arms and legs. I'll be up in the rigging keeping an eye on things while Samphire and Lorimer prepare to entertain the crew."

"Who are they?" Gilbert asked, jiggling with excitement. "My head's in a fast spin."

"A mermaid and a lobster," snapped the gull.

"Silly old me, I should have known."

"And don't be surprised if Jamie gets involved. Come to think of it, the dog's likely to stick his oar in too. Before you ask, his name's Pongo and he's Pogo Pixie's pooch." The Siamese cat's love of alliteration was rubbing off on the seagull.

Peg zipped off again, leaving Gilbert and Leo choking with laughter.

"Well, tickle me pink, chumlet. It sounds as if we're the star turn at the circus. Let's hope the ringmaster doesn't discover what we're up to and throw us to the lions."

"Hold back the elephants and bring on the clowns, is what I say, Gilb."

The Giant Rat threw caution to the wind along with the sailcloth. "No elephants, I'm glad to report, but the clowns have arrived. There's a spectacularly attired lobster swinging claw over claw across the rigging with a broom-wielding Bosun on his tail. What a lark!"

"You're not taking this seriously, Gilbert, are you?"

"And when was the last time you saw a mermaid wearing a balaclava?"

"It's not that cold, surely?"

"Sorry, just kidding. I haven't actually seen Samphire yet but, if Lorimer's anything to go by, we're in for a treat."

"Get your head back in here, before someone clocks you."

17

The Fairy Queen was emotionally drained and still recovering from the wound inflicted by the anklet but, thanks to the bravery of Kismet and Minxie, the Harpie was finally vanquished. The dark secret at the heart of Sylvania had been exposed. Celestina was devastated to discover she had a monstrous twin sister but she wanted nothing kept from her loyal council after everything they been through together.

Hamish was ashen-faced and angry. "Did you know about any of this, Indigoletta?"

Creel raised his head to look at the Royal Raven as she shifted uncomfortably on her perch in the small reception room. Jock stood on the arm of the old fisherman's chair and Grimpen lay curled up at his feet. The rest of the Clandestine Council were present, except for Alfie who was still under the care of the Banshee. Pogo was there in his place with Cassandra resting on her lap.

The Royal Raven's voice was clear and steady. "I believed Princess Celestina to be the only surviving twin. Her sister was stillborn. This turned out to be a blessed accident of fate as the baby bore the birthmark indicating she was from the dark side. I informed the Prince of Cobalt-Sibilance immediately but we did not divulge this information to anyone other than Queen Daria herself. The doctor and midwife had seen the distinguishing mark and knew its significance but their silence was assured as trusted members of the royal household. The whole business was hushed up and the dead infant was taken care of according to ancient law. The Queen decided her remaining daughter should never know the truth. What was the point of upsetting her unnecessarily?"

"Clearly something went wrong though."

"Apparently so, sir."

"There's no apparent about it, Indigoletta."

Celestina put a restraining hand on her husband's arm.

"If anyone's at fault, it's me," said Sammy. "I had the remains of the princess exhumed before I came here and the baby turned out to be nothing more than two bags of sugar wrapped in a shawl. I believed the infant to be dead, for which I was profoundly grateful, and had no reason to suspect anything was amiss when the sealed box arrived for interment. Clearly I should have been more thorough."

"I won't have you taking the blame," said Indigoletta. "I was the one who told you she was dead. You never even saw the baby. Only those present at the twins' birth can be held responsible."

"The doctor made a mistake," said Jock reasonably. "Everything else happened as a result of that."

"But the real damage was caused by my wife's dishonesty." Creel looked directly at the Prince of Cobalt-Sibilance. "She was trusted with delivering the baby to you, sir. She told me she left Queen Daria's rooms with it concealed in the carpet bag she always had with her when she attended a birth. As Royal Midwife she was trusted absolutely. When she discovered the baby was alive she knew what the birthmark represented and yet she still stole her. We desperately wanted a child of our own but Kedda's obsession must have driven her out of her mind."

"She's paid a heavy price, from what you've told us," said Celestina sadly. "But you have suffered so much yourself. Killing your demonic step-daughter to save your wife took enormous courage and what a terrible burden to carry all these years. How did you finally discover the information that brought you here to warn me?"

Creel lifted a work-worn hand and stroked Jock's tail feathers.

"I was horribly troubled by the eruption on the Island of Long Forgotten Dreams, Your Majesty, and that, coupled with a growing preoccupation with my drowned daughter, took me up onto the cliff to the spot where we buried Feya's toys and trinkets as a memorial to her. I hate going there as I always relive my last day with her in harrowing detail, but the island is clearly visible from the clifftop. When the dragon flew past, the hunched figure on its back looked at me with such hatred I knew with absolute certainty Feya was behind its eyes. I confronted Kedda and she confessed what she'd done. I'm sorry I didn't get here in time."

"So, she didn't drown after all," said Sammy. "Feya must have fallen prey to an opportunistic Harpie. These parasitical creatures absorb their victims like a malignant sponge and live off them." The Attendant to the Royal Raven shuddered. "There is only one requirement, Will, and you don't and never will qualify. The blacker the heart, the more attractive it is to a Harpie. Maligna fed on Feya and grew supremely powerful. The entity she lived off was the epitome of evil and created her longing for control of Sylvania in the first place. Harpies are not ambitious or single-minded as a rule and they don't usually possess a weapon as deadly as the anklet. Maligna failed to take control of Sylvania the first time and, with the anklet restored to her, wasn't about to let that happen again. Those long years in the sink-hole had fuelled her hatred making her more determined to succeed. How she came by that destructive magic is lost in the distant past. There has been much speculation but my own belief is that she stole the anklet from one of the last great necromancers. This isn't the first time our world has been stalked by evil."

Celestina's voice was flat and empty. "My dark half created the monster that was Maligna."

"Dear child," said the Royal Raven, dispensing with all formality. "She is not your other half. She is the exact opposite of you. Identical in appearance but that is all."

They sat in silence for a while then Will asked the question on everyone's lips. "Surely you noticed your step-daughter bore an uncanny resemblance to your Sovereign, Creel?"

"All this happened a very long time ago and I've never seen Her Majesty at close quarters until today."

Pigsblanket secured the rowing boat underneath one of the rope ladders on the starboard side of 'The Cheeky Monkey' and the starry bow light switched itself off.

The boy addressed the kilt and sporran in the most serious tone he could muster. "Do you think you could stop bickering at least until we've achieved our aim? A skirt on a ship is bad enough without it being heckled by a purse."

"Right enough, lad. You can rely on us. Isn't that right, *Invincible*?"

The kilt swelled with pride and its pleats expanded accordingly. "Florin and I are a team and that's a fact."

Pongo ached to go with Sandy who was cautiously making her way up the ladder towards the gundeck. "Do I really have to stay here? I feel so useless."

"I can't see an alternative," Pigsblanket said sympathetically. "Rope ladders are tricky if you've four legs. There's a swell in the harbour so, if I were you, I wouldn't risk it."

J Milne

Jamie leapt onto the swinging ladder and followed Sandy without the slightest hesitation.

"I didn't know he was going to do that," gasped the amazed dog.

"Neither did I. Who'd have thought he was so nimble?"

"Or so brave. He's a rare beast."

Sandy arrived unscathed at the top of the ladder and disappeared over the side. Jamie jumped into her arms and draped himself round her shoulders like a fur collar. She leant out and gave a hasty thumbs-up before concealing herself behind the nearest cannon.

There were hurricane lamps dotted around but large areas of the gundeck were in shadow.

She unfolded the pencil sketch Pigsblanket had drawn for her and the magic stars formed a map-light above the scrap of paper. There was an 'X' marking the all-important coil of rope and a smaller one above the locker where the lobster creels were stored. She crept along the gundeck, ducking under muzzles of cannons.

A group of sailors were assembled in neat rows, with their backs to her, receiving a dressing-down from Pestilence Grimshaw. She couldn't see the infamous buccaneer but she could hear him clearly over the wind. As she passed the foremast, Peg gave the agreed signal from the rigging where he was acting as lookout.

Pigsblanket had assured her the cupboard was never locked.

The creels were in among a jumble of fishing nets and crab-pots. She pulled one out and grabbed a couple of lengths of rope.

Peg gave the all-clear and she darted back across the deck, skipping from one patch of shadow to another. She jinked behind an oildrum when a grumbling bunch of matelots came towards her from the gundeck. She could see Gilbert and Leo's hiding place from where she was and experienced a stab of excitement.

When Sandy stepped out from behind the drum she came face-to-face with Cahoots. She was extremely startled, never having met a dragon before. Jamie was in full bristle mode and wouldn't have looked out of place on a witch's broomstick.

"Who are you?" asked Cahoots brightly. "I'm sorry if I scared you both. Does he always travel like that?"

"Only when he's feeling too lazy to walk."

"You cheeky monkey!" said the cat.

"That's the ship's name," replied the amused dragon. "Me Cahoots."

The cat gave an extended sigh. "I'm Jamie and the lippy child is Sandy."

The dragon's eyes grew large. "Are you the one from Irvine everyone's banging on about?"

"Yes, but could you keep your voice down? I don't want anyone to know I'm here."

"Okey-dokey." Cahoots lowered his head and his voice. "Not even the Captain?"

Sandy's eyebrows shot up. "Especially not him!" She'd blurted it out before she could stop herself.

"Don't worry about that. He's in a foul temper and I'm staying well out of his way. Gilbert and Leo have done a bunk and he's livid. I really miss them, they were my friends. I don't suppose you know where they are?"

"Actually I do, which is why I'm sneaking around in the dark. We've come to rescue them."

"Oh, goody! Maybe I can help."

Sandy looked doubtful. If she refused his offer he might decide to blow the whistle, so why take the risk. "I'd appreciate that. Perhaps you could act as a mobile screen. You're certainly big enough."

The dragon was delighted. He'd even forgotten about Maligna. "Size is not an issue with me as long as I'm out of doors. Give me a few more hours at the current rate of growth and I could walk past Captain Grimshaw with the entire crew behind me without him spotting a single one of them! What's the knitted cage for?"

There was a commotion by the foremast before she could reply.

"Get ready to catch him, men," yelled Leitzoff as he took an almighty swipe at Lorimer with the broom.

The lobster swung clear at the last minute, throwing in a spontaneous display of somersaults and half turns worthy of the trapeze act at Gilbert and Leo's circus, before plunging deckwards with a fixed grin and a crowd-pleasing 'taa-raaah'; ever the professional performer. He only escaped being smashed to atoms by Sandy's automatic response which had her running across the deck to catch him in the creel as if he were a tossed pancake and not the marine equivalent of Humpty-Dumpty.

His relief was short-lived when he realised where he was but there was no time to get in a lather, at least not about that. The Bosun and a group of sailors had them surrounded.

"I'll take the lobster," said Leitzoff with a lopsided smirk. "Me and the lads could do with a slap-up dinner. We're sick of saltbeef and crackers." The others nodded vigorously. "There's good eating in that there crustashun. She fills out her bathin' costume very nicely."

"She?!" Lorimer was outraged and almost forgot the predicament he was in. "I'm not female. They're much fleshier. I'm not worth the trouble. All shell and gristle. I'll only get stuck in your teeth."

"That's not somethin' I have to worry about, bein' as I'm near enough out of gnashers." Leitzoff thrust his head forward menacingly. "I'll suck the meat out of you instead."

"Sorry, Lorimer, but you're safer in there for once." Sandy closed the lid of the creel and hugged it to her chest. "This lobster stays right where it is. Take one step towards me and I'll yell my lungs out." She was pretty sure the Bosun wouldn't want Grimshaw on the scene, that would put paid to his plans for dinner. Her gamble paid off.

"Now, don't you be too hasty. We means you no harm nor your collar," he said with a snigger.

"Perhaps we can come to some arrangement," said the 'collar'. "I too am partial to lobster." Lorimer gazed anxiously at Jamie from inside the creel. The cat winked at him. "Preferably cooked, which is where you come in."

"Traitor!" he said, playing along with Jamie. "You won't let any of them eat me will you, Sandy?"

She tweaked his tail surreptitiously to reassure him. "That depends."

Leitzoff became lights on. "Now yer talkin'." He turned to the sailor nearest him. "You keep an eye out for the Skipper while I comes to an arrangement with this here lad in the skirt. You're not from around here, are you?" She shook her head. "Name your price."

"I want safe passage off this ship with..." She never finished the sentence, something that happens a lot in this tale.

A strangulated snort came from Cahoots who had caught sight of Pestilence Grimshaw. He was striding towards them from the gundeck. "Quick, get behind me, the Captain's heading this way. He's so angry he looks as if he's been spit-roasted."

Sandy broke through the circle of sailors and dashed behind the dragon only to find the Bosun and his men heading towards her from the other direction.

Grimshaw went into full buccaneer mode, all 'Jolly Roger' and no jollity. "What are you playing at, you barnacle-brained bedbug? Come out at once and bring those yellow-bellied scumbags with you."

Sandy grabbed the Bosun's arm and whispered urgently. "The lobster's yours if you don't give us away." He nodded and nudged his men out from behind the dragon.

"Sorry, Cap'n, one of the topmastmen thought he'd seen ratty's tail sticking out of that coil of rope, so I thought we ought to have a quick shufti."

Sandy practically collapsed and Lorimer could have made good use of smelling salts. Jamie remained calm on the outside but his heart was hammering against his ribcage.

"It turned out to be a false alarm."

Florin relaxed his seams and Vince loosened his buckles.

Cahoots remained where he was with what felt like a very silly expression on his face. "Any news of mother?" he squeaked when he could no longer bear Grimshaw's penetrating stare.

"Nothing as yet, nephew dear, but she's a tough old bird. She'll be back to annoy us soon enough, so why don't you come and have something to eat before we sail? It's time we got this ship on the high seas while there's still a remote chance of getting away."

"I think I'll stay here a bit longer, if that's OK with you," he said, trying to sound morose rather than over-excited.

"Suit yourself." Grimshaw turned and headed back to his cabin. He called out to the Bosun. "I want a word with the First Mate. Have him report to me at once. You men get about your duties and find the prisoners. Maligna will tear your heads off with my blessing if you don't."

Cahoots was overjoyed to see his pals again. The reunion was necessarily low-key but emotionally charged, Sandy hugged a purring Leo to her chest before thrusting him into the creel which Lorimer readily vacated. She attached the ropes in an impressive series of knots learned from her seafaring father.

Gilbert climbed out of his rope den and sat patiently awaiting instructions. Jamie introduced himself. "You're some size," he said with a visible shudder. "A cat's worst nightmare in the fur and flesh."

"My dear chap, you've nothing to fear from me," said the rat gallantly. "I'm positively delighted to meet you and hope I may return the favour one day."

"Thank you, Gilbert, but I hope that won't be necessary."

"Fall in behind me, you lily-livered scoundrels," hissed the dragon. The rat's serene expression was wiped from his face. "Sorry, I couldn't resist that. When you're ready."

They set off along the deck under cover of Cahoots and parted company with him when he fell in with a group of deckhands who were debating the merits of lobster tails as opposed to lobster claws. "The bigger the claw the sweeter the meat" sent Lorimer skittering across the deck and under a cannon.

"The rations on this tub must be pathetic," whispered Florin. "Everyone's obsessed with food."

"Something we don't have to concern ourselves with, thankfully," said Vince.

Sandy borrowed Gilbert's neckerchief and waved it at Pigsblanket and Pongo. The cabin boy waved back. "Here goes, Leo."

"Bon voyage, little chum. Watch out for those crosswinds."

"Don't worry about me, Gilb. Take care of your own skin."

Sandy carefully lowered the rope with the creel attached until it was hanging above the dog's head. Pigsblanket grabbed hold of the contained cat and placed him beside Pongo who flashed his teeth in a welcoming smile. Conchita set about removing the ropes with a skilful combination of foot and beak manoeuvres in response to the dog's detailed instructions.

"How are you when it comes to climbing backwards down a rope ladder, Gilbert?"

"Inexperienced, Sandy. If it goes horribly wrong I'll take my chances in the sea. Would you mind giving me a leg up?" The Giant Rat put a dainty foot into her cupped hands and she heaved him onto the gunnel. Gilbert swung his rear over the side and hung precariously until his toes connected with the ladder. "Tally-ho!" he cried and began a nifty descent towards the rowing boat.

Lorimer darted out from under the cannon towards Sandy. She gathered him up just as the Bosun grabbed her from behind, pinning her arms to her side. The lobster flew out of her hands and landed awkwardly on his back, spinning like an upturned tortoise. Jamie scowled at Leitzoff from Sandy's shoulders in an attempt to unnerve him but he needn't have bothered. The Bosun was thinking with his stomach.

"You wasn't about to throw that crustashun overboard, was you, lad?"

"Of course not," she lied. "I was trying to loosen the ferocious grip he had on my arm before I handed him over. That bad-tempered lobster just savaged me, you're welcome to him."

Leitzoff's attention had begun to wander and he was gazing past her. A smile spread across his grubby face.

"Here, lads, come and look at this. In all my years on the Sylvanian seas I've never seen the likes."

Lorimer had managed to right himself and was high-stepping along the gunnel with Samphire sitting side-saddle on his back. The magic stars had turned themselves into a

reason

sparkly bridle and reins which the mermaid was holding. "Well, hello there," she called to the gawping matelots. "It's showtime!"

The lobster reared up like a circus pony and the mermaid gave a suitably refined 'yee-hah'.

The sailors stamped and hollered their appreciation when Lorimer became a bucking bronco and Samphire added to the drama by waving an arm above her head, looking as if she might be thrown and trampled under claw at any moment.

Sandy slipped away while this preposterous spectacle was being played out. She tip-toed past Cahoots who was laying it on thick. "They're terrific together. It would be a shame to split up such a talented double-act by eating one of them."

"What makes you think we won't scoff 'em both?" shouted the Bosun to a rousing cheer from his men.

"You're not leaving so soon, surely?" Sandy spun round and found herself staring down the muzzle of a flintlock pistol. "You haven't enjoyed my hospitality yet, unlike your ungrateful pussy-cat and his bumbling sidekick. I hope that thing round your neck has better manners. Do forgive me, I haven't introduced myself."

"There's no need for that, I know who you are, *Mr* Grimshaw."

The buccaneer was furious at the slur but buried his anger under a steely smile. "Don't try to outsmart me, my dear. It's very unwise."

"Is that right?"

"You said that without moving your lips. I'm almost impressed."

"Well, I'm not."

"Neither am I."

"Nor me," said Sandy, deliberately adding to the confusion.

"There's nothing to it really."

"I couldn't agree more."

"That's settled then."

"Enough!" bellowed Grimshaw, well and truly losing his cool.

"There's no need to raise your voice, Florin."

"I didn't, Vince."

"I'm sorry, it must have been someone else."

"I've heard Mr Grimshaw's loud and aggressive, perhaps it was him."

"Surely not?"

"It wouldn't surprise me. You know what pirates are like."

"Don't talk about me as if I'm not here," screeched the buccaneer.

"Did you say something, Florin?"

"No, Vince. Perhaps it was Sandy."

Leitzoff had turned his short attention span to his boss and the lad in the skirt, vaguely wondering if he'd missed something. There were too many voices for the number of people involved.

Pestilence had the sort of dangerous look in his eye that would have sent Jem Slack scurrying behind the bar at The Mischief Maker. "I don't know what your game is, child, but one more word out of you and I'll chop you into chunks."

"Don't rile him, lad. It's best to do as he says."

"And you should know more than most, eh, Leitzoff? You're wrong about one thing though."

"What's that, Cap'n?" he asked warily.

"This lad, as you insist on calling him, is the female child from Scotland, you dolt. The combined brains of this crew add up to less than those in a can of sardines. Damn it, man, it's a wonder we haven't been murdered in our hammocks!"

"You sleep in a bunk, Cap'n, so you'd be all right."

Grimshaw snapped and lashed out with the pistol. He caught the Bosun on the side of the head and Leitzoff stumbled backwards into Sandy. "Sorry, miss," he said as he sank to the floor, blood running freely from the wound on his temple. "I doubt I'll be needin' that crustashun after all."

She knelt down by his side and pressed a hanky to the wound. "If this is how you treat the crew of 'The Cheeky Monkey' no wonder the whole ship's a shambles. You're nothing but an arrogant bully."

Leitzoff felt for her hand and gripped it anxiously. "Shoosh now. Let him be, that's the only way."

Grimshaw pulled her up by the wrist and shook her until her teeth rattled. "Here's the deal, you little brat. If you stop being disrespectful I might just consider letting you join your friends in the rowing boat. I see you're surprised I know about that. Did you think you could sneak around here without anyone realising what you were up to? I'm only sorry I was unable to prevent Gilbert and Leo's departure. There's one other teensy thing. I want that treacherous, back-stabbing cabin boy. I'm tempted to demand the rat's return as well, but I'm feeling generous."

"I'll never agree to that."

"Oh, I think you will." Grimshaw reached out and snatched Jamie from her shoulders. "What an exquisite collar. Diamond and sapphire if I'm not mistaken, but I digress. If you don't accept my terms, I'll break kitty's elegant neck."

"He's bluffing, Vince."

"I'm sure you're right, Florin."

"Am I, or aren't I? Anyone want to place bets? And you, my dear, will stop throwing your voice. I can't tolerate attention-seeking children."

"Is that so?" said the sporran before he could stop himself.

Grimshaw viewed Sandy through narrowed eyes. "That really is very good, you know, but I stand by what I said. One more word and you'll be a finely chopped pile of mince at my feet."

"You can't, Pigsblanket. We won't let you." Pongo was agitated and didn't care who knew it. "What exactly did Sandy say, Peg?"

"You mean to *Mr* Grimshaw?"

"I do wish I'd been there," said Gilbert twiddling his whiskers. "What a wonderful put-down."

"She won't let you give yourself up, no way."

"That's Sandy for you," said Leo shaking his head, "very determined."

The cabin boy's cheerful confidence had melted away and he looked small and frightened. "That doesn't change anything. Once Grimshaw's mind's made up there's no shifting him, particularly when he's been drinking. I better get up there before he goes berserk."

Pongo placed his paw on Pigsblanket's arm to restrain him. "Don't be so hasty, Sandy'll think of something. After all, she can't come to any real harm in Sylvania."

"I'm not willing to take that risk."

Leo had grown close to the boy during their short acquaintance. He jumped onto his lap. "He'll kill you. Please stay here with us."

"Listen to my wee pal," pleaded the rat. "He's no fool and I should know. He's kept me out of trouble even though I've unwittingly gone out of my way to thwart him."

Pigsblanket's tone was flat and his shoulders sagged like a tired old mattress. "I'm sure it won't come to that."

"Say it like you mean it." Pongo was sick with anxiety for his friend. "Look at Conchita, she's frozen with fear. You can't desert her."

"Great Scot, Pigsblanket, there he is! He's dangling Jamie by the collar." The Giant Rat had the ridiculous desire to hide his head under the cloak. If he couldn't see the buccaneer, then maybe the brute wasn't really there. A childish reaction, but compelling nonetheless.

"It's your choice, Pigsbreath!" bawled the pirate. "I'll throttle this fancy kitty if you don't get yourself up here at once. And bring the resurrected parrot. I've unfinished business with her too."

Sandy gestured wildly at Pongo. As the boy reached for the ladder, the dog hurled himself into the air and knocked him into the harbour. Pongo hit Pigsblanket with such force he overshot and plunged into the sea as well.

"Ye gods, that mutt needs some discipline." The buccaneer leant out over the gunnel. "You've all forfeited your freedom thanks to the dog's unruly behaviour," he yelled. "Get them up here right away, Leitzoff. Take as many men as you need but make it quick."

"There isn't time for that, Captain Grimshaw." The voice was calm and authoritative.

Pestilence stepped back in surprise and collided with the sailors nearest him. They scrambled out of his way. "So you've deigned to join us at last, Mr Malahyde. Where have you been?"

"Trying to sail off into the sunrise ahead of the boarding party; the one that's making its way across the harbour as we speak."

"Why wasn't I informed?"

"Consider yourself informed now," he said in a glacial tone. "I'll take the cat."

"I'm perfectly capable of strangling a moggy, Jedediah." Pestilence was expecting a deferential titter from the crew but they didn't react, they were too busy watching the First Mate. The air was heavy with tension.

Grimshaw tightened his hold on Jamie's collar and swung him towards Sandy. The cat's eyes were closed and he hung limply. The buccaneer kicked her when she tried to put her hands under Jamie to support his weight. "Oh no, you don't. You're too late anyway. Poor puss. The dog's next and then the others, one by one, and you get to watch every time. Are you still here, Leitzoff? If it's a flogging you're after, it'll be my pleasure."

Jedediah Malahyde squared up to the pirate captain. "We can do this the hard way or the easy way, it's up to you. But, if you don't unhand the cat, I'll throttle you myself. Mr Leitzoff, I'm taking command of 'The Cheeky Monkey', do you have a problem with that?"

The Bosun had never been asked his opinion on anything quite so important before. He shuffled his feet and looked skywards for inspiration. His face brightened. "Seize him, men!"

"Bravo, Leitzoff! You've earned yourself a reprieve and a large tot of rum. I knew you'd have no stomach for mutiny."

The crew were in no doubt what the Bosun had meant. They fell on Grimshaw who couldn't believe what was happening to him. He dropped Jamie in the scuffle and they hoisted the buccaneer above their heads.

Leitzoff wiped the blood from his face with his shirt sleeve and gave a heartfelt salute.

"The men was wonderin' what you'd like 'em to do with this nasty piece of work, *Captain* Malahyde."

Sandy held Jamie in her arms while she watched the boarding party coming towards the brigantine. The cat had survived his dreadful ordeal, due in part to him having the presence of mind not to struggle. It had been touch and go; Malahyde's intervention had come just in the nick of time.

On Jedediah's orders the Bosun raised the royal ensign over 'The Cheeky Monkey' with the full approval of the crew. It was time to go straight and, with Grimshaw removed, the men were eager to start over again.

Trencher Halibut left the galley and made a rare visit to the gundeck. The generously proportioned cook arrived with two apprentices in his wake carrying trays of fairy cakes soaked in rum.

"It seemed appropriate now that we're working for Her Majesty," he said when he noticed Jedediah's raised eyebrow.

Grimshaw was under armed guard by the foremast. He was thoroughly disgusted and made his feelings plain. "You'll be enrolling the men in country dancing classes next," he scoffed.

"Now there's an idea, Mr Leitzoff. Perhaps you'd like to look into that for me."

"Right away, Cap'n Malahyde." Jedediah started to laugh. "You're pulling me leg. Sometimes I'm not too tightly wrapped."

Cahoots watched the buccaneer from a safe distance.

"Where's that mother of yours when I need her? To think I helped her escape. I must've been soft in the head."

"Minxie's heading this way and she looks well pleased with herself," said the dragon bursting with excitement.

"That's all I need and pray tell me when she isn't full of herself?" His eyes followed the wazwatt as she banked and headed straight for him.

"Party hats all round," she yelled, looping the loop. "Maligna's been defeated." She turned an aerial cartwheel and knocked Grimshaw's feathered tricorn from his head. "Oops! Careless little me."

"I don't know what you're so pleased about. I thought you were on the Harpie's side," he called after her.

"Heavens, no. What in Sylvania gave you that idea?" She landed on Leitzoff's bristly pate and dodged out of the way when he made a playful grab for her.

"You acted as our go-between. She trusted you, as did I, even though you're an exasperating, jumped-up know-all. I really believed you were on our side."

"That's what you were supposed to think," she said, treading air. "I make a good double agent."

Cahoots was practically beside himself. "But Minxie, what's happened to mother? She's not dead, is she?"

"Most definitely not, but I think it's time you and I had a wee chat. You didn't really think that old sea dog was your uncle, did you?"

"Uh-huh. Why shouldn't he be?"

"Jings! This is going to be more difficult than I thought. My approach from now on is going to be more pragmatic."

"Prag-what-ic?"

The wazwatt giggled. "That word's too advanced, methinks. Let me simplify things for you while we take a spin round the deck."

The Commander of the Queen's Imps-at-arms spoke briefly to Pigsblanket and Pongo before he agreed to let them go. He ordered two of his unit to stay with the rowing boat and, with Sandy and Jamie safely installed, gave the order to row ashore.

"Hey, wait for us!"

Gilbert looked quizzically at Leo. "I didn't say a word."

"Over here!"

Pongo barked enthusiastically. "Lorimer, Samphire, how the devil are you?"

Sandy leant out of the boat and whisked the lobster out of the harbour with Samphire clinging to his tail.

"That was some display," she said. "Did you catch any of it down below?"

"You betcha. We saw the whole thing. You two have a future on the stage."

Samphire laughed coyly. "I wouldn't go that far, Pongo."

"Well I would, my dear, you were superb."

"Thank you, Gilbert," she said flicking her hair over her shoulder with studied carelessness.

"What puzzles me, though," said Leo, "is how you came by that fantastic glittery costume."

"You mean this boring old bathing suit? I had it on anyway, it's part of my day wear collection."

The gull hopped towards the lobster. "Perhaps the Bosun might fancy you for his dinner after all? I could make enquiries, if you like."

"Very amusing, but Mr Leitzoff wouldn't dream of eating me now. We're good pals."

Peg landed beside the cabin boy. "I nearly forgot to pass on the message from Captain Malahyde. He was wondering if you'd care to take up a new position on 'The Cheeky Monkey'? Now that he's in overall charge he's very much in need of a First Mate. Would you be interested?"

The boy stopped rowing. "Are you serious?"

"I'd never joke about something like that. If you give me your answer, I'll fly back and tell him."

"He say 'yes, pleeze'." For a moment Sandy thought 'Bandolero' had materialised out of thin air to perform a celebratory Mexican hat dance.

Pigsblanket recognised the Spanish accent immediately and whooped with pleasure that the parrot had finally broken her long silence. "Chita's got it in one. Tell Captain Malahyde it would be an honour to serve under him."

Pongo erupted with pent-up emotion and went twice round the rowing boat, neatly avoiding everyone, even though it was packed. He turned a faultless somersault and landed in front of the parrot. "I didn't know you spoke Spanish."

"With a name like that, what did you expect, Norwegian?"

"Very droll, Jamie. I see you're well on the way to being your old self again. That throttling hasn't made you any less outspoken." The dog leant towards the parrot. "*Gato arrogante y sarcástico*," he said, pointing at the Siamese cat.

"*Muy bien, Señor Pongo*," she replied, winking at Jamie.

"You're not wrong, Conchita, my Spanish is very good." The dog's eyes twinkled. "Perhaps you would take me through some irregular verbs when you have a spare moment. I'm finding some of them rather tricky."

Celestina found Feya in a chair by a window in the infirmary. Her sister stared blankly into the middle distance. She was dressed in black silk. The choice of colour had been Feya's own.

She turned to face Celestina. "Do I know you? You're very familiar."

"I'm your sister," said the Queen choking with emotion. "Don't you remember our conversation on the beach earlier?"

"No." Her eyes slid away from Celestina. "Would you like some tea? Perhaps your mother might care to join us."

"Our mother's dead, Feya."

"What a shame. We could have had such a nice chat. Some other time, perhaps."

The Royal Raven could see how distressed Celestina was. She flew to the Queen's side. "Don't put yourself through any more today. It's so dreadfully upsetting."

A nurse knocked on the open door and stepped into the room. "Excuse me, Your Majesty, the doctor would like a word."

"Matricide is a vile crime. The shock of discovering who she really is and what she's done has turned her mind. Your twin sister may have come from the dark side, Your Majesty, but that's of little significance now. The Harpie dined long and well on the evil that was Feya and what is left is little more than the outer shell; a blank canvas, if you like."

The young doctor got up from behind his desk and threw his notes to one side. "Picture an artist painting with watercolours in the rain. An unlikely scenario, I grant you," he added in response to Indigoletta's doubtful look, "but bear with me. Each brushstroke lasts for a fleeting second before it is washed away leaving the merest trace of what it might have become. The curve of a shoulder, perhaps, or the bloom on a peach. Feya's short-term memory is like that, probably for evermore." He faltered, briefly mistaking the Royal Raven's intense stare for disdain rather than rapt attention.

"Do go on," she said.

"There's not much more to say, I'm afraid. The creature sitting in the other room has no identity. Maligna has abandoned her in search of new prey and Feya herself exists in name only. With the evil gone, there's nothing left."

"How pitiful." Celestina was scarcely audible but she quickly recovered herself and the confident authority came to the fore again. "I will look after my sister. She's completely harmless now and I must do what I can to make her feel secure and comfortable."

"Can you really forgive her?"

"I have to, Indigoletta. She is a victim of her own destiny."

18

"Surely there isn't time to organise the Fairymass celebrations before Sandy has to go home?"

"Indeed there is, Hamish. Some excellent perks come with the job of Fairy Queen and bypassing the organisational palaver for this annual event, fun though it is, happens to be one of them."

Celestina sashayed across the room towards her husband. She planted a light kiss on his cheek. "Shall we go?"

"Go where?"

"Why to Fairymass, of course. It's all arranged and everyone's waiting for us."

"They are?"

"Here's Tabitha now. Doesn't she look wonderful?"

Their daughter ran into the room wearing a pink and black spotted flamenco dress. At first sight the layers of the skirt looked as if they were trimmed with fairy lace. The child started to dance around her parents and the dress came alive. The lace consisted of troupes of tiny black poodles running in opposite directions round the separate layers of the skirt. They barked and capered in high spirits as they scampered around the dress.

Tabitha stopped to catch her breath. "What do you think, Father? Isn't it wonderful?" Her hair sparkled with diamond-slippered fireflies and trails of stardust swirled out from her with every move she made. The little dogs stopped and gazed at Hamish expectantly.

"You look like a fairy princess. Your mother's a very talented dressmaker and a fine breeder of elfin poodles."

Tabitha grabbed hold of his hand and dragged him across the room. Some of the younger dogs were left behind but they romped after the frock in a jumble of curls and caught up with it by the door. "Everyone's waiting for us. Are you coming, Mum?"

"I must have a quick word with Crawford first, sweetles."

"It appears Grimshaw jumped overboard when they were bringing him ashore, Your Majesty. I've only just heard about it."

The crow was dressed in his finest togs for the forthcoming celebrations. His cream silk waistcoat was complemented by a foxglove-pink bow-tie embroidered with seed pearls.

"Pestilence struck out for the harbour mouth, although what he imagined he was going to do when he got there is beyond me. The boat turned to go after him but, before the guards could fish him out of the water, he let out a ghastly scream. A most horrible to-do followed with Grimshaw begging to be saved as he struggled against a ferocious whirlpool which had come out of nowhere. The imps-at-arms didn't have the strength to pull him back into the boat."

"So, the Harpie's very much alive and has found her next victim. She's likely to live well off Pestilence Grimshaw. I don't think we need lose too much sleep over that, however. He was many things but his vision did not extend to the destruction of Sylvania. Greed and cruelty were his prime motivations. The anklet is safe again and the Prince of

Cobalt-Sibilance is working on a compendium of spells to decommission it for all time. We'll tie up the loose ends after Fairymass but, in the meantime, let's give Sandy and her entourage a good send-off. Do you know if Will's woken them up yet? The poor dears were in need of a good rest before the celebrations."

Fairymass takes place once a year in the meadows behind the palace complex. It lasts for one golden day and is the highlight of the year for the residents of Crawdonia. The festival is anticipated with mounting excitement and the preparations usually start months in advance. This year was the exception and the town awoke to the sound of the Queen's Own Musicians playing the rousing music that heralds the start of the festival. Fairymass had been brought forward by royal decree.

Every conceivable instrument was employed for the occasion, including upsized knitted bagpipes based on Spondoolicks' unique design. The town was filled with marching bands all keeping perfect time with the music blasting out of loudspeakers all over Corvine.

Notices had been posted at every street corner pronouncing the defeat of the Harpie with a short paragraph giving details of all that had come to light as a result. The rescue from Maligna of the Fairy Queen's hitherto unknown twin sister was documented in the last paragraph. No mention was made of Feya's part in the death of Queen Daria. "That's more than my subjects need to know and what possible good could come of it?" Members of the Clandestine Council were of the same mind and so the matter was laid to rest.

The proclamation ended with the rapturously received news that all the demons had been driven from the land and the roads and woods of the shire were no longer places of fear. There was also a pardon for Jedediah Malahyde and the entire crew of 'The Cheeky Monkey'. Pestilence Grimshaw was posted as missing, presumed drowned.

The guests of honour arrived with the Royal Party. Kismet was a shining rainbow of colours and lit everything around him. Sammy sat on the cat's head with Wainscot and Spondoolicks. The snake wore his ceremonial crown, an ornate gold castle with filigreed silver turrets, diamond windowpanes and walls studded with zircons and sapphires. This lavish crown is a scale model of the ancient seat of the Cobalt-Sibilance family.

The passengers in the howdah travelled down to the waiting crowds on a struntie wool carpet with Archie, the Queen's flying poodle, circling overhead. "Deeply unoriginal magic, but the carpet's a Fairymass tradition," said the Queen, catching hold of a boisterous Pongo before he tumbled over the edge. "Look! There's the flock whose fleeces made this year's model. The poor souls are still in shock as it all happened so quickly."

The shorn strunties stood in an anxious huddle watching the carpet's descent. When it settled on the grass, delivering its cargo safely, they let rip with their own version of the Sylvanian national anthem at the cracking pace of twelve bleats to the baa.

When the row subsided and the crowds settled down Hamish turned to Sandy. "What do you think of my wife's Fabulous Fairymass Frock?"

"I've never seen a dress like a restless sea before. Those maribou feathers look like waves on a stormy night and they're the colour of Indigoletta's plumage by firelight. The dark jewels are how I picture Sammy's cave when the Giant Sapphire's asleep."

"It's all things to everyone," said the Prince. "Your view of it sounds very beautiful indeed. The silk worms have worked so hard this year, we've ended up with extra material."

Tabitha produced a parcel out of nowhere and handed it to Sandy. The ribbons fell away from the wrappings and the tissue paper dissolved in a sparkling mist.

"We thought you'd like your own Fairymass dress," said the Queen. "The material is the same as mine but the design is more youthful though by no means practical, that would be far too boring. All you have to do is choose the colour."

The dress floated above the ground, a shimmering confection of silk, lace and feathers. It turned a deep shade of lavender.

"What a good choice," said Tabitha clapping her hands . "I love purple."

Celestina saw Sandy glance anxiously at Vince and Florin and stepped in to prevent an awkward moment. "I was wondering if you boys might like to lead the Scottish country dancing. Indigoletta's keen to partake of some jigs and reels and she's hoping you'll team up with her."

"It would be an honour, Your Majesty," said the kilt solemnly. "Is that not so, Florin?"

"Invincibly, Indubitable," said the flustered sporran, making everyone laugh.

The Fairy Queen took up her place on the canopied stage to open the proceedings. Gathered round the flying carpet were palace staff and officials, from the most exalted right down to the junior scullery maids and kitchen porters. Everyone works shifts on Fairymass, so no one misses out on the fun. The crowd was mainly Crawdonian but Celestina had flown in a few special guests from the shires.

Estella stood at the front with Mervyn and his family and Pongo rushed over to greet her. They ended up rolling around on the grass with his nephew Scruggs. "Thank goodness you're still willing to mix with us commoners," said the small version of Pongo, "you're quite a celebrity now."

"Don't encourage him," said Estella with a chuckle. "He's bad enough as it is."

"And you're still a cheeky wee article."

"Can I have your autograph, Uncle Pongo?"

"I'll supply the paw if you provide the ink-pad, Scruggsie."

Estella pushed past them. "Quiet, you two. The presentation's starting."

Celestina awarded Kismet and Minxie Necklets of Honour studded with gemstones from the Cave of Sublime Spirit. The centrepiece on each was cut from the Giant Sapphire itself. The difference in size of the recipients was cause for much mirth.

Before the Fairy Queen declared the festival open she asked Pogo to join her at the front of the stage. The pixie rose to her feet uncertainly and Celestina beckoned her forward.

"I have wonderful news which I'm eager to share with everyone," she said. "Wee Alfie Elf was gravely wounded by a scrogwit during the conflict. Thanks to Jock Craw, Grimpen and the unequalled skill of Marta, the Banshee, WAE, as he's affectionately known, is here today along with his pony Celia who was seriously injured in the same attack."

A space appeared in the crowd and Alfie stepped forward. He bowed to Celestina and smiled at all the well-wishers. Estella ran across to her father and flung herself into his arms.

"Where's Celia?" she asked, looking round for the pony.

"She's over there with Marta and Angus," he said. "You can't miss her, she's decked in garlands of flowers and Jock's standing on her head."

The Banshee was unrecognisable to those who knew her. She'd had a shower installed in her home in the tree and bought herself some snappy new clothes.

"Marta scrubs up well," Pongo said cheerfully. "Isn't that Captain Malahyde giving her the eye?"

"Don't you start any rumours," said Lorimer, happily splashing around in a spacious salt-water aquarium on a stand nearby. There was a sign in front of it which read 'All the Way from Scotland for One Day Only.'

"I suppose that was the lobster's idea."

"Aye, Jamie," said the gull. "Lorimer's very much the showman now. He's constantly changing."

"Colour?"

"No, bathing suits! He woke up from his nap earlier and found a whole pile of new cozzies beside his silver bucket. From the wee princess no less."

A crowd had gathered to watch the highly anticipated display of Scottish country dancing led by Indigoletta wearing Vince and Florin who had resized themselves to fit her perfectly. Crawford had set aside his black patent shoes with the shiny silver buckles and was dancing around the Royal Raven barefoot. The shoes were all very well but when it came to energetic jigs they were too much of a hindrance.

Indigoletta heeled and toed as she advanced towards Crawford, sweeping him off his feet in both senses of the expression. Gilbert joined in and had his first taste of applause and approval. It was intoxicating.

"He's some dancer," said Leo as Jamie pranced past to join the Giant Rat and Pongo for an Eightsome Reel. Sandy dragged an embarrassed Pigsblanket onto the floor and, with Indigoletta and Crawford, they only needed one more. When they failed to persuade Grimpen to join them, Indigoletta insisted Will make up the set. A photograph of their wild cavorting made the front page of *The Corvine Herald* as one of the highlights of Fairymass.

Peg Leg and Conchita sat together watching the dancers while they alternately sipped watermelon sorbet through a shared straw. "I don't know if you're familiar with this style of dancing, Chita, but it's all in the footwork."

"And you should know, *amigo.*"

Lorimer appeared behind them wearing a violet and pink lurex swimsuit. "Hatching plots, are we? Or should that be hatching eggs?"

"Do I detect a hint of jealousy, Thermidor?"

"Not likely. I'm in no hurry to get hitched although I'm promised to a show-stoppingly gorgeous crustacean called Rita Petita. She came over on an exchange scheme from the Gulf of Mexico."

The gull looked sceptical. "That's the first I've heard of it."

"I'm surprised I haven't mentioned her before, but these last few days have occupied centre stage in my mind." He clattered up over the back of a chair and onto the table to help himself to a couple of crab claws. "You'd like Rita Petita, Conchita."

"You made her up just so you could say that!"

"I did not," he replied indignantly, "but you have to admit it is rather funny."

"What about your fans? They'll be disappointed to find an empty tank or did you leave a sign saying 'Back in Ten Minutes'?"

"I left Samphire in charge. She's organising the seahorse racing while I go and watch the Junior Dragon Sprint. Fancy joining me?"

Cahoots made his way to the starting line with the other young dragons. Minxie had added his name to the list of competitors. "Let's see what you can do up against your own species. It ought to be a good laugh if nothing else."

He eyed up the competition. The others were about his size in shades ranging from red to brown and they all had bright green eyes. A blue-eyed, purple dragon would stand out from the rest of the field, something which had not escaped Cahoots.

The competitors were banned from flying and had to have at least one foot on the ground at all times. The race was more of a thump than a sprint and always drew large crowds.

Cahoots went into the lead early and was well ahead of the rest by the halfway mark. He shot a quick look behind him to make sure no one was gaining on him and stopped dead.

The crowd 'oohed' in surprise. There were shouts of "Get on with it, you big wuss!" and "Are you nuts, or just stupid?" but Cahoots wasn't listening. He was staring at a huge purple dragon surrounded by her children. She returned his stare and then began counting her brood. She frowned and counted them a second time.

There was a cheer from the finishing line but most of the spectators were caught up watching Cahoots and the family of purple dragons.

"Bless me," she said, genuinely astonished. "I'm one short. This is the first time I've counted you all since before the earthquake." Cahoots was rooted to the spot. "Do you have nine little moles on the end of your tail, dear?"

"I don't know, I've never looked," he called back. One of the youngsters ducked under the rope which marked the edge of the racetrack and cantered across. She grabbed hold of his tail and let out a yelp of pleasure. "Nine moles in the shape of the letter 'S', mother," she shouted. Then, "Welcome to the family. I'm your sister and that annoying bunch over there with Mum are your sisters as well. Eight eggs all female, can you believe that?"

"Well I'm not," he snorted, sending out a torrent of smoke rings which elicited a roar of approval from the crowd and a proud smile from his mother.

"It's amazing we ever met up. We're only here for Fairymass, then it's back to Kelpien. We moved there after we'd hatched. Mum thought it was getting too dangerous in these parts."

A shadow crossed his face. "Is Kelpien a long way from here?"

"Yes, but what's that got to do with anything?"

"I like it here in Crawdonia."

"That shouldn't present a problem. It's no distance at all as the dragon flies. Now, come and meet the rest of the family. I'm Broonhilda. What's your name, bro?"

"It's Cahoots."

"What kind of a name's that for a dragon?"

"Don't you start," he said with narrowed eyes and a giggle. "There's someone you must meet. You remind me of her, actually. Her name's Minxie."

It was his sister's turn to look surprised. "You know Minxie the Wazwatt? I don't suppose you could arrange an introduction to the Royal Steed as well."

"That's easy. I'll throw in Sandy too, if you want, and Jamie."

"I think I'm going to like having a famous brother and Mum'll be delirious to have a son at long last. You're going to be so spoilt."

"There's just time to watch the Bareback Pony Stakes before we head back to 'Corbie Cottage'. Jock and Celia are presenting the Whiteraven Trophy to the winner."

"Is it really time to go home, Pogo?"

"Not quite, but you do have to leave before nightfall." The pixie lowered her eyes unable to hold Sandy's morose gaze. "Queen Celestina would like to see you before the race. She asked that you bring Jamie and Leo with you."

Pongo had been romping around with Scruggs and Estella. He skidded to a halt. "I can't bear it after everything we've been through together."

Jamie tried to sound upbeat. "I thought you'd be glad to see the back of us, me at least."

"Of course not. I feel as if I've known you all forever and I can't imagine life without you now."

"Scruggs is going to be staying with us for a while, Pongo, so you'll have two of us to play with."

"Estella's right," said Sandy, swallowing hard. "You three have had a rare tear today."

"You'll soon settle into the old routine." Alfie didn't believe what he was saying and neither did Pongo. "Come on now, don't let's spoil the rest of the time we have together. Her Majesty's in the pavilion next to the main stage. We'll wait for you down at the starting line."

"Can I go too, WAE?" asked a lacklustre Pongo.

"I'm sure that'll be fine, but if the Queen asks you to wait outside, you must do as you're told."

"OK."

Pogo and Alfie swapped worried looks. The dog had well and truly lost his sparky effervescence if that was all he had to say.

"If it comes to that, Pongo, I'll keep you company."

"Thanks, Jamie, you're a real pal." His naturally sunny temperament kicked in and his tail went up again. "Last one at the pavilion's a burst haggis."

Pongo darted off into the crowds barking a none-too-polite request for everyone to get out of his way. He barged past Smidge, Filch and Jimlet who'd lived to tell the tale after all, thanks to Jedediah ignoring Grimshaw's orders to dispose of them.

Jimlet was boring the breeches off a group of mates about his pivotal role in recent events.

Mabel Mince happened across them on her way to the seahorse racing. She yawned loudly and took a bite out of a toffee apple as big as her head. "Put a sock in it, mister. Everyone knows you're a waste of space."

"I'd like you all to have something to remember us by. I'm glad you brought Pongo with you, I've a present for him too."

"Nothing will ever take away the memories of my time here. I wish I didn't have to go home."

"Even after everything you've been through? You weren't meant to get caught up in our troubles, Sandy."

"That's what makes it so hard to leave. I'm part of Sylvania now, not just an invited guest from Scotland who also happens to be looking for her cat."

"You would miss your family and friends terribly."

"I know you're right and I did get very homesick at one stage but Crawdonia has depth and substance now. It's no longer a collection of sketchy images from childhood stories. Alfie, Pogo, SSS, the Giant Sapphire really do exist. It's the most wonderful discovery, life-changing. I can't go back to 'Woodburn' as if this never happened. It isn't a dream that will fade with time. I longed to meet the Queen of the Fairies when I was little but time passed and I grew out of that sort of thing and all at once there you were, more noble and magnificent than I could ever have imagined, and such fun too with the best frocks I've ever seen. Then I met Indigoletta, Crawford and everyone else, how can you ask me to give all that up?"

"Because you belong in Scotland, that's where you're supposed to be."

"But fate brought me here at this significant time, Your Majesty. How do I know where my future lies now?"

Jamie, Leo and Pongo sat huddled uncertainly at Sandy's feet.

"You'll have to trust me on that. Going back to 'Woodburn' must seem a bit tame after all you've done here and the thought of school doesn't appeal much either, I suppose."

"Not exactly."

"You're likely to get good marks for that essay on Robert Burns if you ever get round to finishing it."

Their eyes met and they both burst out laughing.

Celestina handed Sandy a shiny box. "I thought you might like to take Vince and Florin back with you as well, if I can persuade Indigoletta to give them up. She's fair taken with them. There's also the dress you're wearing. Everyone should have something frivolous in their wardrobe, don't you think?"

The box was lined with black velvet and appeared to be empty. Celestina smiled when she realised what was going on. "I suppose that's your idea of a joke," she said playfully, wagging her finger at the empty container. "Turn yourselves on, you little monkeys."

"The magic stars! I wondered what had happened to them. When Will woke us up to come to Fairymass I noticed they'd gone but I forgot to ask about them in all the excitement."

"They were in need of a rest too. How are you now, stars?"

They zipped out of the box and wrote in elegant script, 'Refreshed, Your Majesty, thank you for asking'.

"I want you to stay with Sandy and light her way through life, particularly during those dark nights of the soul. That doesn't mean you can't enjoy yourselves but don't get too carried away."

Celestina opened a drawstring velvet bag and removed a small sapphire and diamond crown. "This is for you, Jamie. It should go very well with your collar."

"Woah! You'll look the business in that," said Pongo, nudging the cat in the ribs. "Even more regal than you think you are already."

"I never dreamt I could take the collar back with me, let alone a matching crown. It's nothing short of sublime."

"Here, let me help you. I've had a lot of practice with crowns over the years." The Fairy Queen placed it between his ears and tipped it forward over his left eye. "It's very you. I think you should keep it on."

"If you insist, Your Majesty." Jamie adjusted his pose to one more befitting a royal cat. "It's exactly the right size."

"And so it should be if I'm doing my job properly."

Celestina knelt in front of Leo. "Curiosity is a fundamental part of a cat's nature and how were you to know Angus was going to involve you in such a huge adventure when you decided to find out what was on the other side of that arch?"

The cat gazed at her feathery frock barely able to control his desire to pounce on it and rip it to bits. Until he'd met birds who could talk, his attitude towards them had not been so benign.

"This earring belonged to Pestilence Grimshaw. It seems fitting that you should have it." She dangled the solid gold hoop in front of Leo who couldn't resist giving it a good whacking. "I'm glad you like it. Perhaps you could hang it above your basket as you don't have a pierced ear. Do promise me, you won't have one done specially."

"There's no chance of that, Your Majesty, I'm too squeamish."

"Now, Pongo, I know you're a practical sort of beast so a crown was not an option. This is to thank you for helping Sandy find Leo, even if your way of going about it was not what I would have wished." The dog shuffled around at her feet and began to strut back and forth whistling the national anthem. "I knew you wouldn't thank me for a jewelled collar but I thought you might like to hang this next to the tag on the one you're wearing." Green light radiated from a small spherical gemstone. "Not too plain for you, is it?" she asked, attaching it to his collar.

"On the contrary, Your Majesty. That's definitely got my name on it."

"No it hasn't," said Jamie with a smirk. "That's what your tag's for."

The Queen laughed and stroked the Siamese. "I'll miss you, Jamie. You're good company." She turned back to the dog. "This rare Kelpien emerald will protect you as long as you wear it. Not that you should need its protection now that things are back to normal round here."

Pongo was clearly impressed. "The Royal Raven wears an emerald round her neck. Does that make me the Royal Dog?"

"Absolutely. Now run along and watch the pony race; I wouldn't want you to miss it. I won't be seeing you off. I must remain at Fairymass with my people. Kismet will take you all back to 'Corbie Cottage' to collect your bits and pieces. Ralph knows when to expect you home. Do think of me when you bite into your first slice of birthday cake."

Sandy wasn't expecting to take leave of Celestina so soon and the lump in her throat was making her ears ache.

"It's better this way, really it is. Take care of Gilbert for me, I'm very fond of him but, like you, he belongs elsewhere. I thought he'd like a neckerchief embroidered with the Royal Crest. Actually, there are two in case he loses one, you know what he's like."

The animals went on ahead to give Sandy time on her own. She walked away from the pavilion slowly, wanting to prolong the moment, then turned to wave at the Queen who blew her a kiss.

She was suddenly overwhelmed by the extent of the loss she faced and called out, "Will I ever be able to come back?"

But Celestina had vanished and in her place was a constellation of twinkling blue stars.

They stood together in front of the hedge at the exact spot where they'd first come through. Lorimer clung to Sandy's back and Leo was tucked down the front of her V-necked jumper. Jock and Peg stood on her left with Gilbert and Jamie flanking them. A small suitcase sat on the grass beside Lorimer's ornate silver bucket which was crammed with bathing suits.

Sammy broke away from Alfie and Pogo and slithered across to Sandy. He coiled himself round her arm one last time. "Take care of yourself and give your Dad a hug from me. Open the other present now," he added gently. "It's from all of us."

The sporran raised its flap and Sandy fished out a small box. Inside was a tiny treasure chest. She held it up to the light. "It's beautiful, SSS. Thank you."

"The present's inside the cas-s-sket."

She cried out when she saw the ring.

"We couldn't let you leave without your very own piece of the Giant Sapphire."

"It's a wonder there's anything left of it," said Pongo with a grin.

Sandy planted a kiss on the tip of Sammy's nose.

"I've never been kis-s-sed before."

"No wonder, you're a big scary reptile!"

"Thank you for pointing that out, Pongo. It hadn't occurred to me."

The oval sapphire was suspended between two narrow bands of gold. "I hope you like the design. I thought the stone deserved a simple setting. I couldn't decide on white or yellow gold so there's one circle of each. It should fit whichever finger you choose to wear it on. If not, complain to the management."

She slipped it onto the third finger of her right hand. "You won't get any complaints from me except when I have to take it off to go to school. The rules say quite clearly: 'No jewellery allowed'. I doubt they'd make an exception if I told them how I came by it."

"They'd probably lock you up if you did that," said Jamie.

"Next to you, if you wear that crown in public."

"Pongo!"

"Yes, PP?"

"These delaying tactics won't prevent them from leaving. I'm sure you know what I'm going to say next."

"Pipe down?"

"Words to that effect."

Sammy moved off across the grass to join Indigoletta.

Crawford was trying to keep his emotions in check. He fiddled nervously with his monocle and cleared his throat. "You're not travelling so light this time, but I've allowed for that in my calculations."

"I knew I could rely on you, Crawf," said the Royal Raven warmly. "I hate goodbyes, don't you, dears? It's as well not to prolong things."

Hosepipe Snout scurried across and took up his position by the hedge. The hairy hedgehorn gave three loud blasts which made Indigoletta jump.

"Look," said Sammy, "the arch is starting to appear."

"I'm sorry we didn't catch up with Cahoots before we left, but at least we had time to say cheerio to everyone else. I haven't missed anyone out, have I?"

"I could do with another cuddle, if there's one going, Sandy."

"Dearest Pongo, of course there is." She stooped down and hugged him to her chest.

"You're squashing Leo," he said quietly.

"I'm OK," said a muffled voice.

Pogo caught him by the collar. "Come away, boy. It's time for them to go."

"The route back to 'Woodburn' is direct," said the Prince of Cobalt-Sibilance, "You'll see your destination as you leave us. Jock'll explain, he's made the journey often enough."

"It'll be like, em..., stepping through an arch," he said with a rueful shrug.

"Most illuminating, Jock." The raven gave a brief sigh. "The Craw Cauldron is in dire need of attention if you are ever to receive pictures from Sylvania again. We've arranged for Ralph to hand it to you as you enter the arch. You must take it from your Dad and give it straight to Alfie. Our two worlds will be synchronised so we'll be able to to look from one to the other. It's been forty years since Ralph saw us and a very great deal longer since we saw him. It's potentially risky but there's no reason why anything should go wrong, particularly as you'll be the last one through."

"I'll be on your shoulder, to make sure you're OK."

"Thanks, Jock."

On a sign from the Royal Raven, Alfie and Pogo moved towards the arch with Estella, Pongo and Scruggs. "That should do it," she said. "If we're too far back Ralph won't be able to see us. We'll send your luggage on ahead to make sure everything's working properly."

"The arch is starting to shimmer," said Crawford, counting from one to three. "And there goes the case and the cozzies."

Pongo exploded with joyous barking. "It's Minxie and Cahoots, Indigoletta!"

"Blow me backwards off a branch, how absolutely splendid!"

The dragon landed by the river and ran across to the hedge with the wazwatt whizzing around his head like nobody's business or a swarm of angry bees, depending on your mood.

"Cripes, we only just made it. There was some awful turbulence over Moonglow Lake." Minxie frowned. "I thought Kismet was going to be here."

"I am," he said, emerging from the wooded backdrop. "Wainscot and I were trying to keep a low profile. This departure is proving complicated enough."

"*Right*," said Jock in his most commanding tone. "Best foot forward in order of size. After you, Gilbert, Jamie and Peg." He ticked them off on a mental checklist. "Sandy, Leo, Lorimer, your boarding passes, please. Kilts and sporrans are exempt." It was a lame attempt at humour under the circumstances but it raised a few smiles. The crow flew onto Sandy's shoulder as she walked towards the arch.

By the time she reached the centre of the arch Sandy could see her Dad standing in the orchard with the cat, the gull and a small rodent. "Oh, Gilbert!" she exclaimed when she realised what had happened to him.

As the Craw Cauldron passed from Ralph to Alfie the two worlds swung together in time. Captain Henderson raised his arm to wave at his friends in Sylvania who rushed

J.Milne

forward to return his greeting.

"Hurry, Sandy," urged Jock, "the arch is closing. We must get through."

Estella shrieked as Pongo ran past her towards the vanishing arch. "Oh no you don't!" she yelled running after him. "Come back here at once!"

Printed in the United Kingdom
by Lightning Source UK Ltd.
107158UKS00001B/37-207